HIGHLANDER™
THE SERIES

An Evening at *Joe's*

HIGHLANDER™

THE SERIES

An Evening at

Fiction by the
Cast and Crew

Edited by

GILLIAN HORVATH

BERKLEY BOULEVARD BOOKS, NEW YORK

For Kip Guinn,
I hope he's looking down and laughing

AN EVENING AT JOE'S

A Berkley Boulevard Book / published by arrangement with
Davis Panzer Productions, Inc.

PRINTING HISTORY
Berkley Boulevard trade paperback edition / September 2000

The Penguin Putnam Inc. World Wide Web site address is
http://www.penguinputnam.com

Check out the Ace Science Fiction/Fantasy newsletter, and much more,
at Club PPI!

ISBN: 0-425-17749-1

BERKLEY BOULEVARD
Berkley Boulevard Books are published by The Berkley Publishing Group,
a division of Penguin Putnam Inc., 375 Hudson Street,
New York, New York 10014.
BERKLEY BOULEVARD and its logo
are trademarks belonging to Penguin Putnam Inc.

PRINTED IN THE UNITED STATES OF AMERICA

10 9 8 7 6 5 4 3 2

CONTENTS

FOREWORD

The creative atmosphere on *Highlander* was always very exciting.
Everyone on the crew would read the script. Sounds logical, but isn't
usual. Whenever we split a story between Vancouver and Paris, whoever wasn't filming the second half still wanted to read it. Very
unusual!

But writing?

Everyone wants to; no one does.

So when Gillian first approached me about a collection of Immortal stories written by *Highlander* people, I told her, "Great idea, but
you'll never get them to do it."

In your hands is yet further proof of my wisdom.

Bill Panzer
1 February 2000
London

ACKNOWLEDGMENTS

Ginjer Buchanan had faith where others doubted. Without her, this book would not exist.

Amy Zoll is the muse. What I write is written to entertain her.

Larne, Melissa, Marni, Marion, Kathy, Rachel, Jesse, Jodi, and Pam shared the New Voyages with me. Lydia, Jal, MOS, Starlight, T'Pon, T'Ryn, Velia, and Phoenicia blazed the trail.

Donna Lettow never gave up on making this project a reality. As always, she made my job immeasurably easier.

Marty Greenberg and Larry Segriff at Tekno Books made it all possible with their experience and expertise.

Bill Panzer gave me a sacred trust. I hope to return the favor someday.

INTRODUCTION

This book has its beginnings in a book I encountered in high school. *Star Trek: The New Voyages* and its sequel, *The New Voyages 2*, were published by Bantam Books in the late 1970s. "Eight original Star Trek Stories never seen on screen!" proclaimed the cover copy. It was the birth of the media tie-in book.

The stories in *The New Voyages*, which had been collected from fanzines by editors Sondra Marshak and Myrna Culbreath, were each preceded by a short introduction by a *Star Trek* cast member. *New Voyages 2* went a step further: it contains a wonderful story, "Surprise," written by Nichelle Nichols, who played Lieutenant Uhura. It should come as no surprise that the character portrayals in "Surprise" are beautifully realized, full of the same warmth and humor that made the best moments in the series. Nichelle Nichols was not a professional writer, but she knew *Star Trek*.

The contributors to this volume include actors, a prop master, a composer, a director, and a producer, as well as a few writers. They may not all be professional wordsmiths, but they are each, in their way, storytellers.

And they have something else in common: they all know *Highlander*. They made *Highlander*.

On the surface, *Highlander: The Series* might seem like just another hour of action television, to be watched and soon forgotten. But once in a while, a television show makes a lasting impression. Even a lifetime impression. On the viewers, and on the people who were part of its making.

No one knows which shows will succeed, either in the ratings or in posterity. Thirty years ago, no one predicted the lasting impact *Star Trek* would have on our culture. Thirty years from now, which current shows will still be remembered? I like to think *Highlander* has a better chance than most.

Highlander: The Series ran for six seasons, from 1992 to 1998. Creatively, the show was an unrivaled joy to work on. Story meetings, under Head Writer David Abramowitz, frequently turned into Talmudic discussions on loyalty, friendship, and the nature of good and evil. And these questions became part of the scripts, part of Duncan MacLeod's world. Although we often lamented the lack of a big studio or major network to publicize our show, the fact is that *Highlander* thrived in obscurity. Big studios and networks often mean studio and network interference. Independent production, though struggling with lower budgets and lower profiles, creates the potential for a unique vision, undiluted in committee, to shine through.

On *Highlander*, Executive Producer Bill Panzer created an atmosphere where everyone was listened to and respected. This attitude was reflected throughout the production. As Producer Ken Gord always said, "The fish stinks from the head down." Or in this case, didn't stink. Everyone's contribution was valued—and everyone was expected to do everything in their power to make the best show they possibly could, without regard to ego, on-screen credit, or overtime. We used to joke in our office that "everyone thinks they're the damn Highlander." Meaning that everyone on our crew felt it was their personal responsibility to make sure *Highlander* was perfect, and if that meant that everybody down to the security guard had an opinion on every action of MacLeod's in every script, well, that was the price we paid for having a crew that actually cared what happened on their show. On many shows it's not unusual for on-set crew to film a script without really reading it—it's the director's job to care about the story, the crew is just trying to get the shot. On *Highlander*, the highest compliment I think the writing staff ever received was during season 5, when "Comes a Horseman" was filming in Vancouver and, because the second half of the two-parter was filming in France, only the script for the first hour was distributed to the Canadian crew. The next day we got the call—the crew wanted to read the script for the second half, even though they wouldn't be working on it. They wanted to know how the story ended!

I think a large part of *Highlander*'s ability to inspire that interest in nearly everyone it reaches—crew, guest stars, our loyal viewers—comes from its central premise. *Who wants to live forever?* We all wonder, what would it be like to be immortal? To have more time to see things, and do things, to learn and to love? Wherever I went on the *Highlander* set, everyone, from script typists to caterers to production designers, was asking themselves the same question that the writers, directors, and actors considered every day: "What if it were me? How would my life change? Could I fight and kill to survive? Would I want to?"

When I invited our crew to participate in this project, I asked them to investigate those questions, any way they wanted. On the series, though we explored many stories in our 119 episodes, there were always stories we couldn't tell. Because there were things we couldn't show on television. Because there were ideas we couldn't afford to stage. Because not every story is exactly forty-eight minutes long. Because on a show called *Highlander*, every story was expected to focus on Duncan MacLeod, the Highlander.

But for this book, all bets were off. I told our contributors to write whatever they liked—any style, any length—exploring the world of Immortals. I promised them they would not be edited, other than standard proofreading. Each person's vision would be published just as he or she wished it to be. Perhaps different writers and directors would have different ideas of the nature of the Quickening? Perhaps two authors would write contradictory histories for Methos or Amanda? On the series, those differences would have to be "fixed." But in this book, you will see firsthand the individual, unadulterated visions of some of the key people who made *Highlander* what it is: Composer Roger Bellon, who wrote the music for five seasons out of six; Producer Ken Gord, who oversaw production for the same number of years; Director Dennis Berry, who was there from season 1 to the end of season 6, working in both Canada and France.

Actor Peter Hudson, who played MacLeod's recurring nemesis James Horton, was the first person outside the writing staff to turn in a story. Swordmaster F. Braun McAsh was the second. Their two stories could not be more different—and yet each amazed me in its own way. To each of them I owe a great debt of thanks. It was their early commitment and great talent which proved this book could happen.

Each of our contributors surprised and delighted me by turning in something different from anything that had come before. Some of the actors explored more deeply characters they had portrayed on the show; others did not. More than one writer was inspired in their story by actual real-life events, with a "What if Immortals were real" spin—but no two stories are alike.

In putting together this project, I contacted whatever *Highlander* crew members I could find, many of them scattered to other shows after *Highlander* was shut down. If I could have found everyone who ever worked on the show in six years, I would have issued invitations to each and every one of them, for as far as I'm concerned, every one of them—Wardrobe Mistress or Transportation Coordinator, Director or Director of Photography—is equally qualified to contribute to this project. For without each and every one of them, *Highlander: The Series* would not have been what it was.

Gillian Horvath
September 1999

Letters from Viet Nam

by Jim Byrnes

"JOE DAWSON": Jim Byrnes

The character of Joe Dawson, Duncan MacLeod's Watcher, was added to the cast of Highlander: The Series *at the beginning of the second season. Though Joe (then named Ian Dawson) was originally conceived as a stuffy Brit, Jim Byrnes, well known as "Lifeguard" on the series* Wiseguy, *was cast in the role and soon made it his own. Originally slated to appear in only four episodes, Joe became a major character in the series, who evolved over time to share a number of traits with Jim Byrnes, including his love of blues guitar and his earthy sense of humor.*

The fourth-season episode "Brothers in Arms" revealed that Joe Dawson is a Viet Nam veteran. And although Joe, and Jim, had been a part of Highlander *for two years by that time, that episode was also the first on-screen mention of his cane or his limp. In a powerful flashback to young Joe Dawson's days in combat, we learned that he lost his legs in the war. In his "Letters from Viet Nam," Jim Byrnes draws on*

1

*his own wealth of experience to give us a glimpse of Joe Dawson before
his life was changed by war, injury, and the Watchers.*

⚡

September 17 1969

Dear Catherine,

Hey Sis, long time no hear, huh? Small talk is a little rough out here
in the boonies.

Pre Med must be pretty hard even for you I guess. Mom said you
almost got a B, God forbid, until you aced the final. It must be cool
living downtown, though, instead of next door to Ozzie and Harriet.
Rush Street and the clubs and stuff, jazz, blues, man have I got plans
for when I get home. Even the Art Institute and the Museum of Natural History, just being able to spend your time like that, checking out
history and surrounded by beautiful things. Remember when we'd all
take the train into the city and just spend the whole day doing all that
stuff and then have dinner at Berghof's? Wow. Using your brains
instead of your feet. What a concept! I thought I was in shape playing
sports, well forget it, NOW I am a lean clean killing machine. I kind
of wish I was kidding you. I've done enough walking and running and
running and walking for a whole lifetime.

Anyway, I've got to get something off my chest. Don't think I'm too
weird. The night of Dad's funeral remember I like disappeared and
everybody freaked out and all of Dad's Fire Dept. buddies were looking for me and everything, but you were the one who found me? I was
crying like a baby, it was awful, mortifying, but you were so cool. You
just sat there with me and you never ratted me out to anyone. You
were great, Cath, and I guess I want to thank you because I don't think
I ever did before. But now I have to tell somebody that I feel like that
again sometimes now over here. Paralyzed, so scared. I mean I get
over it, but I just had to tell somebody. Please don't tell Mom, though,
cause it's got to be hard for her with me over here and you not living
at home anymore and all. I know Aunt Rose and Uncle Frank are
around and the neighbors and her club etc., etc., but I just don't want
her to worry too much about me. So don't tell her that, ok?

You know that somebody reads all this before you see it, so I'm not gonna share all our escapades or our whereabouts or anything. Suffice it to say some days are just a real barrel of frigging monkeys and more and more I have to wonder what we're supposed to be doing here. Too many dead boys, us and them. For what? Check this out. Couple of weeks ago we hear on the radio that Ho Chi Minh is dead, and only one other guy even knows who he is! One! I mean if you think he's a Communist stooge or the father of his country, shouldn't you at least know who you're supposed to be fighting? Ours is not to reason why, huh? I guess. Yep, just one big party, living the night life until one day you run out of luck.

So tomorrow we're off on a big walkabout, whoopee! Oh yeah, Cath, I've got to tell you about this new sergeant that got rotated in a while back. Wow, is he a trip! Big, scary looking brother, and fearless, I mean to the point of psychotic. I can't explain it but there is something really different about this guy, spooky. Course sometimes this whole place is spooky. Shadows, tunnels, incense burning in the dark. The haunted house.

When we get back we've got R&R due but I think I'm just going to hang out and bank the pay again. I figure when I get back to Chicago I should have about enough for a trip to Europe what with that grad money and all. I really hope you and Mom come for part of the trip. We could all meet in Paris, you know. The Eiffel Tower and all. Remember when we used to talk about that all the time? Sometimes I can. Seems like another life.

I've got to write Mom yet tonight so I will finish this up. After tomorrow I won't be able to send any mail for a while, so . . . Really I'm ok, Cath, but thanks for being there, huh? Just, when you're talking to your Psych major friends, I'm hypothetical all right? Not your chicken-shit little brother. And ixnay with Mom, swear. Hey, good luck at school and good luck meeting that mysterious foreigner you're planning to marry, whoever he might be. (Ha, ha, ha)

Semper Fi, kiddo.

Your bro, Joe

Sept. 17, 1969
Dear Mom,

  First of all, I'm sure sorry that it's taken me so long to write you
back, but I'm sure you can imagine that it's hard to find the place and
the time. I mean, it's not like we don't have any spare time but usually
the conditions ain't so hot, so I have to wait til stand down. Thanks a
million for the package you sent; you don't know how much it means
to a guy to have something from home when you're so far away. The
big winner is that Skin So Soft from Avon. I gotta wonder what they
put in it, but it sure keeps the bugs off. Hey, remember that year you
were an Avon Lady? Ding, Dong . . . Avon calling. Just like on TV.
That seems so long ago.

  I know in your letter you said you were so worried from watching
reports on Walter Cronkite and stuff but please don't worry, Mom, it's
not so bad. I've met some pretty good guys here from all around the
country which you know I like 'cause I want to travel when I finish my
tour and all. I met one guy who's from Chicago, too, and his uncle
plays blues guitar with some of the really heavy blues greats, so I can
meet them when I come home. Cool, huh? Really, mostly it seems like
all we do is walk and hump and cuss and walk and try to stay dry or
warm up or cool down or something. And I do try to go to Mass when
the chaplain's around, but sometimes it's impossible. Anyway, I'm just
trying to say don't worry too much, ok? I know you think I should
have taken that scholarship and gone to University, but I'm pretty sure
that Dad would be proud to know that I joined the Marine Corps and
I hope you're proud of me, too. I mean I know you are and everything
but I'm just trying to be a man, and do what I think is right, ok? Sometimes that's hard to know, I'm finding out. But, I promise you that I'll
be careful and always try to do my best. Just another six weeks and I'll
be out of here (but who's counting, ha, ha?) and then I'll be home on
leave for Thanksgiving. We'll have the time of our lives, Mom, I
swear. We'll get a big gang together and Catherine will be home from
school and we'll sing and laugh and it will be just like old times,
alright?

Oh yeah, speaking of Cath here's a funny story. Remember when I was just a freshman but I was playing defensive safety in that junior varsity championship game against Assumption? That guy on their team keeled over and dropped the ball and instead of just picking up the fumble and running I called time and helped him off the field. And then it turns out he'd had an appendicitis attack and all, so Cath and all these senior girls, Maureen Kelleher and the Cusamano twins and everybody started calling me "Boyscout" which of course I hated and it took me two years to get another nickname? Well get a load of this. Since my last letter we had a new top kick rotate in, Sgt. Cord, a heavy duty guy like I've never seen in my life. This guy takes chances you really can't believe, I swear it's like he thinks he can't die or something. Well, anyway, second day with us he wants to check out our perimeter, so he walks up to me and says: "Hey, boy scout, you're my man, let's take a hike." Boyscout! I couldn't believe it, it's like some kind of weird curse. Please don't tell Cath or I will never hear the end of it. Please.

Well, it's just about lights out for me so I'll say so long. If you talk to Mrs. Fields tell her I said hi to Betsy and I'll try to write soon, but we're heading for the boonies again tomorrow so I might not get a chance right away. Say a prayer for me, Mom, and keep a light in the window. You never know when I'll be coming home.

Your loving son,
Lance/Cpl. Joseph P. Dawson

Train from Bordeaux

by Gillian Horvath

ASSOCIATE CREATIVE CONSULTANT: Gillian Horvath

"Creative Consultant" is a title that's used in television for any member of the writing staff who, for whatever reason, isn't billed as a Writer, Story Editor, or Producer. I joined the Highlander *team at the beginning of the second season as the Assistant to Creative Consultant David Abramowitz (the Head Writer); for the next four seasons, under various "Consultant" titles, I worked with David Abramowitz, Dave Tynan, and Bill Panzer to plan and oversee the character arcs and freelance writers.*

This story, written in December of 1996 when the "Horseman" episodes had been filmed but not yet aired, arose out of a piece of business Richard Ridings, the actor playing Silas, added to the work. During the scene in the asylum director's office, while Kronos and Methos threatened the doctor, Silas stood in the background whittling on a piece of wood, which was finally revealed to be a simple flute. Although this unscripted bit of action is barely noticeable in the final cut of the episode, it caught my eye while watching the dailies and

*started me thinking about Silas and his relationship with his three
"brothers," particularly Methos.*

⚡

I thought I'd be able to sleep. I thought I'd have to. For two weeks
I've had one eye open every night, watching, planning. Caspian would
kill me in my bed with half an excuse, always would. Kronos doesn't
sleep, he doesn't need to, so I couldn't sleep either, not if I wanted to
keep up.

We think alike, we always have.

I've had to, these last weeks. I've had to put myself in Kronos's
head, to somehow try and imitate that great, twisted imagination of
his, to see where he's going before he gets there. No wonder I
haven't slept.

And now they're gone. Dead. Kronos, and Caspian.

And Silas.

I lay my head against the chilly pane of the train window, slouching
down into my woolen overcoat. I'm safe now, at least my head is safe,
and I should be able to sleep.

But I can't.

I like to have my axe in my hands.

You always had a blade in your hands, didn't you, Brother? When
you weren't hacking men limb from limb you were whittling away
with that knife of yours, turning discarded bits of wood into square-
haunched horses and humpbacked camels, children's playthings.

Did you have toys as a child, Silas? Did a doting foster parent put
hand-carved dolls in your cradle? Or were you abandoned and
unloved, like so many of us? Is your little wooden menagerie your way
of rewriting history? Of taking what you were never given?

I never asked. A thousand years we rode together, fought together,
bled together, but I never asked. It's not a thing men talk about—not
men like us.

I look out the window at the green and brown French countryside.
A farmhouse here, a road there. Otherwise it looks the same as it has
every time I've passed this way, every time in five thousand years.

I'm the one that changes. I've been a different man every time I've crossed these fields. Two thousand years ago, or two hundred. Or two weeks. Two weeks ago when Kronos brought me down here, I was a Horseman. I had to be, to survive. It doesn't matter what I was think-ing inside, it doesn't matter if I wanted to kill Kronos with my bare hands and run, because I didn't. I looked out this window and saw these hills with Horseman's eyes.

That's the part MacLeod will never understand. He wants an expla-nation. He wants to hear me say I never meant to do it.

He hasn't lived long enough to know it doesn't matter what you meant to do. All that matters is what you did.

You don't know anything about me.

I said it to Silas. It's the last thing I said to him before I killed him.

But I could have said it to any of them. To Kronos, who thought he owned me. To MacLeod, who thought he changed me. To Cassandra, who thought she loved me.

None of them have any idea who I am.

How could they? In five thousand years I've been five thousand men. To while away the time I start listing them to myself, the lives, the identities. Farmers and scholars. Butchers and executioners. Hus-bands and lovers.

It's like counting sheep. I sleep.

It's a cold night in the desert and we've got the fire burning high. Travellers are told to keep their fires low for fear of being spotted by raiders, but we have no such worries. We are the Raiders. We are the Horsemen. We are four men who have chosen to be the Bringers of Fear.

The sky is clear and the stars are out. I'm lying back on my bed of skins, finding the animals in the sky. I've just learned the legends of the stars from an old scholar we had prisoner. The maiden, the lion, the twins. The old man told me the stories to save his life, a gap-toothed, shriveled old Scheherezade. He lived twelve nights.

Now I'm telling Kronos about the hunter and the bull. Not because he's interested, but because he likes to hear me talk. He's lying so near to me I can sense every inch of him, though we're not touching. My skin prickles with the

awareness, knowing every muscle and sinew of him as I do, I know how eas-
ily he could reach over and kill me, but I know he won't, not tonight.

I can smell Caspian, lying on the far side of the fire, sleeping, snoring.
None of it means anything to him—not the star stories, not the warmth of
the fire, not the exquisite awareness that binds us four together, body and soul.
To him, only the killing matters. The killing, and the women.

Silas and I are back to back, as we so often are, in battle and in company,
leaning against each other, with no thought of fear or mistrust. Like a dog
and his master, we travel together, serve one another, keep one another whole.

He's pretending to listen to my story but I know he's not. I glance over at
his moving hands, the small knife working the wooden block. I can't see what
he's making. It doesn't matter, he'll pitch it in the fire before we move on any-
way. It's just something he does, this carving. Who he is.

I wake with a start, the feel of Silas's broad back leaning against mine
still fresh in my mind, and for a moment I feel him in me, my brother
now in life and death, before I remember where I am, who I am . . .

Who I've killed.

In an age of warlords, he was a king. In an industrial age, he was
nothing, a man living in the woods, awaiting the day when his master
would call him into service again.

Waiting for Kronos.

Waiting for me.

It doesn't do any good to think about that. This is a new day. I'm a
new man. The Horsemen are no more.

I reach in my pocket and take out the flute Silas carved last week,
put it to my mouth, and start to play.

The Star of Athena

by Laura Brennan

SCRIPT COORDINATOR: Laura Brennan

Laura Brennan joined the Highlander *writing staff as Script Coordinator at the beginning of season 6. Raised in Monaco by American parents, Laura has the distinction of being the first staffer at the Los Angeles office to be fluent in French as well as English, a fact much appreciated by the crew in Paris. Laura later went on to be Associate Creative Consultant on* Highlander: The Raven.

The character of the Immortal Amanda, later featured as the lead of Highlander: The Raven, *began with a single appearance in* Highlander's *first season. From there, this charming cat burglar, played by the beautiful Elizabeth Gracen, grew in importance as a continuing character, appearing more and more frequently as the series progressed. Though she was initially seen as only a rogue and a "bad habit of Duncan's," layers of characterization were added to Amanda over the years, revealing her staunch loyalty to her teachers and friends. In the fifth season's "Forgive Us Our Trespasses," she even demonstrated a deep understanding of the moral issues facing*

*Duncan MacLeod, and all Immortals—even as she was framing him
for jewel theft.*

*In "The Star of Athena," reminiscent of a classic caper film of the
'30s, Laura Brennan gives us an affectionate look at the jetsetting
adventuress Amanda, who could win and lose a million dollars in
jewels in one night, just for the rush.*

⚡

Nowhere on earth was quite so magical as Monte Carlo in the
springtime. The scent of azaleas floated through the clear, balmy
night. The moon had risen, and a million glistening fragments of
reflected silver danced over the Mediterranean.

Yes, Amanda thought, dangling from a rope forty feet above the
waves, this was by far the worst vacation she'd ever had.

She paused to catch her breath, and to curse the moonlight. Not
that there was much risk of someone noticing her from below. The
Monte Carlo Loews Hotel jutted out directly over the ocean, and by
now any straggling ships were safely in the harbor, and out of sight.
She'd be fine, as long as no doe-eyed newlyweds came out for a snug-
gle on their balcony. She edged up another foot. Maybe they'd all
make a night of it at the Casino. Preferably, losing. The thought
cheered her.

It was, after all, gambling that had gotten her into this mess. The
unexpected loss at blackjack. That unfortunate hour at the roulette
wheel. Then, to top it off, the disastrous high-stakes poker game, ille-
gally held in the private home of an exiled Romanian prince. Prince,
my eye, she thought spitefully, inching her way up the side of the
hotel. He was probably run out of the country for fleecing innocent
young women with a shot at an inside straight. She reached up, her
fingers searching for a solid handhold.

And then she got the Buzz.

Startled, Amanda lost her grip. She dropped a yard and scrambled
to stabilize. A forty-foot tumble into the sea wouldn't be fatal, but it
would attract attention. Besides, she hadn't known another Immortal
was in town; she didn't want to be "out," and vulnerable, if the Immortal in question turned out not to be a friend.

One thing she did know: whoever it was was getting closer. Time for a change of plans. She pulled a grappling gun from her waistband and aimed at an upper balcony. The hook caught on the wrought-iron railing. She tugged at it experimentally. The rope held.

The Buzz grew stronger. She pulled out a hunting knife and in one quick motion severed her line to the roof and kicked herself off from the wall. She swung across the side of the hotel, her momentum carrying her away from the unknown Immortal. She felt their connection grow weaker, then disappear, as she let go of the line and landed softly on the balcony of a darkened room.

Amanda jimmied open the sliding door and crept into the room. It was empty—her first bit of luck all night. Sixty seconds later she was on the street. Not the cleanest of getaways, she reflected, but at least she had what she came for. Amanda checked her watch—10:30. Half an hour till her rendezvous with the buyer. Time enough to get a good look at the merchandise.

She slipped into a nightclub, already crowded with tourists, and locked herself in the restroom. Now that she was safely away, Amanda allowed herself a moment to gloat over her success. The Star of Athena, one of the most famous sapphire necklaces in the world. And for the next twenty-five minutes, it belonged to her. Gently, she shook the necklace free from its black velvet pouch and held it up to the indifferent fluorescent light.

Everyone in Europe knew the legendary Star of Athena. The center stone was an enormous star sapphire, spectacular because of a tiny flaw in the smoky blue-grey that reflected light into a brilliant, perfect star. The sapphire itself was set in white gold, and it hung on a necklace literally dripping with diamonds. Fashioned centuries ago, it had been presented to Jeannette du Vaulier by King Louis XV, as a tribute to her divine beauty and, possibly, in gratitude for her other, more earthly, gifts.

Amanda looked at the necklace for a long, long time. Then, with an impatient shake of her head, she returned it to the velvet pouch. Time to meet the buyer.

Entering the small, relentlessly modern and outrageously expensive bar at the Hotel de Paris, Amanda spotted him immediately. She frowned. He was early, already restless, clearly not on his first drink of the night. Not the kind of man she would normally do business with. But then, the Baron du Vaulier was surprising in a number of ways. She had seen him watching her at the blackjack table, and she wasn't surprised when he followed her out of the Casino. He'd caught up with her there, grabbing hold of her arm and asking her if she'd come to Monaco to steal his wife's necklace, the Star of Athena.

"Don't be ridiculous," she'd replied, trying to move past him. But that's just what he was, standing there blocking her way: a ridiculous little man with sweaty palms and sudden boldness.

"But you must," he'd said simply. "I'll give you one hundred thousand francs if you'll do it."

Now the Baron was waiting for her in a booth at the hotel bar, as instructed. He saw her approach and jumped to his feet.

"Do you have it?" he asked in a hoarse whisper.

"You know," Amanda told him, motioning him to sit down, "most mistresses are happy to receive earrings, maybe a diamond tennis bracelet." She hoped Isabelle Jauverne, from whose room she'd retrieved the necklace, had gotten at least that much from the Baron before demanding to wear the famous Star. At least the affair wouldn't have been a total loss.

"You really mustn't give away your wife's jewelry," she continued. "It's disloyal. It's dangerous. And you won't always find someone with my expertise to retrieve it for you."

He didn't seem to hear her. Even in the dim light, Amanda could see that his hands were shaking. "Do you have the Star?" he repeated.

"There is a package at the front desk," she answered carefully. "In it is the necklace I found in Madame Jauverne's safe."

The Baron made a quick movement, as if to rise, but Amanda's voice stopped him. "Haven't you forgotten something, Marco?"

"Of course, of course." He clutched her hand to his chest and bobbed his head enthusiastically. "A million thanks!"

"A hundred thousand would do," Amanda replied drily, extracting her hand with some difficulty from the Baron's grip.

"Of course," he repeated, floundering. "But, Mademoiselle, you must understand, it is difficult to raise such a sum. . . ."

Amanda sighed inwardly. "You lost twice that much at roulette last night," she said flatly. "Besides," she added, "I haven't told you under what name the package is being held. Of course, Madame Jauverne might also be interested in recovering the item. . . ."

At the mention of his mistress's name, the Baron crumbled. "Women!" he grumbled, reaching into his portefeuille. "I am plagued."

Amanda slid the wad of bills into her purse. "Find the hotel concierge," she told him. "Tell him you need the package left for your aunt, Mary Poppins."

"Marr-ee Poe-pins," he repeated the unfamiliar name slowly.

"Close enough." Amanda shook her head as he tottered away. The French could be so exasperating. Before he was out of sight, the Baron was already forgotten, replaced by a more pressing question: who could the mysterious Immortal have been?

The next day passed without a whisper of the break-in at Loews—not that Amanda expected any. Isabelle Jauverne could hardly report as stolen a necklace that so famously belonged to another woman—a woman who, by all reports, had just returned to Monaco, in time for the premiere of a new play at the Theatre Princesse Grace. The Baroness du Vaulier wouldn't miss the opportunity to vaunt her family's fortune to Monaco's elite. No wonder her husband had been in such a panic to retrieve the Star.

Readying herself for the theater, Amanda chose her gown and ornaments with more care than usual. The entire upper crust of Monaco would be there, but it wasn't for them that Amanda dressed. Above the stairs in the theater lobby, shining over the assembly, hung an exquisite portrait of Monaco's First Lady, radiant, full of the delight of life.

Amanda had only met Princess Grace once, when the international circus competition, and a small fortune in rubies, had brought Amanda to town. Grace had been both regal and refreshingly real, down-to-earth, joyous, and vibrantly alive. Amanda paused at the top of the stairs to pay silent tribute to the portrait of the Princess, alive now only in memory. For an instant, she was overwhelmed by how fragile, how fleeting, mortal life could be.

The moment passed. The crowd engulfed her. She was swept up the stairs with them, and emerged into the light of the upper landing.

Amanda saw the Star of Athena before she noticed the woman wearing it. She didn't need the dawning Buzz to recognize the tall, handsome man at the Baroness' side. He turned, sensing her. Their eyes met across the landing, and Amanda remembered. . . .

Monaco, January 8, 1297

Amanda fingered the coins in her pouch and sighed. She had enough for dinner, perhaps even for a bed for the night. Tomorrow would have to take care of itself.

She could, of course, liberate a coin or two from unsuspecting passersby, but few of the figures scurrying through the darkening streets looked more prosperous than herself. Voyagers, mostly, seeking safety for the night behind the fortified walls of The Rock. And soldiers, of course, hired to protect the strategically important fortress in the Emperor's endless battle against the Pope.

Amanda shook her head. It was no surprise to her that neither His Holiness nor the Emperor were putting their own necks on the line. Typical mortal warfare. At least Immortal combat was one-on-one, not sacrificing other lives from a distance. . . . Suddenly, her attention was caught by a procession of brown robes and tonsured heads as a small band of Franciscan monks entered the gates. As tradition demanded, they would be given shelter for the night, even in this Imperial stronghold. She watched the skulk of monks with growing unease—and certainty. One of them was Immortal.

She scanned the faces of the monks, searching for the one who would be searching for her. It took only a moment to find him—tall, with piercing blue eyes. A stranger. Amanda joined a group of women offering water to the holy newcomers. Taking up a small ladle, she and the stranger managed to step away from the group.

"I am Philippe Canella." He kept his voice low, and Amanda guessed that his fellow travelers knew him by another name.

"Amanda," she said simply. She offered him his portion of water; he drank gratefully, and Amanda relaxed. He had not come for her, she told herself. He traveled with a band of holy men, men of peace. . . . For the first time, Amanda took a good look at the other monks. They all seemed to defer to one man, short and dark, who moved silently among them. He bent for a sip of water, and his traveling cape billowed slightly; for a fleeting instant, Amanda caught the impression of a sword hilt hidden under his holy robes.

Then Philippe was in front of her, blocking her view of his leader. She looked up at him. He, she knew, would have his blade on him, for those were the rules of the Game. But the other man was a mortal, and, she was beginning to suspect, no more a monk than she was. She met Philippe's eyes; he knew what she had seen.

"You and I have no quarrel," Philippe told her. "It would not be wise of you to create one."

Amanda thought of the sour dinner and hard bed that awaited her, and weighed it against the inconvenience, if not danger, of a nighttime journey. The mortal with the hidden weapon was moving toward them; others were now in hearing. Amanda made her decision. "I wish I could stay and receive your blessing, Brother"—she smiled demurely—"but I must leave now if I'm to make Roquebrune by nightfall. My mother," she lied, raising her voice slightly, "has taken a turn for the worst."

Philippe looked startled, then nodded his approval. "I'll remember her in my prayers," he said, adding quietly, "You'll want to stay off the main roads." He chose his words with care. "You never know what thieves and cutthroats you might encounter."

"You never know," Amanda agreed.

The two Immortals parted. Fifteen minutes later, Amanda was

already well out of the fortress, headed inland, far from the imposing ramparts.

It was a week before the news caught up with her: François Grimaldi, known as Malizia, "The Cunning," had, with a small band of men, wrested Monaco from the Ghibellines. There were conflicting reports as to how they had infiltrated the well-guarded stronghold, but these were laid to rest by history when the new Grimaldi prince designed a coat of arms. It featured two monks, armed with swords.

Theatre Princesse Grace, Monaco, The Present

Amanda had seen him since then, of course—it was a small world, they were bound to bump into each other every few hundred years. But Philippe had never been quite so unnerved at the sight of her before. She crossed to him, and he dutifully bowed over her hand. His eyes were still the clearest of blues, and they betrayed his annoyance at being forced to introduce Amanda to the woman at his side.

Draped, as always, in black, the Baroness du Vaulier was almost as well-known as the necklace glittering around her neck. She held herself ramrod straight, almost a parody of stuffy aristocracy. And yet, despite her sallow skin and etched face, there was an unassailable dignity to her. She was, quite literally, the last of her kind. But for her and the Baron, the family name had already died out. There were no children, no heirs; this generation would mark the end of the du Vauliers. And so the Baroness fought against oblivion with the only weapon she had: money. She founded Marseille's Musée du Vaulier, rebuilt Rome's Teatro Vaulieri, and endowed the Du Vaulier Chair in the history departments of both Yale and Harvard. The du Vauliers might disappear, but the Baroness had made sure they would never be forgotten.

Amanda was introduced to the lady just as the Baron himself joined their party—already drunk on the free champagne, flowing in honor of the premiere. All told, Amanda was flattered at his reaction when his bleary eyes finally focused on her. His mouth fell open, his eyes bulged; his patchy red face resembled nothing more than a gaping fish.

Before he could recover, the Baron was hit by another outrage. An irate woman marched up to the group, glared spitefully at the Baroness' necklace and began to curse the Baron soundly and with flair. She topped the moment by throwing her champagne in the Baron's face, then turned on her heel and stomped off. Amanda found herself smiling as the crowd broke out in astonished murmurs and discreet laughter. Madame Isabelle Jauverne had just given the finest performance the Monegasque audience had seen in years.

The Baroness had remained completely still throughout Madame Jauverne's histrionics, and made no move to help her husband as he mopped the champagne from his face. This was not, Amanda guessed, the first public scene between her husband and an ex-mistress. Mustering the shards of his dignity, the Baron held out his arm to his wife.

"Shall we?" he asked. The Baroness laid her hand on his. Without a backward glance, they disappeared into their box.

As soon as they were out of sight, Philippe turned to Amanda. "What are you doing here?" he demanded.

"Philippe! I missed you, too."

"If you've come to steal the Star of Athena," he said bluntly, "forget it. The Baroness is cousin to Prince Rainier. She is under my protection here."

"Lucky lady." Amanda smiled up at him. "Still the Grimaldis' knight in shining armor, are you? Or," she mocked softly, "would that be, friar in shining armor?"

"You won't get the necklace, Amanda. Not this time."

"Sounds like a challenge."

"I hope not," he answered. There was an awkward silence. The lobby lights began to blink, warning them to take their seats. Philippe took a step toward the Baroness' box. He stopped, looked back uncertainly.

"Run along, darling," she told him. "You're perfectly safe. I'm on vacation."

She wiggled her fingers at him, in what she hoped was a reassuring wave. He turned and disappeared. Amanda rolled her eyes and snagged

a glass of champagne from a passing waiter. Why did the French have
to take everything so seriously?

She disappeared into the ladies room to touch up her makeup and
steal a moment of peace. The curtain was about to rise; she could
count on having a few minutes alone. And then the door opened. A
dark figure brushed in. Amanda glanced in the mirror and saw the
uncompromising reflection of the Baroness du Vaulier standing
behind her.

"You are Amanda Montrose." The Baroness didn't wait for an
answer. "Philippe tells me you are a jewel thief."

Amanda finished putting on her lipstick. "Philippe is indiscreet,"
she said finally.

"How much will it cost to have my necklace stolen?"

Amanda smiled, gathered her things. "A hundred thousand francs
seems to be the going rate."

"Done." The Baroness threw a handful of bills on the counter.
"Half now. Half when the necklace is gone."

For the first time, Amanda looked directly at the Baroness. "You're
serious?" The Baroness didn't answer. "Why?"

"I am not paying you to ask questions," the Baroness snapped. "I'm
paying you to make the Star of Athena disappear into history, now,
tonight." She paused, fingering the necklace at her throat. Amanda
thought she detected a note of panic behind the steely voice. "Will
you do it?"

Amanda shook her head. "Let me get this straight. You want me to
steal the jewels from around your neck, with no preparation time, no
plan, in front of three hundred witnesses?" The Baroness nodded
once, quickly. There was a moment of silence.

"Okay," Amanda said.

All things considered, it was one of the smoothest heists of Amanda's
career. It helped, of course, to have a willing victim, not to mention a
slightly drunken crowd pressing en masse to the front doors once the

final curtain had come down. It took twenty-two seconds to cut the electricity, another minute to get from the fuse box back to the lobby. The Baroness was exactly where Amanda had told her to be. The crowd dutifully panicked in the sudden darkness, and Philippe found himself stranded near the coat check. Apart from a slight gasp as the Baroness felt the necklace slip from her neck, she made no noise, no move. Amanda slipped out the stage door a moment later. Perhaps Monaco wasn't so unprofitable after all, she decided.

She had ten minutes alone before Philippe pounded on the door of her room at the Hotel de Paris.

"Darling!" Amanda flung the door open. She took in Philippe's glare, the Baroness' composed face, and the professionally bland looks of the Hotel Security team standing behind the Immortal. "If I'd known it was a party, I'd have ordered room service."

"We're going to search your rooms," Philippe began. "If you try to stop us—"

"But why ever should I do that?" Amanda asked. She swung the door open wide. "Come in, boys. Make yourselves at home."

Philippe brushed past her; the others followed. It took less than ten minutes for Philippe to work his way to her jewelry box. He lifted it, felt for a false bottom before he even bothered to open it up. When he lifted the lid, Amanda heard his sharp intake of breath. The room froze.

Gently, Philippe drew the necklace from the box. Light danced over it, sparkling, brilliant, unmistakable.

Philippe approached the woman in black. He held out his hand, bowed his head slightly. "Madame la Baroness," Philippe asked formally, "is this your necklace?"

"I—"

"Don't be absurd, darling," Amanda's voice cut in, languid, bored. She rose from the chair she'd been lounging in. "Why in the world would the Baroness wear paste?"

Philippe whirled to face her. "What?" he asked.

"Paste. Fakes. Falsies. Here"—she tossed her jeweler's loupe at him—"Take a good look."

He did, peering through the glass at the glittering necklace for what seemed an eternity.

"I had a copy made some time ago," Amanda continued. "What can I say, Baroness? The Star of Athena is so beautiful, so legendary, so difficult to fence." She turned back to Philippe. "I couldn't have the real thing, of course, but I saw no reason not to have a copy. Childish, perhaps, but illegal?"

"The real one's here somewhere." Philippe nodded to the security team, who continued their search. "If I have to rip through every pillow, tear down the walls—"

"You'll have quite a hotel bill on your hands. And you won't find it, Philippe," Amanda added, quietly. "I promise you. You won't find anything at all."

And he didn't. Forty minutes later, Philippe and his men were forced to admit defeat. The Baroness, who hadn't spoken a word during the entire search, abruptly rose from her chair, glared once at Philippe, then disappeared out the door. The security men looked to him, then, reluctantly, followed the Baroness. Amanda smiled gently at the Immortal.

"Sorry, darling. Win some . . ."

He didn't let her finish. Philippe grabbed her arm, hard. "This isn't over, Amanda," he managed finally. "We both know it's not over." And he was gone.

Amanda packed quickly. Not that she'd be able to shake Philippe forever, of course, but she might be able to buy some cooling-off time. She checked her watch: 1:40 A.M. Maybe she could rouse one of the helicopter pilots and get a private flight out. . . .

It was not to be. Amanda felt the Buzz the moment she stepped from the hotel. She cast around; Philippe was nowhere in sight. She dropped her bags and moved carefully around the side of the building, her back to the wall. A wide stone walkway, deserted at this time of night, ran behind the hotel, linking it to the Casino. She found him there, waiting for her, sword in hand.

"We have no quarrel, Philippe." Amanda circled him cautiously.

"Draw your sword," he answered.

Amanda heard the regret in his voice, and the uncompromising steel. Reluctantly, she obeyed. Her blade appeared as if by magic; centuries of wielding it had molded the hilt to fit her as if she'd been born with a sword in her hand. Which, in a way, she had.

She parried the first blow and felt a familiar rush of excitement, her confidence in her own ability to survive mingling with a flicker of fear. But her exhilaration was short-lived. Philippe was a powerful fighter, an experienced swordsman. She could only duck and parry so long before she would be forced to kill, or be killed. And, attached as she was to her own neck, Amanda didn't want to be the one to end Philippe's extraordinary life.

She deflected another attack. "Philippe," she began, "listen to me." She backed up slowly, leading him up the stone steps to the courtyard behind Monaco's Casino. She quickly judged the distance between her and the ornate, second-story balcony, then made a run for it. In three great strides, she hurled herself straight up the terraced flower beds. She leapt as he dove for her legs; grabbing the iron bars of the balcony, she swung herself up and over the metal railing. It was a feat, she knew, that Philippe would not be able to duplicate, and it bought her a few precious moments.

"I will be damned," she continued, catching her breath, "if either of us loses our head over a worthless piece of paste."

"Bon Dieu!" he roared, as he desperately looked for a way to reach her. "Now you mock me!"

"No, Philippe, really, I—"

She jumped back as Philippe slammed his sword through the railing, narrowly missing her ankle. His voice shook with anger and frustration. "Where is the Star of Athena?"

"I have no idea. . . . Brussels?" she ventured. "Vienna, possibly. Oh, not the whole necklace, of course," Amanda continued. "The diamonds would have been sold off long ago. But the Sapphire itself, she would never have been able to get rid of it, it's too well-known. . . ."

"She? She, who?"

Amanda looked down at him pityingly. "Why the Baroness, of course. Who did you think?"

. . .

"At first," Amanda explained, "I thought Isabelle Jauverne had the copy made, knowing the Baron would try to get it back." They were back at the Loews Hotel, in Philippe's suite. He had ordered champagne and room service in exchange for the full story—and a cessation of hostilities.

"How did you know she hadn't?"

"If she'd known the necklace was paste, I don't think she'd have been as eager to tear the Baron's heart out with her bare hands," Amanda reminded him. "And the Baron himself would never have paid me a hundred thousand francs to retrieve a fake."

"Aha!" exclaimed Philippe. "Then you admit you stole the necklace from Madame Jauverne?"

"Of course not," she replied, indignant. "I returned the purloined necklace—which just happened to be a brilliant fake—to its rightful owner, the Baroness du Vaulier."

"Who then paid you to take it off her hands."

"Who better?" Amanda smiled and allowed Philippe to refill her glass, just to show there were no hard feelings over his attempt at her head. "I think she knew when she married him that the Baron had, shall we say, a weak heart?" Amanda continued. "She had the fake necklace made in case he was ever tempted to buy affection with the legendary Sapphire. What she didn't realize was that the Baron also had an uncanny ability to lose at cards."

"So she was forced to sell off the diamonds, one by one, to cover his losses."

"And protect the family name."

"Yes," he agreed, "that does seem to be a concern."

"It's more than that, Philippe. It's her immortality." Amanda paused to sip her champagne. "When she realized I was in Monte Carlo, it must have seemed that all her worries were over."

At that, Philippe raised an eyebrow. She shrugged, modestly. "With my name in the report, do you think the insurance company will doubt for a moment that the Star of Athena was really stolen?"

"You do have an unsettling effect on insurance adjusters."

"It's a gift." Amanda smiled at him. "One of many."

Philippe raised his glass. "To your many gifts . . ." He reached over and gently began unbuttoning her blouse. "And to unwrapping them all. . . ."

Amanda closed her eyes as Philippe's lips brushed her neck. She did so love the French.

Words to the Highlander

by Peter Hudson

"JAMES HORTON": Peter Hudson

British actor Peter Hudson is one of a number of one-time guest stars on Highlander: The Series *who made such a positive impact that they were brought back for additional apperarances. Hudson was originally to appear as evil Watcher James Horton only in two episodes (the first-season finale, "The Hunters," and the second season premiere, "The Watchers"), and in fact he died rather convincingly at the end of "The Watchers." But on* Highlander, *dead doesn't always mean gone, and in a series of spectacular revivals, Horton returned to the show again and again.*

Even after he was conclusively killed, ways were found to bring him back, at first in flashbacks, then later as the embodiment of all the evil at loose in the world. Although the role came to be dubbed "Ahriman," in fact Ahriman (the Zoroastrian name for the forces of darkness) was only one face of the universal character he portrayed— and it is a great measure of Peter Hudson's success in the role of James Horton that he seemed the natural choice to give a face to the greatest evil in the world, that which different cultures call Set, or Ahriman, or Satan.

In the end, Peter Hudson made a dozen appearances on Highlander, *including showing up in five out of six season finales.*

⚡

Hello. This is James. A voice from the past. It's been a long time! Whatever that means for someone like you, who would seem to be free of it. Time, I mean. Who can range unfettered across the pages of History, and rise up laughing after suffering mortal wounds. Or for me, come to that. Because, like it or not, understand it or not, you have only once been sure that I was finished, and that was the very first time, when my dear cousin, Joe, sent me spinning off the back of that boat into the sea. And you all thought I was gone for good. It was understandable. In other circumstances I would have called it human error, but in your case I don't feel justified. It's true they found my body down the coast. They cleaned me up and even gave me my last rites, or so they thought.

I can still see your face as you turned and recognised me again, the dust from my tombstone eddying around you, the sledgehammer poised for another strike. You had to prove I was dead, because you were so sure that I wasn't immortal. If I was really back, then the simple division of the world into recognisable mortals and immortals was thrown into question, the narrowing of the numbers of the powerful, ever fewer and ever stronger, down to the last, the one, would be jeopardized, YOUR POWER, MacLeod, would be undermined. And do you know what I saw in your eyes at that moment, one of the moments of my existence I have most cherished until today? I saw fear.

Later, when I lured you once again onto holy ground to finish you, once and for ever, I made a grave error. I underestimated the desperate strength that fear gave you. Your force was doubled as you rose up and ran me down, sent your blade sliding between my ribs towards my heart. And then you hesitated. Even as I felt myself slipping away, I noticed it. And I knew you were asking yourself, "Should I take his head? This mortal I've found so hard to kill? Should I draw the sword that lies concealed behind me, so close it feels within me, and strike off that blond head, strike the light from those unsmiling eyes forever, and wait for the quickening I cannot believe will come? Then at least I will be sure."

Why didn't you do it, MacLeod? Was it foolish pride? Believing that if *you*, Duncan MacLeod, saw to it that I was dead then dead I must be, and for ever?

Or was it a terrible knowledge, growing inside you like a dark flower, even as you heard my rasping breath, that there could be no quickening, no sudden surge of raw power shuddering through your frame, but that I *would* be back? I think so, Duncan—I can call you Duncan, can't I? The last time I asked you, you didn't answer me— Deep in my soul I know it to be true.

There is a very fundamental difference between us, Duncan, and its repercussions are not, I think, those that most would expect. Let us get *back* to fundamentals. You are, in your way, a holy man. That's why you high-tailed it off to that little monastery to look for inner strength. But I, too, am a holy man in *my* way. My battle against your kind is for the soul of humanity. The experiences we have shared over the years have taught me what that vitally important difference is:

You are a *prisoner.*

You are admired, adored, envied for your remarkable powers. I will even admit, that in the beginning my own hatred of you was not devoid of envy. At the start. For hundreds of years you have been a warrior defending what you perceive to be good. And people think "what a gift, to live forever, to have no fear as the brief candle burns down." But I have come to learn the truth, which is that you are trapped. Trapped *in* time, trapped *by* time, going only one way, for-ward, ever forward, with the desires and aspirations of a mortal and the terrible solitude of always losing that which you cherish; and always going on to lose again. You are a man who tries to resist the ter-rible temptation to look back over his shoulder, searching for a last glimpse of something, someone, you have lost but cannot bear to lose. For ever.

I, on the other hand, who am not immortal in terms that you can understand, by my very mortality can do what you cannot. When I understood this, my envy of you died. I have learned over these years that the true power of immortality can only be attained by those for whom physical death is inevitable. Indeed, this is one of the lessons of the figure of Christ himself.

But access to immortality is a terribly dangerous thing, Duncan, because of the surging power, much greater, much more all-embracing than a quickening. And this is the power of Ahriman. Yes. We now must speak of good and evil. I believe that your brand of good, MacLeod, is limited, and dangerous, and I have shown you why. I have seen terrible things, Duncan, horrors I cannot begin to describe, which you will never know, unless you pass over to the other side, and that, you cannot do. The potential for evil out there, beyond the looking glass, is so huge as to make me deeply fearful, in a way that you have never made me fearful. I have seen Ahriman face to face. I have supped with him and, for a time, he beguiled me, won me over to use me against you and others like you.

And now we come to the reason for this missive. You see, Duncan, I have realised, that though my sentiments concerning immortals, and yourself in particular, were founded on genuine beliefs and were even justified, I was *misguided*. Far greater evils menace mankind than you. In fact, I have realised that, though you too are misguided and naive, your hostility to Ahriman is a thing of value in the middle-term. For he must be opposed. He must be fought against, overthrown and crushed in the dust if mankind is to have the slightest chance of survival in a civilized world. And that is why, Duncan, I wish to make a truce. We have fought hard and long and I can now admit that I have grown to respect you, despite, perhaps even because of, your weaknesses. I flatter myself to believe that you have a little respect for me, too.

Duncan, we must unite! Bury our hatred and unite to destroy the powers of the black rose, coloured by the blood of the innocent. There has been enough useless killing. In that you are right. If we do not unite, if we squander our forces on mutual hostility, Ahriman's plan will succeed and the planet will plunge into a darkness that even our most pessimistic prophets have not foreseen. Meet me, Duncan, and let us make a plan. I have learned much, and have much to tell. I have been told that you feel the time is come to retire from the battle, to hand your power on to another, just as yours was passed to you so long ago. This is something only you can know. But if you do so, Duncan, then that immortal will be even more vulnerable than you are. Make him come to me, to speak, to learn, to make vows. To conquer Ahriman.

I live in hope.

James

Pants

by Donna Lettow

ASSOCIATE CREATIVE CONSULTANT: Donna Lettow

"Creative Consultant" is a title that's used in television for a member of the writing staff who, for whatever reason, doesn't fit one of the traditionally defined writing jobs. Donna Lettow joined the Highlander *staff as Script Coordinator at the beginning of season 3; she was promoted to Associate Creative Consultant at the start of season 6.*

Regarding the evolution of "Pants," Donna tells us: "Not every television show has a staff archaeologist, but for seasons 4 through 6, Highlander *had its 'Dr. Amy.' Sadly, every summer, we would lose Amy for several months, as she went off to the ruins of Pompeii to teach field archaeology techniques . . . and to attempt to rescue the Immortals we all know are still buried there beneath the ash. Once we got over our initial jealousy of her other life, we missed her terribly, and would mail her story outlines from new episodes, stills from dailies, and occasional bits of foolishness to brighten the lonely nights she spent in a stifling tent with a dim flashlight and no TV. 'Pants' is a story I wrote for Dr. Amy while I was watching the 1996 Summer Olympics and wishing I could share them with her."*

⚡

INT. JOE'S—DAY

MacLeod and Richie sit at the bar; Dawson's behind it. They're all transfixed by a television sus-pended from the ceiling at the end of the bar. Forget the blues, we're in Joe's Sports Bar.

> MACLEOD
> (intense)
> Go! Go! Go!

> RICHIE
> C'mon . . . c'mon . . .
> (standing)
> Come on!

No one notices Methos enter.

> DAWSON
> Run, boy! Move your ass!

> METHOS
> (oblivious to the TV)
> Hi, guys.

The guys are oblivious to him, caught up in the race on the TV. They yell and cheer along with the crowd on the telly.

> MACLEOD
> Go! Go!

> METHOS
> (to Dawson)
> How 'bout a beer?

                          DAWSON
                (to the TV)
             Watch it! He's coming up behind
             you!

                          METHOS
             Ah, it's every man for himself,
             I see.

He edges past Dawson, begins to draw himself a
beer as the race reaches its climax. From the
guys' reactions, it's clear they each backed a
different runner.

                          RICHIE
                (imaginary high-fives)
             Yessss!

                          DAWSON
             Aw, he was robbed!

                          MACLEOD
                (to Dawson)
             Okay, Dawson, pay up.

                          DAWSON
             What?
                (off MacLeod's look)
             Your guy came in second.

                          MACLEOD
             Win, place or show--you know the
             rules.

Grumbling, Dawson opens the till and fishes out
some money he begrudgingly hands to MacLeod.

                          DAWSON
             Don't spend it all in one place.

A national anthem begins to play. Richie watches
the screen, a little starry-eyed.

> RICHIE
> Now that's what it's all about.
> You got your flag. You got your
> song. You got your medal and
> you're the fastest guy in the
> world. Life doesn't get any
> better than this.

Methos takes notice of the TV for the first time.

> METHOS
> (disinterested)
> Watching the Olympics, huh?

> RICHIE
> (a little irritated)
> Don't tell me. Been there, done
> that, right?

> METHOS
> (a wry smile)
> Well, you could say I'm familiar
> with the commute between
> Marathon and Athens.

> DAWSON
> (grinning)
> Don't let him fool you, Richie.
> I've seen the old Chronicles--
> this guy had laurel leaves out
> the whazoo. He's just being
> humble.

> MACLEOD
> Humble? Him? That'll be the day.

                    (off Methos's feigned look of
                      humility)
                  You probably wrote those
                  Chronicles yourself.

                              RICHIE
                      (to Methos)
                  Then you should know all
                  about the Olympic spirit.
                  Brotherhood . . . teamwork . . .

                              METHOS
                  Bullshit.
                      (beat)
                  All this neo-classicist Olympic
                  flame crap is complete and utter
                  bullshit.
                      (gesturing at the TV)
                  Petty nationalism, sacrificing
                  your health for a piece of
                  metal--where'd they get this
                  stuff? That's not what it was
                  about at all.

                              RICHIE
                  Okay, Mr. Podium-on-Mt.-Olympus,
                  what's it all about?

Methos points to the runner on the TV.

                              METHOS
                  Pants.

                              DAWSON
                  You just lost me.

                    MACLEOD
Oh, this should be good.

                     RICHIE
Pants?

                    METHOS
You heard me. Pants. Trousers.
Or more precisely, the lack
thereof.

                    DAWSON
   (light bulb goes on)
Ahhh . . .

                     RICHIE
So you're telling me the true
spirit of the Olympics is not
about the "human drama of
athletic competition," it's
about not wearing pants.
   (beat)
Sorry, professor, I'm not buying
it.

                    METHOS
   (rolling his eyes)
My, you are young.
   (to Dawson)
Explain it to him, Joe. Make
sure you use small words.

                    DAWSON
It's about women, Richie.

                    MACLEOD
So the entire Olympic movement

started as a way to pick up
chicks?

                    METHOS
Absolutely! And it worked
brilliantly, too.
(off their dubious looks)
Think about it. You've just run
26 miles. You're a hero! You're
hot, your muscles glistening with
sweat, your virility hanging down
to China, and there you are on
the winner's platform in nothing
but laurel leaves and a smile.
   (beat)
No woman alive could resist
that.
   (reminiscing, with a smile)
Some days the Vestal Virgins
would be so thick, you'd have to
beat them off with sticks.
   (re the TV)
No, Richie, this is but a pale
imitation. Keep your medal, keep
your record books, I'll take a
priestess of Hera any day.

As Methos walks toward the door to leave--

                    RICHIE
   (to MacLeod and Dawson)
Twenty-six miles? Man, that's
gotta chafe.

Consone's Diary

Excerpted from "The Consone Journals"

by Anthony De Longis

"OTAVIO CONSONE": Anthony De Longis

Very rarely were parts on Highlander *cast for swordfighting ability.
Guest stars were cast for their acting chops, in the belief that the skills
of our star, swordmaster, and film editors could make the swordfights
look good. And quite often they could. But when actor Anthony De
Longis, a swordmaster in his own right, appeared as Lyman Kurlow
in the second-season episode "Blackmail," everyone saw the difference.
The final swordfight in that episode was a stunning showpiece, and
Adrian Paul asked to have his extraordinary opponent brought back
for a return engagement. The production team was happy to agree,
and the writers and producers kept Anthony on their short "wish list,"
but it was three years before the ideal role was found—and again, it
occurred in an unusual way. For just as roles were not usually cast
with swordfighting ability in mind, neither were scripts usually based
on swordfighting styles. But when Anthony came to Head Writer
David Abramowitz with a suggestion for a story revolving around the*

Spanish "Mysterious Circle," at the same time as Adrian Paul was studying flamenco dancing, something clicked.

The "Duende" episode features a number of complex rapier-and-dagger fights which could never have been accomplished without the skills Anthony and Adrian brought to the set. This episode stands out in the memory of many as one of Highlander's finest.

Regarding "Consone's Diary," Anthony De Longis reports:

"When Bill Panzer and Gillian Horvath invited me to contribute to this book I was delighted. I am thrilled to be a part of the Highlander family. I have had a lifelong love affair with the blade and the opportunity to offer my skills as actor and swordsman to the Highlander legacy has been one of the great rewards on my journey.

" 'Duende' was the culmination of an amazing team of talented artists. The writers, the unflagging support of producers Bill Panzer and Peter Davis and Ken Gord, director Richard Martin, and the excellent crew—everyone went the extra mile to make this episode special. This was especially true of Adrian Paul, who demands the best from himself and who delights in challenges that expand his creative envelope. Swordmaster extraordinaire Braun McAsh welcomed my ideas and encouraged me to co-create the very complex rapier and dagger choreography. Both of us labored hard to balance historical inspiration with dynamic character action. The rain that fell the entire final day and night transformed the fighting surface into a virtual ice rink and eliminated any rehearsal prior to filming our climactic sword encounter. That uncomfortable combination gave the fight a real edge and the downpour added million-dollar production values (God is a teriffic Art Director). We took the impossible in stride and made magic.

"Given this second chance to live in his skin, here are some reflections about one of the most fascinating characters I've ever portrayed. Otavio Consone, master of the sword, perfectionist, obsessive, Immortal, and, I dare say, the only man to have twice defeated Duncan MacLeod in a duel."

December 21, 1997

After his death at the hands of Duncan MacLeod four days ago, I managed to discover and retrieve Otavio Consone's diary. The full text is on file at the Watcher Institute. I have noted entries that refer to his history and association with Señor MacLeod because I thought they might be of special interest to the Society.

Carmen de la Vega, Watcher

August 10, 1851

Only one thing worth noting happened today. A madman appeared from nowhere, a barbarian from the wild hills of Scotland. He's a fighter and he hates the English. That alone would be reason enough to teach him, but there is much more to recommend him.

In truth, his intrusion provided a welcome relief to my usual routine. I had just finished another tedious session with the spoiled and lazy son of the Minister of Finance. These ill-formed creatures who call themselves the "nobility" seem stamped from the same imperfect mold. Their fathers built an empire, the sons have difficulty rising before noon. Not one of them will ever amount to anything with the blade. They will hire their killing done, having neither the skills nor the courage to handle their own affairs of honor.

No sooner had my inept pupil departed than this *estranjero* stomped into my studio. I'd have had no trouble hearing him even if I hadn't felt the vibrations of another of the Chosen. He announced himself as "Duncan MacLeod of the Clan MacLeod," every bit as proud as any courtier to the Catholic King. He proclaimed himself the son of a Chieftain, as if that made him any less the savage.

With that, the young fool unsheathed a magnificent specimen of the Japanese swordmaker's art and launched a stroke that could have split a fully grown ox. His katana was perhaps the finest blade I have ever seen and was as curious a contradiction as the man himself. He handled his sword like a slaughterhouse butcher, all fury and power,

but what power. And it is obvious he has had training, for there is sub-
tlety and strategy at the heart of his movements.

It was a simple matter to avoid his mad charge and the half dozen
mighty strokes that followed, delivered with a speed and endurance
that was impressive. A lesser man than I could not have avoided serious injury. Three times I deflected his blade and drew his blood.
Three times he knew I was his master. Suddenly he stepped back, lowered his sword and grinned with obvious pleasure. He made a small
bow to acknowledge my skills but clearly offering no apology for his
own. MacLeod declared that I was every bit as good as he's heard and
that he's crossed oceans to study with me. No fawning, no pretense,
just a hunger to learn how I so easily defeated his best efforts.

Although MacLeod lacks refinement, he's intelligent and he has
heart and he's utterly determined to learn. He's traveled half of Europe
to seek me out and he won't take no for an answer. This one should be
careful what he wishes for.

I told him to return tomorrow to face my decision.

August 11

Sleep is impossible. I have thought of little else but this mad Scots-
man all night. MacLeod knows he is no match for me, yet he risks my
challenge and his own destruction. He's obviously a warrior, a man
who has fought in many battles in many lands. More important, he's
one of the Chosen, who has kept his head when others more skilled
than he, I have no doubt, were confident that they'd have both his
head and essence. Yet somehow he triumphed. Somehow he lived to
arrive at my door. That our destinies are linked is obvious.

He is a man that bears watching. To accomplish this I must keep
him close. The danger of this appeals to me greatly, for what is life
without risk? I have no doubt MacLeod would fight me if I demanded
it, even knowing it means his certain death. This is either a very brave
or a very stupid man and I do not think he is "stupido." Perhaps he
realizes I have no interest in such an easy victory. But is it wise to train
him? He will not be satisfied with the small disciplines I offer to the

chattering masses. MacLeod knows he is gifted but he recognizes his limitations. He wants my treasures, the subtle refinements that will transform him from barbarian to a true master of the blade.

Will he take my skills and use them to conquer me the way I defeated so many of my own teachers? It was the best way to make certain they could never reveal my former weaknesses. Only the great Ramirez escaped and I was glad not to have to be the one to take his head. I liked him, he was my friend.

But MacLeod is my problem now. The cautious man would send him away or kill him and be done with it. The exceptional man would make him a student, a disciple, perhaps even a companion. It's been a long time since I've called anyone "amigo" and truly meant it. Most candidates don't survive the tests. Besides, a friend will eventually relax his guard and expose the secret, fatal weakness he hides in his heart of hearts. That will give me the necessary edge whenever I choose to utilize it.

So be it. MacLeod's training begins tonight. If he proves himself worthy, I will have an ally, a protégé, and ultimately—an opponent worthy of my skills.

August 15

MacLeod has agreed to put aside his Japanese blade and enter the modern age. I introduced him to the only true weapon for a gentleman, the Spanish rapier. A masterpiece of design and evolution, its long slim blade is honed on both edges and tapers to a needle sharp point. The rapier is the great equalizer, it recognizes neither rank nor privilege, only ability.

I select a cup hilt guard for MacLeod. It will offer him the best protection for his hand while he is learning. I have to smile at how confusing he finds the extended cross-guard until he discovers how readily my own curving quillons trap his blade and wrench it from his fingers. I never have to show him something twice. I have waited a lifetime for such a student.

August 30

MacLeod is without patience. That is his great weakness. He tires of my endless exercises and demands to know my "botta secrete," the secret killing techniques. Whenever you face another in mortal combat, you have only the skills you bring with you that day. There are no second chances. I must make him understand, he is not ready.

I invite MacLeod to attack me with his best effort, to hold nothing back. His first attack is flawless, but unsuccessful. This angers him and he rushes his next pass only to find my blade tickling his throat. I remind him that any challenge outside of the practice studio can have only three possible outcomes. You lose, in which case you die. You tie, in which case you both die. You win, in which case you live. Not the kind of odds that encourage rushing. You might lose your head.

September 28

MacLeod has embraced the Spanish rapier like one born to it. It was not easy for him to abandon his familiar ally, his katana. But a swordsman evolves or he dies. So it is with the sword. So it must be with the Chosen.

Time and again I demonstrate the superiority of the *estocada*, the speed and efficiency of the thrust over the cut. The cut still has its uses, but its use demands the precision of a surgeon. The time for the lopping of limbs belonged to our primitive ancestors who knew no better.

October 17

I've told MacLeod each man has a thousand bad cuts and a thousand bad thrusts. Few swordsmen live long enough to rid themselves of this fatal baggage. My gypsy student, my *gitano*, spends hours in the studio, practicing, tirelessly repeating his lessons over and over. There may yet be hope.

He was ready for the first secret. Strategy. A duelist asks himself four simple questions. What is my opponent doing? How is he doing it? What can I do about it? And most important, can I do it?

Secret number two. Simplify. Action is an exercise in minimalism. Speed does not come from greater effort, but from doing less and doing it better. A smaller, simpler move is more efficient and speed is the natural result.

The hunger in MacLeod's eyes reminds me of my own insatiable appetite for knowledge. It is both exciting and chilling. I haven't felt this alive in years.

October 29

Duncan MacLeod does not know how closely I watch his progress. I see each small discovery, each subtle nuance in technique. Sometimes he finds more than I have shown to him. He is becoming his own teacher, the path of a true master.

November 12

Now MacLeod has the eyes to see, the ears to hear, we can truly begin. Tonight I invited MacLeod to enter my secret world and discover the "Verdadera Destreza," the true art of the fence. Time and again he has demanded to know my "magic." How do I always seem to know his next move, even before he makes it? We walk the lines and patterns, the *rectitudines*, and they come to life like new yet familiar friends.

My Mysterious Circle defines distance in terms that are absolute. Between you and your opponent exists an invisible boundary between life and death, the "lineas infinitis." Outside this line, he offers no threat and merits no response, simply vigilance. When he crosses this line, you have him, he has entered your killing zone. It requires only three inches of steel to finish the job. The Circle creates an impenetrable barrier which your foe cannot invade except by your invitation.

The Circle diagrams scientifically your most direct route to wound, maim or instantly extinguish the life of your foe.

MacLeod struggles to understand, but comprehension teases, then eludes him. Again I invite his *ganacia*, savouring his dangerously skillful attacks. Again and again I foil every cut, every thrust. Always he finds my own blade poised at his vitals, ready to incapacitate or kill.

All at once, MacLeod steps back, the shock of discovery lighting his face. With one step and a subtle adjustment of my body and blade he realizes I've programmed him to attack openings that seem easy and vulnerable, only to find me ready and waiting. MacLeod sees, he knows. The "magic" is the simple application of all that we've practiced.

November 26

Today we drilled the "stesso-tempo," the single move that is both defense and counter-attack in one simultaneous action. The angle of the blade, so subtle and delicate. The timing of the deflection, so hair's-breadth critical to success and survival. The gentle removal of the body and the power unleashed as both hips and torso return to take possession of the center line and drive your blade through your opponent's defenses by superior position and leverage.

Swordplay is a science. The artistry is in the details. Small adjustments have profound effects.

December 14

I remind MacLeod that a true Master of the Circle cannot be defeated. He has already fought the battle in his mind and body in his practice a thousand times before. He waits confidently for the move he knows must come next. Each response has been mastered and repeated, each problem analyzed, solved and converted to action. The mind of the Master is sharp, his body ready, his spirit calm. The victory is his before the fight ever begins.

The Circle is now a part of MacLeod's soul. He breathes it like air, he craves it like sunshine, practicing day and night. I have to chase him out so I can train myself. I have started to be more selective about what I reveal to him. He has gotten that good.

I have chosen well.

December 17

I surprise myself, often speaking to MacLeod about secret things close to my heart and unshared for longer than I care to remember. It is the easy talk of comrades who understand much while saying little.

December 21

MacLeod is ready for another secret, understanding the nature of fear. Fear is a tool to be wielded like a blade. It must be snuffed out in your own heart and fanned like raging wild-fire in the breast of your adversaries.

I favor the "flamberge" blade with its undulating waves of naked steel. This is no accident but a calculated choice, part of the subtle mind game I wage against the confidence of my opponent. He knows that any contact with my blade will disrupt the rhythm of his attack as his blade catches against the enveloping folds of my own. He knows too well that even such subtle delays make him vulnerable and create opportunities for my potentially fatal response.

Perhaps worse, the curves of my blade are designed to inflict ugly wounds, macerating rather than slicing cleanly, literally chewing any flesh it contacts. I want him thinking about such things. It encourages doubt. Doubt breeds hesitation. This is key. Break your man's concentration and you shatter his confidence. Make him doubt himself for even an instant and he is yours. He will hesitate at a crucial moment. That is the opportunity you must seize. It will only appear for an instant. You must be ready.

December 28

MacLeod is the best I have ever produced, a mere student no more. This is no real surprise to me. It was my destiny to prepare him for the others he must face. Someday the master may have to fight the student, but hopefully, that is many lifetimes away.

January 4, 1852

MacLeod and I enter the Circle and begin our daily dance of training and discovery. To enter the Circle is to stand alone, to face your fears and vanquish them.

The Circle is a mystery that a man must embrace boldly. Like a mistress, she will only reveal her secrets if you give yourself fully and completely. Prove yourself worthy and she will open her treasures for you to savor and enjoy. She will make you invulnerable, unbeatable, the master of men, and perhaps even the final victor in the battle among the Immortals, the Chosen Ones.

January 15

It is a new year and many things are changing. I have allowed myself to have a friend in Duncan MacLeod. This is still very new, but I have come to accept and even savor the pleasure of his companionship.

Perhaps this is why I now find myself falling in love again. It has been a long time since a woman stirred my heart and my passions. Not just the physical needs a man must satisfy, but the deeper ache that even one of the Chosen feels in his heart. The need for a mate, someone to share your life with, to give yourself completely to, to share and savor every breath of every new day, even for an interval as brief as one mere lifetime.

The sword has been my life's blood, the Mysterious Circle my passion. I have given her my heart and soul and she has found me worthy and gifted me with my heart's desire. No man can best me, no man dares challenge me. I have earned my reward.

Now I find myself with feelings for a woman again. I deserve happiness. I will allow these feeling to run their course, come what may. I will court and win Theresa del Gloria.

February 2, 1852

I have discovered where my errant student goes in the evening. MacLeod dances flamenco in a taverna that features peasant dances and gypsy entertainments. I had told him his footwork was insufficient and that he must take every opportunity to improve it, but I never expected his studies to take such a route. He is full of surprises, this friend of mine.

February 26

I have decided to take Theresa del Gloria for my bride. I have watched her from afar and she is magnificent. We have only spoken a few times, in the most formal of circumstances, but I know now that she is the one for me. Theresa makes my heart sing, and every day is a little more precious because she is alive. I cannot wait for her to be mine, fully and completely. She will be my mate and we will crowd a millennium into our time together. I see her for what she is, an exceptional flower waiting to blossom. I will inspire her, teach her, mold her and give both my body and my soul. I will create a world for us. With her father's connections and my skills, the sons of the most powerful men in Spain will flock to my studio. I will teach them and bind them to my will. Soon both they and their fathers will fall under my influence and I will heap Theresa with the riches they will pour into my pockets. But Theresa will be my most treasured possession. I will make her happy beyond her wildest dreams.

I must speak to her father, Don Diego del Gloria, at his earliest convenience.

March 3

I take Don Diego del Gloria to the gypsy taverna to see my student, Duncan MacLeod, perform his dance. His partner is a beautiful gypsy woman and they move with fiery passion. I have no doubt that they have danced together before.

To Don Diego's surprise, his daughter Theresa has come to the taverna in secret with her Duena as her only companion. He is appalled at her forwardness, but I am amused and delighted by her spirit of adventure.

I introduced them both to MacLeod, who flirted with her Duena and made everyone laugh at the old woman's pleased discomfort. When Duncan offered to escort the women home, I took the opportunity to open negotiations for my marriage to Theresa with her father. I was confident that no harm could befall her on the journey home with MacLeod as her protector.

March 14

Today I feel so old, a cold emptiness fills my chest where my heart used to be. In spite of all I have done for him, MacLeod has betrayed me. My friend has fallen in love with my Theresa. He, a half-civilized barbarian, dares to look at her with love, with the eyes of desire. I, who love her so myself, can hardly blame him, but I cannot permit this outrage. My only choice was to banish him from Madrid and send him far away.

I will miss him terribly, but if he stays, I will have to kill him.

March 15

I discovered them together, in the garden, in spite of my warnings. There was no choice but to fight, and no doubt as to the outcome. I ordered Theresa from the garden. She thought it was to spare her the sight of her lover's death. Perhaps that was part of my reasoning, but I did not want her there to see the Quickening. It is too soon for such a revelation.

Theresa amazed me and offered a deal. If I spared his life, she will give herself to me freely, and never mention this episode, or Duncan MacLeod, again. If I killed him, she promised to be in a convent by nightfall. She would be lost to me forever. I must give us this chance. She will learn to love me. All I need is time, and I have plenty of that.

Then too, MacLeod must be made to pay for what he has done. The pain will be much greater, the burden much heavier if I spare him. He must live every day with the knowledge that I defeated him, that he owes his life to the woman he loved but wasn't man enough to win.

One day we will fight again, and I will kill him. It is our destiny. Let him suffer until that day.

September 4, 1853

She has cheated me, they both have. All I asked was for Theresa to give us an honest chance. But every day and every night, MacLeod came between us. Even in the bed chamber at night, he was there, her eyes accusing me, holding me at a distance, denying me her heart. She offered only the exercise, never the love of a wife and mate given freely and completely. It was a torture for us both.

Finally, it was too much. I put her out of her misery. She rests at peace but I did not get off so lightly. My torments continue.

There is the passage of many years before Duncan MacLeod again enters the life of Otavio Consone. I have picked up their story with their next meeting in Paris, in 1997.

Carmen de la Vega, Watcher

December 17, 1997

It is time for the final step in my revenge against Anna Hidalgo. I promised her back in 1971 that the death of Raphael was only the first cut. Again, a faithless woman shattered my plans and stole my dreams. All I wanted was to make her happy, and she returned my love and my favors with betrayal. So be it. I returned the favor by taking from her the thing that sustained her, the dance. But I wasn't finished. She thought that the dance was her whole world. But growing inside her was the fruit of her deceit, her daughter.

I waited, biding my time, watching her child grow into a beautiful woman. The child is delightful, almost as beautiful as her mother. Luisa Hidalgo is full and ripe like sweet fruit waiting to be tasted. She is very young and no challenge to my powers. Her seduction was a delight. We both took such pleasure in her youthful exuberance and curiosity.

Now is the time to complete my vengeance on Anna Hidalgo. I will carry her daughter far away. Perhaps I will kill her, perhaps not. But Anna will never know. The last of her dreams will die once and for all with the loss of her child. First dreams with her lover, Raphael, then her dreams of a career in dance, and last, her dreams for her child. She will spend the rest of her days wondering, waiting for word that will never come. Anna will live to regret her betrayal with each and every day.

But that is not the best of it. To make my reward complete, my old enemy returns to pay his debt in full. Once again, Duncan MacLeod tries to interfere in my affairs. Once again he comes sniffing around my women. His life is forfeit. The day of reckoning is at hand.

MacLeod is so easy. He must play the hero, he cannot help himself. It will be the work of a moment to provoke him and put an end to his meddling forever. He will rush to rescue the beautiful women. He cannot help himself. He is a professional hero. It amazes me that he has lived so long. Perhaps his skills have improved enough to give me a real challenge. I shiver at the thought. The element of risk is what makes life worth living. Without the victory over a worthy opponent, how can I be worthy to be final One?

I have looked into the eyes of those I have defeated at the moment of truth, the instant before the final stroke that brings death for the last and final time. I saw deep into the wells of their souls. Then came the Quickening. All that they ever were belonged to me. I wrested it from them by right of combat. Their most private dreams and terrors were a banquet for my appetites. To the victor go the spoils.

Perhaps it would be better if MacLeod and I had never met. We would not have been friends but I would never have felt this pain, this ache that gnaws at my guts and sucks my soul. I gave him my trust and my friendship, I shared my life and my dreams and he repaid me by stealing my woman. Like a thief, he stabbed me in the back and robbed me of all that I valued most. I am what his betrayal has made me. Only my sword and the Circle gives me peace and a reason to go on. Once I was alive. Now I only exist to win. I pass my nights in meaningless conquests and my days in even more meaningless contests. Perhaps that is what I cannot forgive.

I hunger to see the look on MacLeod's face when he must again acknowledge that I am the master. Perhaps then I will have peace at last.

Down Towards the Outflow

by Roger Bellon

COMPOSER: Roger Bellon

Composer Roger Bellon was the savior of many a Highlander *episode in his five seasons with the series, adding his haunting and playful music to the episodes under the pressure of a daunting international delivery schedule.*

For "Down Towards the Outflow," Roger told us he wanted to explore something that the series really hadn't covered: the near-death/after-death experience of an Immortal coming back to life.

And just for the record, it's pronounced with a French accent: Ro-zhay Beh-lohn.

Doubled over in pain, her guts, oozing, are held in with bloodied and mud soiled hands. Her head reels, her face contorts with the pain of life moving swiftly from her nine hundred year old body. "Ah shit, this is the second time this month . . . fuck this war and fuck this god-forsaken planet!" Eyes shut, suddenly wrench open with fear and panic. Once again she will die and once again her life will painfully

flash before her eyes, an experience, to this day, she cannot comprehend. "Christ not again, how many times am I going to see my mother
yelling at me for smoking in the bathroom when I was a kid. Ma,
please I'm sorry . . . I feel bad about it, but fuck, that was eight hundred and eighty-five years ago . . . give me a break with this shit . . .
will ya!" Light slowly engulfs her. The pain seems to fade into the
background as she feels herself being propelled like one of those little
round steel balls being shot down the chute of a pinball machine
towards a rubber bumper. Faster and faster she speeds towards a faint
light. The closer she moves towards the light the less she remembers
about her death. She feels a warmth and calmness that she has never
felt before and realizes that "Heaven" is the light at the end of the tunnel. Way in the distance she can make out what appears to be a neon
sign. Blinking off and on, pulsating with that low Tesla buzz.
"HEAVEN, THIS WAY . . . what the fuck . . . and who in the hell is
that?" Behind a white iron gate, a rather paunchy man, dressed in
white robes garnished with feathered wings, seems to be motioning to
her. "Wait a minute . . . the sign says Heaven is over there. Then why
is he, hey . . . hey you . . . wait a minute . . . I thought I was going to
Heav . . . what the fuck, who's that?" She whips past the angel smiling
and waving at her . . . "Maybe next time darling . . . have a good
life . . . again!" he says. Try as she may she can't seem to slow down or
make herself move towards that white iron gate she so desperately
wants to enter. Her speed suddenly accelerates towards a secondary
light, not white. She is starting to feel a tinge of anxiety creep into her
cells. "I don't get it, and who are they?" Two people wave at her, a man
and a woman. They are standing in front of a door with a sign on it
that reads "IMMORTALS, KEEP RIGHT." "Boy, they both look
familiar, isn't she, hey wait a fucking minute . . . is this a joke or what?"
The woman is dressed in a tight Betty Boop cocktail dress, her breasts
bleed out from the top. She has short platinum blonde hair, big red
lips and a large toothy smile. The man is bare chested wearing tight
black Eldridge Cleaver cock pants. His brown hair is in a pony tail
with the prerequisite ear ring in place. "What the fuck . . . those are
the two bozos from that dumb TV show I used to watch as a kid. What

were their names? I think his was Duncan and hers was Amanda. That's it, Duncan and Amanda . . . what the hell are they doing here?" As she speeds by, they both smile and wave her on as if she is rounding third base on her way to home plate in the seventh game of the world series. Her emotions seem to be turning to that of anger even rage as she whips by on her way to what looks like an EXIT sign. The sign is red and is above a dark brown hole. The closer she gets the worse she feels. Even the air has a hint of putrefied life in it. She can hear something in the distance, it seems to be the sounds of people yelling at each other. "Where the hell am I going now . . . Hell?" But it wasn't Hell, or was it? "God damn, I recognize those voices . . . that sounds like Captain Panzer screaming at Sergeant Paonessa again. What the fuck did he do this time?" Her speed is now in deceleration moving toward the brown hole, her stomach tingles and her ears whistle, her body feels heavy and constipated. Without warning she is sucked in, the smell is unbearable, the pressure agonizing. She is being pushed down and down a long slimy tube that hugs her with its ribbed walls. She feels fear, pain, and all the complex emotions of an approaching event unknown. "Oh god this hurts, I can't breathe, I can't move . . . oh no NO Please!!!!!" Ear crushing decibels spew forth the pulsing sounds that punctuate her spiraling movements down towards the outflow. The apex is shattered with the reversing noisy suck of her birth, again.

Silence, calm, stillness, repose ripped by her desperate gasp for air. Chest heaving, the knotted cramped pain of re-birth line her underskin to the tip of her tongue. The pungent moist odor of this atmosphere's air is the first sign of life she tastes. Her mind is blank, she knows what has happened, but cannot focus on the truth of her experience. Heavy eyelids cautiously unclose. The first image is of the night's deep blue ether holding the four moons of URR hostage. Such beauty only seems fitting after her recent purge. . . . "Lieutenant, lieutenant, I've been searching for you since this morning. Are you alright, where have you been . . . Commander Ginsberg is mad as hell and needs to speak to you at once. It seems your squad's attack on quadrant 32-H has failed. Not only have the NOLLEB fled the planet

intact, but the entire operation has gone over budget and I am personally getting flack from fleet Commanders Ginsberg and King at
Gauttlemont headquarters." "Slow down Corporal Hillman, slow
down. Can't you see I feel like shit . . . what the hell happened to our
men, what day is it for christsakes, where is everybody . . ." "Lieutenant, don't you remember, your squad was hit by . . ." "Oh god, Corporal, when I think of the fucking paperwork I could just . . . hold on,
hold on . . . does the Commander know all the details of what happened here?" "Not yet, Lieutenant, a final report is being compiled as
we speak." "Well then, Corporal, get me Master-Sergeant
Abramowitz. He's been through enough of these episodes to give
those shitheads at headquarters what they want. I'll be damned if I'm
going to take the fall for this disaster. And besides, if we don't give
them the kill numbers they want, our plans to spin this sequence off to
a wider alien congregation is history. Captain Panzer put it best when
he said, 'Boys, they'd better not fuck with my retirement,' and you
know what, Corporal Hillman?" "What, Lieutenant?" "I agree one
hundred percent with him . . . so get your ass in gear and get Master-
Sergeant Abramowitz on the communicator before URR and the few
of us left here become one with the cosmos. OR DO YOU THINK
YOU CAN LIVE FOREVER. . . ?"

The Methos Chronicles
Part I

by Don Anderson

ASSISTANT PROPS MASTER: Don Anderson

*Props on a television series include anything on the set that's not
nailed down or being worn by an actor. On a week's notice, the props
department could be called upon to come up with anything from gro-
ceries for MacLeod's kitchen to an "antique" tea set for a Japanese
flashback.*

*Don Anderson's eagerness to contribute "The Methos Chronicles" to
this project is just one more example of how* Highlander *managed to
capture the imagination of its entire crew. While the props department might not be the first place you would think to look for script
ideas, on* Highlander *it seemed that everyone was putting their cre-
ativity to the test, imagining their own stories for the characters they
came to know and love.*

|

When I was born, the world was still new; the morning dew of life clung purposefully to tree branches and walls, in hopes of surviving the inevitability of the rising sun that would extinguish it for another day. We were far luckier than that. We not only survived, we flourished in our home in the desert. I was welcomed into a large, happy family that occupied the same oasis as my father's grandfather had, long ago. My people had lived there, without interruption, for much longer than that, but our oral history contained specifics for only the last 100 or so years.

Nothing about my childhood was in any way remarkable, compared to the others in my village, or for that matter, from my own siblings. I was the second son of three boys and two girls by a father who claimed vague relation to an extinct royal court and a mother who descended from a line of traders who had settled in the area when she was just a baby herself. I did not lack for attention or love from my parents or my extended family that populated the immediate environs. We lived gratefully together under the limited shade of the fig trees and palms that grew around our home, giving us resources to barter with the many traders who passed through our oasis with items that we desired which remained unavailable to us by other means. In this way we continued with our lives, joyously greeting each new day as another opportunity to improve our condition. When I consider my past from this present perspective, I realise that my entire world was contained in that place with those people, surrounded by a sense of belonging that I have never known since that time. My life has always been about surviving, in one way or another, but the meaning that it had to me then, with the people that I loved and admired, has shaded somewhat in the ensuing years of my existence. The perfect simplicity of that time and place has left me searching for a replacement that I can never find.

Our home was surrounded by an unforgiving desert, which is now called Egypt, that tolerated no mistakes by unprepared travelers. Attempting to ford its expanse without the proper provisions was a fool's errand: certain, parched death awaited those who made a single mistake while fording the cruel distance between oases. Many of the childhood lessons that I learned were centred around tales of the sand engulfing unwary caravans who had fatally misjudged the ferocity of the sun overhead, or the amount of water necessary to complete the journey between the sanctuaries of population. Nothing and no one lived for long outside the boundaries of the settlements that grew around those sources of liquid. Water is the most important substance in that land, the currency of life itself.

It so happened that when I reached my 28th birthday, our home was visited by a terrible calamity. My father was made aware that the well from which we drew our sustenance had dropped in level more than ever before. It had been low in the past, as the underground streams that fed it ebbed and flowed, but never had it sunk to such a desperate mark before. There was an assembly of all the people in our settlement, so that we could decide upon a course of action that would permit us to continue living without it.

We had to move from there, and soon, but where could we go? None of my family had known any other place except this one, only a few of our people had ventured beyond our immediate borders for long. We recounted the tales of other oases that we had heard from the traders who had rested here, and tried to decide which ones might be close enough for us to travel to. We also had to consider whether any of those potential destinations might be occupied by a clan that would be hostile to our arrival. That turned out to be the least of our immediate concerns.

II

When the Bedouin scouting party found me, I was certain that I had died, but they revived me with water from their gourds and carried me back to their camp. I was so disoriented that at first I could not understand what they were saying, but I gradually awakened and explained to them what had happened. As the caravan from our village followed the bearings to our new home that my father was taking from

the sun, we saw a sandstorm forming in the distance. We became completely disoriented and lost track of each other when the maelstrom
hit; the sky became darker than night as we were engulfed by the
swirling sand. I crouched on the ground and huddled into a ball, protected by the cape that I wrapped around myself to shut out the insane
sounds of the turbulence. It seemed to go on forever, because day was
indistinguishable from night until it finally stopped and I emerged
from my cover to find that I was alone. I struggled to find some trace
of my family, but the landscape was completely different, having been
dramatically reformed by the storm. It took two days before I came
upon the realisation that I should continue following my father's
directions to the oasis and hope that the others had done the same.
With only a small amount of water left in my container, I knew that I
had to begin moving again or I would perish in that unforgiving terrain.

I grew weaker and weaker, it was apparent that I wouldn't make it
much further; I was seriously disoriented from my lack of food and
water. The last thing I remember was thinking that if I could just take
one more step, I would make it to safety. . . .

III

These Bedouins were masters of riding camels across the parched
land and I begged them to go out and look for my family, taking them
some supplies and providing guidance back to this oasis. Four days
later the riders returned to confirm my dreaded fears that none of my
family had survived. While I sat there in shock, the Bedouin elders
went away and discussed among themselves what they were to do,
returning to offer me the safety of their camp. They taught me their
ways of the desert, how to find water and food, and eventually they
learned to accept me into their flock. We lived together for many
years, until it became obvious that I was not growing older. The elders
had me brought to their meeting tent, where one of the men from the
original party who had found me was growing noticeably older. They

passed their talking stick around and they debated what I could be, this man who didn't change appearance with the passage of time. They decided that I was either a god or a demon, both of which were unwanted in their home.

During a ceremony to honour the next full moon, I was forced to fight their best warrior to the death. That was the second time I died. When the sun rose the next morning and I had revived again, they tied my hands together and I was banished from the oasis. I was transported away by a small party, whose job it was to ensure that I was left far enough from their camp that I could not return. I was sent out into the vast solitude with no weapon and no water, left to die far from the only home that I knew. I watched them fade away in the distance as they made their way back. I was as terrified as they were. I had no way of knowing what I was, any more than they did; there was absolutely no frame of reference for these things that were happening to me. I stumbled upon a pile of bones and used them to rub apart the strands that bound my hands together in front of me so I could continue into the unknown, able at least to defend myself.

I found my way along a traveled path to a hidden settlement that would later be called Petra, the next place I settled, and began to live with the Nabataeans who camped there. I was so angry with the Bedouins for sending me away, that I swore an oath to return and kill them all for what they had done. That anger took a long time to disappear from my heart. While those years passed, I learned how to carve out caves from the sheer stone walls that protected their camp's location. I lived and grew stronger as I worked each day; I thought about who I was and what I was supposed to do about it. It eventually became apparent to everyone that I was not aging, and I knew that I could not stay there any longer.

It was in this way that I became aware that I was never going to be able to live among other people for very long. My life had become a journey between the cracks of civilisations in which I did not fit. I had already survived longer than anyone I had ever heard of; lived in many strange places and soon found myself wondering if there was anyone else like me out there. I was alone, confused and angry at a world that I didn't understand, so I resolved to continue searching in the hope of finding a family again, somewhere that I belonged.

IV

As I made my way among Mortals, I noticed that certain people I met gave off a unique feeling; as though I somehow knew them: I could actually sense their presence and assumed that they could feel mine. We never took each other by surprise. At this time I was, by my best estimation, 603 years old, and the world had changed much for me in that time. I began to encounter more of these strangers who recognised me in this new way, one in particular—Elijah—with whom I finally broached the subject of this strange ability. He spoke of a man named Menahem, who told him a tale that attempted to explain much of what I felt. He was the first of those strangers that we eventually came to call the Ancient Ones: Menahem had lived for 750 years.

Apparently we were far from alone. He had met many others like us, sprinkled throughout the known world, with some of them speaking languages that he did not recognise. They had each died at least once and returned from that event to the astonishment of their families. Menahem didn't know how to account for this ability, but he was confident that there was a simple answer, if we could just learn how to see it. He said that some of our kind that he discovered had inspired in him an immense feeling of anger, even though they had just met for the first time. He said that he had wanted to kill these ones as soon as he laid eyes upon them, for no reason that he could explain.

There had also been a woman he met who made him feel this strange sense of recognition, but he had not wanted to do battle with her. Instead, they had talked of their experiences in an attempt to make sense of them, just as Elijah and I were doing now. Menahem mentioned that this woman had once encountered a man who she sensed before seeing him, whom she saw fall from a great height and have his head torn away from his body, an injury that he did not awaken from. She felt that she had absorbed something from him immediately after he died in this way, and seemed to understand many things about him and his life that had been unknown to her. She had stayed with his body, waiting for him to return to life again, but he did not.

From this information, Menahem surmised that we had to protect our heads from such damage in order to survive, for it was the only example of an accident to one of us that had resulted in a permanent death. Elijah and I did not know what to make of this information, yet.

V

In order to avoid more displays of alarm from Mortals, I continued to wander from village to village, never putting down any roots. But at the same time, I started to resent these Mortals for their fear. I wondered if they so fear those of us who cannot die because their entire existence is so wrapped up in preserving their own, brief lives. Not that Immortals are fearless, but we certainly don't share their immediate concerns. I found that I was feeling increasingly alienated, less and less as though we had anything more than our bodily form in common. Certainly I preferred the company of other Immortals to Mortals; at least I had figured out how to use my ability to recognise them, and that was slight comfort to me.

Soon I had my first real battle with another Immortal. Everyone knew how to use a sword and I fortuitously recalled the thing that Menahem had spoken of while I was in combat with a particularly unlikeable Immortal named Joseph. During our confrontation, I recalled the way to stop him for good and decided to take advantage of his weakened condition in an entirely new manner.

Often had my fights with another Immortal ended with their death, but I had always quit at that point, never engaging beyond it. The fact that I had proved able to defeat them had always been enough to discourage a future engagement with any given individual, for I had grown quite adept at these acts of aggression. This time however, hatred was boiling inside of me, so when he fell to his knees I tried this new idea: I swung my sword deliberately at his neck. His head came off of his body in a single clean sweep. As I stood over those two separate pieces of him, amazed by the simplicity of the deed, I felt a great trembling arrive from all around me. It was as though the earth beneath my feet was shaking and rolling. I was grabbed, as if by another being, and thrown to the ground where I was thrashed about as though by a great wind. I became like an empty vessel having something flow into me with tremendous ferocity. My thoughts were confused and my memories did not seem to be my own; there were conflicts, experiences, pain and doubts swirling through my being. Visions of places I had never attended and people I had never known came into my mind, along with some things that were known to me, but not in any perspective that seemed familiar. Then, as suddenly as it began, the tumult around me ceased and my mind was quiet again. I recognised my own thoughts and collected myself and my weapon, leaving that place as abruptly as I could.

I went back to my home and fell into a deep, dreamless sleep from which I awoke feeling energised. Certain that I had been hexed by some type of magic or sorcery, I undertook to quit that place.

As I traveled far away over those next few days, I considered the possible implications of that event. I felt as though I had incorporated Joseph into myself. This was rather disconcerting to say the least, for my dislike of him was intense.

VI

I wandered towards an inland sea that I had heard about from other travelers, where I sought solace from the thoughts that were swirling in my mind. I could not understand these thoughts of someone else's existence that felt like they were now my own. Something strange had been added to me, and I felt stronger than ever before. However, it would be some time before I would attempt such a manoeuvre again.

In the next location that I settled, my distaste for Mortals continued to grow even more vehement. I had started to inwardly reflect their distrust of me back at them. That is when I first met other Immortals who shared my sentiments for these despised beings.

Kronos was one of the new friends I met who shared my distaste for

Mortals. He felt that they were in our way and should not be accorded any sympathy at all. It was his friend Silas who first had the idea that we could use our power over them to extract a price. Caspian was the last to join our little band. We got along quite well, the four of us, fusing together over the concept of acting like lords of the Earth. It was agreed that we had been given this control over life and death for a reason; to fail to use it would be a terrible waste of power. So we began to take by force whatever we desired for ourselves, confident in our birthright to do so, and wreaked havoc upon any who displeased us or possessed items we desired. We became known as The Four Horsemen and we ruled the countryside for several hundred years. Occasionally, we might allow a few Mortals to live so that they might spread the word of our existence and create more apprehension among them. We finally got out of control, sometimes killing Mortals just for the smell of their fear of us, leaving the spoils for whoever might wander across our handiwork. We wore full regalia that concealed our faces from those who we allowed to live, in case we ran into them again in a place where we were caught unprepared.

VII

On one of our raids, we encountered an Immortal who had been living in a small village with Mortals who accepted him despite of his inability to age; he was their spiritual guide and protected them from outsiders. We had all sensed him there, and I had assumed that he would die along with the Mortals and revive after we left. As far as I knew, I was the only one who had ever received another Immortal's essence by intentionally separating him from his head. But as we swept through that village, Kronos met him before he could prepare a defense. He swung at him as he passed by on horseback, catching his throat with his sword, and the feat was done. Knocked off of his mount by the momentum of the exchange, the sky opened up and Kronos was enveloped in a display of lightning and fury that brought the other riders to a halt. So entrancing was this exchange of power that we watched wordlessly as Kronos received the stranger's essence, even as the Mortals were allowed to escape. There had been nothing in the world before to compare it to. Afterward, we helped Kronos back on his horse, for he was weakened, and returned to the site of our camp, breathless with discovery. I admitted nothing of my own previous experience with this transformation, and simply followed the discussion as it made its inevitable way to the realisation that we could kill other Immortals after all, accompanied by a reward whose purpose was not yet understood.

All things must come to an end, and this was to be ours. Now we had all seen and understood that there was much more to each other than our fraternity. As of that moment we all became targets, something else to be taken by force. As we listened to Kronos recount the sensations that he had experienced, my heart sank. I realised that Silas and Caspian were hungry to gain a similar amount of power, and I doubted the strength of our bond to keep me safe from them. Word of this transformation would spread quickly through our world. The balance had shifted from us together to our betrayal of each other.

VIII

Our attitudes toward each other had changed; nothing regarding our future was stable anymore. The thirst for individual power had corrupted our ranks, with Kronos declaring himself to be above any other and Silas and Caspian conferring about how to join in his ascendance and regain equality. All three regarded me as weak for not thrilling in the discovery of this new quest. Perhaps if I had not already experienced it myself, I would have been more open to its immediate possibilities. As it was, I searched my heart for answers: Was this what we were here to do, kill each other? Were we really above the Mortals we had slain? When would any of it end? With these issues in mind, I struck out on my own before I became fodder for the aspirations of the two new apprentices. I avoided all contact with other Immortals for the next few years, fearing the inevitable return of my brothers from the band and my own apparent weakness to oppose them.

IX

I began to put some of the pieces of the puzzle together. I reasoned that if I was going to live for a very long time (hopefully), there must be issues of more substance than fighting each other to concern myself with. The exploits that I had willingly performed as one of the Horsemen were fundamentally wrong: we had claimed a justification for our acts without considering any greater purpose for Mortal existence. This denial of their right to exist without our subjugation is to consider ourselves to be much closer to a deity than I am now prepared to assume.

Although I have very mixed feelings towards Mortals because of the way I have been shunned by them, I understand that they are acting out of fear, not rational judgement. To gain insight into these layers of comprehension regarding our inhuman condition is a burden that Immortals must bear, in pursuit of its truth. We have the privilege of an enduring perspective that they do not. There is a difference between what is right and what is wrong; we are not sufficiently above such concerns to give us the right to dismiss them as irrelevant. We will probably be held responsible for our actions in the future.

X

I soon found myself living in Ur of the Chaldeans. It happened that I met another Immortal who I found to be most agreeable in temperament to mine and we became close friends. Abraham and I found work together, assisting in the building of the many new structures that were being created for King Ur-Nammu. We laboured for many seasons, finding solace in physical work being performed in the service of a fair and just ruler. Also, it gave us plenty of time to share the fragments of information about our kind that we had each gathered.

We compared our versions of those we had heard of, as well as partaking in extensive discussions about the true potential of our Immortal condition. I never brought up the subject of the centuries I had spent as a murderer, although he had heard of the Horsemen and believed that they still rode on, leaving horror and destruction in their wake. From time to time we met other Immortals, many of whom were newly formed and without malice toward us because they were just beginning their roaming ways, and had not yet learned how to live among Mortals. Abraham and I had already realised that it was necessary to move on every twenty-five to thirty years to avoid being identified as different for our failure to age. We shared what little knowledge we had with those who wanted to listen, but most of them ignored us and continued on their own way, to find things out for themselves, or die.

One of our favourite topics was the unusual way that we had to identify each other by feeling another Immortal's presence. We decided that it was a warning system that allowed us to avoid being caught unarmed by one who desired battle. It had now become well known among Immortals that we each carried a reward within us. Some had made it their obsession to try and capture as many of these trophies as possible in order to become stronger and further their individual purposes. Abraham and I had both fought others who sought to collect from us in this way, and those battles were always to that end. We had joined in this gathering of power because to do otherwise would have meant a very short life; there were many who carried much strength within them from their conquests and it became necessary to protect ourselves from joining the ranks of the fallen. In fact, it was during just that type of combat that we were made aware of another most interesting protective device that we had within us.

XI

Abraham and I had been working together to finish one of the many buildings that were currently in progress, when an Immortal who Abraham had met previously made an appearance. He was called Joshua, and he was collecting heads. He was barely 100 years old, but had recently learned of this way to gain power and was very dedicated in his pursuit of the task. Because he already knew Abraham, it was him that was desired for combat. I accompanied my friend as far as I could, in case I might be of some help, although I had no intention of interfering in their affair.

Abraham was over 500 years old, much younger than my 1380, and well versed in warfare so I was confident that he would be victorious. Neither of us had any respect for the men like Joshua who were so concerned with their acquisition of raw power that they usually completely neglected to learn how to do anything with it other than apply it as might against weaker individuals.

It was without much sympathy for the plight Joshua had made for himself that I followed them at a discreet distance to the place they were to meet, outside of the city walls. As they engaged, it was apparent that Joshua was all brawn and had little skill at actual combat; he had probably enjoyed considerable success by intimidating others with his size and great strength. I was confident that he had met his match in Abraham, who was a student of strategy and technique: I had learned a great deal from him myself, from our many practices together over the years. It was no surprise to me when Abraham repeatedly frustrated Joshua's bullish challenges stylishly, while conserving his own energy for the kill. What was surprising was that as they fought, they approached the boundary of an old burial ground, used long before people moved inside of the city walls for protection, and it made my senses tremble. I had never felt anything like it before; it was a dread so deep and specific that it was immediately apparent to me, and I assumed, then, that there should be no warfare upon that place. This knowledge was so acute that it was as though it was inside of me, like the life force of another Immortal when you take his head. Observing Abraham's face made it clear that he felt it too, but Joshua's look betrayed no such emotion.

He continued to attack, but with considerably less energy than when they began. I could hear Abraham speaking quite clearly; he was asking Joshua if he felt this strange force but received no reply, so Abraham began to edge away from him to exit the boundary that they had crossed. At that moment he stumbled, losing his grip upon his sword, and was caught without protection. Joshua struck him with a mighty death blow.

At the exact instant of contact between blade and neck, Joshua's sword stopped as though he had struck solid stone and he disappeared, his weapon landing on the hard ground where he had stood only a moment before. It was as though he had never been there. A profound silence occupied the space that had just been full of the sounds of battle, and I moved quickly to remove my friend from it. My mind was racing for an explanation for what we had just witnessed; I had never heard of anything like this happening before, even as I knew the answer: no sacred site could be desecrated by the combat of Immortals. The insensitivity of that act was somehow not permitted by whatever forces ruled our existence. What that energy might be and what else may be forbidden was not something that I was prepared to consider at that moment. I knew only that we had been warned, perhaps by magic or one of the gods that they worshipped in the city. Whatever it was, neither of us was prepared to define it at that moment. We left those grounds as fast as we could, not even stopping to erect Joshua's sword as a warning, and returned to the safety of the city and its comforting sounds of life.

XII

After considerable discussion, we decided to stay in Ur for a while longer so that we could try to figure out what it might mean. Joshua's disappearance caused Abraham to seriously consider that he had been a sorcerer and the whole event was a warning to us that we could not do as we pleased without facing retribution for our actions. I found that hard to believe: If Joshua was magical, why didn't Abraham vanish? It made little sense to me that the punishment would be administered to the enforcer of unspoken laws, especially since we had both felt the dread and Abraham had actually warned Joshua that they should move elsewhere to continue. Abraham hadn't tried to stop their fight, he only wanted to finish it in a place that was safe. I was unable to assist him in resolving his fears about this apparent sorcery that he would carry to his death, nearly eight hundred years later. He was a good friend and his absence from the world still causes me great sorrow.

XIII

After Abraham's death, I decided to make my way to the City of Jerusalem to join the world again. I had always avoided big cities before, because I desired anonymity from Mortals. However, I reasoned that there was no better place in which to be faceless than where there were too many people living to keep track of each other. There was plenty of construction going on there at the time and I, having become a very good stone cutter, had no difficulty in obtaining employment as a master cutter.

There were many other Immortals being drawn to the cities at the same time as we had: some for similar reasons to mine, others because there were so many heads to be collected in these places. I began to enjoy my life, and shared in the bounty of camaraderie prevalent among the various groups of Immortals. Allegiances were being forged and organisations formed between like-minded persons, some based on status or trade, but many were dependent only upon shared ideals or aspirations of the moment.

This was also the place where the Watchers first became known to me as a serious association. They had existed previously as small groups of men and women who were obsessed with sourcing out the tales of people who greatly outlived their normal lifespan, which was about 75 years at that point in history. One night, I overheard a group at a nearby table discussing certain Immortal names that I recognised, while I was enjoying the company of some co-workers at a drinking house. My interest was piqued, so I allowed myself to be observed displaying interest in their conversation. Eventually, acquaintances were struck and I was invited to a meeting the following evening.

My intention was to find out who they were and why they were so interested in Immortals, but since I needed to be cautious so as not to tip my hand, I decided to appear interested in their Organisation for primarily social purposes. In this way, I would not be taken too seriously at first, and I could make use of their rather unorganised ways to find out exactly what they knew.

I soon met Ruth, a tall, lovely woman who I would have been pleased to make the acquaintance of whether she was a Watcher or not. She possessed a long mane of unruly hair with a personality to match. She was outspoken about her beliefs on every topic, with an education to back it up. She had taught herself to read and write so that she could study various subjects as they interested her. Certain men found her enthusiasm towards education to be off-putting; she was often the most well read person present at their meetings, and not many men appreciated her for it. I was definitely not one of those. Ruth had an exhilarating zest for everything that she did, and in any other time she would have led the group. Later on, she did, but only after changes had occurred with regard to respecting women's rights in their social structure.

In order to avoid recognition as an Immortal, I chose the name Alexander to be used as long as I lived among them. Certainly they had heard of Methos, I reasoned, and such effrontery would easily tip my hand. I was disappointed to discover that I was virtually unknown to their records, having been mentioned only in passing. Apparently my rather low profile had paid dividends of anonymity. I eventually became a member and gained access to a treasure of information. There was a good deal to be learned from them; their records confirmed a lot of what I already knew and added much more to my knowledge of who we were and where we all were located. Still, I was uncertain about what purpose this association with them might serve, other than my own curiosity.

XIV

Ruth and I, however, found a great number of shared interests outside of the work we performed for the Watchers, and we became man and wife in 904 B.C., soon after I shared my secret with her. She told me that she had seen something in my eyes that had betrayed me to her, so she was not hard to convince. I was disappointed to find out that fathering a child with her was something that I was unable to do, now that I was with someone who inspired me to become more firmly rooted in a proper life. Upon further consideration, I realised I had never heard of an Immortal man or woman having children. Towards Ruth I felt more deeply and with greater respect than I had ever known or thought possible to exist between men and women. My entire outlook was inexorably altered and I became a better man for the experience she gave to me.

The Watchers, meanwhile, continued to grow in membership and reach, even as it began to diverge in direction. Various smaller groups were beginning to form within the Organisation, with most of them supporting the official policies, but a few held more extreme beliefs regarding the presence of Immortals. The official hypothesis was that Immortals should be watched in order to protect humanity from an outcome similar to the abuses committed by the Horsemen. They were much more knowledgeable about the Immortal condition than I was because they had the benefit of an immense store of information, gathered over many hundreds of years. I was only aware of those I had personally met or heard of from the few Immortal friends with whom I shared such confidences. The renegade groups, however, were of the opinion that Immortals were an abomination of creation and therefore not worthy of any life. Tempers flared at the meetings and I listened to speeches by some really spiteful individuals who were, in my opinion, embittered by the limitations of their own Mortality.

XV

There was a lot for me to learn at these meetings. They inducted me into their ranks with a ceremony and a complete (as much as they knew at the time) explanation of the who and why of Immortal existence. Some of this information was welcome because it confirmed and explained a great many questions and feelings that I had had over the last 2,050 years. For example, I was very interested to learn that the exchange of power from a beheaded Immortal was referred to as a Quickening and could increase a warrior's power greatly.

They also confirmed for me that Immortals were not able to have children but there was no finite number of Immortals yet; more were being born all the time. Apparently, we were the participants in a struggle that they referred to as The Game, with a Prize being granted to the last surviving member who was going to rule the Earth with great powers. This was the central tenet of separation for the Watchers' rank and file; the majority of members were content simply to observe and record our Immortal conquests, but the extremists were concerned that an evil one would win and the earth would be doomed to eternal subjugation. Since the Immortal victor was to be granted an Immortality that would be free of other competitors, he or she would then be unable to be killed by human means and it would be too late for them to affect the outcome.

The extremists proposed killing us all now, before a winner was declared and it was too late, regardless of the individual Immortal's inclination towards method of ruling. At least they agreed that Immortals were the same as Mortals; either good or bad by individual choice. I appeared to be the only one who felt that the odds were at least even that the champion would be one who walked a more discerning path, so I kept my opinions to myself for the time being.

All of these discussions proved extremely informative to me, in that I could now tell if trouble was in store for any of my friends and make an effort to assist them.

Ruth and I were in complete agreement with respect to trying to positively influence the outcome of The Game, although she recognised that we were treading on dangerous ground. How were we any more entitled to make those choices than someone that we considered to be holding divergent views? If we sought entitlement, she cautioned that we couldn't deny it to those who would use the same information to hunt Immortals. After considerable discussion, we agreed that it was an improper use of the Watchers' database to forward such a personal agenda. My previously malleable moral structure that had permitted me to ride with the Horsemen was beginning to develop into a more cohesive substance.

XVI

Not long after, I had to leave my building job and devote my full attention to the Watchers because they needed the help. There were not enough agents to cover the individual Immortal assignments; each Watcher was trying to cover two or three often very disparate people. This started to involve frequent travel in order to keep tabs on them, and Ruth and I turned down several assignments because we didn't want to move anywhere else quite yet. We reasoned that there were enough Immortals who were passing through Jerusalem that we could observe them and concern ourselves more with the organisational structure that was emerging.

Because of my status as an Immortal, we knew that we would have to leave sometime, in about 15 to 20 years, because I would not be showing any advancement of age by then. Hopefully, we would be able to take an assignment following an Immortal who had settled some-where far enough away for me to maintain my cover when the time came.

I was becoming concerned that I would eventually end up running across an Immortal that I knew or one who wanted my Quickening. In this town I would be found out pretty fast if I picked up my sword against someone who was being covered by a Watcher. If I was exposed, my main worry was what would happen to Ruth, both within the Organisation and regarding her personal safety from the radical elements who could use the opportunity to justify their anxiety towards Immortals. The events that would follow my exposure would also serve to drive the Watchers deeper underground, making it harder for me or any other Immortal to ever infiltrate them again. If I had to choose between concealing my identity and revealing Ruth's involvement, I knew that I would give myself up to them, hoping that eventually Ruth and I could escape and start over somewhere else.

XVII

Just as I was preparing myself for the potential of a confrontation, my most dreaded fear came true; Kronos found me as he was passing through the city. I had always figured that my unfinished business with him would reappear and require closure, so I wasn't completely unprepared for his arrival. However, I was unprepared for his response to finding me. He wanted to pick up where we had left off, having changed his ways and attitude towards Mortals not a bit. He was quite amused at my having married a Mortal and agreed to a trade for my freedom: If I would tell him all I knew about the Watchers and supply the information that they had on him, he agreed to let me continue my charade. I discussed the matter with Ruth right away, and she agreed to provide me with the necessary materials to pull it off. We knew that he was not to be trusted, so we also planned to take an assignment immediately and disappear from Jerusalem. It pained me greatly to see her sacrifice so much for me, but we both knew that it had always been inevitable.

When the day came for the exchange, I made arrangements to meet him at a location where I could conceal my sword beforehand and guarantee my own safety, or at least a fighting chance. As I had suspected, Kronos attempted to turn the tables and forced me to fight him. Short-sighted man that he was, after all this time he still desired power more than information. I fought well considering that I had not trained in a long time, and I found myself with an opportunity to take his head. I knew that the course of my life with Ruth would change if I should change by assimilating his wicked temperament into myself in a Quickening, but I was still considering it when the sudden appearance of Ruth changed everything.

XVIII

She came into view with a group of Watchers that I knew, who apparently also knew Kronos by reputation, since they had brought restraints for his upper body and a cart with which to transport him away. They swarmed us, filling me with apprehension because I had no idea of their intent. They made themselves clear only when they completed binding Kronos firmly and bundled him into the cart.

They were prepared to take him to an underground chamber that had been an ancient prison, where he would remain trapped for eternity, unable to escape or get assistance, due to the remote location. In return for their co-operation, Ruth and I were to leave immediately on assignment. They would not divulge our secret. Ruth was moved by their actions, and tried to tell them how deeply she appreciated their concern for us, but before she could say any more, they bade her to say no more. Although clearly disappointed with her for betraying them by knowingly marrying an Immortal, they felt that little would be gained by turning me in and upsetting the entire Organisation.

To them, this trade was more valuable, in that it allowed Kronos to be interrupted from his campaign of terror against Mortals, than the internal upset of revealing my secret to the other Watchers. Besides, they did not think I was in danger of being an evil ruler should I win The Prize.

We stood together for the last time, with our friends and my enemy Kronos, and I thought about the lessons that I had learned from these people. The fact that they trusted us enough to do this touched me deeply and restored my wavering faith in Mortals. We waved goodbye and went our separate paths forever; I knew that Ruth would never see these friends again, yet she relinquished it all to be with me. I made up my mind to make it known to her that she should never underestimate her importance to me, and how much I would treasure her for the rest of her life.

XIX

After the happiest 52 years of my life, Ruth died. Those glorious years that I had spent married to such an incredible woman had forever altered my existence, so in tribute to her memory I decided to seek some of the larger answers, or at least, I sought to find some of the questions. I decided to travel to Asia to learn more about the spiritual side of existence. I had heard about the religious orders of the East from other traveling Immortals and decided that I was finally ready to study among them.

I made my way to Tibet, a mountainous region that was sufficiently secluded from the world to ensure that I would not be distracted, and began to seek out a master to assist me in my quest. I met many men there who had dedicated their lives to the search for greater meaning in this life, as a means of preparing for the next one. Far from the prying eyes of outsiders, I began as a helper in an old monastery, where I cut and hauled wood and water in service of the monks who lived there. When I was given an opportunity to study the written language of their people, so that I could read from their magnificent collection of created works, I virtually leaped at the chance. These quiet, humble men asked no questions about my past, but had many piercing inquiries about my future intentions. What did I desire from my life? Who did I wish to be? I answered them as truthfully as I could.

I chose to live the life of a warrior who understood the value of each breath, and I wanted to become a man who faced life's uncertainties with the strength of one who knew why he was here on earth. My answers surprised them, for they had met very few outsiders who had seriously considered such issues. Most travelers that they had been exposed to were primarily concerned with finding an immediate cosmic key to happiness or instant peace within their tortured souls. I assured them that I was here to stay and study, not to grab at the first solution and return to the world to build a fortune as a holy man. When they had satisfied themselves that my intentions were true to their purposes, my training began, but not in the way I had imagined.

XX

It was like being in the military, with physical exertion and plenty of weapons training. It was necessary to understand your animal side before one could walk with peace in his heart, my master Lin Chi told me. The man who is unable to defend himself must always be wary of others, and will therefore be too distracted to notice whether he is headed on the path towards enlightenment, the art of emptiness and fullness. He taught me how to read another person's intentions simply by observing the manner in which he carried himself. Twenty years after I began to seek truths, my teacher told me that the time had come for me to study with his master, a man of great understanding with respect to the particular question that I faced. I asked him how he could know what my question was, when I did not even know it myself. Lin Chi laughed, and told me that he had known it in his heart since the day I arrived. He made me a present of a beautiful white robe like his own and instructed me to wear it on my arrival at my new master's. With those words, an old man who worked as a groundskeeper at this temple entered the room wordlessly and motioned for me to follow him.

XXI

We trekked for three days, much farther up into the mountains, until we came upon a gate that opened into a simple garden. My guide spoke to me for the first time, reminding me to put on the robe that Lin Chi had given me, then to continue up the pathway that would lead to the temple I would find in only an hour's walk. With that, he turned and left, going effortlessly down the rugged trail as if he was merely out for an afternoon stroll. I changed my clothes and began to ascend the path that lay ahead of me. I wondered about this new master that I was to meet; whether he would find me worthy of serving him, and if I was ready to be in his company. Soon, I would know much more than that.

As I climbed over a small rise in the terrain, a surprisingly large structure came into view. It blended perfectly with the surrounding landscape and gave me the impression that it was an extension of it. A man was standing at the doorway, like a guardian of that remote place. He showed no emotion as he opened the single door and motioned me to enter. I walked into the entrance hall and felt the presence of another Immortal. It was my new master, Sun Tzu, and I became immediately at ease when he smiled and gave the secret greeting that

Lin Chi had taught me to use whenever I met another member of their order. I responded with the correct reply and he welcomed me to his home. He said he had been here for nearly 1250 of his 1577 years, instructing apprentices and studying the ways of men. He explained that he had no personal use for The Prize that other Immortals sought. He felt that he was not fit to rule; his role was to help others find their own truths so they would be able to decide for themselves whether or not they desired permanent Immortality from The Game, but none had come to him before. I could hardly contain myself from asking why he thought himself unsuited to lead the world into the next great event of humanity, when he answered my question before I could ask it. He told me that those who are skilled in combat do not become angered, those who are skilled at winning do not become afraid. Thus the wise win before they fight, while the ignorant fight to win. Obviously I was in the right place for the instructions I sought and realised that I, like the man who guarded his front door and my master Lin Chi, would lay down my own life to protect his.

It was easy to stay on the mountain with Sun Tzu. There were only the three of us to look after and Li Quan took very good care of the vegetable garden that kept us all healthy. Somehow the brothers at the other temple always knew when we needed fresh meat and the occasional treat. Whatever supplies we needed but did not have would appear mysteriously at our doorstep at precisely the right time. I asked my master why no one thought it strange that he had lived so long. He replied that as far as they were concerned, he was a different person every generation, drawn anonymously from the ranks every fifty years or so and the foods were merely traditional gifts to the resident of the temple, whomever he may be.

XXII

After many years of training both physical and mental, when we finally began to discuss what role in the world's development was to be played by the winner of The Game, Sun Tzu explained the details of his philosophy to me. In his opinion, the champion must be one who walked an enlightened path, because the forces of the universe that ultimately controlled us could not permit otherwise. If there was a benefic Creator, and he could not imagine that there was not, He would not allow the rest of His creations to suffer under a ruler that would treat the rest of humanity with disdain. That would be too great of an injustice to a world that had done nothing to deserve it. Thus, the widespread concern that a potential tyrant could gain The Prize was intrinsically delusional. Everything about living on earth is about balance, he explained, with each living thing playing its own necessary part in the greater whole. To ensure that somewhere else an adjustment was made to compensate. Things had always been this way, he said, and would always remain so, for as long as there was life on the planet. Occasional imbalances might occur from time to time, but something or someone would always intuitively know how and when to adjust it when the correct time came. Those who were intended to make such adjustments might even be the most unlikely to recognise in themselves the ability to evoke these changes.

I explained to him about the Watchers and my involvement with them in the past, as well as my intention to continue monitoring them. He was not surprised to hear that they existed, since people are basically social beings, and shared my concerns about their potential to cause disarray. He cautioned me to remain guarded about exchanging my information about them with other Immortals, even to those whom I trusted, because I could not guarantee that the information would be used wisely.

XXIII

About 800 B.C., our keeper of the temple, Li Quan, died and we were indebted to carry him back to the lower temple so his body could be returned to his family for burial. While we were there, Sun Tzu spoke at great length with Lin Chi, who was growing quite old. When I questioned him while on our return home about what they had discussed, Sun Tzu said that Lin Chi had commented to him upon the lack of change in his physical features, despite the advance of time. Lin

Chi had been just a boy when he was sent to train under Sun Tzu some 70 years ago and although he understood that it was common for members of their order to live for 90 or even 100 years he wondered why his teacher looked exactly as he had when they first met. I told Sun Tzu that such circumstances were a common problem in the outside world, precipitating a change in location every generation to preserve my identity. He said, with reference to our new guardian—Wang Xi—who was traveling back with us, that he always told the truth when the end of life came to his students. If he had trained them well, they had gained enough wisdom to understand.

When his time came, he would tell Wang Xi the same thing, if he asked. I was his first Immortal student, and he had been pleased to see that one of us had come so far to seek answers. It was uncommon for Immortals to do this, he said, because the immediate concerns of The Game could be very distracting from a life of contemplation. I took that to be a compliment and never asked him about it again.

XXIV

As I approached my 2200th birthday, I possessed renewed hope that the questions I sought to understand were someday going to be within my reach. My master and I had explored the existential concept of Immortality, along with a program of physical training that would assist my mind in its deliberations, for nearly a century. This had awakened in me a rejuvenated spiritual sense that I had not known since I was a boy and I stared at the night sky, entranced by its infinite mystery of creation. Certainly I had not been able to comprehend, at that young age, the infinite possibilities of my lifetime and my potential to impact upon the world in a positive way. Now I was beginning to recognise a glimmer of light in a world that had previously been cast in the shadow of my own ignorance. I had learned enough to understand some of the basic responsibilities and contradictions of human experience, that I felt truly free to begin to explore the true potential of a life, any life, that was lived in worthy pursuit of a purposeful existence. I knew that I had come a long way to find out that my real journey was just beginning and I was thankful for the opportunity. Every new day was a rebirth of my soul, full of forgiveness for my past and the promise of new beginnings. I felt more alive than ever and the chasm of emptiness was becoming instead a covenant of expectation left to fulfill. It was the most exciting period of my life.

Sun Tzu acted to use this opportunity to pour his wisdom of warfare into my newly constructed chassis. We began training earnestly in the methods of physical technique necessary to accompany my development into a philosopher-warrior. He demonstrated the necessity of balance between my soul and mind, in order to avoid the trap of arrogance. I discovered how to win without fighting. He instructed me in the art of strategy and endurance of the mind, to assist me in the judicious use of my strengths. Our new guardian/groundskeeper Wang Xi allowed us to know that he was trained in the fighting style of his native region, and he generously taught me several new techniques.

XXV

And so I began the next phase of my life. Sun Tzu had been hinting at a new level of progression that I needed to ascend, without elaborating any further at that time. Now he did. He told me that I had been a good and worthy student of all that he had taught me, but the time had come for me to return to the world and apply that which I had absorbed. He assured me that I was welcome to return to him for more instruction as I felt the need, but he was of the opinion that I was unlikely to do so in the near future. I had learned a great deal while living in that refuge with him, but he was concerned that I had lost touch with my social abilities among ordinary people. He intended to do the very same thing himself, he said, returning to his home province in order to renew his contact with the perspective of ordinary people, as well as to confirm the sights and sounds of his own beginnings. I argued that I had much more to learn from him before I would be ready to go forth again, but my complaints fell upon deaf ears. The date of my departure was set in stone at two weeks hence, in order that I might prepare myself mentally for the challenges ahead. That time was to be spent in contemplation of all that I had observed while in this retreat, and how it might be best applied to my future actions.

My heart was heavy with regret when the moment came for me to go. I changed into a suit of clothing that Sun Tzu had obtained for me, which he said was contemporary dress for the period that I was rejoining. He asked me to make my way alone from the temple I had called home for 126 years, and so, on the morning of the proscribed date, I walked down the mountain to meet my future. I was 2271 years old and felt like a new-born lamb that was being led in from the wilderness as I began my expedition to rejoin civilisation. I headed for the city of Rome, familiar ground upon which I could begin again.

From the Grave

An Excerpt from the Journal of Richie Ryan

by Stan Kirsch

"RICHIE RYAN": Stan Kirsch

No character on Highlander: The Series *experienced more change and growth over the course of the series than Richie Ryan. The first character we see in the very first scene of the first episode, Richie is a defining force throughout the series as he learns the lessons of the Immortal Game, first as an observer, then as a participant.*

Actor Stan Kirsch, too, was there from the start to the finish, one of a very small number of cast or crew to be a part of all six seasons of Highlander. *For a surprising perspective on Richie's past, present, and future, Stan gives us his voice, "From the Grave."*

⚡

October, 1999

I've been safely tucked away in the afterlife for several years now. Fortunately, I've managed to make excellent use of the time. I've immersed myself in books, absorbing literature and art, educating and enriching myself in ways I never had the occasion to before. After all, a brief life spent watching one's back, attacking and defending, constantly sheathed in a protective shell, doesn't leave much opportunity for inspiration or reflection.

I'm aware that my sudden and unpremeditated decapitation at the hands of my illustrious mentor was not his intention. Ironically, however, it was MacLeod who introduced me to the notion that "there can be only one." Alas, it was not me. Who was I kidding to think it might be? I'm sure MacLeod grieved. He is not a man without feeling. Nevertheless, he has taken many lives and seen many loved ones die. I'm certain he will move on.

I lost great friends whom I miss dearly and have yearned for the chance to bid them farewell. Recently I befriended a messenger at the gates of Saint Peter, and it seems he will do me the favor of relaying a single correspondence to a few of my cohorts on earth. I have decided to take him up on his offer and put words to paper. I'm sure this is a rare privilege and I am thankful for it. Incidentally, I imagine that the therapeutic benefits of such an exercise can be quite enormous. I will embark on these letters now.

Dearest Amanda:

I'm certain this letter finds you deep in drink and mischief.

It's a large responsibility being the life of the party, but you seem to manage quite well. Come to think of it, I miss the rebellious thrill of a wild detour from the path of righteousness. Those nights we spent together in Spain will always remain our precious secret and very dear to me. I will never be able to smell the aroma of cheap Castillian wine and not think of you.

I understand that you settled in New York and I hope it's worked out for you. Be careful—the cops there can be relentless. I know this from experience. I am terribly envious at any rate. I would certainly love a bite of the Big Apple right now. Speaking of which, be sure to take in the food, particularly Little Italy. It's as close to the real thing as you could possibly imagine. Knowing you, on the other hand, you'll be spending a good deal more time at the Metropolitan Museum of Art. Those poor security guards have no idea what awaits them.

Amanda, thank you for encouraging me to look into the face of adversity, stare it down with strength and pride, and always maintain my sense of humor. I would have looked forward to a lasting and enduring friendship between us.

Live long and happy, work hard and play hard, and never look back—just like you taught me. Thanks for the memories.

> Yours truly,
> Richard "The Lionheart"

Dear Joe:

I have an unopened bottle of fine tequila sitting right here, beckoning you. It's not that I'm pessimistic about your life span, but if you continue to travel in such dangerous circles, you're bound to run into trouble sooner or later. Take it from me.

I was stubborn, should have listened to you and Methos. Too bad you weren't there with a gun this time. At any rate, I've made some good contacts up here and I look forward to showing you around. It may be centuries before I run into Amanda, Methos or Mac, so I'm not holding my breath. Don't worry, I'm not angry or bitter. I'm certain Mac didn't knowingly harm me.

I'm actually at peace for the first time. My life was spent running and ducking, and although I made good friends, such as yourself, I never really found a home. I've submerged myself in books and art and taken to many creative pursuits. I've even met a wonderful woman.

It was lonely at first, but I've come to appreciate my life of tranquility. Still, I would love the chance to spend one last evening at Joe's. Speaking of which, give my regards to everyone. I hold on to the notion that I am missed, and I'd certainly hate to be wrong.

I have great respect for you, Joe. You are a man of courage and fortitude (and perhaps, insanity) to live the life you've chosen. I'm grateful to have known you. Your counsel was invaluable and your friendship priceless.

Best of luck with your music and don't forget to bring your guitars when next we meet. For now, enjoy every moment. I know how mortals value their precious "time on earth" and I'm certain you'll continue to make the most of yours. And when that fateful moment comes, fear not. I'm right here for you with those drinks and many more. After all, if it's good to you, it's good for you. Take care, Joe.

Your Friend,
Richie

Methos:

It may come as a surprise to you hearing from me. Given the opportunity, I wanted you to know what a great pleasure it was to make your acquaintance and get to know you. For the record, I'm sorry I ever questioned your identity. I was plagued by both naivete and stubbornness, a deadly combination. I should have listened to you and Joe. Famous last words—I'm sure you've heard them before.

Over several thousand years I'd imagine you've touched many people, and I can assure you I'm one of them. I'm certain your sarcasm and irreverence belie a caring and a genuinely good nature, although I don't doubt that you, too, have your faults. I wonder what my life would have been like under your tutelage. But as we both know, "In the end there can be only one," and my likelihood for survival may not have been any better.

I look forward to a time when and if we meet again. Until then, take care. Be generous with your wisdom, Methos. Many could benefit from it.

Sincerely,
Rich Ryan

Mac:

Where to begin? I suppose the first thing I'd like to tell you is that I forgive you. I'm aware that what happened wasn't your intention. As it wasn't the first time I was confronted by this type of trouble either, I'm fairly certain I was doomed anyway. You were the brother and the father I never had. You welcomed me into your life and introduced me to some excellent and fascinating people who became very dear to me. We certainly had our moments of difference, but that's par for the course. You also guided, defended, and relentlessly looked out for me. I'm no longer bitter or angry about what happened. Actually, it may have been a blessing in disguise. I was always searching for something on earth, never quite happy or settled in who I was. Like your shadow, I looked to you for all of life's answers and never really developed a mind of my own. It seems sad now, painful to bear, and even a bit pathetic.

I do wish that you had encouraged me to take greater advantage of my time on earth and enjoy it more, as opposed to focusing so much attention on training to defend myself. Sometimes I think I was ill-fated from the start and that it was only through wits, chance, and the generosity of others that I was able to survive as long as I did.

I know you meant well, Mac, but I am finally at greater peace with myself and my surroundings than ever before. I even have a beautiful woman in my life and we don't live under a veil of secrecy.

In an effort to occupy myself, I have taken to a great deal of reading and writing and particularly familiarized myself with the works of William Shakespeare. Bill, as I refer to him now, has given me a passport to worlds foreign to me and my limited experiences on earth. I especially came to like this fellow Hamlet, perhaps because I identified with him so closely. We were both confused young men, caught up in tragic circumstances, very torn and feeling betrayed.

I think back on our time together and can't help but feel as if our lives were littered with tragedy. Quite honestly, I don't know how you continue to bear it. I admire your perseverance and your courage. You are a man of great principle and you taught me a great deal. For this, I thank you.

Take care of yourself. While I have faith that in the end you will be "the one," I would certainly look forward to seeing you sooner. Give my best to everyone and toast me once in a while.

All the best, my friend.

Until next time,
Richie

What a fantastic opportunity this has been. I feel better already. I do hope these letters reach their intended recipients. My friend, the messenger, is a trustworthy sort, and I am therefore very confident. At this time I am reminded of a passage from that William Shakespeare play for which I have such an affinity. I will leave you with this:

"What a piece of work is a man, how noble in reason, how infinite in faculties, in form and moving how express and admirable, in action how like an angel, in apprehension how like a god: the beauty of the world, the paragon of animals—and yet, to me, what is this quintessence of dust?"

Postcards from Alexa

World Enough and Time

by Gillian Horvath

The love story of Methos and Alexa is like an iceberg in the High-lander world—only the tip rises above the surface of the series. Although Ocean Hellman, who portrayed Alexa so beautifully, appeared in only one episode, the impact of the character was felt throughout season 4. In "Timeless," when they meet. In "Deliverance," when Methos mentions to MacLeod that he left Alexa in Athens. In "Methuselah's Gift," when Methos is in pursuit of the Methuselah Crystals to save Alexa's life. And Head Writer David Abramowitz decreed that we would find a place in the show to let Methos have his moment of grief for her loss; that place was found in "Through a Glass Darkly," when Methos and MacLeod stand at Alexa's grave.

In creating these few scenes referring to Alexa's off-screen death, we found that we had created an off-screen life for her as well. Over six or eight months, beginning in December of 1995, Donna Lettow and I took turns writing a series of vignettes, known collectively as "Postcards from Alexa."

It had seemed like such a good idea at the time. With a bone-weary sigh, the man who was calling himself Adam Pierson stripped off his mud-soaked clothes and dropped them on the floor of the hotel bathroom. The cuts and bruises had healed already; the clothes were a total loss.

He'd wanted to start their trip at the Grand Canyon, even though it meant driving more than twenty hours straight through while Alexa dozed in the back of the van. He'd wanted to be there at that moment when she stepped out of the van and saw the canyon spread before her, to see that look of wonder and awe as she tried to assimilate the broken landscape. He'd been there a dozen times over the years himself, and had yet to become immune to the absolute amazement he'd felt the very first time he'd seen it. Next to this work of Nature every human problem seemed small, and even he, with five thousand years of memories weighing on him, seemed young.

He hadn't counted on the driving rainstorm that had caught them as they crossed the Rockies, or the flat tire that had them almost in a ditch outside of Flagstaff. On the darkened road the fall rain was less a gentle shower than an aggressor, and he'd been soaked through in seconds changing the tire. He'd lost his footing as he struggled to push them out of the mud the van was mired in, and taken a tumble down a scraggly bank which seemed to have been planted strategically with briars. There was less damage to his body than to his mood—the perfect day he'd planned had been turned into a disaster, and even Alexa's attempts to turn it into a joke had fallen flat. It didn't matter, she said, but it did matter—they'd never get this day, their first day, back.

They'd finished the drive in silence, and he'd stayed in the van, too mud-soaked to venture inside, while she'd checked them into their hotel. She'd handed him a key and disappeared into the next bungalow over, and he couldn't say he blamed her. His charm seemed to have abandoned him back in that muddy ditch. He didn't feel much like spending the night with himself, either.

Pushing muddy hair out of his eyes, he reached for the shower knobs, then cursed fluently in a couple of dead languages. The quaint hotel, apparently designed for romantic getaways for couples, had foregone installing a shower in favor of a big whirlpool tub, and he stood shivering in the tiled bathroom while it filled slowly.

Finally lowering himself into the steaming water, he wasn't surprised when it turned brown immediately. He leaned over to try and scrub some of the mud and grit out of his hair, and succeeded only in getting filthy water running into his eyes. He blinked it away, then blinked again. Alexa was standing in the doorway, wrapped in a white robe with Coronet Hotel stitched on the pocket, looking warm and scrubbed.

"My room has a shower," she said quietly, by way of explanation.

"Maybe I should borrow it," he replied, painfully aware of what a sight he must be, with barely diluted mud smeared from head to toe. "I'll never get clean this way."

"You might try clean water," she answered wryly. She crouched down to his level, reached past him to pull the drain. He forced himself not to move as the muddy water drained away; her eyes stayed locked on his, a tiny smile playing on her lips. She was enjoying this, damn her! Bless her.

She turned the taps back on and sat on the edge of the tub as it started to fill. "Turn around," she said softly, and he did as he was told, drawing his knees up, leaning against the padded tub wall next to her. She nudged him forward with her knee, scooping up a handful of water to splash over him. He allowed himself to relax as the hot water rose around him, his head dropping forward as Alexa's tiny hands ladled water over his head in warm half-cupfuls. He could feel her fingers brushing against his skull, against the tops of his ears, as she went over his head seemingly strand by strand. Senses heightened, head bowed, he could see the ripples on the smooth surface of the water as he breathed, he could feel every fiber of her terry robe where his shoulder brushed her thigh.

When the last handful of water over his head ran away clean, her hands dropped to his shoulders for a moment, then moved off. She shifted position to kneel behind him and reached past him for the soap, and when her hands returned they were cool and slick with lather. She made her way over his shoulders and down his chest, the

last of the mud disappearing as she repeatedly cupped clean water over
him and smoothed away the last of the soap. Her chest pressed against
his back and her breath was warm against his ear as she leaned foward,
her hands running down his arm from shoulder to elbow to wrist. She
lifted his hand to soap between each finger, and he closed his eyes,
feeling his breath catch at the touch of her hands against the sensitive
webbing.

Then her finger traced a circle on the inside of his wrist, and his
eyes flew open to see her staring at the Watcher tattoo, tracing its
intricate design with one gentle finger.

"And here I thought you were some geeky travel writer with his col-
lege van." She raised his arm out of the water for a better look. "Didn't
figure you for a guy with the kind of checkered past that includes a tattoo."

"You have no idea." He looked at the tattoo with new eyes, trying
to see it as she saw it, as a sign of a troubled youth. She raised the wrist
toward her mouth and he shuddered slightly, anticipating the kiss,
then shuddered again as she surprised him with no kiss, instead blow-
ing gently on the exposed wrist until the bathwater evaporated, then,
all but imperceptibly, running the tip of her tongue around the tattooed circle.

The inside of the wrist, jammed with veins and nerves, is one of the
most dangerous places on the body to be tattooed—hence the
Watcher ritual. And hence his reaction as her tongue touched the sensitive skin. He turned in the tub, scooped her up in both arms, and
pulled her in on top of him. Her robe turned into a sponge as he settled her in his lap and kissed her, holding on until he could feel her
breath go short. He pulled back a fraction of an inch then, looking
into her eyes, and there it was—the look of wonder and awe he had
wanted so much to see. Here, in this tub, in this bathroom, they were
looking at a work of nature older than either of them.

Maybe their first day wasn't ruined, after all.

Postcards from Alexa

World Enough and Time II

by Donna Lettow

Alexa had tried to tell him a little rain didn't matter, but you know the way men are. And it was very hard not to laugh when he returned to the van, stiff and scratched and covered head to toe in mud, although she suspected his pride was bruised more than his butt—no, bum—was. Bum. Just the sound of his voice spoke of all the adventure and exotic far away places she'd thought she'd never see. Not until she met Adam . . .

When they'd pulled out of Seacouver yesterday after tearful good-byes to Joe and a solemn promise to write, she was brimming with excitement, but after nearly eighteen hours, the road had taken its toll on her. She had harbored a faint hope they would stop for the night at some cozy hotel in northern Utah, maybe even one with a honeymoon suite . . . she'd flushed a bit at the thought. But Adam had his own plans. His heart was set on being at the Grand Canyon as the sun rose. She reminded him with a gentle laugh that the Canyon had been there longer than either of them and it would still be there tomorrow. Adam said nothing, just smiled and gazed at her with those bottomless eyes that pleaded "but we've got so much to do . . ." Alexa melted, allowing him to build a cozy nest for her in the back of the VW.

Her body was exhausted and crying out for rest, but her mind was racing and she couldn't sleep. Mile after mile, long into the night, she watched him drive, his face silhouetted in the glare of oncoming lights. For the first time in many months, Alexa allowed herself to think—about her life, about her past . . . and about her future. Funny how less than a week ago her life was set, an endless cycle of doctors' offices and shifts at Joe's. A safe, mindless routine, comforting in its sameness. No need to think, no reason to plan, just wait for the inevitable. Her mother would have been proud—a quiet death borne stoically, not bothering, not beholding to anyone.

Then Adam came . . .

And suddenly her life had value to someone, although she would never understand why someone as wonderful . . . as *magical* as Adam could care about her, could want to climb the slow, painful mountain with her. He had offered her the world. And she, who had never been more than 50 miles from home in her whole life, accepted it. "First stop," Adam had chattered excitedly as they packed his microbus the previous morning, "the Grand Canyon. You'd never believe a bit of rock could be so beautiful." Alexa could believe anything he said. "After that, Bourbon Street in New Orleans, up the Atlantic Coast to Washington, then a little piece of West Virginia that only God and I know about. By then my friends will have your passport waiting in New York and we'll be off to the wonders of Egypt!" Alexa had sensed that even a landfill would be wonderful, if she could see it with him. Later, in the back of the van, she had only wished her sense of geography hadn't been so poor—that she'd realized just how far away the Canyon was.

Far away from home . . .

The rain had started well after midnight and the only sound was the incessant patter of rain on the plastic roof, the swish of the wipers, and Adam's breathing. Occasionally she could hear him humming a snippet of some song. He seemed so far away, this man she barely knew but had given the rest of her life to. She looked out the window—no moon, no stars, no signs of life, just the inky black of the rainy night—and suddenly felt cold and alone. And afraid. Alexa never allowed herself to be afraid, it was counter-productive and a waste of time. But in the van in the dark a few tears came unbidden and she choked back a little sob. Adam quickly turned in the driver's seat, full of concern, but Alexa buried her head in her pillow. It wouldn't do for him to hear her crying. Better to let Adam think she was sleeping.

Adam . . . She wondered if he knew she'd lied to him. She'd had maybe a year to live in Seacouver—with the treatments, the pills, the needles, the tests. Cut off from them, who knew? A couple of months, maybe more. Maybe less. Her doctors thought she was crazy, but they could only offer her a longer death. Adam had offered her a chance at a dazzling life, no matter how brief the candle. She would see Egypt before she died. And maybe Greece—she'd always wanted to see Greece. Maybe if she asked, Adam would take her there. . . . She would see Greece with Adam. Comforted by visions of Adam/Adonis, Alexa finally slept.

When she awoke an hour or so later, she was truly alone. The rain coming down in buckets on its roof, the van was empty and listing to one side. "Adam?" she called out. From outside the van she heard a strained "Out here," then a clank of metal, a thunk, and a muttered "Oops." Alexa opened the van's side door and started to step out. "No, no," she heard Adam warn. "Wouldn't do that if I were you. Nasty bit of weather we're having."

Alexa stepped down from the van and looked around. The VW was mired in a ditch by the side of the road, one tire flat. "A little rain won't kill me," she told him. "Let me help." Poor Adam. He looked like a drowned kitten, his hair plastered to his head, water running in his eyes as he attempted to push the van from the ditch.

"Wouldn't want you to think it wasn't raining," he said sheepishly.

"Let me at least get you an umbrella."

"Too late for that, I'm afraid." He wiped his eyes, looking a little haggard. "Besides, a little rain won't kill me, either. How about you drive while I push from here?"

Alexa climbed into the driver's seat. Her feet barely touching the pedals, she started the engine and stepped on the gas, but the VW made no attempt to move. "Adam," she called out the window, "nothing's happening."

"Are you sure you've got the parking brake off?" Yes, the parking brake was off. She tried it again. The engine roared but still nothing. She could hear his frustration. "Did you put it into gear? It's a clutch car." Oh. She shifted into first and stomped the gas pedal with all her strength. The van rolled backwards, then leaped forward onto the highway shoulder.

"Adam, we did it!" There was no response. She opened the driver's door. "Adam? Adam!" After a long moment, when she began to fear she'd killed him, she saw him drag himself out of a patch of briars by the ditch.

"Go back inside, Alexa," he said carefully. "I'll change the tire."

When he finally got back in the van ten minutes later looking like a broken toy, she couldn't help but giggle. His hair was caked in mud, rainy streaks punctuating the mud-smeared face. His long coat was torn and stuck through with brambles. He glared at her wearily. "Not funny, Alexa."

She couldn't help it. All the tension, all her fear and sadness, and all the feelings she had for this man, feelings that might actually be love if she allowed that, all came spilling out at once and she laughed. She laughed at the little mud-caked clump of his hair that stuck up like Alfalfa's, the twig sticking up out of his collar, and especially the dollop of mud on the tip of his nose. She laughed until it hurt.

"That will be quite enough," Adam enunciated each word, closing the driver's side door with more of a bang than necessary. He didn't look at her. Like a scolded puppy, Alexa retreated to the farthest corner of the passenger seat.

• • •

They rode on for another hour in silence—to Alexa it seemed like days—before he stopped the van outside a quaint motel. "Are we here?" she asked brightly.

Adam shook his head. "We'll never make it in time. Might as well pack it in, get some sleep. Start out again tomorrow." It wasn't so much his face as the droop of an ear, the sag of a shoulder that told her how incredibly disappointed he was. She was sure he was disappointed in her, as well.

"Why don't you get us some lodgings?" He indicated the lobby. "I'm afraid I'm not very presentable at the moment." He made an attempt at a wry smile.

"I noticed," she answered, trying to match his tone, and instantly regretted it as he quickly looked away, embarrassed.

The night clerk didn't seem fazed when Alexa wanted a room at four in the morning. She'd filled out the paperwork and he was about to hand her the keys to the room when she stopped him and asked almost shyly, "Do you have . . . a honeymoon suite?" The clerk grinned broadly, reached under the counter, pulled out the keys to a different room and handed them to her, saying, "Whirlpool. Water bed. Would you like champagne? On the house . . ." Alexa turned toward the front door and Adam's van, wondering if he liked champagne as much as he did beer, and watched him throw their bags to the sidewalk, then slam shut the van door, hitting it for good measure. She turned back to the clerk with a sigh.

"No, no champagne. And maybe you'd better give me those other keys, too."

It wasn't until she'd dropped her bags inside the door and sat on the decidedly not water bed to remove her shoes that she realized she'd given Adam the wrong room. She hoped he'd enjoy the whirlpool. Right at the moment, she wanted nothing more than a good hot shower.

Later, clean and snug in a terry cloth robe, Alexa combed her long, sleek hair in a mirror and thought about her promise to Joe that she'd

write. She could see her first letter now. "Dear Joe, we've only been
gone a day and already I've disappointed him. I think he hates me now.
Please come get me. . . ." She stared at herself in the mirror—trying to
see what it was Adam saw. All she could see were the telltale marks of
the battle her body was waging with itself, the wrinkles, the stress and
fatigue, and worst of all the scars from the tests and the treatments.
She knew what Joe's response would be, what Joe's response always
was: "There's nothing between two human beings that can't be
resolved by talking things out." She thought about it and decided, fine,
she'd apologize to him. And then she'd explain that she wasn't who he
thought she was, that she couldn't be that person. She wasn't perfect . . . and she certainly wasn't beautiful. And if he hated her, she
knew the way back to Joe's.

When Alexa knocked on the door of Adam's room and got no response,
she let herself in with the second key. She was determined to say what
she'd come to say, and if Adam was asleep, she'd damn well wake him
up to hear it.

But Adam wasn't sleeping.

She found him in the tub, up to the waist in dirty water, trying in
vain to get the mud from his hair, looking tired and vulnerable and
more than a little bit . . . lost. Her stern resolve melted at the sight. "I
guess I got the one with the shower," she said.

"Alexa." She couldn't miss the way his face lit when he saw her. It
seemed his whole body changed, like the weight of a thousand years
had been lifted from his shoulders. She moved to him.

"Cleaner water might help," she suggested, unstopping the drain to
allow the muddy water to run out. She busied herself gathering soap
and towels and shampoo as the water ran low around him and then
was replaced by water that was clean and hot.

She started with his head, lathering the short bristly hair on top,
massaging deep into the scalp until she could feel him begin to relax.
Then, cupping her hands, she scooped up water to rinse and poured it
over his head like a baptism, again and again and again, until finally

the water ran clear. She breathed in the fresh, clean scent of his hair, her chest rising and falling against the terry cloth robe, as she traced the outline of his ears with a soapy wash cloth. Such wonderful ears, and she explored every wrinkle and fold with her cloth.

"Alexa . . ." Adam said, his voice huskier now. She placed a finger over his lips, quietly shushing him, and began washing his face, bathing him like a baby, tiny, circular motions above his brows, beneath his eyes, across his cheeks. She could feel the blood pulsing in his temples. Then down the nose—a very nice nose, a splendid nose—and across his lips. She wanted so badly to linger there, to kiss those lips, to finally taste Adam for the first time, but she continued on. Down the chin and under, small tentative swirling motions of terry and lather. She heard his breath catch and felt his entire body stiffen as she reached a sensitive area around his throat, and then he relaxed, as if giving himself over to her touch.

She dug the washcloth hard into the muscles of his shoulders. His bulky sweaters and baggy coats had hidden a finely muscled torso, an athlete's body, or a dancer's body. So many things to learn, so much to discover. She could feel his breath slow and deepen as her fingers moved across his chest leaving soapy trails. She rinsed it carefully and laid her head against it as she reached for his arm. His other hand came up to clutch her head closer to him and he buried his face in her hair, inhaling until she thought he'd burst and exhaling with a sigh as she continued down his arm with her ritual cleansing. Each finger she washed individually, lingering on the sensitive webbing between them. She fought back the urge to take a finger in her mouth to suckle.

She stopped in surprise when she encountered the tattoo on his wrist. "I didn't realize you had this much of a past," she murmured. The words came out breathier than she'd intended. "You have no idea," he responded, gently. She followed the outline of the tattooed circle with a corner of the washcloth. It fascinated her, its very exis-tence hinting of the secrets she longed to know about her mysterious Adam. Impulsively, she kissed the mark that spoiled the perfection of his body and heard him gasp as she traced the winged symbol with her tongue. He reached out for her then, pulling her into the tub with him.

They kissed. A deep, soul-exploring kiss. A kiss that seemed to lock them together for eternity. He was at once gentle and savage, aggressor and supplicant. And when he finally released her from the kiss, she knew her world had changed forever.

He rose from the tub and scooped her up in his deceptively muscled arms like an infant, soggy robe and all, as she gazed into his bottomless eyes with amazement. He carried her to the waterbed of her honeymoon suite and lay her gently upon it, staring at her with wonder as well. She saw him fully at his most vulnerable—Adam/Adonis indeed.

Kneeling beside her, he reached for her robe and she tingled as he pulled it off her shoulders, pushed it away from her breasts. But she stopped his hand as he moved to untie the sash. "Adam, no . . ." she begged, "please . . ." She turned away slightly.

As if he hadn't heard her, he continued to carefully untie the sash, removing the robe from her abdomen. Placing an arm around her waist, he bent and began gently kissing her scars. Slowly, he moved up her body, kissing the tender spot between her breasts, the base of her neck, her throat, her lips, her nose, and finally her forehead. She was crying as he said, "You are the most beautiful woman in the entire world, Alexa, and *nothing* will ever take that away from you."

Tears streaming from her eyes, she reached out for Adam and pulled him onto the bed beside her. Maybe tomorrow they would see the Grand Canyon. For the rest of tonight, they had other wonders of nature to explore.

Postcards from Alexa

World Enough and Time III

by Gillian Horvath

Alexa's sodden robe clung to her, tangling around her as he laid her gently on the bed. Her skin was flushed delicate pink from her hairline to where the tops of her breasts were revealed by the folds of the robe. He leaned down to kiss her throat at the join of neck and collarbone, his other hand going to part the robe tentatively, afraid it was too soon but unable to resist. She didn't shy away; she arched toward him with a tiny moan of pleasure as his mouth moved across the line of her breasts. He moved his hand downward, pushing the robe aside, and felt her freeze beneath his touch as his hand brushed lower on her stomach.

"Adam, no . . . please." It was a plea, a sob, and he froze in place, horrified by the reaction he'd provoked. He started to back away and then he saw it, the tracery of puckered red lines and chalky white patches, the scars that had made her try to turn from him. Medicine had come so far, he knew, and yet the marks left here by oncologists and chemotherapists looked to him no better than the burns and bleeding scars left by shamans and charlatans of earlier times. They had kept Alexa alive, but at what price? She was afraid to look at her own body, afraid to share it with the man who loved her.

He couldn't let her see the anger that filled him. She'd think it was directed at her. She'd never believe there was a man who could see past what was happening to her. And from what he'd seen of the world, he couldn't blame her. Men of his apparent age of barely 30 who would have known her for what she was, loved her for as long as she had, were few and far between.

Then he saw the resignation in her eyes, the slight turning away, her hands moving to pull the robe back together. He didn't let her do it. He kept his hand on her abdomen, keeping her in place. She was so tiny that his oversized hand all but covered her from hip to hip. Wordlessly, as softly as he could, he ran a finger along the crescent curve of a neat ridge of scar tissue that traced the lower edge of her belly, just above where the silken blonde triangle disappeared under the folds of the robe, and felt her shiver in fear and pleasure. He leaned in to kiss just above his hand, running a line of kisses up her body, between her breasts, as slowly as he could bear to. He stopped when he reached her face, raised himself up to look at her. Her eyes were closed, her fists clenched hard at her sides. So filled with rage and sorrow, she couldn't make room for joy.

He was good at being what people wanted him to be, at telling them what they wanted to hear. It had kept him alive more than once. He wanted to do it for Alexa now, to say whatever it would take to soothe away her pain and sadness, to restore her for just one moment to the woman she had been a year ago, before she had known how mortal she was. But he didn't know what to say, wasn't sure there was anything good enough, cute enough, wise enough, to heal her. So he just said what he was thinking:

"Alexa . . . You are the most beautiful woman in the world. The most beautiful woman I've ever seen. Nothing will change that. Nothing."

He heard the sob that broke his voice and cursed himself for it, for not having the strength to hide it from her. But she reached for him then, tangling her hands in his hair, pulling him down onto her with a fervor that surprised him. This time when his hand slipped between them to push the robe aside, she did not resist.

Postcards from Alexa

Natural Wonders

by Donna Lettow

"Closed? What do they mean, *closed?*" Adam was indignant. "How do you *close* a very large hole in the ground?" Two cars ahead of the VW, the Arizona State Police were systematically turning cars away from the main gate to the Grand Canyon.

"Guess we should've been watching the news," Alexa noted.

"Looks like the government's closed again." And when they approached the State Trooper blocking the road, the trooper confirmed that the largest natural canyon formation in the world was closed due to governmental shut down. Adam, lowering his voice, leaned out the window and tried to explain to the Trooper about Alexa, about how they were on a bit of a tight deadline. Whether the Trooper believed him or not, there was nothing he could do. He ordered Adam to turn the van around and head back out the access road.

"What is the point of having a government if they're going to shut down? What do they think they are, the fishmonger's?" Adam fumed as they rode back down the highway away from the Canyon. Putting on his best blue-haired pensioner voice: " 'Sorry, luv, tea time, you know. Pop back 'round at five.' "

Alexa laughed until she grimaced. "It's not all that bad," she said. "Maybe they'll be open tomorrow. The Trooper did say that Congress was working as fast as they can."

"Oh, there's a comfort."

"Let's just go back to Flagstaff and check into the hotel. I've never been to Arizona before, I'm sure there are all kinds of things to see here." He found her optimism invigorating. "And then later, we can have a nice dinner . . . relax . . ." She reached across the narrow gap between the driver's and passenger's seats and placed a hand on his knee. "Or not . . ." She gave what she hoped was her most wanton smile as she drew her hand up along his inner thigh.

She heard him growl slightly as his foot pressed harder on the accelerator and they both laughed.

Just outside of Flagstaff, Adam pulled the VW into the drive of a huge Victorian house. "This is it," he announced as he helped her from the van. "The Crow Canyon Bed & Breakfast."

"Have you been here before?" Alexa asked.

"No, but it comes highly recommended. I've got colleagues in the area." No need to tell her that the last time he'd actually stayed in Flagstaff, he'd been brought there by a Sheriff's posse and was to be hung at dawn. Thank goodness for Sundance.

As Adam removed their bags from the van, a large, matronly woman hustled down the steps of the house, her obviously Native features a bit incongruous with the extremely European architecture. *"Greetings, honored mother,"* Adam said in flawless Hopi as she approached. The woman broke into a huge smile, while Alexa looked at him with astonishment.

"You are most welcome here," the woman answered in the formal tongue of her people, then switched to English. "You must be Adam. Garrett warned me you were a linguist. Mary Crow, pleased to meet

you." Mary shook Adam's hand vigorously. "And this must be Alexa. Come on, dear, let's get you inside. You must be exhausted." Alexa's "no, really, I'm fine" was lost as the innkeeper wrapped a motherly arm around her shoulders and swept her toward the house. Alexa shot Adam an accusatory look, but Adam could do nothing but shrug his shoulders with a smile and gather up their bags to follow.

As he entered the parlor, he could hear Mary talking as she gave Alexa a tour of the downstairs. "Your Adam went to school with my son Garrett."

"I didn't realize Adam had gone to school in the U.S." Alexa filed it away with the few other sketchy facts she'd learned about Adam in the past week.

Mary went on with the tour. "Here's the breakfast room. I generally have breakfast on by eight for the guests, but if you kids want to, you know, sleep in, by all means, take your time." Then she explained, "They went to a special school in Geneva, about ten years ago."

"Switzerland? Really?" Adam had told her he had traveled a lot, but it piqued Alexa's interest all the same.

Adam caught up with them in the dining room and broke in quickly. "Only for about a year. It didn't really work out for me. Where should I put these?" He indicated the baggage he was carrying to Mary, exaggerating its heaviness. He knew she didn't know much more about what Garrett Crow did for a living than what she'd already said, but he'd much prefer a different conversation all the same.

"Follow the stairs all the way up. You've got the whole third floor to yourselves. Go on up, it's unlocked. Give you a hand?"

"No, no, that's all right." He started up the stairs. "Why don't you show Alexa the view from the back deck. Garrett tells me it's spectacular."

"But you have the same view from your—" Mary started to call up to him, but Adam cut her off by clearing his throat. "Oh, right . . . Do you like kittens?" Mary asked Alexa as she led her to the back of the house. "There's a brand new litter under the porch. . . ."

Adam hurried up the stairs with the baggage and opened the door to the third floor suite. Perfect. Everything was just the way he'd requested it. He pulled the drapes closed—he hadn't planned on arriving in the daylight—and went around the room lighting candles that had been strategically placed. Digging through his duffel, he pulled out his CD player and speakers and made a place for them on a dresser, then selected just the right CD. Looking in the mirror, he ran a quick hand through his hair and licked his lips. Everything was ready. Turning on the CD player at a low volume, he left the room and went back down the stairs.

When Alexa and Mary returned from their trip outside, Adam was leaning casually against the wall at the bottom of the stairs. "You were right," Alexa told him excitedly, "I have never seen such a view. The way the light plays on the mountainside—c'mon"—she took his hand—"you need to see this."

A smile played over his lips. "I'm told by a reliable source that the view from upstairs is even better. Care to see it with me?" he asked, reaching down and scooping her up in his arms.

"Adam!" Alexa laughed, "what are you doing? Put me down!" She struggled playfully and turned to look toward Mary for help, but the motherly innkeeper simply said, "It *is* a very nice view," grinned broadly, and walked away as Adam began to carry his precious burden up the stairs.

"Adam, I'm too heavy for this. You'll hurt yourself." But to Adam she was as soft and light as the newborn kittens under Mary Crow's porch. He silenced her with a gentle kiss. There in his arms he could sense how delicate she was, how fragile, how . . . mortal. And how much he loved her for that. As he climbed the last flight of stairs, he nuzzled his face against hers and whispered "It's time we finally did this correctly."

Alexa lifted an eyebrow. "I wasn't aware we were doing anything incorrectly." They arrived at the door to the suite and Adam realized, a bit awkwardly, he'd have to set her down to get the door open again. He let her feet touch the ground just long enough so he could open the door with his free hand, then he scooped her up again. "What *are* you doing? I can walk," she protested.

"Carrying you over the threshold, milady," he responded solemnly, and he carried her into the room he had prepared for her.

The scent reached her before her eyes adjusted to the candlelight—the scent of the hundreds of roses that adorned every surface of the room. She looked around in wonder—roses of every hue, long-stemmed in vases, buds woven into wreaths, and gentle, delicate petals strewn an inch thick on the canopied bed upon which he finally set her down. "Adam . . . I . . ." She was speechless, struck dumb with wonder. But her eyes said everything Adam had hoped he would hear.

He had planned their marriage bed practically since the first moment he'd seen her, weeks ago in Joe's. Across the bar he could see her surrounded by roses, their perfection echoing the perfection of her skin, their purity the purity of her spirit. And while theirs was not a marriage by modern definition, legalistic and bound by the dictates of governments and modern religions, he sought marriage with Alexa more ancient than any of that—a uniting of their bodies, their minds, and their souls, for as long as they had.

When they had been delayed on their journey, he was afraid they had been deprived of this place, of this moment. His disappointment had turned to anger, and his anger had nearly driven her away. But Alexa was strong, he'd seen that strength before he'd ever even asked her name, and she'd come to him and healed him and purified him. They had discovered wonders about each other that even he, after so many years, had never imagined. Last night was a night of exploration and learning, a night when two people became fully whole after living half empty for too long. Today, those two would become one.

He sat on the bed beside her, picked up a single white rose from the nightstand, and handed it to her. "I hope you like roses," he said, a bit of a shy grin playing around his mouth.

Alexa's eyes were bright with unshed tears which reflected the glow of the candles. "I hope you removed the thorns," she said, trying to keep the moment light.

He held her close and looked into those eyes. "I promise you, every thorn that it is within my power to remove." And then he kissed her. He could feel the warm path of her tear on his face, then another as they glided down her cheeks toward her lips, where both he and Alexa tasted their bitterness in shared communion as their tongues sought each other.

His first taste of Alexa, his first taste of a woman in years, had been an explosion as senses he had thought long dormant reawakened and fired into urgency. Now, though his senses still thrummed, he could savor the moment. He held her close, drinking deep of her essence, enjoying the feel of his tongue as it rubbed against her teeth, delighting in the tiny sounds Alexa made in the back of her throat. Bodies unmoving, their entire lifeforce focused into their lips, their mouths—he was content to remain that way forever.

But Alexa, not having forever, was hungry for more. Without breaking the kiss, she reached behind him and began to pull the Irish fisherman's sweater he wore over his head. She succeeded only in getting it hopelessly entangled around the two of them. The kiss finally broke as they began to giggle, the sweater caught over both Adam's head and Alexa's.

"Whoa, whoa, Tiger, not so fast," Adam laughed as he freed them from the tangled wool.

"And why not?" she asked, taking the sweater and tossing it at the nightstand, leaving Adam shirtless.

He smiled, pleased at the changes he could see in Alexa after only one night of affection and attention. A closed blossom, ashamed of her body and afraid of intimacy, was slowly beginning to flower. "Because the night is still young, and I'm an old man," he teased.

"Old man, my ass," she laughed, tracing the definition of his biceps with a finger. He stood and reached for his duffel, and she watched the movement of his sinewy torso in the candlelight. "Guess I must just have a thing for older men."

Adam removed a green jar and a small box from his duffel and set them on the nightstand, then kicked off his shoes. He stood before Alexa clad only in his jeans. "Besides, this isn't about me. It's about you."

"Sounds ominous." Alexa looked at him with mock wariness. "Should I be afraid?"

"Never be afraid of me," he said, reaching for the clips that bound back her hair. He carefully unclasped them and Alexa shook her head, allowing the hair to tumble down, long and loose. He fingered a long, silken strand, let it fall, then kissed her on the top of the head. Her head against his chest, she reached out to clasp him around the waist, but he stopped her. "Not yet," he admonished, a twinkle in his eye.

"Tease," she accused.

"Wouldn't have it any other way," he said, reaching for the hem of the oversized tunic which concealed her body from the light. He pulled it up and over her head and dropped it on the floor behind him, and her flowing hair framed her milky shoulders like a painting. She smiled her encouragement as he sat beside her, but her eyes crinkled mischievously when he reached behind her to unfasten her bra. He was thrown for an instant when he found no fastener whatsoever, until Alexa reached around and guided his hands to the front. He had encountered and conquered countless variations on women's under-garments, from chastity belts to corsets, but this fastener stymied him. He gave her his best hurt puppy look and she relented, raising her arms, allowing him to pull the offending garment off over her head.

"You did that on purpose, didn't you?" he said. She laughed and said, "Moi?" as she pulled off her shoes and then looked up at him expectantly. "What next?"

She was radiant as she sat under the canopy of her rose-covered marriage bed, her face a gentle pink in anticipation. There had been many marriage beds, of different cultures and different faiths, and many women, more perhaps than one man should be allowed—per-haps five thousand years were more than one man should be allowed. But he had loved each one as much as he could, for as long as he could, whether it was one year or eighty, and he cherished the memory of each in his heart forever. But in this time and in this place, Alexa out-shone them all. He reached for the box on the nightstand, knelt before Alexa on both knees, and handed it to her. "I want you to have this."

As she opened the box, he once again glimpsed her look of wonder and awe, until she reluctantly closed the box and handed it back to him. "Adam . . . I couldn't . . . you've done so much already."

"Please. For me."

She looked into his eyes as he knelt before her, and relented. He opened the box and pulled out the necklace, its gemstones twinkling in the candlelight reflected by its golden bangles. It took her breath away. She couldn't imagine what it might be worth. "Adam, how could you—?"

"It's an old family heirloom," he interrupted her. "Please wear it."

"Now?"

He got up from his knees and sat on the bed behind her. "Please," he said simply. He placed the necklace around her neck, fastening the clasp in the back, then turned her toward him, admiring how the bangles and stones caressed her throat before dipping down to end in a flawless crystal perfectly positioned between her breasts. A young bride's parents customarily bedecked her with whatever gold and jewelry the family could afford in preparation for her union. But Alexa had no family, no one to escort her to the bridal chamber, no one to give her away. No one, now, except Adam.

"It's lovely," she said, a bit breathlessly.

"*You're* lovely," he corrected, the barest hint of a catch in his voice, for she *was* beautiful indeed, and he knew how fortunate he was to have found her. He stood and offered her a hand to stand as well. He reached his arms around her tiny waist and unzipped her billowy gauze skirt, which fell in soft folds around her ankles. She stepped out of the skirt, her body covered only by her silken panties, and Adam scooped her up in his arms once again.

"Ad-am," she scolded in jest.

"Last time," he grinned. "I promise," and he carried her to the center of the bed and laid her carefully down in the midst of the rose petals.

She arched in pleasure at the cool touch of the gentle petals and settled onto the bed with a sigh, her hair spread out in luxurious waves behind her. Adam gazed at her, arranged across the pillows like Venus come to earth, veiled only by a narrow strip of palest silk, and he suddenly wanted her more than he had ever dreamed. The urge to take her, then and there, was stronger than any he'd felt in centuries.

But he didn't. Couldn't.

This was her marriage bed, and he would never give her cause to fear him. As he'd assured Alexa earlier, this wasn't about him and his needs, no matter how strong. This was about her.

He picked up the green marble jar and sat close to her on the bed. She reached out for him, wanting him as much as he wanted her. He took her hand and kissed it, savoring for a moment her scent mingling with that of the roses. Then, summoning the discipline of a monk, he placed her hand on her tummy.

Alexa rolled to one side to look at him. "Adam?" she asked, half in frustration, half in fear. "Is something wrong? Did I—?"

He placed a calming finger to her lips. "Shhh, it's okay. You'll like this part. Trust me."

"Don't I always?" she said, a bit halfheartedly, and he realized she was retreating to that place she went when he scared her, her refuge when she thought she'd angered him. He'd have to work to rebuild her trust. He held out the marble jar and twisted the lid free. He took a little of the ointment inside and rubbed it into his fingers. He allowed the fragrance to waft over him, to envelop him and enter him, and for a moment he was lost in the memories the fragrance stirred up in him, memories of life and pleasure and pain and death. He dipped the tips of his fingers into the precious liquid again and gently but carefully, with long deliberate strokes, massaged the oil into her temples, across her forehead, around her eyes which had closed at the first touch of his hand to her face, and into her cheeks, which grew rosier as the warmth of the oil penetrated her skin.

She took a short, tentative breath and her eyes opened and grew wide at the unfamiliar scent. In Alexa's world, sense of smell was the least useful of the five senses, handy for letting you know when the milk went bad. She'd never encountered a smell that claimed you, possessed you, tried to make you one with it. Involuntarily, she inhaled deeply and allowed the almost living scent to fill her. She held her breath as long as she could bear, then exhaled slowly, trailing off into a little sigh.

"Like it?" he asked with a grin, already seeing the answer in her face, in her eyes. His fingers, warm and throbbing from the oil, danced along the contours of her face, massaging the ointment into cheek and jaw and chin. He lingered around her mouth, tiny careful strokes, kneading the skin, the lips, knowing each pass of his hand set nerves atingle, brought those lips to life. She opened her mouth as he drew a long finger across her lower lip and she caught the finger between her teeth in a delicate nip. "Hey! You don't play fair."

She released his finger with a laugh and spoke between deep cleansing breaths. "Me? You! My God, Adam, what is this stuff?"

He showed her the green marble jar full of milky yellow liquid and spoke a word in a language already dying when he was young. Switching to a tongue more recently dead, "Olibanum," he said. "Frankincense."

"Frankincense?" she repeated, incredulous. "Like the Wise Men?"

"Like the Wise Men."

" 'Gold, frankincense, and myrrh,' frankincense?"

"With a little oil of jasmine and a few other surprises." He poured some of the mixture into his palms and began rhythmically kneading it into her throat, her neck. "Believe me, you wouldn't like myrrh. Nasty stuff." Myrrh was reserved for the anointing of the dead. They would both know myrrh soon enough. Reaching under her hair, he rubbed the ointment into the join of head and neck and spine until he felt it relax and he guided her head gently back to a pillow.

Alexa was lost in her childhood Bible lessons. "Thou anointest my head with oil. My cup overfloweth." Not some dry words on a page, it was beginning to make her feel warm and vibrant and alive.

"Exactly. Although if you think I'm going to stop with your head, you're sadly mistaken." He poured a dollop of oil directly in the well between her breasts, under the crystal necklace. The cold oil made her gasp as it touched the tender skin, but almost immediately she could feel its warmth start to reach into her chest. Using firm, deliberate motions, he began to work the oil and where his hands went, fire reached into her soul.

In Canaan, the women gleamed like the sun as they approached their bridegroom. In Egypt, the scent was darker, muskier; the priest's unguent thick and rich. In Babylon, the mother of the groom anointed the bride in preparation for her son, but he had had no mother and so the queen herself prepared his chosen one. He massaged the precious oils into Alexa's tummy, and then, even more tenderly, into her scars. Modern medicine, so quick to reject the remedies of the past—over time the ointment could have softened them, made them less notice-able, and the simple act of touching them would have helped Alexa accept them as part of herself. The Babylonians had used a different ointment for this nearly sacred area of a woman's body, consecrated oils to promote fertility and ease the pain of childbirth. But both he and Alexa were doomed in their separate ways to never know the joy of children.

Standing, he moved to the foot of the bed and, covering his hands with oil, carefully rubbed it into her feet. The Chinese believed pres-sure points in the feet had power over the heart, the mind, the emo-tions. Even the Christians, with their deep hatred of the human body, considered anointing the feet sacred. The feet were second only to the hands in sensuality and Alexa's, in addition to being sensitive, were apparently also ticklish, but her sudden "Hey!" quickly settled into something not unlike a quiet purr as his thorough massage continued.

Finally, he could stand it no longer. He pulled her to him and kissed her deeply once again, relishing the taste that was so uniquely Alexa. He could drink her soul, sample her essential lifesblood. It spoke of strength and passion and goodness. It mixed with the frankincense and jasmine coursing through her veins. And there, subtly, almost imper-ceptible, another taste all too familiar—the bitter tang of death, wait-ing. It flavored her body like it flavored her life. As his lips crushed hers perhaps more forcibly than he'd intended, as if to prove he would not be driven away by the taint of death, Alexa cried out and, tangling both hands in his hair, pulled him down with her onto the bed of roses.

Not one scribe in a hundred generations could convey the sweet sound Alexa made as the two became whole, husband and wife, bound together. His own voice rumbled in the base of his throat, the deep trill of meditation, as he felt her protect him with her body. Time seemed to stop as he savored the oneness with Alexa, two souls sharing a single body, united forever in the moment. And, as one, they became aware of the rhythm of the earth and sky and sought together to match it.

But after a short while, Adam also became aware of the rhythm of footsteps on the stairs, a niggling sensation on the border of his awareness. And when the footsteps stopped just outside their door, he was jerked roughly back to reality.

"Yes, mother?" he asked of the Hopi woman he knew was standing outside the suite after a moment of awkward silence.

"Is something wrong?" Alexa whispered to him urgently.

Mary Crow's voice was obviously embarrassed. "I, um, it's almost dinner time and I was wondering if you kids were hungry yet."

"Not for food, no," Adam answered, a bit exasperated, and Alexa giggled into his chest. He liked the way that felt against his skin. But it was obvious to him that was not Mary's primary reason for inter-rupting them. "And . . . ?" he encouraged her to continue.

"And . . . Garrett just called. I'm sorry, Adam, but you're not going to get to see the Canyon. Congress adjourned 'til after the holidays. They've called out the National Guard to keep trespassers away." Alexa may not even have noticed the shadow that crossed Adam's face, then disappeared as quickly as it had come. "I'm so sorry," Mary con-tinued, outside the door, "I know how much it meant to you . . . for Alexa . . ."

Alexa, though disappointed by the news, told her, "Don't worry, Mary. It's okay, really."

Adam dismissed Mary with a bright "Thanks for the news. No need to hold dinner on our account." Then, after he was sure he heard Mary start back down the stairs, he gave Alexa's ear a quick tug with his teeth. "Now, where were we . . . ?" he teased, as rose petals flut-tered to the floor around them.

Mary Crow found Alexa later that evening curled up in a tight ball on the bed covered by a woven Indian blanket. She could tell Alexa had been crying, but the Indian woman tried to put on a bright face, knowing the cause. "On his way out, Adam said he thought you might want something to eat." Mary put a tray next to her on the bed.

Alexa didn't look at her or the tray. "That was nice of him," she said, all inflection drained from her voice. "I don't suppose he told you where he was going? I woke up and he was . . . gone."

"He just said he had to run into town to get a few things." Mary saw Alexa's shoulder shake as she choked back a sob. "Honey, is everything all right?" she asked.

"No," Alexa said, turning to face her, "no, it's not all right." She sat up on the bed, still wrapped in the Indian blanket. "I just . . . there's just no pleasing him. Everything I do . . . everything I say . . . it just turns out all wrong. I tried to make him happy . . . and now he's gone. He hates me, I know it."

Mary put a hand on Alexa's shoulder. "He doesn't hate you. I've seen a hundred young couples come through here, and there's always some awkwardness and doubt at the beginning. It's natural. I'm sure he's feeling just as scared and vulnerable as you are."

"I'm not the one who disappeared as soon as we'd . . . as soon as . . ." Just thinking about it brought more tears, and she couldn't get the sentence out. Mary put her arms around her and held her close.

"There, there," Mary whispered, gently rubbing Alexa's back as she would a child's. "Is this the part where I give you the All Men Are Pigs speech?" She could feel Alexa laugh in spite of herself. "Why don't you eat something," she continued. "My cooking's not quite as good as sex, but it'll do in his absence."

As Mary reached for the tray of food, Alexa sat up against the head-board and set aside the blanket, uncovering the demure satin negligee she'd put on when she woke up. Mary set up the tray across her lap and handed her a napkin. "We wouldn't want to get that messed up, now would we? It's very pretty."

Alexa wiped her eyes with the napkin, then tucked it in around her. "My boss, Joe, he had a little party for me before we left. A couple of the bartenders gave it to me." Mike and Lou had called it her "trousseau."

"Seems a little tame for bartenders."

"Oh, no, they were like my big brothers. Everybody at Joe's, they were my family." Alexa grew quiet for moment. Mary suspected she was thinking about how she'd never see them again.

"Now it's my turn," Mary said, breaking the silence. "Here's my contribution to the hope chest." She picked a figurine off the tray and pressed it into Alexa's hand. It was a small doll painstakingly carved from a single piece of smoky-red quartz.

"What is it?"

"It's a fetish," Mary explained, "it's kind of like a talisman. My people carved this one from a special type of rock you can only find in the canyons—its magic is to bring happiness and prosperity to young married couples."

Alexa set the stone down. "We're not married."

"You're sure about that?"

"Of course I'm sure. Maybe if we were, he wouldn't have run off. . . ."

Mary looked around, taking in the candlelight, the lingering fragrances, the roses she'd helped Adam prepare. "You know, there's more to marriage than a white dress and a piece of paper. And it's not about legally chaining someone to your side, either." She fingered the crystal necklace Alexa had left lying on the bedstand. "Marriage is what two souls do, on their own, when they're ready."

"Then it'll never happen. Because I don't know him and I'll certainly never understand him. Every time I think I could get close to him, he locks me out. Or runs away."

Mary picked up the quartz fetish and examined it closely. "Garrett's father was probably the oddest man I'd ever met. I don't think he said six words to me the first time he took me out. My father was convinced he was mute. Garrett, poor thing, took after me—you can't shut the boy up sometimes. Anyway, after that first date, I was convinced I'd never see him again, and I wasn't even sure I wanted to. Then he asked me out to the movies and I went. He said hello at the door, asked me if I wanted popcorn or a soda at the theater, then gave me a peck on the cheek and said goodnight when he took me home. So that's what?

Ten more words? The third time we went out, he got down on one knee and asked me to marry him. And I amazed everyone, me included, by saying yes. Because our souls had already decided. The rest is just paperwork." Handing the fetish to Alexa, she stood up and moved toward the door. "I'll be up in a little bit to get the dishes."

Alexa looked at the fetish and then at Mary. "You know, Mary, he's really not a pig."

Mary stopped in the door and smiled at her. "I know. None of them are—once you get to know them."

It was a little after midnight when Adam quietly snuck back into the Crow Canyon Bed & Breakfast. Mary Crow was asleep in an armchair in front of the fireplace, which had cooled to embers. He tiptoed past her and up the stairs. The Indian woman opened one eye to watch him go and smiled.

Adam opened the door to the third floor suite tentatively, not sure what he'd find. It was only when he was in the van on the way to Flagstaff that he had begun to realize what a slap in the face his single-minded determination must have been to Alexa. He could hardly blame her if she was gone. He hoped to God she wasn't.

She wasn't. He found her asleep on the bed of roses, a vision in cream-colored satin and lace. He was struck once again by her beauty, her purity, and how he wished he could share in the serenity reflected in her sleeping face. He stood by the side of the bed, content to watch the candlelight play over the satin as it rose and fell in the rhythm of sleep. As carefully as he could, he set his duffel and the shopping bag he carried down on the floor by the nightstand.

The crunch of the shopping bag woke Alexa with a start and, still half-asleep, she called out to "Adam!" for help. He was at her side in an instant.

"It's okay, it's all right," he comforted her, hugging her to him. "I'm here. Nothing to be afraid of." She melted against him in relief, then, coming more awake, remembered she was angry with him and pulled away. "Alexa?" he asked, concerned.

"So, you came back."

"Of course I did. I would never leave you."

"Could've fooled me." The hurt in Alexa's eyes was nearly more than he could bear.

"Alexa," he dropped to one knee beside the bed, taking her hand and bowing his head to touch it, "I am a thoughtless, pathetic cad begging you for your forgiveness." He looked up at her with eyes wide and pleading.

He could tell she was amused by his melodramatics but trying hard not to show it. " 'Cad,' " she said after a long pause while she thought it over. "Now there's a word you don't hear every day."

"I'm forgiven, then?" he asked hopefully. She laughed and nodded her head. "You have my solemn promise it will never happen again," he said as he stood. "Now get dressed, I have a surprise for you."

Postcards from Alexa

Holy Ground

by Gillian Horvath & Donna Lettow

He pulled the van off the road on a narrow bit of shoulder, shut off the lights, leaving them in a darkness blacker than a city-raised girl like Alexa could imagine. A million stars twinkled overhead, obscuring the familiar constellations in the crowd of lights.

"What are we doing?"

Adam switched on a powerful flashlight, slid open the van's side door and pulled out a stuffed backpack. "It's not like they can put a fence around the whole canyon," he answered, shouldering the pack. "We're hiking in."

"Let me get this straight, we're breaking into a national monument? This was your surprise?"

"Well, technically we aren't 'breaking' anything, we're just, well, trespassing a little. Watch out for that rock." He shone the flashlight around. The trail to the eastern wall of the Canyon wasn't nearly as obvious as it had been a hundred years ago. Somewhere along here the path used to fork near the old pine tree.

"Well, *technically* it's still a Federal offense. When you promised me

I'd get to see things I never saw before on this trip, the inside of a women's prison was not what I had in mind, Adam."

"C'mon, where's your sense of adventure?" He reached back into the van, pulled out a smaller pack and handed it to her.

The canvas was crisp and new, and Alexa guessed the equipment inside was, too. "Have you ever done this?" she asked dubiously.

"I've lived off the land a few times. Don't worry, it's only a couple hours to the rim, easy terrain. Just stick close."

This didn't seem like the time to tell him that she'd never been camping, never been a girl scout, never hiked farther than the stretch along the beach below the university. Alexa shouldered the light pack, took the flashlight he handed her, and followed him into the woods. From farther away than she expected him to be, she heard him start to sing. "Oh give me a home . . . where the buffalo roam . . ."

The incline was gentle, but it was an uphill climb. It only took a few minutes for her to feel it, a tightening in her chest, her lungs tingling, then burning. She breathed through her mouth, the cold night air raw on her throat, her steps slowing as her legs flagged, lactic acid building to sharp aches from the lack of oxygen. She stopped to catch her breath, leaning her head against the nearest tree, her flashlight dipping to point at her feet.

"Alexa?" He was beside her immediately, dropping his own pack with a thud, hastily helping her off with hers.

"I'm sorry . . . give me a minute . . . I guess I'm a little out of shape."

"It's the air," he answered, realization cracking his voice. "We're at almost eight thousand feet." He kicked his pack over angrily, sending it skidding a couple of feet in the carpet of pine needles. "Damn, damn, damn, damn."

"I'm sorry, Adam, I'm sorry, I know how much you want to do this—" Her tears weren't helping her breathing any and she had to gulp for air.

"No, Alexa, it's not you, it's not your fault. I just didn't think . . . We'll just have to find another way." He grabbed up both packs one handed, gestured with his flashlight back toward the van. "Come on. I'll make a few calls."

She followed him back, wiping at the last stubborn tears, forcing herself to breathe deeply. Not her fault, he'd said. Whose fault then? When he'd offered to fill what was left of her life with adventure, surely he hadn't realized that she couldn't run, couldn't climb, couldn't even walk a few miles in the mountains.

She sat at the kitchen table with her coffee, letting the caffeine and hot liquid dilate her lungs, watching through the big back windows as the sun dipped sedately toward the hills.

Garrett's pickup pulled up outside and Garrett himself came in, pulling off his battered straw hat to wipe sweat and road dust from his glistening black hair.

"You kids having fun?" he teased, and, off Alexa's quiet shrug, took another look at her. "Where's Adam?"

"Making some calls. Trying to find someone who knows someone who knows someone who can get us into the canyon." A few calls had turned into a hundred calls, ranging from local rangers to an Under-secretary at the White House, and the day was nearly gone. "I wish he'd just let it go."

Garrett smiled fondly. "Adam tends to get a little bit of tunnel vision. When he wants something, he just goes straight for it. Forgets about everything else. And everyone," he added, catching her eye. "Why does he want to go there so bad, anyway?"

"He told me the whole canyon is a holy place, a place of peace and sanctuary. He said he wants me to feel safe." She shook her head in frustration. "I don't need a holy canyon to feel safe."

Garrett looked at her a long moment, his dark eyes unreadable. Then he clamped his hat back on his head. "Get in the truck," he told her. "And Adam's getting in, too, if I have to carry him."

He drove them in silence out Route 89 to the 64, refusing to answer questions. Adam sat silently against the opposite door, gazing blindly out at the painted desert, ignoring Alexa's exclamations at its beaut until she finally stopped making them and sat quietly between the two brooding men.

Finally, at a right turn-out leading to a line of lean-tos staffed with locals selling crafts and wares, Garrett pulled the truck over. He came around and opened the opposite door, hauled Adam out by one arm. Alexa jumped down after him, watching in astonishment as Garrett dragged Adam past the line of jewelry stands, where the last of the vendors were starting to pack up for the night, and over to the western railing. "Look," he told him simply, almost angrily. "You think that Canyon is the only holy place we got out here? Feds don't own 'em all—not yet."

The sun was setting over the hills, pitching them into sharp black relief; below them, a gorge plunged away to dizzying depth. It might not be the Grand Canyon, but it was the earth at her grandest, her ancient secrets laid out in layers of rock too deep to fathom. Alexa gasped, her breath taken this time not by the altitude but by the view, and Adam turned to her, and his face changed. "Alexa?"

"Adam . . . my God . . . if this is what you wanted to show me . . ." There were no words. She put her arms around him and held on, feeling his heart beat against hers, looking out into what seemed like forever. "It's perfect."

He didn't answer, but she felt his hesitation, his unspoken answer. Beautiful it might be, but it was not what he had planned, not what he had wanted to give her. She tried again.

"I know you wanted to show me the Canyon," she said quietly, "But this . . ." She shook her head, still groping for words. She pointed to an outcropping across from them, where clean yellow stone showed the scar of a fresh break, a thousand feet of rock that had tumbled away in the last freeze. "This is all new. As new for you as for me. It can be *ours*. Not a gift from you to me . . . something for us to share."

She looked up at him expectantly, hoping he would accept this interpretation. Hoping, above all, that he would stop worrying about what he couldn't change, and accept instead what was. Great gifts lay all around them, if he would only get over the Canyon and all it seemed to mean to him.

He looked into her eyes, seeming to look *at* her, not past her, for the first time in two days. "I almost ruined everything, didn't I? I just wanted everything to be perfect."

"Adam, we're here. We're together. There's so much I haven't seen, or done . . . and no time to do it all. Do you think it will bother me if Parisians are rude, or Venice smells like a sewer? Do you think that matters?" She locked his gaze with hers. "Don't let it matter. Don't let it take you away from me. There isn't time."

He shook his head, marveling at her wisdom. She'd had too much reason, in the last year, to be cynical, but she hadn't let it happen. She wanted the world to be a wonderful place, with or without her, and he . . . In trying to make it perfect for her, he had nearly soured it.

He took her hand and walked her down the natural steps made by erosion of the rock, out onto a finger of mesa that jutted like a penin- sula into the chasm. Blue railings were all that stood between them and the sheer drop—and, on a section of mesa off to their right, split off from theirs and at least ten feet lower, Alexa saw the remains of one of the stone posts that held the railings in place. In a few years' time, perhaps, the spot they were standing on would have tumbled into the void, but for now it seemed permanent, ancient, an observation post into the past.

"Listen," he said, and she did, and heard nothing. A hundred feet above and behind them, the vendors were packing up their stalls as the sun set behind them; a hundred yards beyond that, Highway 64 cut through the reservation. But no sound of voices or traffic reached them; not even a bird sang. It was true silence, and they stood in it together for a moment, drinking it in.

Garrett joined them, his arms full of Navajo blankets, fresh off one of the stalls. He handed them to Alexa. "Here. Kate says they'll be back to open up just after sunrise, so try and get your sacred stuff done by then. She'll bring you some coffee. I'll pick you up at 8."

They were spending the night here? Alexa was astonished to find that the idea did not terrify her—as long as Adam was here, she really *did* feel safe.

Adam clasped hands with Garrett, his face shining with pleasure, his voice earnest. "Garrett, I don't know how to thank you for this. . . ."

"Well, you owe Kate two hundred bucks for the blankets," Garrett answered teasingly; then, more serious: "You want to do something for me? Tell me what it was like here before. . . . Before they put up the fences."

Adam stared at his friend for a long moment. There was no challenge in Garrett's expression. No anger. And no hint of doubt. He wasn't asking Adam to confirm what he'd guessed. But he wasn't leaving him any room for lying, now, either. The man deserved an answer.

Methos stepped to the railing, put one long leg over, then the other, until he was standing outside it, on the edge of the mesa. The rock was solid, but the feeling of vertigo was real. He barely heard Alexa's gasp of objection; he put out a hand to Garrett, as once one of Garrett's ancestors had put out a hand to him: "Come."

Garrett came over the fence, stood beside him at the edge. Everything was different here—the wind, as still as indoors just a few feet away where Alexa stood on the other side of the rail, streamed up out of the canyon, tossing Garrett's long hair, ruffling even Adam's short brush cut, carrying the scents of four states, of a whole, young country. In his stretch of lifetimes Methos had felt a thousand winds in his face—ancient desert winds, sweet heathered winds, the killing winds of Atlantic gales. The wind on the Painted Desert was like so much of Garrett's lost culture—you had to know where to stand, where to look, to catch it.

"That's what it felt like," he told Garrett quietly, and Garrett stood a moment, drinking it in; then they both climbed back over the rail.

Garrett was silent, almost somber, as he moved to his truck; Adam put an arm around Alexa as they watched him pull out. One by one the other pickups with local plates pulled away, bearing the families who ran the tourist stalls, and they were left alone, watching the shadows of the setting sun against the immense canvas of colored rock.

He took one of the brown and white woven blankets from the pile in her arms, spread it on the edge of the mesa, as near to the railing as he dared. They sat together in the fading light, the remaining blankets draped over their knees, her head against his shoulder. Every moment of the sunset brought a new color to land or sky, brought a new detail of stone into sharp relief, or cast one into shadow.

"Look at it," Alexa breathed quietly. "You could come here every day for a thousand years and I bet you'd never see the same thing twice."

She was right, again. "Let this be our canyon, then. Forever." He reached out a hand to trace the line of her jaw, down her cheek, curving up to stroke along her mouth. It seemed she could feel every whorl of his thumb against her lip, and her lips parted as he leaned toward her, the sun behind him throwing the planes of his face into relief as dramatic as the rockfaces around them. "Let's make it ours."

His lips met hers and his hand slid down to cradle her neck, and she tasted desert dust and wind in his kiss, passion and relief and a deep sweetness that could only be joy, the same joy she was feeling as she realized she had finally reached him, finally had the chance to be the strong one, the generous one. She would not, could not, be the rescued damsel—and wouldn't let him be the teacher, the father, in all things. She would give as well as take, or there was nothing, nothing between them worth having.

They sipped good Italian wine from the picnic basket Garrett had left them, watching the unbroken sky turn from orange to deep blue to darkest black. When the last of the twilight was gone, they were in a darkness greater than any she'd ever seen. There were no lights on the road above, no lights from homes anywhere—and on her right, somehow blacker than the rest of the darkness, the great chasm of the canyon. Adam was only a shadow beside her, more felt than seen, when finally Alexa whispered, "Are there really more stars here than at home, or do I just feel closer to heaven?"

He answered her softly. "Some people believe that every star you can see in the sky is the soul of a loved one who's left us."

There was quiet again as they both stared at the heavens. He could get lost in watching the stars. Civilizations would rise and fall, loved ones come and go in the blink of an eye, but the stars were always there, had always been there, would always be there. Like the Canyon they were formed long before him and would still be burning bright long after he had finally turned to dust.

"Where do you think I'll be?"

Alexa's quiet voice brought him back. "What do you mean?" he asked.

"With the other souls," she explained. "Where do you think my star will be?"

Adam wanted nothing more than to derail this conversation before it went any further. He didn't need another reminder of how soon he was going to lose her. But he knew it was important to Alexa to talk about it, to share the experience with him—just as he'd begged her to do. "See that bright one there," he said, pointing, "that's Venus, the goddess of love and beauty."

Alexa stared up at the Morning Star. "I see it."

"I think you're going to be right next to her. And the beauty of Alexa will burn so brightly no one will ever be able to see Venus again."

"You're sweet to say that," she said in a tiny voice.

"I only say it because I mean it."

She shivered, from silent pleasure more than from the cold. He felt the tremble run through her, and his arm tightened around her. He cupped her body against his, protecting it, warming it.

"Ummm, this is nice, isn't it?" she murmured, almost to herself.

"Well, except for one thing . . ." Adam extracted one hand from around her waist and reached under the blanket. He removed a stone that had been digging into his leg and held it in the beam of the flashlight to show it to her. "That's better."

Alexa reached out and took the stone. "That's one of Mary Crow's fetish stones," she said as she rubbed the dirt off the smoky-red rock.

"She gave me a doll carved from this. She says it brings luck to young couples."

"Well, we'll definitely hang on to it, then. You and I need all the luck we can get, don't we?"

After a long pause, she asked him a question that took him totally off guard. "Adam . . . are we married?"

"What?"

"Mary Crow seems to think we're married. Do you think we're married?"

He thought back on their marriage bed. Yes, even though he'd made a botch of it in the end, he believed they were married. But he was sure it was not the kind of marriage Alexa had in mind. "Why? Do you want to be? We're not that far from Vegas. We could be there tomorrow afternoon. If that's what would make you happy, I'm sure there's an Elvis impersonator who'd love to perform any ceremony you want."

Alexa shook her head, ignoring the feeble joke, seeing through to the genuine offer underneath. "No, that's not what I meant."

It wasn't? He nearly held his breath, waiting for her to continue.

"I mean, you know, this sounds silly but, our souls . . . our spirits— are they married?"

"I don't know," he said cautiously. "Do you love me?" She looked away at the mention of the word. He tenderly turned her face toward his and looked intently into her eyes. "I love you desperately, Alexa. Do you love me?"

The silence nearly killed him. Then her lower lip started to quiver. "Yes," she whispered, barely daring to speak it, "Desperately."

He took the quartz from her and stood. He held out a hand and pulled her to her feet beside him.

"Alexa Bond," he began, "in this sacred place and in front of the witness of those who have gone on before us, with this rock, I thee wed. I vow to honor and cherish and above all love you with all my heart, in health and in sickness, until death takes you from me, and beyond."

Alexa's heart was breaking with joy. She took the rock from him and

began, "Adam Pierson . . ." Her words cut through him like an angry
knife—a reminder that he could never be truly married to Alexa, that
their souls could never really join. There was so much he was forced
to withhold from her. She could never know Methos, only Adam Pierson. Only a shell of all he truly was. ". . . until death takes me from
you." He reached down and found his wine glass in the dark, offered
it to her. She drank and then gave it to him to drink. Then, placing the
empty glass on the ground, he broke it with his foot.

"I always wanted to do that," Adam said with a little laugh. Alexa
cleared her throat. "What, did I forget something?"

" 'You may kiss the bride'?"

"Oh, right."

She leaned against him, prolonging their kiss, pressing him down onto
the blanket. "I hope this is what Garrett meant by sacred stuff," she
whispered. She used both hands to comb his hair away from his face,
studying the planes of his face, every curve and point, the way the
muscles of his neck angled down to join his collarbone. Making them
part of her, part of this canyon, part of this night, forever.

He reached up to stroke her face, and her eyes slid closed as his fin-
gertips played over her jawline, her lips, her eyelids. Even without
Frankincense, warmth permeated her skin everywhere he touched.
Sensation dancing in places he had not touched, her whole body
responding to his concentrated touch on her face.

"Look," he whispered. His left hand slipped down her back, and in
one smooth move flipped them over so that she was lying on the rough
blanket, gazing up at the starlit sky, pinpricks of light filling her sight,
her senses, so much so that she would almost have sworn she could
feel the stars on her skin, tiny goosebumps running over her body.

He kneeled over her, a dark silhouette against the star-filled sky, as
awesome and implacable as a constellation. And it was as though the
sky, the stone, the whole earth had entered her, sending river and wind
and stars shooting through her body. In that moment she would gladly

have rolled with him over the edge, falling into forever, ending both their lives in this moment of perfect ecstasy, perfect unity.

And then they were back on earth, arms around each other, hearts beating hard and fast, a sheen of shared sweat drying quickly in the canyon wind. Alexa was panting and crying with exertion and joy. "Adam . . . I'll remember this . . . forever."

He pulled another blanket over them, clutched her closer. "So will I, Alexa. I swear. As long as I live."

Postcards from Alexa
The Man with No Name

by Donna Lettow

The sound of hoofbeats was all around him. He bent low over the pommel of his saddle, heels and spurs viciously grazing the sides of the chestnut mare who'd given him her all, demanding she give still more. She whinnied in pain and continued her headlong charge across the dusty flats toward the forest in the distance.

Crack! He heard the sharp report of a Winchester behind him. He turned in his saddle to see that Sheriff Bruton and his men, thundering behind him, were still out of range but gaining steadily as his brave little mare began to flag. He counted eight, plus the Sheriff.

Damn them.

He and the McQuarrie brothers had split up when they heard the posse coming, hoping to raise the odds. There couldn't have been more than 15 of them to start, why did he still have nine? God dammit, someone must have talked. Someone must have told them he'd be the one with the gold. He looked ahead. The forest was getting nearer, but still not close enough. He bent down lower, stroking the foam-flecked head of the exhausted mare, then raked his spurs

across her tender ribs. The horse screamed but was able to respond
with a short burst of speed. But it didn't last.

The posse rode into range as he reached the treeline. A bullet
whizzed past his head and he pulled on the reins, steering the mare in
and among the trees. He wove headlong through the forest as bullets
zinged around him, trying to keep the trees between himself and the
main body of the posse. But Bruton and his men, though hampered in
speed by the trees, made up for it in sheer numbers as they began to
fan out through the woods. He couldn't hide from all of them.

When the bullet tore through his right arm, shattering the
humerus, he was nearly thrown from the saddle. He howled in pain as
he struggled to stay mounted, grabbing the reins one-handed, urging
the mare on. He heard one of Bruton's deputies whoop in triumph.

The next shot slammed into the mare's flank, driving her to her
knees.

He scrambled to get out of the stirrups before she pitched to her
side, dead, and he narrowly avoided being pinned beneath her. He
tugged desperately on her saddlebags but, one arm still useless, he
knew he'd never free the loot.

Grasping his arm to him, wishing he could will it to heal even faster,
he took off running. He dodged through the trees, scrambling
through the underbrush, all the time hearing the galloping horses and
the shouts of Bruton and his men coming closer as bullets found their
marks in the trees all around him. All the time waiting for a bullet with
his name on it to come crashing through the back of his skull.

He ran with all his strength. It certainly wasn't the first time he'd
been hunted like an animal, by an angry mob or a troop of soldiers,
many with much more unpleasant designs on his person than a public
lynching in Fraziers Well. But he couldn't let them take him back for
a trial. Not even the sham mockery of justice he could expect in a
backwater mining town dominated by Sheriff Willy Bruton. A trial
might expose Veronica's complicity in the scam, and he couldn't allow
Veronica to swing with him—she wouldn't come back.

Unless it was Veronica who tipped off Bruton. The revelation hit
him harder than a bullet and he nearly tripped over his own running

feet. Of course. Veronica. It had to be. What could he expect from a whore? Even one who'd sworn she loved him. She'd be one dead whore if he ever saw her again.

His anger lent power to his legs and he ran for all he was worth, lungs screaming, legs screaming, arm screaming, but it wasn't enough. His path was cut off by the horses of the Sheriff and one of his men. He pulled up and turned around, running in the opposite direction, but was met by more men and more horses. He was trapped, a lone fox ringed by a pack of snarling hounds. He stopped and turned back to the Sheriff, slowly raising his good arm in surrender, his wounded gun arm hanging bloody and useless at his side.

"You win, Bruton, you got me."

"I should just shoot you where you stand, Adams," the Sheriff hissed.

An excellent suggestion. "Go ahead," he goaded, "I dare you. Or maybe you're just too yellow-bellied?"

"Of some fancy-pants foreigner?" Bruton cocked his revolver and aimed. His target braced himself for the impact and the two men stared each other down. Then Bruton holstered his gun. "You got balls for a foreigner, but I won't deprive the people back home of the pleasure of seein' you swing." The Sheriff indicated to two of his men. "Tie him to a horse. Let's get him outta here. And you two"—pointing to two more deputies—"go back to his horse. Make sure the gold's all there."

As they rode off, the first two men dismounted. Their prisoner looked around as they approached him, assessing everyone's position, looking for any means of escape. Then, as they tried to grab him, his "useless" right hand suddenly slung the gun from his holster, shooting one man in the chest, the other in the gut.

He whirled before the other men had a chance to react, shot one in the shoulder, knocking him from his horse. He shot two more as they cocked their rifles, then turned and fired at the Sheriff, missing him but hitting his horse in the withers, throwing the Sheriff to the ground.

He tried firing again at the Sheriff, but the gun clicked uselessly,

empty. He quickly shoved it back into his holster. Seven men, six bullets—he'd never liked math. He tried grabbing a gun from one of the
two men at his feet, but one of the men still mounted got off a shot,
winging him in the left shoulder. He took off running again amid
more rifle fire.

Up ahead he could see where the forest ended and he made for it as
fast as he could. As he approached the end of the treeline, he looked
back over his shoulder again—Bruton, mounted on one of the dead
men's horses, and two of his deputies were gaining fast. He looked
ahead again and stopped dead in his tracks.

In front of him the forest floor dropped away into nothing and before
him stretched the largest canyon he had ever seen. He'd heard locals tell
of the great canyon, but he'd thought they were exaggerating—nothing
could be that vast. Another two steps and he would have been over the
side. He looked over the rim—it was a mighty long way down.

The hoofbeats behind him reminded him it was no time for sight-
seeing. His eyes desperately searched the rim for a path or another
way down into the canyon. They would have an advantage over him
down there, because he could sense it was a holy place and rules much
older than the Law of the West would prevent him from fighting here,
but he was counting on the fact that most white men wouldn't enter
the canyon at all, whether from fear of the Indian spirits or the actual
Indians who lived within it.

But there was no path. No way down. He could hear the lawmen
rein in their horses behind him.

There was one way down. He turned to them.

"Say goodbye, Sheriff," he bluffed and pulled his empty gun. One of
the deputies caught him square in the chest with a round from a Winchester rifle and the impact knocked him off the rim of the canyon.

Bruton and his men watched him fall, his body bouncing off a rocky
ledge far below to land, a broken heap, nearly a mile below.

"Shit," the Sheriff said, and motioned for his men to follow him
back to Fraziers Well, empty handed.

• • •

He was pain. A ball of pain. A throbbing mass of pain. Pain was his entire existence. Pain was his awareness. He could not see or hear or even feel, but he knew the pain. It was in him and through him and around him. He gasped for air and it seared down his throat like molten lava.

Hearing returned first. He could hear a great rushing, like a mighty ocean or a river. A river . . . a canyon . . . suddenly he remembered. He remembered the canyon, the lawmen, he remembered Immortality, he remembered so many, so many years. He was no longer pain. He was Methos.

But he was still in pain. He heard a sound like a silent footstep off to his right and he struggled to force his eyes open. He looked up into the sky pure and blue high above him and on either side of him walls of impossible colors jutted up to touch the sky. The feeling of vertigo was so intense he closed his eyes again. A twig snapped, like the passing of a small animal, and he turned his head toward it. Muscles and bones alike protested as he moved. There, behind a bush, he saw a boy not much more than 10. An Indian boy. He locked eyes with the boy for a moment until the boy ran off. He tried to call out to him, but speech had not yet returned.

He lay where he had fallen for a while without moving, feeling the healing, feeling the pain slowly start to recede. He knew he had to get up, to move away before the boy returned, but his spine and his legs could not bear his weight. Finally, still on the ground, he tested each appendage—head, arms, legs—to make sure they worked, then climbed to his knees. The effort exhausted him. He waited a minute and then, feeling stronger, was able to stand.

He looked down at himself, covered head to toe in blood, clothes twisted and torn, and made his way to the river. Removing his boots and duster, his vest, shirt and belt, he waded into the Colorado. The bone-chilling cold of the river recharged him and he fell to his knees, dunking under the water repeatedly to get the blood and the taste of death off of his body.

As he came up out of the river, wiping the water from his eyes, he realized the river bank was lined with Indians. The small boy, his eyes

wide, silently pointed him out to one of the men of the tribe. Then the
Indian man and boy entered the water and walked out to him. The
Indian spoke to him, but in a language he could not understand.

"Sorry," the white man said with a shrug. "¿Español? English?"

The Indian nodded. "I am Crow's Feather and this is my son, Little Crow."

"Pleased to meet you. I'm . . ." Who was he in this situation? He
certainly didn't want word getting around that Ben Adams was still
alive. ". . . lost. Can we go ashore? It's a little cold out here."

The Indian and his son escorted him to the river bank, where all the
other Indians, twenty or more, gathered around him. Some reached
out to touch his smooth chest, his unblemished shoulders. Crow's
Feather said a word and all the Indians stepped back, giving them
room.

"Little Crow says he saw you fall from the Eagle's Nest. Some of
the women saw it, too, from our village."

"I'm afraid that's true. Always been a little clumsy." He tried to read
the Indian, but couldn't.

"Little Crow also says he came to see where you had fallen and you
were like a snake trampled by horses. You were dead. And then he
watched you come back to life." The Indian looked at him, searchingly.

He just laughed it off. "You know how boys are, always exaggerating things."

"My son does not lie," Crow's Feather said solemnly. "And he is
more than old enough to know when someone is dead and someone is
alive."

The two men looked into each other's eyes, each surprised at the
honesty and wisdom they glimpsed there. Crow's Feather went on.

"There are stories handed down from our fathers of beings who live
far beyond the life granted ordinary men. Beings who can only be
killed among lightning and fire. Little Crow tells me you are such a
being. Are you?"

He did not know whether these people would consider him an
agent of good or a demon spirit to be cast out and destroyed, but he
felt he owed them no less than the truth. "Yes, I guess I am."

"Our ancestors say these beings are messengers of the Great Spirit who created these lands and should be treated with honor."

This particular "messenger of the Great Spirit" was sure his great relief could be seen by everyone present.

"Come, Eagle's Flight, we will give you food and warm clothes. We have much to learn from each other."

Postcards from Alexa

Postcards from Athens

by Gillian Horvath

Alexa sat on the little balcony overlooking the old square and tried to write her postcards. She was woefully behind on her correspondence, she knew. There'd been so much to see, so much to do, since she had left home with Adam. Was it only three months? It felt like a lifetime . . . and of course, it was, near enough.

She'd grown to know Adam well enough that his little moods no longer fased her. Usually when his eyes got that faraway look she could joke him out of it . . . or try kissing it away, that usually worked, even when it took a lot of kissing. Once or twice he'd gone so far into whatever place in his head his mystery was, there'd been nothing for it but to leave him alone for a day or two. He'd scared her the last time—he was so distant and distracted, she was sure he was trying to figure out a way to tell her he'd had enough, it was time for her to go home. They'd been in Cairo and he'd disappeared at midnight, sneaking out of the room while she pretended sleep, and she'd lain there for four long hours, huddled in her half of the bed, wondering if he would come back at all or if she would find herself in the morning abandoned in a foreign country on the other side of the world.

He'd come back, covered in sand and sweat, and he'd shed the long coat he always wore with angry haste, flinging it across the room as though he couldn't bear the sight or the feel of it, and then he'd slipped into the bed, trying not to disturb her, wrapping himself into a tight ball. Not wanting to push, she'd waited until she could bear the silence no longer, then had reached for him, found to her astonishment that he was trembling with exhaustion, almost shivering, like a child trying to sleep after a nightmare. She'd pulled him into her arms, trying to offer comfort, and he had reached for her with surprising passion, as though some bottled up need were spilling out, almost beyond his will. All but crushing her mouth with his, he'd tangled one of those big gentle hands none too gently in her hair, spreading the other in the small of her back and flipping her over with him on top, plunging into her with such suddenness and strength that she'd cried out into the kiss, and he'd taken her cry and echoed it back at her, a primal sound from the edge between pain and pleasure, their two bodies locked together in satisfying the need that had, for that moment, consumed him.

In the morning they'd left Egypt for Jerusalem. In the Holy City Adam had returned to himself, the beast that had possessed him for that one night banished back to wherever in his soul he stored the part of him he did not share with her. Alexa questioned nothing, let him have the time he needed, and after a week of respite he'd suggested that she might like to see Greece, and they had come to Athens and taken this little sunny room with the courtyard view, and nothing more had been said of that night in Cairo.

And now there was this. The call had come on Friday and Alexa had been surprised and pleased to hear Joe's voice on the other end of the line—but he'd been hasty, clearly troubled, as he'd asked to speak to Adam, and Alexa had watched the pall settle over Adam as he listened in silence. She recognized the look, the one that said "Don't ask," as he'd turned to her, almost not seeing her. He had to go to France for a few days, business. Joe would call her if there was anything she needed to know, he told her, his tone struggling for lightness. And then he'd stopped in the doorway, very serious, and told her to do whatever Joe said, *anything*. And then he'd been gone, leaving her in an agony of wondering what he'd meant. He wasn't a person who liked confrontations, he avoided arguments whenever possible. Was this his way of avoiding a messy scene—faking an urgent call, urgent business, and then having Joe call her in a few days with the bad news and the price of a ticket home?

Well, if it was, Alexa decided stoutly, she wasn't sorry she'd come. Whatever happened next, she'd had her grand adventure, she'd seen some of the things she'd dreamed of, before it was too late. She had Adam to thank for it, and she determined to forgive him *whatever* he was about to do, even as her heart closed up at the thought of him gone.

And if these were to be the last days of her world tour, damned if she was going to spend them in a hotel room when Athens and all its wonders were right outside her door.

It was an effort of will not to miss Adam every minute. He had been such a splendid tour guide in every city they'd visited, she was painfully conscious of his absence as she negotiated the unfamiliar city with the help of a four-color guidebook's superficial hints and histories. Returning to the hotel each night exhausted from the day's explorations, she tried to force herself not to hope to find Adam waiting there. More than once she thought she saw him at one of the tables at the cafe on the square, huddled in his big coat, watching for her return—and every time it had turned out to be some other young man, an English history student or a French tourist or an Italian local, looking away as she passed.

The guidebook recommended the collection of statuary at the Museum at Olympia, and Alexa, with her nonexistent command of Greek, braved the trip and joined the sparse crowds visiting the collection on an overcast weekday in February. The locals blended into the statuary, a collection of lifesize portrayals of Greek citizens of the second millennium B.C., standing stark and still beside their modern cousins, marble faces as expressive as those of the living. Alexa's eye was caught by two teenage girls gazing blissfully up at a male figure, an athlete, his head crowned with the laurels of victory, slightly bowed in modest acceptance. Alexa moved closer for a better look.

And looked up into Adam's face.

It took her so completely by surprise, the marble features so like his, that for a moment she thought she was imagining it, missing him so much that she saw him where he was not. But the aquiline nose, the expressive ears, the eyes with their distant, disengaged gaze, even the lopsided half-smile she loved so much, had all been captured in perfect likeness some three millennia before either of them was born. Well, almost perfect likeness, Alexa reflected wryly, her eyes straying below the marble waist, where the Greeks had tended to idolize a boy's attributes and Adam was . . . well, anything but a boy.

Adonis, indeed, she thought with a smile, stopping herself from reaching out a hand to touch the so-familiar face. She looked around for the label, found a yellowing typewritten sheet sealed under plexiglass on the wall nearby.

Not Adonis after all, it seemed, but an anonymous marathon runner, some ancient ancestor of Adam's, immortalized in stone. She pulled out her camera to snap a picture, thinking what a kick Adam would get out of this when he got back.

If he got back.

The thought came unbidden, like a kick in the stomach, and she stopped to examine it. Looking through her viewfinder at this ancient heroic image, she had suddenly seen her absent lover with new eyes. She knew by now there was more to him than met the eye. The strong body he tried to hide under baggy clothes. The rich knowledge of history he tried to disguise with an equally encyclopedic obsession with the trivia of modern pop culture. She knew he would deny that he was anything but an eternal graduate student with a hopelessly retentive memory . . . but she knew how much more than that he had been to her. He had rescued her, that was the only word for it—he had saved her. His tools might be different—a walkman and a battered VW in place of an olympic torch or a chariot—but looked at whole, he was as much a hero as his mysterious ancestor, as any Adonis or Prometheus in the place.

She now saw the suddenness and awkwardness of his departure in a new light. The set of the shoulders, the tension concealed by his wool greatcoat, the clipped emotionless tone, had hinted not at abandonment, but at reluctant farewell. He *wasn't* sure if he was coming back—not because he didn't want to, but because he might not be able to. Something needed doing, something he hadn't been sure he could do, something that scared him so much that he'd tried to prepare her for the possibility that she wouldn't see him again.

Alexa shuddered as a cloud passed over the sun, throwing both her and the marathon runner into winter shadow. Who was he trying to save this time, and from what?

In Adam's absence, Alexa had taken to eating in her room rather than endure the constant chore of dining out alone. Juggling her daily parcels of fabulous local bread and cheeses, new film for the camera, and the English-language newspaper, Alexa dug out her key and unlocked the door.

And stopped in the doorway as she heard his voice.

"Thanks for the lead, Joe, you were right about that sword. And about Rachel." He was standing by the window, looking out at the square, phone pressed to his ear. "And do me a favor . . . next time MacLeod's in trouble, remind me to take a sword *and* a gun."

She was barely listening to the words, beyond registering a passing astonishment at the name. Joe's friend Duncan MacLeod had never seemed like a man who would need help from anyone, much less from Adam. But it didn't matter, none of it mattered, save he was safe and whole. And *here*.

She must have made a sound, because he turned in the window and saw her standing in the doorway and smiled at her somewhat sheepishly, waggled the fingers of one hand in a weak wave.

She kicked the door shut behind her, dropped her coat and packages, moved to him, took the telephone from him. "Hi Joe, bye Joe," was all she said before putting the receiver on the cradle. She was peeling off Adam's big wool coat before he even finished lowering the hand that had held the phone. She went up on tiptoe to press her mouth to his, then moved downward, along the muscle that ran from jaw to sternum, tracing a finger ahead of her tongue, and continuing down past the collarbone, unbuttoning his shirt as she went.

"Hello . . ." he said, surprised but by no means displeased.

"Hello yourself," she breathed back, wrapping her arms around him and pulling his shirt free of the top of his brick-colored jeans, slipping her hands up under the loosened cotton to stroke the skin along his spine. She felt him come alive against her as she explored, his breath catching when her mouth reached the tiny hollow where ribcage met abdomen.

He struggled to keep his voice light. "So you missed me?"

She smiled into his chest, tickling it, and felt the half-laugh vibrate his diaphragm. She stopped her careful ministrations to look up at him seriously. "I thought about you a lot. I thought about what you've done for me."

"It's not like that, Alexa." Cupping her chin, tilting her head back, holding her gaze—*needing* her to understand. "You're not a charity project, believe me."

"All the same." She caught a hand in one of his front beltloops, pulled him gently forward, backing toward the bed. She turned with him in her arms, urging him back onto the bed until he was lying under her, his unbuttoned shirt awry, his hands clasped on her waist as she sat across him, her flowered skirt spread over his thighs and stomach, her legs under it clasped around his hips. "Now I want to do something for you."

It took all his willpower to put his hands over hers, stopping them as they slid down his stomach. "Not because you owe me anything, Alexa."

"No." She took a wrist in each hand and pulled his hands away, to the sides, holding them there as she leaned over him, her mouth tantalizingly close to his as she whispered, "Because I want to."

And as her tiny but deft hands slipped the top button of his jeans, he was in no position to object.

The orange light of the Greek winter sunset slanting through the window woke her and she rolled over, feeling the cotton sheets slide against her naked body, to see Adam sitting at the little table, gazing at her. His eyes were intense, thoughtful . . . full of love and something that looked suspiciously like regret.

"What? What's wrong?"

He glanced down for a moment, and she saw what he was looking at—her most recent roll of pictures, developed yesterday, and dropped in the doorway with everything else when she saw him, wanted him, took him.

"You went to the museum at Olympia."

"While you were gone. Yes." His distress was easy to read, but not the reason for it. "Did you want to go together? You hadn't mentioned it, so I thought—" She wrapped the sheet around her and got out of bed, moving toward the table, wanting to bridge this sudden distance. "We could go again. I don't mind."

"No," he answered quietly, "I wasn't planning to take you there." He turned one of the photos around, held it up so it was facing her. The marathon runner. In last night's excitement she'd forgotten all about it.

Her smile returned. "Oh, that. Isn't it funny? It looks just like—" And then she stopped, her smile fading again. Confronted with them both at once, Adam and the photo of the statue, she could see just how close the resemblance was, down to the little divot under his nose . . . and knew, suddenly, paling, that no ancestor could be that alike.

She would hate him for it. She had to. With so much love of life, and so little of it left, how could she not hate a man who had seen a hundred lifetimes and might see a hundred yet?

He had hoped to never face this day, had thought her limited time would mean he never had to explain why he didn't change, didn't age, didn't die. Looking at Alexa now, he realized what a huge mistake he had made, building their love on a lie, asking her to love Adam Pierson as though the man existed, as though he could have life, and happiness, apart from Methos.

He had never felt lonelier than at this moment, in this room, groping for the words to tell the woman he loved all the ways in which he had betrayed her.

There was a long moment of silence after he'd told her. Alexa stared at him, unspeaking, worrying her lower lip with her teeth, not even knowing she was doing it. He could only wait, in an agony of knowing what had to come next. The end. The reason he'd sworn to himself, a hundred times in the last thousand years, not to put himself in this situation.

It wasn't a question of her believing him. They'd come that far, at least—he wouldn't need to pull out a knife to prove his case. She knew the truth of it—that was clear in the tension in her shoulders, the knitting of her fingers that brought out bright white crescents along each knuckle.

It explained so much, Alexa realized. His wisdom, his caring, the way he looked at her sometimes like a fond parent marveling at an infant's tiny ears and toes. His automatic, unthinking understanding of some things—and his incredible naivete about others. He had seen life and death a hundred times over . . . but he had never lived what she was living, never faced death not as trial by combat but as the implacable result of a force so great there was no fighting it, no more than a drop of water could fight the current of the Colorado. What ironic God had plucked him from the stream, made of him a stone in time's river, weathered and shaped by its passing, but unmoved?

It was too much. After all she'd been through in the last year. The diagnosis, the denial, the acceptance that her life was ending, that she would never have the chance to do all the things she'd read about, dreamed about, since she was a little girl. And then Adam, with his promise that she *would*. In some ways that had been the hardest to take. The deadline she was living under had been easier to accept when every day was the same—work, doctor, home; work, doctor, home. Since she'd accepted Adam's offer, and *Adam*, her life had become a thing she could hardly bear to leave.

And now this. This unbelievable cruelty. She wanted to erase it from existence, pretend he had never spoken, go back to last night, when they had been equals, brought together in mutual comfort. Now he was a stranger in Adam's body.

Why had he told her? Why not hide the photo, hurry her out of Athens, lie, do whatever it took to keep this from her? There was no comfort in knowing that Immortality existed, but not for her—that the man she loved was but the tip of the iceberg of a hundred lives lived, a hundred women loved . . .

. . . and lost.

But there was no turning back the clock on this, any more than there had been the day the doctor had told her what he'd found. He was what he was. She could send him away, with his perfect, unin-jurable body and his wounded eyes, and go back to the life he'd lured her from. And try to forget this had ever happened.

Finally she spoke. "You didn't choose this, did you?"

He'd thought he'd heard everything, but he'd never expected to hear that, and his answer was immediate, torn from him without thought: "No. God, no." He tried again: "Alexa, if there was any way on earth for me to share this with you, you know I'd—"

She held up a hand. She didn't want to hear it. He didn't blame her—what good was a promise like that? He couldn't share what he was . . . at this moment, wouldn't wish it on his worst enemy.

"Don't say it. I know." She looked at him for a long moment, exam-ining every fold of his clothing, the bend of an arm, the tips of his ears. He could only sit and let her do it, sure she was replaying in her mind every word he'd said to her, everything he'd done, from the moment they met.

As indeed she was. Every word, every deed, every caress. Finally she made her judgment. "Adam . . . if you can forgive me for dying . . . I can forgive you for this."

He started to protest that that wasn't her fault, and stopped himself as he realized that she was a step ahead of him. They weren't to blame, either of them, for the hand they'd been dealt.

And then, incredibly, beyond hoping or believing, she was in his arms.

Postcards from Alexa

Night in Geneva

by Donna Lettow

Adam moved swiftly down the corridor, matching stride for stride the rapid beating of his heart. As he neared the nurses station he vaguely heard someone call out to him—"Monsieur Pierson? Wait!"— but he ignored them and hurried past, opening the door to Alexa's room. He couldn't stop until he'd seen her, until he knew—

The bed was empty.

Oh, God, he was too late. He sank back against the door post, unable to breathe.

He had tried to save her, had tried *so hard* to save her, and instead he'd lost what little time they'd had left. He'd promised her he'd be there, told her so many times he'd see her through it, and when it finally came, she was alone, abandoned in a foreign city.

Oh, God, what had he done?

"NOOOOOO!" he bellowed in a voice he hoped would crack Heaven as he slammed his head back against the doorframe.

"Monsieur Pierson?"

A nurse was beside him. He grabbed her shoulders forcefully, a dark, evil look in his eyes. "When?" he demanded, shaking her. "When?"

The nurse explained, terrified, "Non, they've taken her to intensive care." A faint light of hope came back into his eyes and he released his grasp on the nurse, his hands shaking. "She's been asking for you."

He ran down the corridor to the elevator with all his strength and pushed the call button repeatedly. There was still time. There was still hope. The elevator doors opened and an orderly stepped out. Adam grabbed him by the arm. "Intensive care? Where?"

"Sixth floor, Monsieur."

There was still time. He caught his breath as he watched her through the observation window, her sleep apparently peaceful and serene despite the banks of monitors and machines and wires and tubing and blinking lights monitoring her every function. Still time, but not much time. He had kept up with medicine enough to know that the news projected on the read-outs and the dials wasn't good. Her doctor only confirmed it.

"I'm terribly sorry, but we've done all we can. It's just a matter of time, now."

"How much?"

"A couple of hours. Maybe a day. No more."

It wasn't enough. It could never be enough. "Is she in any pain?"

"Some. She's refused narcotics. Said she wanted to be alert . . . in case you came back." The doctor's words cut him to the very core. Adam pushed past him and into Alexa's room.

She'd grown so thin, so fragile. He remembered carrying her across the threshold in Mary Crow's inn, how feather-light she felt even then. Now he'd be almost afraid to pick her up, afraid he'd lose her in a breeze. He remembered how, despite her size, she had haggled with the 200-pound gondolier in Venice and had him cowed. And what a little tigress she'd been in Athens, when he'd returned from Paris. He rubbed her cheek tenderly, a tear welling in his eye.

Moving aside some monitors, he crouched beside her bed, frustrated by the metal bed rails that kept him from her. He whispered close to her ear. "Alexa . . . sweetheart . . . I'm here. Can you hear me, baby?" He held his breath as slowly her eyes came open. She turned her head to focus on him and smiled.

"Adam."

"Miss me?" he asked brightly.

"Maybe. A little," she said with effort. After a moment, drawing more oxygen into her lungs through the tube in her nose, she continued. "It didn't work, did it?" It wasn't a recrimination, or an I told you so, merely a statement of resignation and fact.

He could feel his heart break as he had to tell her, "No." His voice caught, then broke, and the tears he could never let her see welled up, uncontrollable.

She tried to reach out to him, to console him, but found herself restrained by the IVs, the wires, the monitors. Her weak whimper of frustration turned Adam's heartbreak into fury.

"Damn them, damn these THINGS!" he lashed out and CRASH went the EKG monitor. As the EKG, suddenly disconnected from its sensors, wailed its flatline tone, he tore the bed rail from the side of the bed and dropped to his knees, burying his face in Alexa's tummy. He let loose a roar of animal rage as she stroked his head as best she could.

After a moment, the cardiac crash cart broke through the door, followed by the doctor and a team of nurses. The doctor sized up the situation. "Monsieur Pierson, get out immediately!" he commanded.

Adam stood slowly, with a seething, burning intensity Alexa had seen only once before, that awful, brutal night in Cairo.

"Adam, no," she begged, but he couldn't hear her.

"No, Doctor, *you* leave. And take this *thing*"—he pushed the crash cart back toward the door, scattering the nurses—"and *this*," kicking the fallen EKG monitor toward them. The incessant flatline silenced. "All of it. Out of here. Now."

"But—" the doctor started, but Adam cut him off.

"Useless. All of it." He pulled an IV bag from a stand and threw it on the floor. One of the nurses scurried after it. "You said it yourself. Useless. If you can't help her, I want it all away from her." He reached down and pulled the plug from the blood pressure monitor.

"You have no right!"

"I am her *husband*, damn you!"

"Not by the *law*, Monsieur," the doctor countered. They were at a standoff.

Alexa, though frightened, was never more proud of Adam than she was at that moment. They had never discussed their "marriage" since leaving the canyon, she'd assumed it forgotten. But he remembered. Even now, he was still willing to commit his soul to hers. She tried to speak, but the men shouted over her.

"THEN CALL THE POLICE!" Adam challenged the doctor.

Alexa pulled an IV from her arm. The scream of the IV monitor silenced everyone in their tracks.

"May I say something?" she asked quietly. They waited while she caught her breath again. She asked the doctor pointedly, "Is he right? Will any of this . . . keep me alive any longer? . . . Or just tell you when I'm dead?"

The doctor hemmed and hawed and finally admitted, "The oxygen, perhaps."

"Then everything but the oxygen . . . goes," she pronounced.

"But, Alexa, you cannot—" the doctor tried to reason with her.

"It's my life, it's my right. . . . No heroic measures. No resuscitation." Her arm finally freed from the IV and the blood pressure monitor, she reached out for Adam, who moved to her side protectively.

"You heard the lady, doctor." They both looked at him defiantly.

At the doctor's signal, the nurses removed Alexa's remaining IVs, disconnected the electrodes and monitors attached to her body, shut down the machinery and rolled it away. Only the oxygen remained, quietly hissing in the background.

"I hope you know what you're doing," the doctor said, following the equipment out.

Adam sat on the bed next to Alexa, still holding her hand. "Now, that's much nicer, isn't it." He stroked her forehead, wiping the hair from her eyes, and asked, "How are you feeling?"

"Like someone's pulling me inside . . . out with a pair of visegrips."

"Ah, about the same, then," he said with feigned brightness. She rolled her eyes at him and stuck her tongue out. "What's this they've got you dressed in?" he went on. "It doesn't even have a back. Who's your designer?"

"All the rage in the morgue."

"Well, it just won't do." He opened a closet and found her suitcase. "I've always found this much more attractive." He brought her the cream-colored negligee Mike and Lou had given her when she left Joe's all those months ago. She reached out and fingered the material.

"You'll . . . call Joe, won't you? . . . Let them know . . ."

He slipped off her utilitarian hospital gown, refusing to acknowledge her emaciated belly, her sensuous legs now gaunt and spindly, her once full and vibrant breasts shrunken and hollow. "Of course I will, baby." He calculated the logistics of putting the negligee on Alexa without dislodging the oxygen, and decided from the feet up was his best plan of attack. "I may need your help here."

" 'Fraid moral support's . . . about all I got left." But like a trouper, she allowed herself to be manipulated this way and that until the feat was accomplished.

"There, much more dignified," he admired his handiwork.

She smiled. "Death with dignity."

"Wouldn't have it any other way."

She coughed violently a couple of times. Adam started forward, concerned, but she waved him off. When her breath had caught up with her, she said, "I'm . . . exhausted."

Adam sat beside her again, stroking her forehead, then her cheek. "Do you want to sleep?"

"No!" she said vehemently, and coughed again. "I'm afraid . . ." She started again. "I'm afraid if I close my eyes again . . . they'll never open."

"And what would be so wrong with that?" he asked tenderly.

"I don't want to leave you," she whispered so low he could barely hear her. "I don't want to lose you."

He wished there was something he could say, some platitude, some bit of religious dogma to assure her that some day they'd be together again, that something wondrous waited for her on the other side, but the other side of what he didn't know, and he'd tried on and discarded

more religious beliefs than modern man knew existed. And he still had
no answers. All he knew to do was hold her and tell her he loved her
over and over again.

And he did.

After a while, as he noticed her skin become cooler and her breathing more labored, he reached for his duffel and pulled out the gold and
crystal necklace he had once given her. "Remember this?" he asked.

"Bed of roses," she answered, with a faint smile. He placed it around
her neck.

"You're still beautiful, Alexa."

"Prettier than Venus?"

"Still prettier than Venus."

"Guess you'd know." She tried to laugh at her own joke, but the
laugh became a cough, then a series of wracking coughs as she gasped
for more air. All he could do was watch, helplessly, until finally the
coughing subsided and she could get her breath.

He reached into his duffel and pulled out a jar of purest white
alabaster. He opened the lid and inhaled and, although the aroma was
pleasing to him, it sent an involuntary shiver down his spine. He tried
hard to close his mind to the memories the scent invoked in him,
memories better repressed. Dipping his fingers into the oils, he began
anointing Alexa's head and face.

"Frankincense?" she asked, then took a tentative, labored breath.
The scent was smoky, bitter, with a taste of cinnamon. "Not frankincense."

"No, Alexa," he said, blinking back a tear, "not frankincense." He
rubbed the oils into her throat and neck, then began with her fingers
and worked his way up each arm.

"Myrrh?" she asked. He nodded sadly.

"How did you know?"

"In Jerusalem. Shrine of the Holy . . ." She coughed once, but the
ointment seemed to free her breathing a little. ". . . Holy Sepulcher.
Mary Magdalene came to an . . . anoint Christ's body with myrrh . . .
and spices." She looked him in the eyes. "Myrrh is for the dead."

He looked back at her with eyes tearful but honest. "Yes, it is."

They held each other's gaze for what seemed forever before she nodded for him to continue and turned her head away, closing her eyes to stop the tears.

When he had finished his ritual, he sat beside her once more on the bed, watching her with sad eyes. Even with the warming effect of the ointment, her skin had grown even colder and she'd begun to drift in and out of awareness.

Suddenly she began to shiver uncontrollably. She called out to him, "Adam! Adam!"

He stroked her hair. "I'm here, baby, I'm here."

"I'm so cold.... Could we ... light a fire?" Without a second thought, he climbed into the bed with her, embracing and enveloping her with his body, willing the heat of his body into hers. In time, her tremors subsided and she seemed to rest more easily. Time passed as he lay there, caressing her face, stroking her hair, trying to give comfort to Alexa, and to himself, but he was unaware of the passage of time.

Somewhere in that timeless void, her eyes opened again, and she gazed at him with such love and longing he thought his heart would break. "Adam," she said. "I'm sorry ..."

"For what, baby?"

"... I'm so tired ..." Her voice was barely a whisper. "... have to sleep now."

"Then let it go, Alexa. It's time."

He kissed her, one last goodbye.

"Methos ..." He looked at her in surprise—she'd never called him that, could never bear to think of him as a creature who might live on forever—but he could barely see her through his tears. "Remember me," she commanded.

As she closed her eyes, he whispered, "For eternity, my love."

He needed no monitor, no warning light to tell him she was gone. Not long after she closed her eyes, he could tell that all he embraced was an empty shell. The soul he'd loved as Alexa was free, off to join the other stars in the endless sky. God, did he hope so.

It was two hours more before the nurses could persuade Adam Pierson to finally leave Alexa's side.

He Scores!

by Ken Gord

PRODUCER: Ken Gord

Taking over the Producer's reins of the series at the beginning of season 2, Ken Gord oversaw production on 97 out of 119 episodes of Highlander. Both in Vancouver and in Paris, Ken was responsible for hiring and supervising set designers, wardrobe and props personnel, location managers, stunt drivers, and actors.

Ken tells us about "He Scores": "When Gillian asked me to write a story, my first reaction was, are you crazy? In over one hundred episodes David A., David T., Gillian, and Donna covered every angle imaginable . . . and then some. What other story could there possibly be to tell? But then I got to thinking. We did flashbacks in Mongolia, India, China, Japan, France, England, Mexico, Germany. . . . But we never did a flashback in Canada. Now, I'm not a big nationalist but I am Canadian. The show's Canadian; the actors and crew and writers and directors were, for the most part, Canadian. So was this some kind of nefarious American plot to keep Duncan MacLeod south of the forty-ninth parallel? I decided it was. 'He Scores!' is my

homage to all the polite, loyal, Canadian Highlander *fans who never
saw Duncan MacLeod playing the ultimate Canuck. Happy reading,
eh?"*

⚡

FADE IN:

EXT. MAPLE LEAF GARDENS—NIGHT

February 21, 1974. Maple Leaf Gardens, Toronto,
Ontario, Canada. Famous throughout the world as
The Shrine of Hockey. The billboard shows the Buffalo Sabres in town against the Maple Leafs.
Though the game is just about to start, hundreds
of people still throng on the sub-zero sidewalks,
shouting, negotiating with knots of scalpers under
the who-cares gaze of Toronto's finest.

INT. MAPLE LEAF GARDENS—NIGHT

The Garden's been sold out for every game since
it was built in 1931 as home to the Toronto Maple
Leafs and tonight is no different as 16,182 wor-
shippers pack the old "cathedral" to the rafters.

The voice of hockey is Foster Hewitt, a voice more
recognizable to Canadians than Frank Sinatra's and
as the broadcast begins on this freezing winter's
night, 20 million Canadians from Nova Scotia to
the Arctic Circle settle into the warmth of their
armchairs and Foster's Sermon from the Mount.

                    FOSTER HEWITT
          (O.S.)

               Hello, hockey fans in Canada,
               the United States and
               Newfoundland. Welcome to Hockey
               Night in Canada.

INT. MAPLE LEAF GARDENS—ICE—NIGHT

The puck is dropped to the cheers of the crowd. The Maple Leaf center in his home whites wins the draw and stick handles around the gold and black Buffalo center, racing like a devil for the Sabre defence.

CLOSEUP

The Leaf centerman. Duncan MacLeod! As he barrels toward the Buffalo net . . .

ANGLE ON BUFFALO GOAL

MacLeod dekes out the Buffalo defenceman. There's nothing but clear ice between him and the Buffalo goalie. MacLeod winds up and without missing a stride takes a blistering slapshot at the Buffalo net.

                    FOSTER HEWITT
          (O.S.)
          He shoots! He scores!!

And as his teammates swarm him, MacLeod raises his fists in the air, overcome with the excitement of scoring.

The organ leads the fans in a cheer. Dum dum dum dum, duh dum . . . !!!

                    DAWSON
          (O.S.)
          Wait a minute. Wait just a gosh
          darn minute.

The organ dies like a flattened bagpipe as we abruptly:

CUT TO:

INT. JOE'S—DAY

MacLeod and Dawson sitting at a table. MacLeod's
innocent boy-scout eyes do nothing to convince Joe
Dawson that he's not being had.

                    DAWSON
          MacLeod, you expect me to
          believe that you scored a goal
          right off the opening faceoff?
          What kind of a dummy do you
          think I am?

                    MACLEOD
          All right, I didn't exactly
          score off the faceoff.

Off Dawson's look . . .

                    MACLEOD
             (cont.)
          And I didn't exactly play for
          the Toronto Maple Leafs.
             (brightening)
          But I *was* at the game.

                    DAWSON
          Since when are you a hockey fan?

                    MACLEOD
          I'm not. I was in Toronto for a
          symposium on antiquities at the
          Royal Ontario Museum. Got a call
          at my hotel from this guy, said
          he was concerned for my safety.
          His brother was some kind of

dangerous psychopath . . . with a
hit list. I was on it.

                    DAWSON
So you did what any normal
person would do upon hearing he
was on the wrong end of a
killer's bad mood. You took in a
game.

                    MACLEOD
Exactly. The guy sent me a
ticket.

                    TRANSITION TO:

INT. MAPLE LEAF GARDENS—1974—NIGHT

MacLeod is in the first row, directly behind the
penalty box.

Directly in front of him a fight is in progress,
two opposing players grabbing, pummeling each
other until the referees are able to break
it up.

                    MACLEOD
          (V.O.)
Said to wait there, he'd make
contact. I'm waiting, looking
around. Who is this guy? Someone
in the seats? The peanut vendor?
The usher?

The fighting Buffalo Sabre enters the penalty box
in front of MacLeod. And as MacLeod continues to
look around him . . .

> SABRE

I know what you are. You're an
Immortal.

MacLeod is stunned. The Sabre continues talking
but doesn't turn around.

> SABRE
> (cont.)

My brother graduated three
months ago from an institution
called the Watcher Academy. He's
a loony tune but he's smart.
Ranked first in his class out of
eighty-two. That's the good
news. The bad news is he's out
to get you.

> MACLEOD

Who is he?

> SABRE

Just listen. I can't tell you
any more right now. All I can
say is that my brother is a
dangerous man and he has vowed
to destroy you and your kind.
Meet me tomorrow at the Sheraton
Hotel in Buffalo.

As the penalty gate opens to allow the player back
on the ice he turns and looks at MacLeod. He's
tall, strong and good-looking, 44 years old. He
smiles at MacLeod.

> SABRE
> (cont.)

Watch your head.

And he charges back onto the ice as MacLeod stares, dumbfounded.

                              TRANSITION TO:

INT. JOE'S—DAY

                    MACLEOD
          Turns out he should've watched
          his.

Dawson looks at MacLeod with concern.

                    DAWSON
          What do you mean? What happened?

                    MACLEOD
          He gets in his car after
          the game. On the highway from
          Toronto to Buffalo there was
          a car crash. He died.

                    DAWSON
          Sonofabitch.

Joe is quiet as he takes this in. He looks up at MacLeod.

                    DAWSON
             (cont.)
          What was his name? This hockey
          player.

                    MACLEOD
          Horton. Tim Horton.

Dawson looks at MacLeod.

                    DAWSON
          Tim Horton? *The* Tim Horton?

                    MACLEOD
          The very same. The one and only
          brother of your brother-in-law,
          James Horton.

And off Dawson's reaction...

                                              CUT TO:

INT. MACLEOD'S LOFT—LATER

MacLeod has fired up his computer and punches some
keys as Dawson looks over his shoulder.

                    DAWSON
               (reading)
          "No finer person, teammate, or
          hockey player ever lived." "One
          of the finest gentlemen ever to
          wear the Leaf colours."

He's upset. He walks over to the bar and pours
himself a drink.

                    DAWSON
               (cont.)
          So James graduates from the
          Watcher Academy, tries to enlist
          the help of his brother, Tim.
          Gives him the whole routine, how
          Immortals have to be wiped off
          the face of the earth. Only Tim
          doesn't bite. In fact, he's a
          good guy. He decides to warn
          Immortals. So James kills him.

                    MACLEOD
          Not exactly. Remember how he
          used Xavier St. Cloud to do his

dirty work for him? That wasn't
the first time he used those
tactics.

                    DAWSON
Then who did it, dammit? Do you
know?

                    MACLEOD
Oh, I know alright. Took me
almost fourteen years to catch
up with the guy. It was 1988, in
Spokane, Washington. Not far
from here.

He pours himself a drink and joins Dawson on the
couch.

                    MACLEOD
         (cont.)
I was playing center for the
Spokane Chiefs of the Western
Hockey League . . .

                    DAWSON
Wait a minute. Wait just a gosh
darn minute. We've been through
this already. You've already
admitted you are not a hockey
player so what in blazes are you
trying to hand me?

                    MACLEOD
Well, actually, I was a hockey
player. But only for one game.
As it turns out, that one game
was all I needed.

He takes a sip of his drink.

                    MACLEOD
        (cont.)
    Joe, how much do you know about
    hockey?

                    DAWSON
    Not very much. Why?

                    MACLEOD
    Let me tell you. Hockey's a
    rough tough game. I would even
    go so far as to call it a
    violent game. There are all
    kinds of mean, dirty things
    players can do to each other--
    elbowing, checking from behind,
    clipping, cross-checking,
    charging, interfering, tripping,
    board-checking, slashing,
    butt-ending, spearing the other
    guy with your stick. . . . Most of
    these infractions will draw a
    two or five minute penalty. I
    mean, even if you drop your
    gloves and fight, you only get
    five minutes in the box. It's all
    considered part of the game.
    What's more serious is when you
    draw blood. Jabbing your stick
    in someone's face, knocking out
    a few teeth and drawing a bucket
    of blood will get you a one game
    suspension.

                         DAWSON
I know you're leading me
somewhere, but I'm not sure
where it is. Do you want to cut
to the punchline?

                         MACLEOD
I was given a *lifetime* game
misconduct. Actually . . . *two*
lifetimes. We fought with
sticks.

                         DAWSON
   (incredulous)
You had a swordfight with your
hockey sticks?

                         MACLEOD
A dandy. But that wasn't the
worst of it.

                         DAWSON
I'm all ears.

                         MACLEOD
I tripped. Don't forget this was
my one and only hockey game and
he was much more proficient on
ice. He started to undo his
skate.

                         DAWSON
He was taking off his skate?

                         MACLEOD
Yeah. But the thing is, I
managed to remove my skate first.

I must add that nobody in any
game had ever before seen a
player remove his skates during
a fight. The crowd went wild.
There was a Gary Glitter rock
song blasting from the speakers.
The entire arena was on its
feet, loving it, roaring for
blood.

Dawson stares at him, hanging off his every word.

                    MACLEOD
          (cont.)
          The guy tried to reason with me.
          He said since hockey was the
          religion of Canada, a hockey
          arena should be considered Holy
          Ground.

                    DAWSON
          And? You agreed with him?

MacLeod smiles sheepishly.

                    MACLEOD
          Not exactly. I got caught up in
          the moment. I pandered to the
          crowd.

                    DAWSON
          You did it? You actually did it?
          Right there?

MacLeod shrugs.

                    MACLEOD
          I gave the people what they
          wanted.

Joe Dawson stares incredulously.

MacLeod takes a sip. He smiles, nods to himself as he reminisces.

> MACLEOD
> (cont.)
> Those blades are sharp.

And as Dawson's jaw drops open . . .

FADE OUT.

WRITER'S NOTE: Tim Horton was born in Cochrane, Ontario, on January 12, 1930. He played nineteen seasons with the Toronto Maple Leafs, including four Stanley Cup winners. He was finishing his career with the Buffalo Sabres when he was killed in a car accident on February 21, 1974, on his way home to Buffalo after a game in Toronto. Horton had opened thirty-five coffee shops before his death. There are now some thirteen hundred of them in Canada and the United States. Brad MacLeod played one game for the Spokane Chiefs of the WHL in 1987–88. He did not score any goals.

The Staircase

by Valentine Pelka

"KRONOS": Valentine Pelka

Casting for the role of Kronos, the leader of the mythical Four Horse-men in Highlander's *historic "Revelation 6:8," was pivotal. Actor Valentine Pelka wasn't the most physically intimidating of the men who auditioned—in fact, in person he is almost unassuming!—but he had a way of becoming Kronos that was impressive, to say the least. Even on badly lit, badly shot audition videotapes, Valentine made the part his own. It's impossible now to imagine anyone else as Kronos. And, like many of the other recurring actors represented here, Valen-tine made more of the role than had originally been planned, return-ing for two additional episodes after his character had been killed.*

Though not set in the world of Highlander's *Immortals, Valen-tine's story offers another perspective on the universal human themes of life, death, and the battle for survival.*

⚡

Dedicated to my wife, Noriko, without whose encouragement and patience I would never have taken the top off the pen.

I

They had been anticipating this moment all day with a sort of impending dread. Dark, grey clouds hung around listlessly like celestial undertakers tired of waiting. The normally boisterous city traffic was sullen and hushed. People sat behind half-misted cafe windows and stared out, ruminating upon existence while others, seemingly anxious to avoid an end that might be nigh, scuttled bad-temperedly about clutching their inadequate umbrellas and silently loathed their fellow man. As the hidden sun finally sank below the horizon it was as if the city breathed a sigh of relief that the day had finally been put out of its misery. And somewhere a clock sounded four o'clock, perhaps out of respect for the deceased.

II

"So, Mr. Morris, how can I help you?"

The question took him by surprise. "I rather had the impression, doctor, that I was paying you to tell me that."

She smiled, indulgently. "First of all, Mr. Morris, I'm not a doctor. Secondly, this is a consultation to assess if I can help you . . . there is no charge." She was not French, that much he could tell, but the accent was quite definite, Polish perhaps or Czech? "I have already talked to your specialist but I would like to hear from you why you think Dr. Gueritoimeme has referred you."

"Passing the buck, perhaps?" He shifted in his seat . . . mildly irritated by the directness of her approach . . . she expected answers from him and he had only brought an overnight case packed so full of preconceptions and skepticism that little room was left for objectivity. "I have absolutely no idea . . . you'd have to ask him that." He could feel a surge of his old irascibility mounting in his chest. "Look, doctor . . . I'm sorry, Mrs. . . . ." He looked up at her impatiently, waving his hand generally in her direction. "Mrs. . . . ?"

She smiled, "Kolyatowski, Miss. I'm not married."

"All right, Miss Kolyatowski. Look, I'm sorry to be rude but this . . ." He searched the air for the correct phrase but without success. ". . . THIS! It's just not me. Do you understand? This whole alternative, aromatherapy, sniff your way to a healthy life thing! Hm? I mean, contemplating your navel while breathing deeply and thinking nice thoughts is no doubt fine for some people but I don't happen to be one of them. I have a tumour the size of a small grape-fruit and it is malignant. That's a fact! Can't alter that fact, caught it a little late, that's all. The bloody treatment isn't working and I've got six or seven months to live. Maybe a little more if I give up cigarettes! For God's sake, can you believe he said that to me? Can you believe it!" He was very agitated by now, breathing heavily, tripping over himself as he searched his thesaurus of invective. "I'm going to die. I am going to die! Why don't we just cut all the bollocks . . . pardon my French! . . . and just admit it? I don't believe in God, Father Christmas, or the innate goodness of Mankind. It's too late to become a Buddhist and I can't stand spinach. Is the picture becoming clearer . . . ?"

"Helena . . . my name is Helena. . . ." She walked over to her desk and reached down into a drawer. "Do you mind if I smoke?"

III

"There are two ways of looking at your predicament, Mr. Morris. Your interpretation is that you are dying and there is nothing anyone can do. Dr. Gueritoimeme sees things slightly differently and hence his suggestion that we meet. Basically he feels that all things being equal you have a fighting chance of responding well to your treatment. But all things are not equal, are they, Mr. Morris?" She looked at him very pointedly as she stubbed out her cigarette. "That wasn't a rhetorical question."

It was like a game of chess and he sensed she had spotted his weakness very early on. "What do you mean?"

Her next move was direct and decisive. "Dr. Gueritoimeme believes that the obstacle to your successful treatment lies not within the invasive nature of your tumour and his ability to treat it but rather inside your own head."

His contemptuous "Pah!" was a tad too theatrical to be truly convincing and he knew it. . . . "That is typical . . . just . . . I mean . . . I mean . . . oh, God!!" The vehicle of his indignation had just run out of gas and he was having to get out and push.

"How many psychiatrists does it take to change a lightbulb, Mr. Morris? . . . Do you understand my point? Your doctor can do very little to help you beat your cancer if you have not yet resolved the question of whether you really want to live or not. And yet, given all you have said, I can't help wondering why you are here." She let that hang in the air for a few moments and then, very softly, said, "I'm a hypnotherapist, Mr. Morris. I try to help people in your position to tap the enormous potential of the brain to find its own solutions when all artificial means appear to be failing. But you have to want to live . . . otherwise we'd both be wasting our time, wouldn't we?"

IV

He was in a wheelchair, and spinning the wheels as fast as his blistered hands would allow. He daren't look over his shoulder and what good would it do anyway? He knew it was behind him and gaining on him with every hour that passed. The landscape was tarmac as far as the eye could see, with here and there the rusting frame of a supermarket trolley. There was light but seemingly no source and he cast no shadow as he careered along. To call it a road would be misleading because nothing existed either side of it and "it" didn't appear to lead anywhere but he had an instinct that this was all. The road was all, leading everywhere and yet nowhere. Choose a direction and the road would accommodate you with its effortless tarmacadam glide. There were no trees, no weeds, no streetlights, no pedestrians, no lines on the road because there was no traffic and no need to distinguish one side from the other. There was nothing on the horizon in any direction to look forward to or to aim for. The smooth, dark grey mass undulated to a never-ending perspective fade-out. Stranger still was the lack of breeze. . . . The speedometer on his chair was needling ninety m.p.h. which seemed a trifle fast for an invalid carriage and yet he was more concerned about the lack of atmospheric resistance. There was no wind! In fact there appeared to be no climate at all. Where was he? It was no world he had ever encountered and yet it seemed to him to be familiar. The sky was there because it was above the land, such as it was, but it wasn't blue, or grey, or any colour . . . and yet there it hung above his head, a flat, colourless, empty space seemingly without dimension or content.

Suddenly he heard a sound behind him which started quietly at first but steadily built until he recognised it to be laughter, deep, mocking, goading laughter. It seemed to echo inside his skull and the noise level grew and grew until he thought he could stand it no longer. He covered his ears with his bloodied hands and shut his eyes tight as if he could negate the sound but it was impossible. The laughter in his head had built to such a level that he thought his skull would split and it was only the fact that his hands were clasping his head so tightly that prevented this from happening. Eventually he could stand it no longer and as he felt the warm trickle of blood trickling from his ears and down his neck he let out a desperate scream and . . .

∨

. . . he fell off the couch in a heap on the sitting room floor. He decided to stay still. "Better not make any rash decisions at this juncture," he thought. He had a fair idea what was awaiting him and, in truth, he was putting off the inevitable. In his experience, and recently his research in this area had been extensive, any position approximating to the horizontal was pretty safe. The side of his head reclined on the rather worn Afghan carpet, the left cheek puffed and squashed out like that of a lop-sided Botticelli cherub. He'd never liked the pattern and had made a fuss about it at the time but his ex-wife had bullied him into buying it. How she would enjoy his present predicament, his mouth half-full of medium pile Afghan shag, arse in the air, his nose being forced to sniff the accumulated dust of a failed and bitter marriage. "Should have thrown it out together with her bloody Barry Manilow albums," he thought.

His mouth was as dry as . . . "Try again." . . . his mouth was as dry as . . . no, it was no good . . . he knew all too well that metaphors and hangovers made very uncomfortable bedfellows. His tongue had performed its customary night time trick and appeared to have doubled in size and welded itself to the roof of his mouth. Talking articulately wasn't to be top of his "things to do today" list and neither, for that matter, was any strenuous form of physical activity due to the, by now, usual pains in his joints. On the other hand, he knew he couldn't stay like this all day. For one thing his neck was starting to hurt and for another his bladder was asking to be taken for a walk. After a great deal of thought he opened one rather bloodshot eye and as it swiveled in its socket his complaining retina registered the debris of the night before. The two empty wine bottles and the glass on its side with its red, crystallised residue and the chip in the rim, the ashtray overflowing with passports to international smoking pleasure, the small, portable black and white television in the corner showing Loony Tune Cartoons rendered even more insane by Gallic translation, the underpants hanging limply from the dormant radiator and the congealed remains of his "sad bastard" meal for one which had borne as much resemblance to coq au vin as . . . as . . . "oh, sod it!" he sighed . . . "oh, sod it!"

VI

Two hours later and he was lying on his bed, his face a contorted mask as he did battle with his pain. The pills he'd taken were just starting to do their numbing work but it would be difficult to move for a little while. At no other time in his life had he ever felt as alone as he did on these occasions.

He'd got into the habit of taking his mind off the discomfort by giving his brain the task of compiling lists. The subject could be arbitrary but the theme was always the surreality of human existence. "Ambition, vanity, possessions, sex . . . aaagh! Breathe, breathe! In, out, in, out, ohhhh! . . . you bastard!" He stopped doing anything but hurting until the spasm passed and after a few more deep breaths he was ready to continue.

"Tupperware parties, fashion, sock suspenders, heated toilet seats, machines for trimming nasal hair, garden gnomes, the colour beige, devices for attaching plantpots to drainpipes," which he knew were crap because he'd been daft enough to buy several. "Home electrolysis kits, kits in general, the patent do-it-yourself jacuzzi, the solar-powered cat-flap. Life, death, and the detritus of detail in between. We're born, we clutter the world with the worthless garbage we call a life and then we peg it." People who collected stamps, for example. Why? He'd read in the newspaper the other day about a couple in England whose hobby was, wait for it . . . collecting paper bags from all over the world. . . . What was that all about? And, then of course, we come to the totally incomprehensible pastime of . . . trainspotting! When he used to teach in London he'd see them at London Bridge station, huddled at the end of a platform with their 1973-style Youth-Hostel Association anoraks and their notebooks, cheap biros poised, waiting for the 9.53 from West Croydon and as it trundled in, late, of course, and filthy, they'd all jump up and down in their Rohan outdoor trousers and their Clarkes all-weather shoes and all because the third carriage from the front was being carried on the old 728 Bogey with its specially streamlined grommets! Grown men, for God's sake! Not children. Grey, boring introverts who hid behind their glasses and their beards and looked for any distraction at all from their sad and lonely lives.

Not unlike himself, he suddenly realised. Not unlike himself.

Here lies Charles Morris, Principal Lecturer in Philosophy at the University of the Sorbonne who died of loneliness and cynicism at the age of fifty three. The funeral was attended by the gravedigger!

Somewhere in the building a young man played the Spanish guitar . . . a reflective, melancholy piece. His eyes wandered about the untidy room . . . the half-full wardrobe still permeated by the ghost of Chanel, the little oil-lamp whose light had softly illuminated their kisses and the rest from fifteen years before, the now redundant dressing table with its dusty mirrors and empty drawers. As he lay on his side his eyes came to rest on the empty photo frame next to his bed . . . memory spoke gently to him of once happy days and here, alone with his thoughts, he wept.

VII

He had no idea how long he'd been asleep but dusk had descended outside, suffusing his room with a pale half-light. The tattered remnants of a late winter sunset streaked across the horizon and somewhere in the city a bell announced the half-hour. He closed his eyes for a few moments and dozed. A faint noise of traffic and the more present cooing of the pigeons, their claws scratching the lead covering of his bedroom window roof, created an atmosphere of peace . . . he felt rested, he was pain-free.

A faint tapping noise drew itself to his attention. Three taps and then a muffled voice. He lay there, not wanting to disturb this rare moment of peace. But then it came again, the same tapping, slightly more urgent, and the voice.

"Monsieur, monsieur Morris, vous êtes la?"

Slowly he got up and, rubbing his face to wake himself up, he opened the door.

"Monsieur Morris, excusez-moi, je vous ai derangé. Je reviendrai plus tard."

"That's o.k., madame Klarsehen, I was already awake. What can I do for you?"

"I've come to ask your advice, monsieur. I know you don't like to be disturbed, but I didn't know who else to ask. I don't really know the other tenants in the building very well."

He'd been living there for the last twenty years and can't have exchanged more than a dozen "bonjours" in all that time with this rather eccentric old lady but, as other tenants came and went over the years the fact that they were a familiar fixture on the landscape established a curious bond between them. They were neighbours.

"What seems to be the trouble, madame?"

"Well, monsieur, I wondered if you had lost a cat. You see, I found one about a week ago and it seemed to be lost. It's quite young and appeared to be well looked after but it was very hungry and I gave it some scraps of food whenever it appeared. I rang the authorities and I told them about it and they asked me if it had a collar. I said no and they said that that meant it was technically a stray and if it was still around in a few days' time they would come and dispose of it for me. I wish I'd waited now . . . I feel awful, it's such a beautiful little thing . . . it's not yours, is it, monsieur?"

The very idea! "No madame, I haven't got a cat and I'm never likely to."

"Well, you see, monsieur, I would love to look after it but I'm too old and I don't think I could afford it. But I feel guilty. I'm sure it's been abandoned. Perhaps the family has moved house and when they called it it was too far away, or got lost, and when it returned they'd gone. I feel awful, now. I'm a silly old woman, I should have kept quiet!"

He was getting slightly impatient, now. "I'm sorry, madame . . . I'm afraid I can't help you."

"Ah, well," she said, and she turned to go.

He looked at her twisted figure as she cautiously descended the narrow stairs, one swollen arthritic hand grasping the banister as tight as she could, the other lifting the hem of her dress so she could see the stairs. He started to close the door and then, for no apparent reason, he stopped, his eyes pressed closed, and just stood there. It was a defining moment. "Look at yourself in the hall mirror," the voice said. And then more urgently, "Look!" He opened his eyes and turned reluctantly towards his reflection. "Listen very carefully," the voice grew deep and had assumed a rather ominous quality. "Ignore these words at your peril . . . listen to me . . . ignore these words at your peril . . . if you don't move in this apartment, nothing does," and as he thought about these words they started to echo louder and louder inside his head. He broke out in a cold sweat and, almost without being able to stop himself he called out, "Madame Klarsehen! Madame Klarsehen!" He descended the stairs quickly for him and he caught up with her on the landing.

"Yes, monsieur?"

"I've been thinking. If nobody claims the cat in the next twenty-four hours, perhaps . . ."

The old lady's face suddenly became very animated and her hands shot up in the air as if someone had stuck a gun in her back, "But, monsieur, why not look at the little thing first, it's downstairs in the courtyard. I left it some scraps from my lunch . . . come." She started down the next flight of stairs and although he protested that maybe he should wait until tomorrow her hearing aid was obviously on selective mode and she was having none of it.

Reluctantly he followed her down the stairs and through the high, ornate, double doors and into the courtyard. The light, by now, had all but disappeared and it was difficult to make anything out. She blew extravagantly theatrical kisses into the darkness calling for the cat. "Here, little one, here. . . ." They strained their eyes into the corners of the courtyard and then suddenly they heard a cat's cry from behind them in the entranceway. They both turned. To begin with he couldn't see where the noise had come from and then he saw him, a thin, sleek, jet black form brushing its body against the edge of the staircase and limping slightly. The cat turned its gaze towards him and he was transfixed by the sheer beauty, the absolute liquid clarity of the eyes, large eyes, deep bottomless pools of black with irises of amber gold. For a moment he held his breath . . . and then the moment passed.

"What's wrong with its leg, madame?"

She shrugged in her eccentric way, hands in the air. "I don't know, monsieur. He seemed to start limping the day before yesterday. Poor little thing. Pretty, though, isn't he?"

He walked outside to buy himself some time to think. As he stood looking up at the now cloudless sky he was on the verge of making a decision. "Looks like there might be a full moon. It might freeze tonight," he thought. Suddenly he felt something brush against his leg and, looking down, he was met by the expectant gaze of the cat. Bending down he advanced his hand towards the cat's face and, after initially recoiling, the animal cautiously advanced and sniffed his fingers. He straightened up and walked back to where the old lady stood. Just before he entered the lobby, he felt the brush against his leg again and, once more, he saw the cat by his feet staring up at him. "Well, monsieur?"

He fidgeted a bit. "Well, madame, it would be a shame if he were put down just for not having a collar . . . so I . . . I suppose I'd better get him one."

VIII

"What seems to be the problem, monsieur?"

"I woke up this morning and found him like this by a radiator in a very dark corner of the sitting room. I was pretty worried so I thought I should bring him here as a precaution."

The vet nodded. "O.K. let's have a look at him."

After about ten minutes the vet turned to him and said, "Well, monsieur Morris, the news is not too good, I'm afraid. He's limping because he's broken a toe. Now we can strap that up and, in time, say three to four weeks, that will have healed as good as new. The problem is that as a result of the break he's developed an infection and he's got a temperature of 103 degrees which in a child would be high but in an animal of this size it's pretty much off the scale and is potentially fatal. Now, he's not your cat as such and you may not feel that you want to assume the costs of treatment which could be quite high, in which case . . . we would have no option but to put him to sleep. There are enough unwanted cats as it is on the streets of Paris and in cases like this our hands are tied by the authorities."

Something in him sank.

"The cost is of no concern to me . . . but does he stand a chance?"

The vet absentmindedly stroked the cat's neck. "Whether he survives or not is entirely down to him. If he really wants to live, then, together with treatment, I'd say he's got a fighting chance."

IX

It was late afternoon and he must have been asleep for a couple of hours. His first reaction was to look down at the cat. Its breathing was deep and laboured and he could feel its paws spasmodically twitching as the instinct for survival and the illness fought it out. It was touch and go. He knew it, the vet knew it, and, without being fanciful, he had the distinct impression that the cat knew it too. Any attempt to move him or distract him in any way was met by a low, deep-throated growl. All he wanted was to concentrate very hard and focus deep within himself and fight this thing. So here they both were, the cat wrapped in blankets on his knee and struggling for life. All of a sudden there was a gentle knock at the door followed by the familiar call of Mme. Klarsehen. "Monsieur Morris . . ."

Having carefully laid the suffering animal on the couch beside him he dashed to the door as quietly as he could and as he opened it he put his finger to his lips. "What is it?" he whispered.

She looked a little taken aback. "I'm sorry, monsieur, have I come at a bad time?"

He'd been rude and his conscience prompted him. "Not at all, Madame, come in, please, but we must keep our voices down."

She asked if she could see the cat and he ushered her into the sitting room. "Oh! The poor little thing!" she whispered.

He explained to her all the vet had said. "We shall know in the next twenty-four hours."

She sat next to the animal on the couch and gently stroked its head. "Monsieur, is there anything I can do to help?"

"Actually, madame, there is. Would you mind holding him while I give him his antibiotic tablet?"

"Of course, monsieur." She gently picked the cat up and carefully placed him in her lap. He reached for the old driving gloves he'd decided to use as a precaution against scratches and as he offered them to her her mouth twisted into a curious smile and she said, "I won't be needing those, thank you, monsieur."

"Well, if you're quite sure." He knelt in front of the old lady and reached for the pills, carefully reading the indications on the label. "One tablet to be given three times a day." He looked at her and smiled nervously, "I've never done this sort of thing before." He nervously took the cat's head in his left hand, a faint rumble of complaint vibrating deep in the animal's throat and his sides were heaving with the added effort.

"That's it, monsieur, now gently ease the jaw down with your fin-ger, that's it, and now drop the pill to the back of the throat." The cat swallowed. He looked up at her with a worried expression on his face. "Is that it?"

Her eyes sparkled, "Well done, monsieur. Yes, that's all there is to it," she whispered.

He looked amazed and relieved, and his hands had started to shake very slightly. He started to laugh quietly and then, all of a sudden, pain jolted through his abdomen and he fell to the floor groaning. Far from panicking, the old lady carefully placed the cat on one side and looked about her. She saw a bottle of tablets with a prescription label on the old sideboard and so she eased herself up from the couch and hurried into the kitchen to fetch a glass of water. Coming back, she took the pills and read the label. What she read seemed to confirm something.

"Monsieur, monsieur, are these what you need?" He was breathing very erratically, three or four deep lungfuls and then a stop as he groaned through the pain with clenched teeth followed by a further desperate need to breathe. He nodded vigorously in reply to her ques-tion and after some initial difficulty with the childproof top, she suc-ceeded in opening the bottle and shook out a tablet. The next thing he knew she was kneeling by his side and holding the water in front of him, the pill in the palm of her other hand. "Here, monsieur, take the medicine."

He put the pill in his mouth and as he reached for the glass, his hand shaking, she said, "Allow me," and very tenderly she placed one hand behind his head and with the other she raised the glass to his lips.

When he came to, his head was resting on a pillow from the bed-room and he was covered by the bedspread. All was dark in the room. He looked about him and as he began to stir the light by the couch clicked on and Madame Klarsehen sat looking at him. "How are you feeling, monsieur?"

He felt a little awkward, as if he had let slip something that was sup-posed to be a secret and now someone else knew. He got up slowly and started to fuss with the pillow and the blanket. "Have I been asleep long?"

She looked closely at him before replying, "Not long, monsieur. Perhaps for an hour. I thought it best to . . ."

"I . . . I . . . I think I'd better take over from you now. You must be tired. I mustn't keep you, I'm sure you must have things to do. Thank you so much. . . ." It was a heavy hint and he regretted its clumsiness immediately.

The old lady, however, didn't look at all offended. On the contrary she seemed to understand the situation perfectly . . . as if she was sensitive to a conversation where the meaning was to be found between the lines, somewhere in the ether of what was not said. "Of course, monsieur. It's you he needs. You must see him through the next few hours. You sit here, that's it, monsieur. Let me put the hot water bottles on your knee, that's it, and now the cat. Voila. Don't worry, I'll let myself out. Goodnight, monsieur."

The door closed and he listened as her hipshot steps echoed slowly down the creaking staircase. He felt he had handled the whole thing so badly. He couldn't have given the cat its medicine without her help, and while he'd been less than useless on the floor she'd held him on her lap and kept him warm. "Stupid man," he berated himself. "Stupid, careless, selfish man!"

The cat appeared to be sleeping quite deeply and hadn't stirred when he was transferred to his lap. He reached over carefully to his coffee table and poured himself a glass of wine and placed the plate of untouched sandwiches next to him. Having turned off the light he sat in the gloom and listened to the silence. The old house creaked now and again, and through the open window the city beyond could be heard playing out its twilight symphony, while here, in the concentrated seclusion of a dusty apartment, the man waited fearfully for the outcome of a struggle between life and death.

×

The first thing he became aware of was that he was shivering. Falling asleep on the couch had become something of a habit for him over the last couple of years, and, if he was honest with himself, and he wasn't very often, he suspected that deep down, he was afraid of going to bed alone. Afraid of the dark . . . how ridiculous at his age! Ever since childhood, scared of those waking moments as you lay in your bed, staring at the blackness that was the bedroom ceiling and waiting, waiting to fall asleep. It was the falling he feared . . . the conscious descent into the unknown.

Remembering the cat he lifted his head to look down . . . the blanket was open and the cat was gone! He was a little surprised but reassured at the same time. It must be a good sign if the cat felt like moving around. Calling him brought no response. He was probably hiding somewhere, cats did that, didn't they? He began looking in corners, under the bed, behind the couch but without success so he widened the search to include the top of the wardrobe but he wasn't there either. It was only a two-room flat so there were a limited number of places he could be and a faint sense of panic was starting to set in. He found himself opening kitchen cupboards, looking inside the washing machine, the spin dryer, and the laundry basket but the cat was nowhere to be found. He even went into the bathroom and lifted the toilet seat and then spent the next thirty seconds feeling very foolish. As he came back out of the bathroom and headed for the kitchen he suddenly stopped in his tracks and the blood drained from his face. "Oh, God! The window, you stupid arse, you left the bloody window open!" He dashed into the sitting room and yanking the window open further he thrust his head out, straining his neck muscles as he looked down, a drop of nearly seventy feet to the street below. Could he have fallen? He looked left to his neighbour's balcony but their windows were shuttered and the cat was not to be seen. Looking to his right he figured that the fire escape was a possibility but it would be a pretty risky jump. He looked down again to the busy pavement below but could see nothing. At that moment there was a knock at the door and he was so startled he nearly lost his balance. "Oh, bloody hell, who can that be?"

He yanked the door open and there was madame Klarsehen holding the cat.

"Well done, monsieur. He's better!"

XI

"Can you make me bark like a dog?" The worried expression on his face showed he was being absolutely serious.

She started to laugh again. "No, Mr. Morris. I can't make you hop around the room like a kangaroo either. You are entirely conscious throughout the whole process. If, at any stage you're not willing to proceed you can abandon the session yourself. I can't 'make' you do anything. I can, however, help you to achieve a desired result by tapping into the enormous power of your subconscious. And to do that you need to be in as relaxed a physical and mental state as possible. So I ask you to close your eyes and I talk you through some relaxation techniques. After that the initial session will last for about thirty minutes."

He looked doubtful and extremely nervous.

"If we are going to go ahead, now is as good a time as any . . . what do you say?" The first thing she'd noticed when he came into her consulting room was a change in attitude. A barrier seemed to have disappeared, apprehension had replaced out and out cynicism, which meant, she hoped, that he had decided to give it a try.

He took a deep breath and nodded.

"Excellent . . . first of all, as I am constructing these sessions to compliment and support your clinical treatment, when are you scheduled to commence your next period of chemotherapy?"

Reaching into his inside jacket pocket he pulled out a university diary. "I have my first session in three weeks' time . . . the 24th. January."

This was noted down and then she put away her spectacles and got up. "Right, Mr. Morris, let's have you up on the couch with your shoes off and please loosen your trouser belt."

At this last command he shot her a very disconcerted look but he complied. Going to the window she drew the curtains partially. She then walked across the dimly lit room and sat down in a chair a few feet away from the couch.

"Now, Mr. Morris, I'd like you to take a nice deep breath and close your eyes. Close your eyes and begin to relax."

What followed was like nothing he had ever experienced before. The controlled breathing and the gentle cadence of her voice with its downward inflections and carefully chosen repetition all conspired to encourage him to relax. His body had been like a piano wire, strung so tight it was ready to snap, and slowly, carefully, she was encouraging him to unwind. After twenty minutes his heart rate had dropped dramatically, his breathing had become shallow and almost inaudible, and his body appeared to have acquired a strange sense of detachment from his sentient self. He was aware of everything around him . . . her words, the far off hum of traffic, the beat of his heart and yet he felt separated from it all, beneath it, as if he had floated down and down and down and had come to rest on a sort of sea bed. He felt heavy and relaxed but free and light all at once. And here, below all the concerns and irritations of his active, tumour-invaded life, he lay calm and expectant.

He had no idea how long he had been lying in this state but her voice came as a mild surprise as if he had forgotten she was there.

"Now, I want you to imagine you are standing at the top of a beautiful staircase which has ten steps and, in a moment, I will ask you to descend this staircase. I will count from ten to one and with each number, with each step, you will descend deeper and deeper into total relaxation. Deeper and deeper. Deeper and deeper."

"Ten."

He started down, as if floating in slow motion, and felt his foot touch the next step.

"Nine . . . eight . . . seven . . ." and then it happened. It felt like he was in a lift and suddenly the brake had failed and the lift had lurched down as if about to plummet and he felt himself involuntarily pull back in panic. How she knew that this had happened he couldn't fathom, but sense it she had and she paused and got him to breathe deeply and steadily until he was ready to continue. It was for him to decide . . . to continue, to take the risk or to pull back. He felt that another defining moment had arrived and it was here that he came to realise how many of these moments he had squandered throughout his life. Here was a chance to change, to feel anew, to shed the bitterness of the past and to live in the here and now, to assume responsibility for his life and to live, to live, to live!

"Six . . . five . . . four . . ."

He saw his feet go slowly down, step by step and he felt his conscious mind drift down, down, down to somewhere darker, quieter, more significant. His eyes were open but there was nothing to see.

"In front of you you will see a door. This door will lead you to a very special place for you, a place where you feel happy and safe and secure. This place can be anywhere you choose. And now . . . step through the door."

He walked onto a beach he hadn't set foot on since he was ten years old. As clearly as if he was there for the first time he could smell the sand left wet by a receding tide . . . he could hear the far-off crash of the waves and the high-wind call of the gulls, he could smell the new-mown hay from the fields at the top of the rocky cliffs . . . he was there . . . Oh! The sea! The sea! His heart felt light, he could feel the sand between his toes and as he looked down at his shoeless feet he smiled and wondered where he had left his brogues.

"I would like you to walk towards the sea to a part of the beach where the sand is wet. Here I would like you to write in the sand, 'I forgive . . .' followed by the names of three people, of which your name must be the first."

It seemed to his waking mind a strange request but his deeper self encouraged him to continue and he felt the coolness of the sand as his index finger began to plough its exonerating furrow. The hand had started to write and without further premeditation he wrote, "I forgive myself, my father, and my wife." As he pulled back to look at the general effect he heard the words, "Watch the waves . . . see the wave come in and over the words you have written . . . watch the wave recede . . . your words are gone . . ." And so he stood for what could have been hours contemplating the sea with its high rollers, one after the other, pushing for the shore and wondering why he had picked the names he had. It had been entirely spontaneous. What did he have to forgive his father for? And his wife?! She had had the affairs, she had walked out on him finally . . . and yet despite his questions he was filled with a sense that something was very right about this moment, the here and now of it, the utter irrelevance of all that was other than this.

And then came her voice again, dropping like a pebble into the smooth water of a hidden pool, "Take a few moments to enjoy your special place, and then I want you to lie on the sand. In a few seconds I will count from one to ten and you will come slowly back to full consciousness. One . . . two, three . . ."

She had left the room to allow him to come round quietly. Very slowly he came to a sitting position on the couch and rubbed his head slowly. His watch told him he'd had his eyes closed for an hour and yet it had felt like ten minutes. Rather abstractedly he did up the clasp on the waistband of his trousers and then the belt and then, slowly, put on his shoes. The sight of his face in the mirror opposite stopped him for a few moments. He was smiling and he had no idea why. Shaking his head he put on his jacket and went out into the reception area. As he filled out his cheque she asked, "How do you feel?"

He tried to speak but all he managed to do was nod a few times and smile broadly. She smiled too. "It was a good start. . . . I know you hesitated to begin with but you went with it and I think you did very well. So, I'll need to see you again in a week. Same time?"

Again he found himself nodding and, smiling inanely by this time, he began to feel an acute urge to laugh. Suddenly he was in a hurry, his need had become urgent . . . he was not panicking but he must leave now or he might make a fool of himself. "Yes, yes, that's fine." He looked at his watch. "Oh, God, is that the time . . . sorry, must dash." With that he snatched his appointment card from the table and rushed out through the door.

She stood quite still for a few moments, and then went back into the consulting room and, after opening the window slightly, she sat down.

She was clearly waiting for something to happen and then she heard it. A man had run into the alley behind her building and had started to laugh uncontrollably.

XII

He was worried about the old lady downstairs. He feared she was losing her mind. She had come up for her now customary cup of coffee and to see the cat who had taken quite a shine to her. Over the last few weeks a strange sort of friendship had started to blossom between them. She didn't appear to need his company, rather he felt he needed hers. She had her life and her routine. Every morning she would go to mass at eight thirty and then on to the cemetery to talk with her husband. She didn't appear at all embarrassed or self-conscious as she recounted how he had said this or that to her. But now she was in the process of recounting to him a dream she had had the night before and which she daren't tell her husband for fear of shocking him.

"You see, monsieur, it was all a bit confused. It wasn't so much the fact that I was having an affair with the Fuhrer, although that was bad enough. But they were hanging Jews at the bottom of the garden and the kitchen sink was filthy!" His mouth just hung open as he tried to think of something to say. "It's the guilt, you see, monsieur. We Catholics carry it around and it just gets heavier the older you get. My husband was Jewish and my family were terribly shocked when we married. We had to run away. It was a scandal!" She was smiling and seemed to be enjoying herself.

He found himself noticing things about her he'd never noticed before. The old-fashioned wedding and engagement rings she wore, the swollen knuckles of her hands distorted by arthritis, the beautifully manicured nails. The Piaf-style coiffure without a hint of grey. The old, two-piece suit with the frayed cuffs but whose original quality was evident—Dior, perhaps, or one of the other houses his wife had frequented. His eyes drifted to her face as she spoke. The eyebrows had been carefully plucked and, with further help, described two graceful arches above her large, pale-green eyes. Vanity and habit still encouraged her to put rouge on her cheeks and her lipstick had been applied in a manner Bette Davis would have approved of.

"When the occupation began, they took us in and hid Bernard in the cellar. We came back to the house one night and he didn't see daylight again for five years! Can you imagine? It's the fact that we were of German extraction, I suppose, and Bernard's brother being dragged off to the camp in Poland and never coming back, my being Catholic and German, oh, I don't know . . . such a confused mess . . . so silly . . . and how could I even dream of kissing a man with such a ridiculous moustache!? But we were lucky . . . they came once to check papers or something but we were lucky. Half way through a search of the house the air-raid sirens went off and they left. They just never came back. My father used to play chess with Bernard . . . he always lost . . . but he really grew to love him. So silly, it's the same God . . . we all pray to the same God. . . ." She just sat there looking out into the distance and sipping her coffee, the cat on her lap, purring loudly. The mantle clock rang the half hour and she seemed to wake up with a start. "Oh! Is that the time? Excuse me, monsieur, I must be going, I'm arranging the flowers at church and I mustn't be late." She limped to the door and as she opened it she turned and looked at him for a few seconds but said nothing. Slowly she began to smile and, nodding her head as if she had resolved a question in her mind, she turned and shut the door behind her.

XIII

At first the only change he had become aware of was that he was smiling a lot. One morning, not long after his first session with the hypnotherapist formerly known as "psycho-quack," he had caught himself grinning in the mirror while shaving and, for several seconds, wondering who the other chap was. He was also, rather curiously, getting better at it. Shaving, that is. His usual performance resembled more a vain attempt to cut his head off by degrees with a safety razor than an essential procedure in the morning ritual of male grooming. After-shave used to be applied as disinfectant whereas now . . .

"You'd think, wouldn't you," he said to the chap shaving in the mirror, "that after doing something every morning without fail for the last thirty years or so you'd at least be good at it."

His change of demeanour had also caused quite a stir in the local shops and the one or two restaurants which were prepared to put up with his irascibility. Madame Klarsehen had had to fend off numerous enquiries from all quarters. Was he in love? Had he come into an inheritance? Had he finally gone mad? Was he safe?! Of course he was oblivious to all this.

Change was working quietly within him and at first he was merely aware of feeling happier about life in general. He hadn't found God, he had no desire to shave his head, wear orange or ask total strangers on the Champs-Elysees whether they loved him; he hadn't become a Buddhist and the contortions of the lotus position were, thankfully, still a mystery. He hadn't become a vegetarian, started jogging, or stopped smoking and he was prepared to resist the allure of yogic flying until they started offering air miles. But yesterday he had noticed a pot of daffodils in a florist's window and he had spent ten minutes just looking at them and thinking of England before he went in and made with the readies.

However the tumour was still there and growing. Over the past few weeks the aim had been to address his negative approach to life. But a few days ago she had addressed the question of his cancer. To help his clinical treatment he had to alter his perception of his problem. He had been a passive onlooker in a fight to the death between his body and his illness. If this remained the status quo he would be dead in a matter of months. On the other hand he could choose to become an active participant, regarding his body as the one precious thing he had which was worth defending and deciding to treat his illness as his enemy.

"Get aggressive with your cancer," she said to him one afternoon. "Don't put up with it, be outraged by it, get furious with it and then do something about it. Channel and focus that anger and, perhaps, and there are no guarantees, but perhaps, you have a chance. Treat it as a battle, plan your strategy, personalise your enemy if you wish,

stage the battle in your mind and work to defeat it. Don't underestimate the power of your mind. Use the power of your brain and your
imagination and give yourself a chance."

XIV

The staircase was different! It wasn't the beautifully carved Gothic
masterpiece he had conjured up in his imagination during all his sessions to date. This was dirty and narrow, set at a steeply raked angle
with rickety banisters, the steps themselves covered in a layer of dust.
He started to breathe deeply, trying to calm himself while he decided
what to do. He stepped very cautiously to the edge of the first step and
looked down into the gloom below. There were more than ten steps!
He couldn't tell how many as they disappeared into what looked like
an unlit cellar. What should he do? This was unexpected, nothing had
prepared him for the eventuality of more than ten steps, and this was
a staircase he hadn't meant to imagine. And yet his spirit was strangely
calm and determined today. "Don't be afraid of falling . . . you cannot
fall, I will not let you fall, have faith in me."

He was floating down, now, sinking gently with each descent then
pausing as his feet crossed and began the next. He eventually became
aware that he had stopped counting. The last number he remembered
consciously was fifteen and that seemed like a long, long time ago.
The gloom about him had started to increase quite appreciably as if
there was darkness and then this more extreme state of darkness visible. And then, quite naturally, he felt he had reached the bottom. It
took his eyes a few moments to accustom themselves to the obscurity
about him but when they did he thought he could just make out the
outline of a door. Behind and far above him he thought he could make
out a faint glow of light and then he heard the following words whispered gently but urgently inside his head. "Beyond this door is
unknown . . . all possibility, all disappointment, all misery and all happiness lie beyond. Carpe diem . . . carpe diem . . . have faith and
enter."

He hesitated initially, his hand hovering by the doorknob, shaking.

And then, in one positive movement he grasped it and pushed. It wouldn't open! Evidently it had dropped in the frame over the years and the bottom edge was stuck. He hadn't come all this way, however, to be thwarted almost at the first hurdle so he grasped the handle even tighter and gave the door an almighty shove with all his weight behind it. It burst open and he found himself looking once again at the wheel-chair and the tarmac landscape. All was as before except for the bit-ingly cold, dry wind which was sweeping dust in diaphanous waves away into the distance to blend with the horizon. He knew he had to move, but in which direction? Perhaps the wind was a clue . . . to go against would be pointless. The wind was so strong he'd be moving just to stand still. Better to let the wind assist you, go with the wind. Taking out his handkerchief he folded it diagonally across the square and tied it over his nose and mouth, knotting it behind his neck. He reached into his shirt pocket for his glasses and put them on and then, his preparations complete, he climbed into the chair and set off.

Hours seemed to have passed, although he sensed that any refer-ence to his watch would be useless. Earthly, corporeal measures seemed to have no relevance in this land with light but no shadows. His speedometer had recently edged towards two hundred and fifty miles an hour, but what thrill can you get out of speed without the sen-sations of wind in your hair and the landscape racing by? One thing occupied his conscious thoughts as his wheels spun, however. He had no impression of being chased as before, rather he felt that he was pro-ceeding headlong towards his nemesis, almost as if he had become the hunter, that he was on the offensive. He began to be filled with a curi-ously exciting sense of anticipation despite the unrelieved monotony of the geography. There was nothing now to catch the eye. Even the rusting super-market trolleys had ceased to litter the racing ground beneath him.

On and on he went, swept on by an unrelenting wind, up and down the gently undulating asphalt. He must have dozed off because the next time he opened his eyes the wheelchair was at a standstill and the wind had dropped ever so slightly. At first he couldn't quite believe his eyes. He took off his glasses and wiped the dust from the lenses with one of the tails of his shirt and having replaced them, he took a second look about him. The gently rolling hills of tarmac had been replaced by a landscape paved in huge slabs of very pale yellow stone. So perfectly uniform were the edges of these stones that you would have been hard pressed to fit a cigarette paper between them. So intently was he looking at the ground he almost missed it. But, there it was, moving languidly before his eyes on the ground. A shadow! A shadow! That meant light, didn't it? Light, goddamn it! He peered up and his eyes were greeted by an intensely blue sky, a brilliant sun and a small rain-laden cloud about fifty feet above him. The cloud and he were being blown in the same direction by the wind and as the cloud started to move away from him he felt a desperation to stay in touch with it, to keep up with it, as if his life depended on it. Mask back in place he set off again in pursuit of the cloud. And now he didn't feel so alone. Every so often he would look up at the cloud and smile as if reassured. He had heard of men in solitary confinement befriending insects but this cloud, constantly altering, seemed to have befriended him and was leading him who knew where?

For a little while now the wind had started to die down and he had had to propel the wheelchair with his hands. But just a moment ago the wind had died completely and as the cloud had stopped he did likewise. The sun shone but with the fresh warmth of an early spring day as he and the cumulo-nimbus waited . . . strange . . . he had the impression that the wind had died down for a reason. Something was about to happen, he could sense it. He scoured the horizon for signs of movement but all was as before. The sky remained empty except for his companion and apart from the hum of the wind and the beating of his heart in his ears there was no sound. And then . . . without warning he began to hear the isolated splats of heavy drops of water hitting stone. Slightly disorientated by the noise at first he finally looked up and there he saw the cloud, its dark grey belly pregnant with its watery load, unburdening itself upon the flagstones below. A curious sight to behold for the rain fell on a very confined area not more than thirty feet in diameter while all about remained arid. He was desperate to feel the water cool upon his dusty face and to open his mouth and to

feel its pure, fresh trickle run down his throat but something told him
that he was not there to participate but to bear witness to something
important . . . perhaps something with meaning for him alone. And so
he maintained his respectful distance and watched. The rain fell heavily drenching the slabs below and a miniature rainbow arced across the
space and shimmered there for several minutes. And then . . . it
stopped . . . as abruptly as it had started and the rainbow was no more.
The cloud above had not changed its position and the horizon was as
empty as before. Nothing moved except for the gentle mists of vapour
steaming from the sun-warmed stone. Seconds passed then minutes
and still he daren't move.

When it happened he nearly jumped out of his chair, so shocking
was the sound in such a profoundly silent world. It was a crack as loud
as that from a bullwhip and every bit as dramatic. He looked here and
there but all was deserted about him. And then his eye was drawn to
one of the stones. Wheeling his chair over to get a closer look he
noticed that the stone had suffered a jagged break running diagonally
from one corner to the other, both portions slightly raised along the
line of the break as if pushed up from below. His mind was racing now
as he tried to imagine what could have such force to break a slab of
stone over seven inches thick. And then, so slowly it was difficult to
swear that it moved, a snub-nosed, pale green tip appeared between
the broken slabs. Up, up it pushed, disclosing more of its bullet-
shaped tip before finally the darker green wrappings became evident.
These began to fill with sap and straighten out as the single stem with
its swollen tip continued its upward progress. After about twelve or
fourteen inches it appeared to halt and then the tip, encased in papery
onion brown began to flower. The cloud's gift surged through the
microscopic sap-laden capillaries as the magnificent yellow trumpet
burst forth its petals and searched with its face for the approval of the
sun.

Some hours must have passed because he awoke cold and shivering.
The daffodil had disappeared as had the cloud and all that remained of
the sun was an afterglow below the horizon. "No time to waste," came
his inner voice. "Remember this, learn the lesson . . . and now pass

on . . . we must return soon and there may be more to discover before the light is gone." And so his aching arms turned the wheels once more in absence of the wind and he continued along his way.

After perhaps an hour (although it was impossible to tell) the ground seemed to rise in front of him. It was such a slight inclination it was hard to be sure but the chair's wheels were demanding greater effort for less return and each time he looked at the horizon it seemed set at a steeper angle. After another fifteen minutes or so the gradient had become very hard work indeed but he had become filled with a determination to get to the summit of this hill before he had to return. His breathing became laboured now, the muscles in his arms and shoulders were screaming for relief and sweat dripped into his eyes and from the ends of his nose and chin. "Just a few more yards," he muttered to himself through gritted teeth. "Come on . . . just a few more yards!"

Without warning he reached a plateau but the effort of the last push had been accomplished with his eyes closed, his face set in a rictus grin of pain. He just sat there panting, concentrating on gulping in the cool dusk air and waiting for the pain to relax its grip. Finally he opened his eyes and the sight that greeted him sent his head spinning. Before him and below were the white stones of what appeared to be an amphitheatre, but unlike anything in size or concept he had ever seen before. Imagine a Coliseum set into the crater of an enormous volcano. A structure made of pure, almost unnaturally, white stone but perhaps twenty miles in circumference, composed of an immense series of elliptical steps at the inverted apex of which was an arena, perhaps a mile below. His mouth hung open and all he could do was blink at the sheer size of it. The wind had begun to pick up and somewhere behind him a lone bell tolled. Here, far far below, he sensed he was meant to stand and fight and strive for the right to live.

XV

Two days had elapsed since his last hypnotherapy session and he was still trying to figure out what it had all meant. It was as if the waking part of him had been hijacked by his subconscious and it had left him not a little rattled. Over the last few weeks he'd followed her advice to the letter. She'd encouraged him to develop the ability to create pictures in his mind and to "do exercises" with the images. He'd started by imagining a grey cube floating in space . . . and then rotating it through 360 degrees. Once he'd mastered this he progressed to writing things on pieces of paper and then watching them spontaneously combust. He could take himself for a walk down country lanes he hadn't visited since he was five years old or fly across the Alps without getting cold. As he got better at it he pictured himself standing on the beach and then moving around himself as if with a floating movie camera seeing his body from the back, the side, extreme close-up, profile, etc. He eventually came to see it as a game he enjoyed playing . . . well, it was better than television after all. He'd become quite the amateur film-maker with the luxury of his own "head cinema" to screen his efforts in. Shows twice daily with matinees on Sunday. Under her guidance he eventually was ready to develop what had turned out to be a highly effective strategy against his illness. After the twenty minutes of relaxation he'd drift down the staircase, walk through the door onto his beautiful beach and lie down. And having closed his eyes he'd focus on the tumour. He'd learned to vary the method of attack, too, first of all visualising it as a huge black balloon and seeing himself take a pin and puncture it and watch it slowly deflate. On other days he would characterise it as a shoal of black fish swimming and devouring all the plant life in the sea and then he would imagine an enormous white whale opening its huge jaws and eating them all up. He'd even managed to get away from monochrome. Dr. Gueritoimeme had shown him the colour scans so he could have some visual link with the enemy. The invasive growth showed as a red blotch attached to one of his lungs surrounded by a sea of blue. Taking this image he'd imagine a technicolour screen and he'd visualise the red area being invaded bit by bit by the blue until in the end it had disappeared entirely.

But now he was afraid. Afraid of the unknown he had encountered, as if there might be another, more frightening adversary to be fought and beaten. He'd rung Helena the day before.

"What do you think it all means? You know, all this wheelchair stuff. That was not my staircase, you know. My staircase has a beautiful Turkish runner with polished brass stair rods and, above all, it is clean. This one didn't have a carpet and didn't look as if it had been dusted in years. It was filthy. And the banisters didn't look that safe either. Oh, yes, and there were more than ten steps. . . . Perhaps I was hallucinating. That bloody chemotherapy can be quite debilitating, you know."

There was no response from the other end of the line. He thought he'd been cut off. "Hello, are you still there?"

"Yes, Mr. Morris, I'm still here, just give me a moment to think this through." About half a minute elapsed and then she came back. "Mr. Morris? Hello?"

"Yes. Well, what do you think?"

"I think you'd better come to my office. We need to talk this through properly. Are you free in an hour?"

Her usually calm demeanour was gone and she'd smoked three cigarettes, one after the other, by the time he'd told her exactly what had happened to him in his last solo session. After a few seconds of intense thought she reached for her cigarettes and lighter.

"You know, you really should try to cut down, they're not very good for you," he said.

She looked at him slightly non-plussed.

"That's a joke."

She smiled. "You've come a long way, since our first meeting." She sat looking at him for a few moments as if weighing up carefully what she was going to say. "Mr. Morris, what I practise is an inexact science. I don't mean this as a cop out although it could sound like one, but hypnosis is not something you can deconstruct into component parts to see how it works. My strong feeling is that to do that would have the same effect as to dissect a bee to find out how it flies. The net result is that you're left with a dead bee. The bee flies . . . your hypnosis appears to be working. I know it's a lot to ask, but try not to analyse it too much. Now, I grant you it's not usual, but I think that your subconscious is trying to tell you something, I won't be any more

specific than that. I told you to get aggressive with your cancer and it
seems that your subconscious is preparing you for some sort of . . .
confrontation. Perhaps your therapy has led you to confront things
from your past that you've avoided facing up to. My advice is not to
fear where it is leading you."

Two hours later he sat and reflected on these and other matters
while his food slowly went cold. He'd decided to eat somewhere different tonight, to break his routine. He'd walked for about an hour to
give himself an appetite and then happened upon this rather quiet and
exclusive looking restaurant near the Place de la Bastille. He had chosen a table by the window and had taken the chair facing out to the
street so that he could watch humanity pass by and be alone with his
thoughts. His mind was naturally preoccupied by thoughts of the
operation to remove the tumour which was a week away. He loathed
hospitals, the very smell, full of sick people, stiflingly overheated . . .
no wonder so many people fainted in them. And for three or four
hours he would be put to sleep and his life would be in someone else's
hands. The thought of being cut open made him grind his teeth and
shiver.

But a further ordeal lay before him. The amphitheatre awaited him.
He only had instinct to go on but he sensed that everything in that
barren, windswept world, the invalid carriage, the cloud, the rainbow,
the flower . . . they all meant something. Perhaps she was right. Maybe
each of them was a key to a door he had shut and locked years ago.
Issues lay unresolved and like restless spirits they had come back to
haunt him. He was scared, very frightened indeed and yet he knew he
had no choice. He noticed his hand holding his half-smoked cigarette.
It was shaking.

It was at this moment that he became aware of someone who had
just come into view and had put down the bags he was carrying as if to
rest for a while. Standing a few feet away from the window and rum-
maging in one of the bags he presented quite a sight to anyone who
took the time to look. It had started raining about an hour ago and this
man's clothes, if you could call them that, were soaked. He was about
forty years of age, quite tall, and thin. He wore a filthy brown tweed

overcoat belted at the waist with an old tie. His dark grey trousers were ripped and tattered at the ends and he only had one boot, the toe of which had come away from the sole and both were held together by a frayed piece of thick, dirty string. The other foot was wrapped in old newspapers and plastic carrier bags and held on with some worn electrical tape. His eyes were drawn to the man's face. A wild, sodden grey mass of wiry hair fell to his shoulders and blended with an equally long beard of the same colour. Very full eyebrows bristled ferociously above a pair of large, sharp blue eyes and this face was made even more impressive to the eye by a prominent nose and full lips. As he watched him rummage in his overcoat pockets and finally produce a huge red handkerchief with which he proceeded to rub his dripping beard he was surprised to note that the man's hand and nails were perfectly clean. Having put the handkerchief away, he undid the tie around his waist and re-folded the enormous coat before replacing it. He then took out a small mirror from another bag and raked his long fingers through his straggly hair as if he was an actor about to go on stage. Having returned the mirror to its bag he paused as if to prepare himself and then turned towards the window and looked straight at him. The eyes knew exactly where to look without searching out their object. The look appeared to be meant for him and he was struck by its momentary severity. He immediately thought, "Oh, God, he's going to come in, ask me for money!" He was just about to call the waiter for some assistance when the tramp suddenly stood up very straight, as if to attention and, with a huge smile he raised his right hand and made an extravagant "thumbs up" sign. It was an awkward moment as the tramp just looked at him, beaming and nodding vigorously. A little taken aback and somewhat ashamed he raised his wine glass to the man outside, which he immediately regretted, realising how condescending it might have looked to the other people in the restaurant. He was just about to reach into his pocket for some change when the tramp went through the whole procedure over again. He rubbed his head with the handkerchief, checked his clothes and hair in the mirror and, just as before, he turned to the window and raised his thumb to the sky, his face brought alive by that wonderful smile. And

then, without another look in the direction of the restaurant, he gathered up his tattered belongings and walked off into the night.

For several seconds he just sat there, as if paralysed, and then he
jumped to his feet and dashed out of the restaurant to the astonishment of the other diners. Turning the collar of his jacket up against the
rain he looked down the street but there was no sign of the tramp.
There was a turning left thirty yards ahead but when he got there all
that he saw was a little dog crossing the dimly lit road and urinating
against the wall of a house. The man appeared to have vanished into
the night and as he slowly retraced his steps he cursed himself for his
presumption and wondered how a man in such a situation could
appear to be so happy on a night like this. He looked so bedraggled
when he came back through the door that the waiter didn't recognise
him at first and nearly asked him to leave.

Coffee and brandy did little to soothe his thoughts and, after having paid the bill, he walked into the night, umbrella aloft, reflecting on
the bedraggled figure who had spontaneously offered him so much
without asking anything in return.

XVI

Dr. Gueritoimeme had paid a visit half an hour before the time of
the operation to have a chat and to reassure him and this had been
closely followed by the pre-med. Twenty minutes later he had been
wheeled in a fairly happy state to a lobby just outside the operating
theatre and it was here that he was then administered with the drug
that knocked him out.

The ceiling was high and afforded him a pretty good view. Fifteen
feet or so below him on the table lay the rather awkward and slightly
overweight piece of flesh he had grudgingly come to accept as his
body. It had been a private joke of many years' standing between him
and his creator that when Heaven had been handing out the equipment he'd been at the back of the queue. How vulnerable he looked,
he thought, without all the paraphernalia we humans use to distance
ourselves from ideas of our own mortality. No glasses to make us look

clever or to hide behind. No cigarette nonchalantly hanging from our lip to make us look moody or sophisticated. No expensive watch to assert our status. No beautifully tailored suit to hide the sagging buttocks or the expanding waistline. This was it . . . the truth laid bare in all its brutal detail. The body of a sick, middle aged man who had only ever been momentarily attractive to one woman in his life and who, after years of self-loathing, had realised he didn't want to die and who hoped it wasn't too late. And here he was, surrounded by machines that went ping and monitors that assured the world that where there was life there was hope.

For quite a while he stared at the scene below and very slowly he was coming round to the realisation that his next trip down the staircase could happen sooner than he expected if that was what he wanted. Below him a group of seven or eight figures in pale blue gowns moved about the table, their heads covered and their faces masked, reminding him of grave robbers who had decided to cut out the middle man. The atmosphere in the room was hushed and expectant as a tall figure, similarly dressed, backed through the double swing doors, adjusting the see-through rubber gloves and flexing his long, delicate fingers. "Alright, everyone, this has been scheduled for three and a half hours but this gentleman's tumour is in a particularly tricky position and I want to be absolutely sure I don't leave any so it might take a little longer." Turning to a nurse standing by the bank of monitors he said, "Yvette, first signs of distress let me know." She nodded and continued to adjust the angle of one of the screens.

"Robert?"

"Yes, monsieur?" The man addressed was standing at the head of the table by three long, tubular gas canisters with pressure gauges on the top.

"If you're happy I'd like to start."

"Quite happy, monsieur."

Dr. Gueritoimeme turned towards the unconscious figure on the table. An area of the chest lay naked and exposed through an opening in the green sheet that covered him.

"Scalpel."

His squeamishness got the better of him and without any apparent effort other than the thought he drifted through the wall to his left and found himself in another operating theatre. The scene was the same. The patient prone on a table beneath the halogen glare of the operating lights, the blood-spattered cover sheet, the various machines blipping out their life-affirming hospital morse. One thing was different, however. Everyone bar the sedated form on the table was laughing. They all looked towards the surgeon who was waving his scalpel around and trying to control his own laughter as he said, "And do you know why she'd never have one of these?" He gestured with his other hand somewhere in the patient's groin area as he looked at them over his half-moon glasses, eyebrows raised in expectation. "She'd never be able to find the shoes to go with the bag!" At this point he could control himself no longer. He leaned with one hand on the patient's leg and laughed uncontrollably for a few seconds together with the rest of the theatre crew.

"I don't think that's very funny."

He started at the sound of the voice. He'd presumed he was alone and he felt guilty, as if he'd been caught doing something naughty, like a child. The brilliance of the theatre lights made the high corners of the room near the ceiling gloomy by comparison but over the other side he could just make out the rather milky figure of a man about forty years of age. He was bald with a long, rather solemn face and slightly sad, watery eyes.

"I beg your pardon?"

"I don't think that sort of behaviour is very professional, do you? Been round any of the other wards yet? I wouldn't bother . . . they all seem to be doing adenoids or hemorrhoids tonight and knowing this lot here the chances of a mix-up must be high. What are you in for?"

"They're removing a tumour, just started actually. Didn't fancy seeing myself get cut open. Thought I'd have a look about."

"Serious, is it? What are your chances?"

"Fifty fifty," he said, nodding. "What are you in for?"

"Colostomy operation. Hence the joke at my expense. Still, I'll get my own back soon."

"What do you mean?"

The rather morose looking spirit seemed to be grinning most horribly in the gloom of his corner. Looking at the surgeon he said, "I'm his dentist. He's booked in for a filling in two weeks' time . . . we shall see, we shall see."

Some sense of urgency shivered through him and he decided he had better get back. "I'm afraid I must be going. Best of luck and all that."

The other chap didn't seem to have heard him. He'd moved down to a position just above and behind the surgeon's right shoulder and was chuckling to himself and nodding vigorously.

As he crossed back through the dividing wall he was relieved to see that all was as he had left it. The team were going about their tasks in an atmosphere of quiet concentration, Dr. Gueritoimeme talking rarely and then only in a calm and measured voice. The only other sound was the rhythmic whoosh, in and out, of the breathing equipment. A brief look at the monitors told him nothing except that they appeared to be working and he was left to presume that the unhurried air of calm was indicative that things were going as well as could be hoped.

He descended slowly and moved about the room. He hovered to the other side of the table opposite the doctor and looked closely at him. His gaze was drawn to his face. The forehead was creased and the muscles about the eyes flickered and twitched with the enormous effort of concentration required. Sweat beaded on his forehead and once in a while he'd take a rest and having closed his eyes and taken a deep breath he'd flex his shoulder muscles and then continue. The doctor was fighting, doing his best to save his life. It was now time he did the same. All that was required to accomplish the intention of the thought appeared to be to think it. He found himself once more inside his body and after taking a long and perhaps final look at the face of the doctor hard at work, he closed his eyes, took a deep breath and began his descent towards who knew what.

XVII

Before him stood an imposing pair of double doors that must have been fifteen feet high. A very dim light filtered through two large glass panels covered in a tracery of rusting wrought ironwork. There was no shadow of movement beyond, although the glass was so filthy it was difficult to be sure. He put his ear to the slight gap where the doors joined in the middle . . . no sound but a faint whistle as of a wind playing through the corridors of an empty house. A look over his shoulder yielded nothing. There was no dim haze of light above in the distance, just blackness all around. Turning back to the door he felt for a handle but there didn't appear to be one. Undeterred he took a deep breath and pushed hard on the doors. The hinges juddered from the pressure as years of rust crumbled and the pins started to move reluctantly in their sockets and the weighty doors swung slowly open. Before him was disclosed a bare corridor illuminated by an old, unshaded lightbulb swaying in the draught and he was momentarily disconcerted. . . . Where was his beach? Where was the tarmac landscape? Was this it . . . ?

He was a little confused and it wasn't until he caught himself watching his shadow sway crazily back and forth across the corridor that the thought occurred to him. "The lightbulb's moving. So where's the draught coming from? Somewhere else of course, you idiot!" He started down the corridor and after about forty feet or so he came up against another door. This one was plain and had no glass but the sound of the wind was quite strong the other side. Apart from a corroded iron doorknob there was also a keyhole and he bent down to be greeted by a blast of concentrated air that made hot salt water stream down his cheek. Through the tears he thought he could make out the dim out-lines of another corridor but also his nose was picking up the dank, musty smell of underground. Straightening up, he took a deep breath, grasped the doorknob in his hand, and pushed. The door swung open easily and he found himself in a subterranean passageway about fifteen feet across and seven feet high, the walls and ceiling of which were made of large blocks of roughly chiseled stone and which ran for about fifty feet before veering sharply to the left. He cautiously began to walk along the beaten earth floor which was hard and dry and looked for footprints or any sign at all that anyone else had been there before him but he found nothing. Turning back would achieve nothing so he decided to follow the tunnel to see where it led.

He'd been walking for quite a while and still the tunnel yielded no hint of where it might be leading. There was no variation in its construction and, as before, no sign of previous occupancy. Every so often the tunnel would turn sharply left or right as if leading somewhere specific but then it would continue on its way, the monotony of its walls unrelieved by a door or a corridor leading off somewhere else. He was just starting to get impatient when the passageway deviated sharply to the right and there before him were a set of stone steps leading up and through the ceiling. Shafts of cold blue-white light pierced the subterranean gloom from above and picked up the swirling motes of dust in the air. At last it looked as if he had reached his journey's end.

He went to the foot of the steps and looked up and held his breath as he beheld a dazzling silver-white moon framed against an indigo sky. After a few moments' reflection and with a heavy tread he started up the staircase, never taking his eyes off the far off stars intermittently pricking through the fabric of an inky universe.

He found himself in an arena at the very bottom of the amphitheatre he had visited a few days ago. Seen from above the scale of the place had been impressive but now, down here, it was, if anything more awe-inspiring. The tiered benches or steps glowed white under the watchful eye of the moon and seemed to stretch up and away into infinity. Here the air was still and cold and not a sound was to be heard except for the crunch of his footsteps in the sand as he walked about trying to take it all in. The stadium was completely empty and yet the place was filled with an intense atmosphere of anticipation. Something was about to happen. He could feel it. It was like a charge of electricity running through him and it was becoming unbearable. He had to do something, anything, to break the spell.

"Hello!"

His voice echoed around and around the arena and he waited for the echo to fade and die and then listened but all remained silent.

This time he shouted a little louder, "Hello! Is there anybody there?"

A cacophony of noise and jumbled up words came back to mock him and he looked about apprehensively . . . why had he been led here if nothing was to happen? What was the point . . . there had to be a point, he had felt it . . . that it had all meant something. Surely . . . and then he stopped in his tracks. All was now silence and he held his breath. The beating of his heart pounded in his ears and he stood there rooted to the spot just waiting. Nothing . . . nothing . . . and then, yes, there it was. From deep down inside the bowels of the arena came the sound of a deep-throated, mocking laugh.

"Who's there?"

Again the laughter, steady, goading, sardonic, confident.

This wasn't at all what he had expected. Trembling with apprehension he took a few steps forward and shielded his eyes from the moonlight with his hand. At regular intervals around the stone walls of the arena shadowy entrances from the tunnels below gaped like rotting cavities in an otherwise handsome smile.

"Come out and show yourself . . . that's what we're here for isn't it?"

An asylum of voices came at him from all directions, reverberating wave upon wave in lunatic repetition of his original words. The tide of sound eventually ebbed only to be replaced by the agonising silent wait and then the slow, assured and derisive laugh.

Suddenly he thought he could hear music . . . a distant melancholy orchestral strain followed by the profoundly sad tones of a soprano. He looked around to see where it might be coming from and there behind him, perhaps fifty yards away, he saw some sort of long box resting on a couple of trestles and what looked like an old wind-up gramophone with a brass amplifying horn placed on the box at one end. Flaming torches, one at each corner, illumined the scene with a rich and flickering glow. Although cracked and slightly tinny, the sound of the old record almost seemed to add to the poignancy of the moment as his eyes feasted on the seductive and solemn beauty of the scene. The passage of time itself seemed to have been frozen as the mesmeric combination of sight and sound slowly drew him forward.

"Requiem aeternam dona eis, Domine."

He could feel something pulling him forward, as powerful and yet unseen as the force that holds a moon and its planet in a suspension of mutual attraction.

". . . et lux perpetua luceat eis . . ."

Approaching the box it was as if he was in a dream and all movement, even that of the very flames, was slow and measured. The lid of the box appeared to be in two halves, the upper half resting against one of the trestles.

"Te decet hymnus, Deus in Sion . . ."

Finally his eyes cleared the top edge of the box-side and there, covered in a pale green, blood-soaked sheet, the face covered in a perspex breathing mask, he found himself looking into his own eyes.

". . . et tibi red-det-ur . . . vot-um . . . in . . . J . . . e . . . r . . . u . . ."

The gramophone had begun to wind down and the moment lost its hold on him and suddenly he saw the face looking back at him was laughing, the same deep-throated laugh he had heard before.

". . . s . . . a . . . l . . . e . . . m . . ."

The record had ground to a halt and as the silence reasserted itself he felt an anger he had never experienced before well up inside him. He turned in one decisive movement and grabbing the gramophone and raising it above his head he smashed it down on the coffin before him. But there was no crash or splintering of wood, no violent shiver as the bones in his arms absorbed the shock of one solid object hitting another. Opening his eyes he beheld an empty scene. The box, the trestles, the record player, even the torches, all had disappeared and no trace of their presence remained even in the sand of the arena floor.

He stood there for a few seconds feeling slightly foolish when he heard again the complacent, self-satisfied laugh coming from the tunnel but before he could react he was distracted by the sight of a little boy carrying a teddy bear who had emerged from the blackness of one of the shadowed entrances. He was about ten years old and seemed vaguely disorientated as he looked about him. Having come about twenty yards in from the edge of the perimeter he clutched the bear to his chest and started to cry.

"I want my daddy back! I . . . want . . . my . . . daddy back!"

He thought that perhaps the boy was lost and, genuinely moved by his distress, he walked towards him.

"What are you doing here," he asked. "Have you lost your father?"

The boy's face was eclipsed in shadow but his distress was all too apparent as he sobbed even louder. "Daddy! . . . Daddy! Why did you die, Daddy? Why did you leave me?"

He had started to shiver as he heard the words the boy had uttered. There was something familiar about him and it troubled him although he couldn't quite pin it down.

"What's your name, little boy?" His words sounded so ineffectual, so impotent in the face of the grief of the child. "Perhaps I can help you? Would you like me to help you?"

The boy didn't seem to have heard him as he continued to cry so he moved to within a few feet of him and gently tried again. "Tell me, little boy, what is the matter. Why are you crying? Come on now, look at me when I'm talking to you."

The little boy stopped crying immediately and stood there for a moment with his head hung low. And then slowly, he raised his head and as the man looked at the face he recoiled a pace or two in absolute horror. The face that looked back at him was that of his father as he had looked in the hospital just before he died. The face leered back at him and with a rather sneering tone the words came out, "Why did you leave me, Daddy? Was I bad? Did God make you die because I was bad?"

The shock of the words struck him down and as he knelt on the ground he began to cry. And then came the laugh again. Looking up, he saw that the boy had disappeared but in his place stood a very elegant lady in a mink coat, swaying slightly unsteadily and smoking a cigarette in a long black holder. In her other hand she held a cocktail glass and her full red lips were twisted in an amused smile.

"On your knees and begging for more . . . now that's the way I like my men! Come on, darling, where's your sense of fucking humour?" She pretended to look shocked. "Oh, pardon my French! . . ."

He was still on his knees, and as the sound of her laughter broke the silence of the night, he held his arms folded tight across his chest and, rocking ever so slightly, the tears streamed down his face.

"How's our little friend, eh? Our mutual friend, Mr. Dickens? Still finding it hard to stand up for long periods, is he? He should get out more, good for the circulation, or so I'm told." She threw her head back and laughed even louder. "Seriously, darling, where do you get your jollies nowadays?" Her eyes had a defocused look about them and she had started, ever so slightly, to slur her words. "Never been one of my problems, I must admit. Never had a problem in the 'man' department . . . except you, of course . . . you were 'in love,' weren't you, or so you once said? You wanted me to settle down and play happy families, didn't you? But I couldn't because my sodding plumbing was up the spout! The stop-cock was well and truly . . . stopped, wasn't it? I could not conceive. I was without fruit . . . barren . . . up the creek without a bloody paddle! . . . You're good with words, darling, why don't you have a go, please, be my guest. . . ."

High up in the "Gods" of the amphitheatre a tiny figure caught his eye. He couldn't see what or who it might be but progress down the steps was evidently made difficult by the things they were carrying in both hands.

"Are you listening to me . . . you self-important little shit . . . did you hear what I said? . . ."

He turned and looked at her. She was crying now, her mascara had started to run and her lipstick had smudged slightly and suddenly he was back in the apartment they had shared before the divorce and he had just come home and he'd found her drunk on the Afghan carpet and crying, just like now. The gynaecologist's test results lay opened on the table . . . and he'd said nothing. He'd left her there, angry that she'd drunk so much, impotent in the face of such pain, physically unable to do what was required. . . . "Unfortunate choice of phrase . . . try again, try again. . . ." That was the problem . . . she'd needed comfort and he couldn't give it. "Just an arm about her shoulder, for God's sake, a hug, a comforting word, what sort of husband were you?" Life is full of such defining moments, stitches in time, ships lost for a ha'porth of tar, a tender kiss and a loving word and perhaps they could have carried on. But no, he'd gone for a walk and waited for her to sober up and pull herself together!

"My God, what have I done? I . . . I . . . I am so very, very sorry." He looked up to say more but she had gone. He jumped up and looked frantically about him. "Margot! Margot! Come back . . . I'm sorry . . . please forgive me! . . ." His words dissonated in wave upon wave rising to a deafening crescendo and then slowly subsiding until all that remained was the fleeting shadow of a phrase, "Forgive me, forgive me. . . ."

"Now do you understand why you are here?"

The words came from behind him and made him jump. He turned to see who had spoken and was greeted by the sight of a thin, disheveled man wrapped in filthy, ragged clothes with wild hair and a long, matted beard carrying a variety of plastic carrier bags in each hand and descending the steps with some difficulty. He was about twenty yards away, but the curious thing was that the voice seemed to have come from inside his head. The man stopped a few steps from the bottom and put his bags down.

"Ah, dear, so many steps, so many steps. Better sit down and catch my breath for a moment." The tramp put his bags on the steps either side of him and as he sat down he pulled a huge red handkerchief out of one of his overcoat pockets and wiped the sweat from his face. "Heh, heh, nearly didn't make it you know. Such a busy day. Still . . . I'm here now, that's all that matters." After a few adjustments to his coat and having run his fingers through the matted strands of his hair he looked up at him and smiled.

"Remember me?"

"What are you doing here?"

Seemingly oblivious of having been addressed he carried on, "What do you think? Will I do?"

He stood there for a moment, confused by the rather dislocated nature of the conversation. "I beg your pardon?"

"I know the clothes are in a bit of a state and the whiskers could do with a trim, but books and covers, you know, books and covers."

"Did you hear what I said?"

The tramp was searching one of the carrier bags and didn't seem to be paying much attention. Eventually he seemed to find what he was looking for and pulled out a little black book. The corners of the cover had been worn down to the cardboard underneath and the spine was falling apart, the whole being held together by a thick elastic band which he took off. He was flicking through the pages rapidly, licking his thumb and forefinger every so often, when he seemed to remember something and looked up.

"Hm? I do beg your pardon, did you say something?"

"I asked you what you were doing here."

The hairy face looked back at him and leaning forward with an air of complicity he winked and said, "Everybody's got to be somewhere. Here seemed as good a place as any." He turned his attention back to the tattered book in his hands. "Now I know it's in here somewhere, but where exactly, that's the point. Don't want to open the wrong one by mistake . . . better double-check . . . let me see . . . aha! Blue bag, red and white stripes! That's it! You're my last one today." He started to rummage in one of the bags, talking to himself all the while. "Bit of a tricky one, old man, but we do like a challenge, don't we?"

"Excuse me. I . . . I . . ."

The tramp stopped his search and turned to look at him. "Well pipe up, don't be shy."

"I'm a little bit confused, you see. Or maybe you don't . . . oh, dear! It's so damnably difficult to explain. I mean, I sense I'm here for a reason but you've taken me a bit by surprise and so, as there's no one else to ask and er . . . and . . . I was wondering, do you have any idea why I'm here?"

"Ah! the eternal question . . . why are any of us here, laddie? Hm?" The piercing blue eyes were smiling mischievously and as he tapped an elegant finger against the side of his nose he looked from side to side as if to check that the coast was clear and said in a loud whisper, "Perhaps we're here to find out!" He let that hang in the air for a moment and then, turning back to the plastic bag he reached in and brought out something wrapped up in old newspaper.

"You wouldn't happen to have the time on you now, would you?"

He looked at his watch and found that the second hand had stopped moving. He shook his wrist and then put it up to his ear but again heard nothing.

"Heh, heh, heh. That wasn't a question, you know . . . merely an observation." He started to untie the string from around the parcel, deftly dealing with a couple of difficult knots with his long, well-kept nails and then started unwrapping the newspaper. He straightened the first sheet out on his knee and held it up to the moonlight.

The Daily Telegraph No. 28 043

LONDON THURSDAY. May 3 1945 and Morning Post

Printed in LONDON and MANCHESTER Price 1£/2d.

BERLIN FALLS: GARRISON LAYS DOWN ARMS

"Momentous day to be born, wouldn't you say?"

He just stood there watching him as he continued to unwrap each sheet of newspaper and once in a while read out a headline that caught his eye. "Ah yes, the Hungarians . . . put up quite a fight, I seem to remember. You'd have been eleven then, wouldn't you? Now, let me see, Cuba, Belgian Congo . . ." He seemed to have lost interest in the various articles themselves and now was merely checking the headlines as if he was going through some sort of inventory.

"I'm sorry, but what has all this . . ."

The tramp waved a hand vaguely in his direction as if he shouldn't be disturbed and carried on in a barely audible murmur, "Algiers, De Gaulle, first man in space! Heh, heh, that's what they think! . . . Kennedy assassination, Martin Luther King . . . te dum, te dum, te dum . . ." And so he went on, muttering to himself, sometimes pausing when a headline caught his eye, but constantly going back to the tattered black book to check a detail or to write something down with the little stub of pencil that he'd produced from yet another pocket in his coat. Every so often he would gather some of the smoothed out sheets into a rough pile at his feet and then having referred once more to the book he would continue to sort the remaining pages. This went on for a few minutes during which time his impatient companion paced up and down looking about nervously until finally he could stand it no longer.

"Forgive me, but you don't seem to appreciate the seriousness of my situation."

The tramp turned a fierce look upon him and said, "That is precisely where you are wrong! These things cannot be rushed . . . i's dotted, t's crossed, that's the only way. Don't want to lose you on a technicality, do we?"

"What on earth are you talking about . . . and . . . and while we're about it, who are you? Hm?"

He fidgeted slightly and looked rather awkward and then finally replied in a reluctant voice, "We're not supposed to say, the manual says it's on a need to know basis and . . . well . . . you're the wrong side of the line. According to the manual you don't need to know."

He could feel the blood rising in his face and his eyes were nearly popping out of his head with frustration as he tried to form the flood of words in his head into a coherent reply but in the end all he could manage was, "What? . . . I don't believe . . ."

The tramp suddenly stood up and pointed a long finger at him. "Be quiet! . . . We haven't got long and I'm sure you'll forgive me if I'm a little short with you but the social niceties have a time and a place and this is neither. Now . . . what is that?" He had taken away the final sheet of yellowed newspaper, letting it fall to the ground, and now, in his hand, he held out what appeared to be an unfeasibly large egg-timer in an ornate wooden frame. "Go on," he said, "have a look at it and see if you can tell me what it is."

"Well . . . it's an hour glass, of course."

"Come on . . . come on . . . you can do better than that . . . have a good look. . . ."

He turned the object around in his hands. It was beautifully crafted and looked very old indeed. It was one of the largest he had ever seen, being about twelve inches long and five inches wide.

"Hell's bells, laddie, for Pete's sake, we haven't got all night . . . what is unusual about it would you say? Hm? Hm?"

He held the glass up to the quicksilver light of the moon and turned it round and round and then the expression on his face changed to puzzlement as he gently shook the frame in front of his eyes. A look of surprise flashed across his face. He turned it upside down and shook it more vigorously.

"Well, anything to report?"

"The, er, the sand appears to have, er, solidified in the glass."

"That's better . . . and? And?"

He returned his attention to the object in his hands and upon further inspection he saw that on the underside of one of the wooden bases there was an old-fashioned label with some writing on it in faded black ink. Out of habit he felt for his reading glasses in his shirt pocket but then remembered they were resting on his bedside table back at the hospital, so he brought the label close up to his face and read the following words:

> Charles Morris Born May 3rd. 1945.
> Deceased . . . ?

The seed of a suspicion that all was not as it seemed had germinated and started to grow as he looked at his name . . . it was his name . . . what . . . ?

"What is his name doing there stuck to the underside of an old hourglass, he is wondering . . . hm?" The bright blue eyes were looking at him keenly, waiting for his reaction.

"I don't . . . I don't quite . . ."

"Of course you don't, that's what I'm here for. By the way, you are literally holding your life in your hands . . . so don't drop it, there's a good chap. That is your glass. We're all given one at birth with varying amounts of sand in them and when the sand runs out . . . well . . . need I say more? And you're looking at your sand now and you're perplexed because it's not moving . . . but, you see, it can't move until you leave . . . and you can't leave until you've found out why you're here, can you? Bit of a conundrum, what?"

All of a sudden everything began to get darker. A blustery wind had sprung up and a few isolated drops of rain had started to slap down in the sand of the arena as they both looked up to be greeted by the sight of storm clouds, heavy with moisture, cutting across the face of the waning moon.

"Quick, help me!"

He looked back to see the tramp scurrying around the arena chasing a few sheets of newspaper that had been blown away by the ever-strengthening wind.

"Come on! We mustn't lose any, that's very important. This is not a time to bugger up the paperwork!"

After a few minutes they had managed to gather them all and they were folded neatly and put away in one of the bags. A low rumble of thunder sounded menacingly close as the tramp turned to him and raised his voice above the noise of the wind.

"It's about to start . . . how do you feel?"

"What's about to start? What do you mean?"

"That's why you're here, isn't it! To fight? You're here to fight for your life, laddie!"

The arena was lit for a split second by a blinding flash of lightning and as he began to shout back his reply his words were drowned out by a massive crash of thunder overhead which shook the arena and resonated deep down in his chest. This heralded the onset of the rain which now fell heavily, driven wildly in all directions by the violent wind and as he anxiously looked about him the moon was eclipsed by a storm-blackened cloud and the world went dark.

"Where are you?" he screamed in panic. "Are you still there?"

He wondered if his voice had carried above the howling of the wind and when the reply came it was as if from far away.

"I'm still here . . . can you hear me? . . . beware, it's about to start . . . be on your guard! And remember, the Devil is in the detail! Good luck!"

At that moment the sky was rent by a jagged split of intense violet lightning and a couple of seconds later the amphitheatre was shaken again by a massive crash of thunder. It was at this moment that he felt a shiver of an uneasy feeling behind him run down his back. He turned but in the darkness could see nothing. The downpour had plastered his hair against his skull and was running down his face and into his eyes, obscuring his vision. He was shivering in his drenched clothes and it was all he could do to keep on his feet as the wind grew stronger and stronger and the clouds above him writhed like vaporous snakes in a boiling sea. He was afraid and he knew it but he was also aware that he had started to feel angry, as if someone or something was playing games with him and he was becoming irritated. And then a brilliant explosion of lightning fissured across the sky and its livid light blinded him momentarily. When he opened his eyes again the blood drained from his face and his heart missed several beats.

The moon had temporarily asserted its presence in the battle for the sky and its troubled light shone on a pale grey figure at least seven feet tall sitting astride a pale grey horse with a white mane which shook its head and pawed the earth impatiently. The figure was clad from head to foot in heavy armour and the shield it carried was plain black with a single, vicious-looking spike thrusting out from its centre. His eyes were drawn back to the knight's head. The helmet was plain black and resembled a steel mask that followed the contours of whatever face lay behind. He strained his eyes for any hint of what lay behind the glistening steel but all he saw was darkness. The horse's head and muzzle were protected by a steel plate which curled up slightly at the edges and a steel spike protruded between the eyes. A caparison of black edged with a pattern of skulls was blown by the wind about its legs and the whole combined to create the effect of a malevolent unicorn. Heavy plumes of condensation issued from the horse's nostrils and it fidgeted and twisted from side to side as if impatient to get on with the job in hand. The wind had, if anything, got stronger and yet he thought he could hear something, someone calling his name. He turned and saw the tramp standing about fifty yards away. Like a decrepit ancient prophet with the wind tugging at his bedraggled hair and beard he now held aloft and was shaking vigorously a large thick book in his left hand.

"Beware! Beware! The fourth seal . . . beware the fourth seal."

Lightning strobed its static flash several times followed by a deafening explosion which drowned out the tramp's words, but as the sound abated he heard the words repeated, "Beware the fourth seal, the Lamb broke open the fourth seal and I heard the fourth living creature say, 'Come!' I looked, and there was a pale-coloured horse. Its rider was named 'Death,' and Hades followed close behind."

The horse and rider had started to move forward and after twenty yards or so they stopped. The knight extended his gloved hand in the man's general direction and beckoned him to step forward. He stood there terrified, shivering more from abject fear than the energy-sapping cold of the rain but underneath, deep down he could feel an eruption of anger in his chest. It was at the core of him and far away but it was unmistakable. Again the knight beckoned and turned his horse as if he expected him to follow as a matter of course. But he stood his ground and waited, outraged almost by the presumption that he would follow meekly without question. The horse and rider paused and then wheeled round. The rider made an impatient gesture with his arm this time and he spoke for the first time. "Come!" This was all he said, one little word and yet the tone of the voice resonated with venomous intent.

He felt as if he was in the eye of the storm as the rain and the wind lashed his body but he was standing firm and his heart was pumping strongly as a burst of anger adrenalised him into action. "No! No, I won't come just like that! I bloody won't, do you hear me? I'm sup-posed to be here to fight, so fight, damn you!"

The horse and rider stood without moving and he trembled at his own temerity as he wondered what would come next.

"That's the stuff, laddie! Books and covers, books and covers. Remember the daffodil, remember! Break stone, move mountains, believe, believe!"

A roar came from the other side of him and he saw the knight draw a huge sword with inverted spikes quilloned a third of the way down its blade and the horse reared and as its hooves pawed the air its eyes and nostrils shone with a sickly, bloodshot glow. "My patience is at an end! Come! Now!"

At last, this was what everything had been leading up to, the final defining moment, the cusp upon which all possibility turned. He looked to the tramp for guidance but all he heard were the words, "It's up to you now, laddie! It's up to you!"

For a moment he stood there, anger and frustration and adrenaline coursing through every cell of his body, looking for an outlet, a release, and then it came to him. He was still holding the hourglass tightly and he looked at it again closely in the moon's intermittent light. He held his breath. "That's it!" he whispered. "That's the point, that's why I'm here!" His face burned as the realisation dawned on him and he felt his outrage about to burst forth. "You bastard! You cheat! I'm not going anywhere without a fight! Look! Look at this and tell me my time has come!"

The knight spurred his horse forward and his words filled the stadium with deep, malicious intent. "Your time is now because I say it is now. It is written and so it must be!" He dug his spurs into the horse's flank and with sword aloft and a terrible cry they charged. He clenched his fists and trembled as the bile rose in his throat. A wave of emotion was erupting within him and as he looked at the hand that had held the hour-glass he saw it was now grasping a flaming sword. The knight was about seventy yards away and covering the ground quickly. His breath came short and fast and a spasm of wrath convulsed his body. He started to run towards the knight, and from his very entrails there came a defiant cry, as if all his pain and frustration and ire had built up behind a huge dam wall which had now begun to crumble and the flood had been unleashed. The two protagonists were twenty yards apart and as he saw the knight bearing his considerable bulk down upon him he heard him laugh the deep mocking laugh he had heard before and it infuriated him. He gripped the hilt of his fiery sword and raised it above his head and as he made to cut at the knight who was almost upon him he closed his eyes against the expected impact.

The next thing he knew he was lying face down on the arena floor and the hourglass was lying next to him. He lay there for a few seconds listening for the sound of hoof beats but all was silent. The rain had stopped and the wind had died and the quick-silver light that bathed the sand about him was testimony that the moon had won its celestial battle and the stars had prevailed. He lifted his head and looked about him but there was no sign of the knight. He was not alone, however. The tramp seemed to have fallen asleep under a counterpane of newspaper and on the other side of the arena, about a hundred yards away, a figure sat at a table illuminated by a small desk lamp.

He got up and walked over and as he approached he saw a little man dressed like a Victorian clerk in black frock coat, high, celluloid collar and black tie. He was bald and a few fugitive strands of grey hair had been carefully plastered across the papery skin that was stretched tightly across his skull. The man was writing with a quill pen in a huge ledger and was muttering to himself. "Oh dear, this will never do! No, no, no! It will all have to be re-written now!"

The little man didn't seem to have noticed him so he coughed. The man didn't look up but waved a hand generally in his direction and said rather curtly, "Wait there. I shall see you in a moment." His patience, however, had run out long ago. He walked up to the desk, snatched the pen from his hand and placed it rather deliberately on the inkstand in front of him.

"You will see me now."

"Really!" The little man looked appalled and the pince-nez fell from the bridge of his nose and clattered on the table as he raised his eyebrows in surprise. "Really, this is quite irregular, you know. What do you want? I am very busy, and mustn't fall behind."

Before the little man could do anything he had snatched the ledger from the table. The pages were vertically divided into three columns each one of which was topped by a heading. The first was "Full Term"; the second was entitled, "Needs Encouragement"; and the third column, in which he found his own name neatly written in an old-fashioned hand, fell under the label N.W.T.L.—(In quiet periods file early).

"I must insist that you return that this instant . . . you people are not supposed to . . . I mean . . ." He'd obviously begun to say something he shouldn't and he was trying not to show it. "Just give that back, there's a good chap, and we'll say no more about it."

"What does this mean"—he said, pointing to the ledger—"In quiet periods file early. What does that mean and why is my name there?"

The little man had begun to look decidedly shifty and tried to avoid his gaze by tidying his desk. "You wouldn't understand. These are technical terms . . . it's just a stocktaking record, that's all."

"I asked you why my name is there. Come on . . ." He turned the book over and saw that the spine had some words printed in gold letters. "Inventory of Cancellations—1998." Turning back to the clerk he tried very hard to keep his temper under check as he said, "What does this refer to then? Hm? What sort of stock do you deal in?" The little man was hesitating. "Did you hear what I said, bloody well answer the question or . . . or . . . or I'll rip this book up! And don't think I wouldn't!"

The clerk jumped to his feet and having pulled a large, rather grubby handkerchief from his coat pocket he started to wipe the palms of his hands. "Very well! Very well, please, just put the book down and I'll tell you. Please!"

"You tell me and I'll put the book down. I like that arrangement better."

The little man appeared quite frightened and looked nervously from side to side and then behind him before he said very quietly, "It records all deaths for the year 1998. There's a book for each year and everyone who dies anywhere in the world is recorded in it."

"In that case," he fumed, "what is my name doing there? And what do those letters mean?"

The clerk rubbed the beads of sweat from his forehead and wiped his palms again. "Oh dear! Oh dear, dear me! Well, you see, they stand for 'No Will To Live' and when we're in a bit of a slack period we're encouraged to make good use of the spare time. So those people who are, shall we say, 'borderline' are . . . well . . ." He evidently didn't want to say any more and just stood there blinking.

"Are what? Don't just stand there shaking, I want answers and I'm not leaving without them!"

"Well, you see . . . oh dear! This is all very unfortunate. . . . Those who are borderline are . . . canceled. There . . . you have it! And I'm afraid you won't be leaving, oh no, no, no, that wouldn't do at all . . . your name, it's in the book."

He was staring at the little man very intently and breathing heavily as his mind raced. This couldn't be right . . . he'd fought for his right to live, he'd shown a will to live, he thirsted for the right to continue his life. There seemed to be no way out until he remembered what the tramp had said. "Aha!" he exclaimed as it began to dawn upon him, "Aha! I've got it!"

The little man started to look quite concerned and was looking for an escape route just in case he might need it.

"Where is the Devil, little man? Come on, everyone likes a little riddle now and again! Where is the Devil? Hm?"

"I'm sorry, I'm not very good at . . ."

Triumphantly he brought his fist down on the face of the book and whispered, "It's in the detail! Ha! Get it? It's in the detail!" With a great flourish he opened the book and furiously flipped page after page as the clerk looked as if he was about to be very ill indeed. "Take a look . . . go on, take a look. Ah, ah, ah! No touching. That's near enough. See? All the other names are in ink. Mine is in pencil! Why is that? Hm? This arrangement doesn't seem to be entirely above board, if you ask me. If some people are sick of life that's up to them. But I've changed my mind! I want to live. I like life! Do you hear me? So let's see how we can rectify this clerical error, shall we?"

"Ah! there we are." He'd picked up a rubber from the desk and he started to erase his name from the record.

The little man's eyes nearly popped out of his head and he began to splutter, "You can't do that . . . you have no authority! I . . . I . . . I . . ."

"And before you think of putting me through all this palaver again take a good look at this." He held up the hourglass and thrust it in front of the clerk's eyes. "Put your glasses on because I want you to see this clearly. There . . . you know what this is, don't you? Of course you do. Now look at the top globe very carefully, that's right . . . notice anything in particular?"

The man wiped his hands again and wore a resigned expression on his face as he sighed, "It's not empty . . . it's still about a third full."

"That's right," he said, "and that, my little bookish friend, is my authority. Now pick up your ledger, and your pens and leave. Now! And tell whoever sent you that if he wants me he can bloody well come in person next time!"

The clerk cut a forlorn figure as he gathered up his bits and pieces and started to walk down one of the entrances that led down to the chambers below. Even after he had disappeared from view the echoes of his receding voice could still be heard coming from below. "They'll take a very dim view of this . . . oh, dear. Oh, dear, dear me! . . . Mind you, strictly speaking, he had a point."

XVIII

He'd found the tramp under a heap of newspapers and snoring loudly. He hadn't wanted to wake him but he was exhausted with everything that had gone before and impatient to return. "Excuse me . . . hello?" He reached down and gently nudged where he thought his shoulder should be. At first there was no reaction and then suddenly he heard an enormous snorting inhalation and then nothing for several seconds. Just as he was about to nudge him again the newspapers erupted and the tramp sat bolt upright. "Aaaagh!" He shook his head and looked all about before he saw him standing there. "Aha! So, you made it . . . thought you would! Are you ready for the off?"

"Er, yes . . . I thought you probably would be wanting this back and I just wanted to thank you . . ."

The tramp accepted the proffered hourglass and started to wrap it carefully in the newspapers that had covered him. "No need for thanks, laddie, just doing my job."

He stood there watching him wrap the hourglass for several seconds and finally the tramp stopped and looked up. "Was there anything else? I thought you'd be keen to get back."

"I have to know . . . who are you?"

He looked at him with a curious smile before he said, "I'm your defining moment, laddie. I am who I am but I'm not what I seem. I'm a putter right of things turned bad and I specialise in lost causes. Now, I don't mean to be rude, but hadn't you better be going?"

"Am I allowed to shake your hand?"

The tramp smiled broadly. "You better had or I'll take it as a slight, my lad."

He clasped the hand strongly and found words difficult. The hand was warm, and strong, and he felt an energy pass through it which made the hairs on the back of his neck stand up.

"Alright, laddie, off you go before we both make fools of ourselves."

He turned to go and after walking up the first few steps he turned and said, "Will I see you again?"

The tramp smiled and tapped the side of his nose with a significant wink. Then he drew himself to his full height and gave him an extravagant thumbs-up.

He turned and started to climb and as he looked up the light of the moon beckoned him on. After a few steps he had a thought which made him smile. "Better feed the cat."

Below him the tramp was checking his reflection in his mirror and running his fingers through his long grey hair.

In memory of my great friend Jacques Leon Salvignol.

Death Shall Have No Dominion

by F. Braun McAsh

SWORDMASTER: F. Braun McAsh

F. Braun McAsh became the Swordmaster for Highlander: The
Series *at the beginning of season 3. He brought to the job an encyclopedic knowledge of fighting styles, adding to the repertoire of Duncan
MacLeod and his opponents. As Swordmaster, he was responsible for
creating the choreography of each swordfight (sometimes as many as
four or five in an episode!), training guest actors, and choosing or
designing the swords for each Immortal appearing on his watch.*

*An accomplished actor as well, F. Braun appeared in three on-
screen roles during his tenure on the series (not counting the occasions
on which he "doubled" for guest stars in sword fights): a homeless man
in "Blind Faith," an innkeeper in "Through a Glass Darkly," and
finally, the role of Lord Byron's cuckolded rival Immortal, Hans Kershner, in "The Modern Prometheus."*

Of his contribution here, Braun writes: "They say, 'Write about

*what you know.' When Gillian approached me to write this piece, I
had already been kicking around an idea for a* Highlander *script
based on the historical Dracula, and, having also played him on stage,
I had done a lot of research on the subject. The challenge was to take
actual history and, without changing it, fill in the blanks and grey
areas with my fiction. So roughly 75 to 80 percent of this story is fact.
You figure out what's not."*

⚡

> "... I am old, so very old
> and will be for as long as God commands.
> Nor will death take this life away from me.
> And so I walk—a restless wandering wretch,
> beating with my stick against the earth
> which is my mother's gate, always my cry,
> 'Mother, let me in' ..."
> —*Chaucer, Prologue to* The Canterbury Tales

I

The miasma of fresh blood hung over the field like a wet woolen cloak.
It suffused all it touched—the clothing, the hair. Some claimed you
could even smell it on steel. But worst of all, you tasted it each time
you inhaled—a sharp, pungent coppery tang that coated the tongue
and curdled in the nose and spoke to the more ancient, fearful part of
the brain. "Death," it whispered and urged the adrenaline to surge and
escape the cause.

Hans Kirschner was, in small part, the cause, and fancied he would
not have been able to summon up the juice to make a misanthropic
gesture if the devil himself were to appear before him.

Kirschner sat on a small knoll, slumping as much as his breastplate
and gorget would allow, feeling every ounce of the fifty pounds-plus of
his armour and the less obvious weight of his years. Below him soldiers
of Prince Stephan of Transylvania walked casually among the contorted bodies of the fallen; violence rarely conferred the dignity of
dying in a comfortable position.

Here and there one would stoop to run a blade across a throat, or poke a misericorde through a helmet's visor, or snag a choice weapon off a belt. Normally, coin-purses would have also hung from these belts for battlefield ransom, but these men knew their enemy. There would be no ransom on this day.

As Kirschner sat watching grimly and mentally cataloging the various aches that were beginning to compete for attention, a tiresomely familiar sensation began to rudely elbow the others aside. It felt to him as though there was an insect trapped under a tankard somehow centered behind his eyes.

Instinctively, his fingers tightened around the grip of his broadsword, which never left his hand while within an arrow's flight of carnage, but loosened as he recognized its source.

"Ritter Hans!" boomed an excessively enthusiastic voice.

"Your Grace," acknowledged Kirschner as he rose with a sigh and a series of muffled clicks as the joints of his harness reseated themselves.

The Duke of Almas and Fagaras strode up beside him, his helm clanking against his side from its suspensor chain. He inhaled sharply, and turned to Kirschner with a wolfish toothy grin.

"Is it not invigorating to smell the blood of traitors? Tell me what could be better?"

Several dozen things came immediately to mind but Kirschner was too familiar with the duke's temperament to give them voice. Instead, he forced his mouth into a shape that was, at least, geometrically speaking, a smile. "It is a great day for your Grace. That which once was yours is yours again."

The duke's grin was humorless and predatory. "Yes. Mine! Fourteen years, Hans. Fourteen years since I was master of this realm, and only two of those years master of my own destiny. Time is the only thing they have robbed of me that I cannot repossess; but what small comfort a throne can afford me, that I will have, and more." Delight had returned to his grin, and it was not a pleasant sight to behold.

If one managed to ignore his disturbing rictus, the duke presented an arresting—some would say startling—physical presence. He was Kirschner's height, about five foot ten, and clad in a fully articulated suit of plate that had been labouriously polished to silver-brightness and trimmed with bands of ornately etched brass. But it was his face that commanded the observer's attention. A long thin pointed nose stabbed towards a wide mouth bordered by thin bloodless lips, both partially hidden by a thick black moustache that drooped to a strong jaw line. His otherwise cleanshaven skin was unnaturally pale, which made his large green eyes stand out like two emeralds set into snow. He had long curly sable hair that, now free from the confinement of his arming cap, cascaded over his shoulders, hiding a thick bull-neck. Encircling his head was a gold coronet with a sunburst in its centre holding a large ruby that sparkled like a malevolent third eye.

"And the smallest comfort I look forward to for now is a steaming tub to wash away the stink of this day's work, and bring some warmth back into these frozen old bones. You and I, Ritter, we are both almost too old for this jouncing about, eh?" He pounded a gauntleted fist on Kirschner's right paulderon, causing the shoulder beneath to momentarily wince with the remembrance of the past five hours' worth of strains and shocks.

Old? thought Kirschner. You're only 45, you blustering bullcalf—wait until you've been at it for over three and a half centuries, then talk to me about old.

A hot bath though . . . that thought brought a genuine smile back to Kirschner's face. The duke had wisely wanted to reach and invest his objectives before the first snows fell and they had barely made it. It was now November the 16th, and the ground was hard as rock, the grasses glittered with frost. They had crept an army of 21,000 through the back door of this country over the high-mountain pass at Bran barely two weeks ago. The wind stunned the body like a kick to the kidneys, icicles grew on moustaches like they were eaves, and anyone fool enough to touch metal with a bare hand could look forward to the joys of regrowing skin. Kirschner almost welcomed the prospect of battle, and the brief warmth that violent exercise afforded. Almost . . .

"Warmth," grimaced Kirschner. "Ah yes, I have a vague recollection of that sensation, or perhaps it's just my dotage come upon me."

The duke uttered a sharp guttural bark that served him as a laugh.

"Come then, grandfather. We'll muster the army and march back to the gates of the citadel. By now the burgomaster will have determined from which quarter the new winds blow and instructed everyone to scrape and grovel in an appropriate fashion. It'll all be hollow cant, transparent as ice, but I'll accept it . . . for now. Besides—bowed heads expose necks. I have lost enough of my life and my honour through treachery. So let them tug their greasy forelocks, bow, and play the lickspittle until their hypocrisy sweats out of them and fills up their boots. If the only homage I'll have for the rest of my days is the puling deference paid a tyrant, then so be it. When once the crown again encircles this brow, the only way they'll get it off is if this head goes with it."

If necessary, thought Kirschner. Time will tell. . . .

"Come," said the duke as he gestured for his mount. "The sooner we grace these lack-bones with our presence the sooner we warm up and eat."

Kirschner accepted the reins of his palfrey from a guardsman, and swung into the saddle. With his massive war-horse in tow, and surrounded by the two hundred–strong Moldavian ducal guard, he fell into a canter behind his current liege-lord. Before them lay the now-open gates of Bucharest, soon to be the temporary royal residence of the Duke of Almas and Fagaras and Prince-Voevod of Ungro-Wallachia—Vlad Dracula.

II

The room was small, but richly appointed. Aromatic woods in the fireplace burned yellow-orange and, together with several brass censers, permeated the chamber with a fragrant bouquet. The flames danced in reflections on the dark and ornately carved wall panels. The furniture was sumptuously carved by a master's hand, especially the large canopied bed. This was obviously a chamber for someone of great consequence.

Prince Vlad and Kirschner sat opposite each other at a small table in solidly timbered high-backed chairs—shields with legs, if the truth be known. The thick oaken door to their left safely barred, the two were enjoying a late supper. The lavish banquet thrown them by the burgomaster was, for Dracula, an expression of his consolidation of power—a feast for the eyes, not the stomach. To have eaten would have been sheer recklessness. In attendance, thinly disguised by laughter and fawning platitudes, were sympathizers or outright minions of Basarab Laiota, the puppet prince installed by the Turks a year ago when Dracula's hated brother Radu the Handsome died. Without doubt there were also agents of Dracula's rival clan, the Danesti, who, for generations, had contested heirdom of the throne. And, of course, the boyars—the noble class—many of whom were recent defectors to Dracula's rising star, leaving Basarab to flounder and flee. The boyars, as a class, had reason to hate Dracula out of sheer principle. In 1456, during his second reign, knowing that those who murdered his father and older brother would number among those who had experienced a certain number of reigns, and having no particular desire to ferret them out specifically, Dracula had five hundred of them impaled. A few years later, ostensibly to remind them of their proper place in Wallachia's political food-chain, Dracula had three hundred of them arrested during his annual Easter celebration. Combining object-lesson with frugality, he then used them as slave labour to reconstruct his castle at Poenari. So neither Dracula nor his captains put morsel to mouth at the evening's fete. Nor did Dracula partake of any wine that did not issue from the pitcher of his personal bodyguard and cupbearer, Ritter Hans Kirschner.

The table littered with half-empty platters and their trencher-loaf plates saturated with the rich gravies of pork and beef, Dracula and Kirschner eased back into the cushions of their chairs and savoured the soporific quality of the spice-laden air and the heady aroma of tankards of warm mulled wine. "You need not perish with heat to preserve my dignity, mien Ritter." Dracula had early on discarded the finery worn to the reception. The heavy ermine-trimmed crimson velvet robe and the russet knee-length hoopelande underdress now regally graced a side-table. He lounged in an embroidered silk-shirt, black

hose, and soft leather boots. The ermine cap with the pearl-lined cir-
clet and plume of ostrich feathers caught up in a clutch of blazing diamonds hung casually but significantly over the knule of his chair—a
nuance not lost on Kirschner. Hans, by contrast, was still garbed up to
the ears. His deep-blue velvet gippon, vertically quilted and falling to
just above the knee, was the height of Burgundian fashion. It was also
becoming like wearing wet towels in the desert, but he preferred a
damp shirt to the revelation of what lay underneath. In addition to the
corslet of steel plates set into leather that guarded his lower abdomen
and kidneys, the high collar conveniently concealed a padded steel
gorget encircling his neck. This last piece of kit had been a nasty and
terminal surprise to more than one rival Immortal, and Kirschner had
no intention of revealing it gratuitously.

"Your Majesty's dignity needs no help from me," said Kirschner
with a deferential bow of the head. "Besides—for the last month I've
felt like an icicle in a drain-pipe. I don't intend to take this off until
spring."

"Then you will do me the honour of riding downwind till then."
The Prince flashed a lupine smile and tipped an ample draught of hip-
pocras down his throat. With a slight raise of his tankard Kirschner
followed suit. The two men sat in silence for a moment.

"It is necessary then that we travel to Curtea de Arges?" inquired
Kirschner.

"Yes, regrettably," replied Dracula with a slight grimace. "But the
church there is the seat of the Metropolitan for the Orthodox faith,
and as such, must perform the coronation."

Kirschner wrinkled his brow. "I'm sure he'll be less than enthusiastic to sanctify the ascension of a Prince recently converted to Catholi-
cism."

"The old larded eel! Don't worry about him. If he could grit his
remaining teeth to crown a lisping sodomite like my late unlamented
brother Radu, or a senile dotard like Laiota, he can damn well find a
way to look elsewhere when I genuflect in the opposite direction. If I
hadn't converted, Mathias would never have allowed my marriage to

his sister, and in all likelihood I'd still be a 'guest' in Solomon's Tower in Visegrad. No—my freedom and my crown are well worth an occasional mass, to say nothing of a son and heir."

Kirschner nodded gravely . . . the less said about the latter, the better. Dracula had spent twelve years as the prisoner of King Mathias of Hungary, during which time he met, courted and married the King's sister, Illona Szilagy. His conversion and marriage into the Hungarian royal family, coupled with the urgings of his cousin Steven, Prince of Moldavia, finally bequeathed Dracula his liberty, and restored to him the Transylvanian duchies hereditary to his title. After a brief campaign into Croatia with his new royal brother-in-law, he settled in Pest where he, the two Princes (Steven and Stephan) and Kirschner spent the better part of a year engaged in the wrangling, arm-twisting, and sundry political machinations necessary to put together an army consisting of four different nationalities and two major religions, half of whom had absolutely nothing to gain by restoring someone many considered a heretic and mass-murderer to the Wallachian throne.

During this exasperating and often futile year, Dracula's new wife presented him with a son, Mihnea. About nine months previously Dracula had slain a young guard officer who he had found inside his house. The fellow had tried to explain his unfortunate presence by claiming to have been searching for an intruder that, strangely enough, only he had apparently seen enter. Far from speculating on the possibility of cuckoldry, Dracula's excuse to King Mathias for this latest homicide was that "one does not impune the dignity of a Prince by entering his domicile unannounced." Apart from offering a possible explanation for the existence of Vlad's "son," it also taught Kirschner a prudent circumspection when dealing with anything, no matter how small, that might impinge on Dracula's monstrous ego.

"So . . . one last impotent insolence. You must ride two days through snow and freezing wind so that they may give back to you that which was always yours." Kirschner inclined his head and swirled the contents of his stein. "You have, naturally, given thought of what will happen to your army once the coronation is concluded."

Dracula shrugged indifferently. "We begin to lose men. Prince

Stephan and his Transylvanians will be lurching through the gate before the holy oil dries on my scalp, and Mathias' Hungarians with him. The men I will miss for their strength of heart as much as their numbers, but Prince Stephan? . . ." His eyes glazed, and he sought a metaphor in the depths of his cup. "If we two had in beard what he has in brain, we'd scarce possess a hair to grace our chin. I have pages with more military experience, and my sumpter-horse has better sense of tactics."

Kirschner unsuccessfully stifled a rueful chuckle. Prince Stephan was undeniably brave, but would charge a cannon if he thought he could reach it before its shot cleared the muzzle.

"He can't even read a war-map. The man could lose his way inside a garderobe." Kirschner refilled Vlad's outstretched tankard. "But all that aside, he's shockingly ill-read for a Prince. Small wonder he doesn't apprehend Tacitus—he hasn't enough Latin to fill a posset-cup. And have you had the pleasure of familiar conversation with this gosling?"

"Of a fashion," replied Kirschner with a slow shake of his head, "if being audience to an oration qualifies as conversation. If you denied him his horse and armour as subjects, the man would be as mute as a stone."

"I fear we burn logs with higher intellect. And it was this man that my erstwhile brother-in-law made second in command of this campaign."

"An appointment promulgated by political expedience, most assuredly." Although Kirschner had the wit not to correct the Prince on this particular subject, he knew full well that King Mathias had decreed Prince Stephan sole commander of the army, at least while within the borders of Transylvania. His two duchies notwithstanding, Vlad was not the most welcome of guests in "the land beyond the forest." The German-Saxon population in particular, cozeners and intriguers with the Danesti, Dracula's most potent political rival, had ample cause to fear his restoration. The Saxons had long perpetuated a trade monopoly that fettered native industry. Dracula hit upon an unprecedented yet undeniably effective method of redressing this trade imbalance—he had over 40,000 of them impaled at the towns of Brasov, Amlas, and Sibiu. It was stories of legendary depredations such as these that, in no small part, inspired King Mathias to intern Dracula for a dozen years and keep him on a short lead in his progress through Transylvania.

"And Prince Steven's host—they will be returning too?" ventured Kirschner, although he already knew the answer.

"Yes, they must return," nodded Dracula. "The Turk is a common threat to all our borders, and I cannot—will not—weaken Steven at my expense. His pledge to me is fulfilled. My only real regret is that he cannot be present at the Curtea to witness my vindication." In his twentieth year, and fleeing the assassins of his father, Dracula found asylum in the court of Prince Bogdan of Moldavia. There he developed what was probably to be the only true and lasting friendship of his life, with the Prince's son and his cousin, Steven. They had vowed to each other that whoever attained their throne first would likewise aid the other. The cruel and untimely assassination of Bogdan had elevated Steven before Vlad, but no princely obligation would compel him so much as a covenant made in honour to a friend.

"But your Moldavian guard . . . they will remain?" asked Kirschner optimistically.

"Oh yes, they will stay—Steven's gift to me. Ironic, is it not," mused Dracula, "that I, Prince of Wallachia, have as my personal guard a Teuton and two hundred Moldavs, because I cannot risk to trust my own subjects?"

Kirschner nodded in commiseration. A less charitable person (or one with a suicidal paucity of discretion) might have been tempted to point out that this condition might have been avoided had the Prince been more judicious in where he exercised his unsavoury hobby. However, after over thirty years' exposure to the realpolitik of eastern Europe, Hans realized that, Vlad's revolting enthusiasm for pointed sticks aside, if he was considered merciless and sadistic, it was only a matter of degree. "So . . . the coronation being concluded, that will leave us with how many men?"

Vlad took a contemplative sip and toyed with a piece of sugared marchepan. "Hmmm . . . the mathematica was never my strong suit, so I would not presume to render an exact figure, but I could speculate . . ."

"Please do."

". . . however imprecisely, mind, that we could expect to be left with . . ." He regarded the ceiling momentarily, then favoured Kirschner with a grin. "Five thousand, maybe less."

"God Almighty!"

"Not counting, of course, the inevitable defections the moment there exists any real threat to our borders, or the throne. The boyars who joined us when we crossed into Wallachia did so by casting aside Laotia, the pretender. It served their purpose then to fasten their lips to a more puissant backside, and I doubt not that when another rump appears more succulent that they will throng, lamprey-like, to it. These fools think to prosper by straddling the chess board, and following whichever king is not in check. Some fancy themselves adept, and so have deluded themselves into believing that it is a game." Dracula paused, then reached over the table to place the piece of candied marchepane he held atop an artistically arranged pile of like delicacies. He studied the stack briefly, then reached out and removed a select piece from the bottom. One whole side of the pile collapsed, rolling little squares of confectionery onto the table in a miniature cloud of sugar-dust. "Games have rules," said Dracula, as he popped a loose piece of marchepane into his mouth and chewed toothily. "Princes do not."

Perhaps so, thought Kirschner as he listened to Vlad foment, gleefully and graphically, against conspirators both real and imagined. But sooner or later you will be entering into a much different game, whose rules you ignore at far greater peril. You have been a wily mariner in the currents of petty politics. We'll see how adaptable your mind is when presented with the possibility of infinity as a playground.

Time, in the short term, passed considerably quicker. The following day, with Kirschner in the vanguard, Dracula left the citadel of Bucharest with a force of over a thousand, and plodded, with grumbling horses, for two days, through biting cold and stinging sleet, to

Curtea de Arges. There, after a brief but poignant theological discussion on the nature of the afterlife with the Metropolitan, Dracula donned his coronation robes, and hung about his massive neck the chivalric order from whence derived his name; a golden dragon biting its own tail, on whose wings was emblazoned a Christian cross.

And so, on November the 19th, 1476, Vlad Dracula, the "little dragon," was reinvested with the crown of Wallachia. A man considered a heretic by the very church that found it prudent to crown him, regarded by the Saxons as a genocidal tyrant, conspired against by the prideful and corrupt boyars, loathed by the Turks, feared by most of the peasantry; whose only true friend and confidant was a centuries-old German mercenary, whose chief concern was to patiently wait out his prince's death.

III

Kirschner threw his blade across his chest in inverted position, just managing to catch the blow that was descending onto the left side of his neck. He could feel the jarring impact all the way up to his shoulder. Almost simultaneously, he swung up with his left arm, catching his opponent a numbing back-handed blow to the inside of his outstretched forearm, knocking the arm and weapon aside. Instantly, from out of his parry position, Kirschner launched his riposte—bringing the blade to horizontal, and slashing left to right across the throat, adding power to the cut by lunging forward on his right leg.

His antagonist, however, was fast—almost preternaturally so. The second Kirschner's knuckles had stunned his sword-arm, he hurled himself backwards, rolling his head and chest to the left, in a frantic attempt to diminish the effect of the blow he knew must follow. His desperate stratagem succeeded; the pronounced curve of Kirschner's blade had foreshortened the slash just enough, and only the last two inches of the point grated unnervingly but ineffectively across the chain mail aventail that depended from his helm.

The knight's reprieve was temporary in the extreme. Off balance, stumbling backwards and too close to use his sword to cut, his assailant's blade rising to renew the attack, he did the only thing left to him. He punched out a thrust from his hip, the point directed to his foe's inside thigh.

Kirschner had already anticipated this action as being one of three possible responses to his attack, and dealt with it summarily. Pivoting to the left, he smashed the blade aside, then, pivoting back and pulling his elbow into his right hip, he arced the sword down onto his opponent's head. The tightness of its delivery put the full weight of Kirschner's torso behind the blow, and the force of it on the parry brought the other knight, already in a compromised balance position, down onto his left knee.

Kirschner stepped back, his blade hovering at his right side. His rival was down but far from out. He had pulled in his right leg and held his sword in a two-handed grip, the pommel tucked into his stomach, and the point angled up to threaten Kirschner. Only a fool would rush onto a man positioned thus. It would be like tilting cavalry against pikes.

Kirschner backed off another three steps. He saw his opponent starting to lean forward in his crouch—a sign that usually indicated his intention to spring into a charge. As if not to disappoint him, the knight leapt from the ground like an uncoiling spring, his sword already swinging down towards Kirschner's right hip. Once again, the walls of the small private courtyard echoed with the impact of steel on steel.

Kirschner and Dracula sparred at least once a week. The Prince was too experienced a warrior not to recognize the value of another's experience. He also reveled in the joys of violent exercise. Here was the one and only place where Vlad could ignore the often strident demands of his towering egoism. Indeed, it was absolutely necessary that he do so, it being impossible to learn such skills if the teacher felt inhibited to point out deficiencies, or allowed him constantly to win. And, to his credit, Dracula urged Kirschner to push him as hard as any squire. Long immured to the fawning and silver-tongued sycophancy of court, Dracula recognized the need for at least one man to speak to him honestly. Here, after bouting, the two men spoke of many things.

The private courtyard was the only concession to Dracula's vanity. He could tolerate being bested in practice, so long as no one else were present to see.

For the moment, losing was not a consideration foremost in Dracula's mind. Switching to a two-handed grip for additional speed, he pressed Kirschner back with a flurry of blows.

Kirschner retreated evenly, drawing his opponent towards him. Even after three hours, Dracula's blows had shocking potency. Come on, my princeling, thought Kirschner as he absorbed a jolting flank-cut, let's get this over with.

Almost as the words formed in his mind, it came: the break in cadence he knew Vlad was setting him up for. As a cut flashed down to Kirschner's right knee, he noticed the blade beginning to turn to its inside flat. Even exhausted, Dracula's swordsmanship was far too precise for this to be unintentional. No, there it was! The right elbow was rising to allow the wrists maximum rotation. Vlad's blade snapped through a left molinello with blinding speed, descending upon Kirschner's head. Hans brought up his blade with the point facing right, making a window-bow of his arm, and stepping out slightly with his left foot. As the blow caught on his edge, he allowed the point of his blade to dip slightly down. Bound by the laws of physics and his own strength, Dracula's blade began to slide, following the curvature of Kirschner's sword. At the very instant of impact, Hans' left hand shot forth like a striking snake to seize Vlad's right forearm. Three things now occurred more or less simultaneously: rotating on the ball of his right foot, Kirschner gave Dracula's now-extended arm a powerful yank, while he drove his left shin into the back of Vlad's right knee. The prince's sword now safely deflected, Hans shifted his weight to the left leg, and brought his blade whistling down to stop with an audible click against the mail on the back of Dracula's neck.

The two men paused in a frozen tableau as though contemplating the ramifications of the last four seconds. There was silence in the courtyard save the whistling of laboured breath. Intermittent puffs of white blew from the holes of their visors and blanched the metal with frost.

Kirschner swung his sword to the side, and stepped away from the prince. He depressed the spring-stud that locked his visor in place and pushed it up.

"Shall we dispute upon those last few moves, my liege?"

His Liege rolled over to sit, and hinged up the klappviser of his bascinet. "Well," he breathed, "as I recall, your sword had a serious difference of opinion with my neck and as a result, my head left home in disgust."

Ass, thought Kirschner. ". . . which would affect, most radically, your ability to govern." Kirschner held up his sword, a Turkish kilij taken from one of his innumerable battlefield victims, and presented it to Dracula.

"Witness the extreme curvature of the upper half of the blade. It provides a grazing surface as oblique as your helm's. Any forceful cut upon the head can easily be deflected to the right or the left, even by an unskilled warrior. The blow itself will bend the man's wrist enough to send your blade on its way, and so you aid the enemy in your defeat." He held the gleaming blunted half-moon motionless as a stone; steam rose slowly from his arm as perspiration leached through the black leather of his practice jupon. "There is another thing . . ."

"I rather thought there might be," sighed Dracula resignedly, as he absentmindedly snicked at the frozen grass with the rebated tip of his blade. "Please . . . continue." He gestured magnanimously with an upward roll of his eyes.

"The pronounced curve of this blade, the width of its tip, and the thickness of its spine, make it an exceptionally deadly weapon for close-quarters combat. The Turkish manner of fighting favours circular slashing moves. When you make a similar cut with a straight blade very little of the edge is involved. Indeed, the closer you are, the more it becomes a tip-cut, as you must haul back strongly on the hilt for leverage. Now observe." He stepped back, and slashed two fluid figure-eights in front of himself, one descending, one rising. Dracula's eyes narrowed with interest.

"With the kilij, the extreme arch of the blade ensures contact with the edge is maintained through the full length of the draw. The closer

you are, the more edge there is employed. But here is the weakness."
Dracula leaned forward intently. "Such a draw-cut must pull the hilt
past the hip to free the blade—as the stroke slides off your armour,
step in, face-to-face, and employ your pommel. Then, as his head
snaps back, retire on your right foot, and slash down diagonally upon
his neck." Hans mimed his way through the moves as he spoke.

"Yes . . . yes," suspirated Dracula intensely, whitening his moustache in a cloud of frosty breath. "And leaving the left hand free to
oppose his sword-arm."

Kirschner nodded sagaciously. "Also, be wary of blows where the
edge seems to face away from you. If your Grace will oblige me with
a high ward in dexter . . ."

Dracula rose swiftly, and made to parry his right chest and neck.
Kirschner brought the blade up slowly, his knuckles pointing to the
ground, and transferring his weight into a moderate left lunge. The
spine of the kilij clunked dully onto the edge of Dracula's ward, but the
blade's arc bent it around the parry so that its thick point touched
Vlad's chain-mail aventail directly above the carotid artery.

"That," observed Dracula, "would be annoying."

"Only for a brief second, I assure you," admonished Hans. "On
such an attack it is necessary to step to the opposite direction, and
slightly forward, to negate the effect of the curve."

Dracula complied, and the point slipped away by eight inches.
"What other vulnerabilities?" he demanded enthusiastically.

"The Turk does not commonly employ armoured gauntlets and, oft
when they do, they are mail. Stand off your man and utilize your
sword's superior reach to advantage. Swing up from a low ward and
fetch him a cut upon the inside wrist, the thumb, or the back of the
hand." Kirschner transferred his sword to his left hand, where he held
it by the blade, signifying the conclusion of the lesson.

"Excellent," grinned Dracula. He looked about him, taking bracing
lungfuls of frigid winter air. "Come, shall we sit?" The two men
walked over and, with a creak of frozen leather, ensconced themselves
on a stone bench, under the lead-tiled eaves of the monk's walk that
encompassed the courtyard.

"Such exercise—it keeps one young, does it not, my Ritter?"

"My intention leans more to keeping one alive. Youth is wasted on the dead."

Dracula chuckled gutturally. "Always the stoic. Often, I think you could have instructed Zeno. Tell me—were you this old when you were younger than you now are?

No, thought Kirschner, it took about a century. "Stoicism implies indifference to both pain and pleasure, your Grace. Since I am immured to one, and jaded of the other, this term could hardly apply to me."

"You are a cynic then?" baited Dracula.

"Pertaining to matters wherein it is wise to be. In all things politic it serves one best to see things as they are, rather than as one would wish them to be."

"If wishes were horses . . ." nodded Dracula, quoting an old homily. "Reality can be an annoying distraction to those whose scepter is a looking glass."

Hans regarded Dracula with quiet deliberation. "One cannot improve a cynic's vision by putting out his eyes."

Dracula's eyebrows raised and he cast an askant glance at Kirschner. "I flatter myself that my vision has been as acute as your own for many years, friend Hans, else I would not have likely survived to make your acquaintance." He leaned back against the wall and gazed up at the grey-granite sky. "Do you find you miss your homeland, Hans? You have been away for many years now."

Twenty-seven, to be exact. Kirschner had departed the Holy Roman Empire in 1439, on the command of Albrect II of Habsburg, to find allies in their fight against the Turk. Finding potential confederates preoccupied with Ottoman expansion on their own borders, Kirschner pragmatically decided to fight them where he found them. He served in the army of John Hunyadi in the 1440's, when that great warrior was the interregnum governor of Hungary. Fate had drawn Kirschner to Italy scant years before Dracula, deposed of his second reign by his Turkophile brother Radu, fled to the court of the Transylvanian Prince. Hunyadi, never one to pass up earning the indebtedness of a prince, became Dracula's military and political mentor for five years.

Years after the event, Kirschner learned that Hunyadi had fallen in the siege of Belgrade, and that his son Mathias was now King of Hungary. Sensing distinct possibilities inherent in renewing an old, albeit vague, acquaintance with new royalty, Kirschner slowly made his way back to Visegrad. At the time of his arrival Dracula had been a "guest" of Mathias for over eleven years. For days Kirschner had experienced the disconcerting presence of the Gift, but had been frustrated in his attempt to identify the source. It was with no little trepidation that he finally accepted that it emanated from Solomon's Tower, whose sole resident was the man known as "Tepes"—the Impaler.

Kirschner thought for a moment, then spread his hands indifferently. "Wallachia is not so dissimilar. The Dambovita is as blue as the Danube, the forests as green, the sky as somber. I have traveled much. Home"—he tapped the slate floor with the tip of his sword—"is where you make it."

"That sounds to me like a convenient excuse to remain rootless," mused Dracula, absently worrying the end of his moustache. "You are demonstrably not a man who shuns commitment. Perhaps someday, when we have our leisure, we might explore the true source of your professed wanderlust. Myself," he said, stretching his legs, "I have always loved this land, and would still were I not its Prince. And I'll be damned if I will allow its crown, or its people, to continue to be simpering vassals to a Sultan."

"From whom I am sure we can expect a reaction presently," observed Kirschner. "Your coronation is a month behind us, and the bulk of our former army has marched back across our borders. I doubt this has escaped notice in Constantinople."

"Oh, I am sure that I do not scratch my backside, but that His Omnipresence takes wind of it. I pity those who dwell by public roads. The nightly din of boyars' messengers must make for fitful sleep."

"When think you we can anticipate an invasion?"

"Soon. I am but lately come again to power, and have gained no new loyalties. My army is the weakest it has ever been, and my allies remote. And, although the boyars have the wit not to conspire against me openly, neither will it serve their purpose to render me aid."

"The season is our chiefest ally," observed Kirschner. "If they wait another month the mountain passes will be snowed over, and without crops they cannot forage. Once here, they cannot besiege; they must commit themselves to a swift, decisive victory else the winter traps them."

"Very true," grinned Dracula accordingly. "So let them come. Since it seems I am not destined to reap the allegiance of my fellow man, I shall curry favour with nature by feeding her children. The wolf and carrion crow shall not lack for sustenance this winter."

Kirschner shook his head in mock disapproval. "You spoil your pets to feast them on such savory fare."

"Don't worry, Ritter," chuckled Dracula as he rose and stomped his feet briskly. "They have long since acquired a palate for boyar, and after we have entertained the Turk, I am sure a fresh supply of such viands will become apparent. Come, sup with me. Exercise and anticipation are always a mighty whet to my appetite."

Enemies swell up around you like the tide and yet you live, thought Kirschner as he followed the prince out of the courtyard. And every ward and wile I teach you only serves to lengthen my wait. Men such as you, he mused, imbued with arrogant recklessness—they seldom die abed. Oh well, he reasoned as he contemplated the evening's repast; if patience is a virtue, there are less commodious places in which to exercise it than the palace of a prince.

IV

The invasion came within a fortnight. Mehmet II, a seasoned campaigner, knew full well that his old enemy would never again be in such a depleted condition. And waiting for the thaw was not an option—by spring he might well end up facing the combined forces of Wallachia, Moldavia, Transylvania, and Hungary. Not their full armies, to be sure, but their combined contingents, under experienced warlords, could easily repel whatever forces he might muster. Thrice he had faced Dracula on the field, and thrice he had led a bleeding army back across the frontier, having each time lost over fifty percent

of his host. Once, while preparing to seige Dracula's capital of Targoviste, the prince had personally led a midnight cavalry charge through
the tents of the encamped Turks. So swift and savage was the assault
that Dracula actually cut a swath to within less than a hundred yards
from the pavilion of the Sultan himself. The bloody devastation of the
attack impressed itself so indelibly on the Turkish consciousness that
it was henceforth recorded in the histories as "the Night of Terror."

But even that could not possibly have prepared them for what lay
ahead. Dracula's forces had retreated following a scorched earth pol-
icy. The sultan's triumphant entrance into Targoviste was somewhat
diminished by the resounding emptiness of its walls. Its people had
fled, its treasures—indeed, anything of the remotest value—spirited
away. Some buildings had been put to the torch, the wells poisoned,
and the croplands burned. It was a hollow victory, and soon to prove
a pyrrhic one as well. A familiar and sickening odour had begun to
permeate through the eye-stinging haze, and it filled Mehmet with
horror and dread. There, outside the city's south wall was found its
source. Twenty thousand raven-ravaged corpses stood in rigid agony
upon as many stakes; Turkish prisoners of war that Dracula felt disposed to return to their master.

Mehmet's eyes clenched tightly shut as memories of that day
returned unbidden, like a frozen hand on the back of his neck.
Stunned numb by the sheer enormity of such a savage deed, he could
manage but a whisper. "What can we do against a man capable of such
a thing?" And then he turned and rode away.

It was then, in desolate and ignominious retreat, that Mehmet
would learn to what depths pure hatred could delve. Dracula still rent
his enemies far beyond the range of a bow-shaft. Understanding well
the "needs" of an army on the march, the Prince had sent into the
Turkish camps prostitutes infected with leprosy and the bubonic
plague. Now, dulled by fatigue and despair, the viruses began to break
forth. By the time they reached the Bosphorous, fifty thousand men
lay dead, smote by a distant prince who wielded a weapon against
which no armour was proof. Mehmet's eyes opened, and stared with
hollow, grim resolve. Vulnerable as Dracula seemed, it was utter folly

to underestimate such a man. But it was strike now, or not at all. As an army of twenty thousand slogged their shivering way to the confluence of the Danube and the Dambovita, Mehmet II prayed that one way or another, the upcoming battle would be the last.

"Here! On this ground shall we meet them." Dracula stabbed a long white finger towards the map spread out on a trestle-table in the tapestry-draped great-hall.

"Since they are determined to march, then let them. We'll not tire ourselves by meeting them half-way. Their force is equally divided between sipahi cavalry and janissary infantry, half whose ranks will be foot archers. At this point"—he tapped the yellowing parchment— "the land is at its narrowest. The river to their left and wooded foothills to their right will funnel their advance. We will present our cavalry to oppose theirs. As their sipahis charge, our horse will wheel onto their right flank and push them towards the river. Our archers hidden on the hillsides shall then loose their bows upon the janissaries, while our own infantry swarms down the slopes to form a line across this new front. We then will strive to push their two forces apart from one another."

Kirschner regarded the small assemblage of knights and nobles. "Pushed into the frozen marsh, their cavalry will lose its momentum. Their infantry, exposed and without support, cannot flank us, being denied the hills. And although their numbers greatly outweigh our own, the lay of the land restricts their ability to bring the full force of their numbers against us en masse."

"Should our infantry falter," said Dracula, with a look that suggested the impropriety of such a possibility, "it shall withdraw back up the hills, with our archers harassing any pursuit. Our cavalry will then wheel left and retreat. We shall then retire to the citadel, and watch them freeze. We are full-provisioned, and the Turk is unprepared to invest a siege." Dracula folded his arms with an air of finality, and looked to Kirschner.

"Nevertheless," continued Hans, "it is our Prince's intention that

the Turk be put to rout. All those who escape our blades we shall simply face again come spring. Let us see what exhausts itself first," he
posed, meeting the eye of each man present, "the sultan's soldiers or
his will."

Kirschner's proposal was met with smiles of grim resolve. "Go then,
assemble your men," commanded Dracula. "Tomorrow, the price of
our vassalage increases once again. Together we shall plumb the
depths of the sultan's purse."

V

Most people, if pressed, will admit to a certain degree of surprise
upon the occasion of witnessing their first battle. Things are never
quite as they expect them to be, which seems to indicate there is a limit
to the normal human mind's ability to contemplate the nature of horror.

The first apparent contradiction is the seeming lack of any obvious
movement; two contending mobs locked as if in a massive football
scrum. Cautiously moving closer, one recieves their first intimation of
violence—first from the larger weapons. Pole-axes, glaives and
berdiches rise and fall like trip-hammers. Then, smaller, faster
motions resolve themselves. Sword blades flailing in a flashing downward blur like metronomes gone mad. The curt outline of the cruel
triangular flanges of a mace poised briefly in midair, then descending
with brutal purpose into the sea of bobbing helmets.

Here and there, the besmirched colours of a pennon or galfanon
dance violently at the end of a pole—rallying, exhorting. The bob and
duck of helmets, and the wrenching twist of torsos, are grim sugges-
tions of actions yet unseen—the crush of contending shields and desperate pistoning of thrusts. And overhead, arcing down like driving
sleet, yard-long steel-tipped shafts rain upon the heaving fray.

Now add the noise. There is no fabled "ring of steel"—blade seldom encounters blade. Instead, a cacophony of dull, crunching metal-
lic thuds, like a thousand madmen beating on tin pots with hammers.
And above this unholy din, barely recognizable as human, a thunder of

inarticulate roars, hoarse and ragged, torn unawares by savage exertion from parched throats. And finally, shrill screams that pierce the ear like needles, and haunt the soul's memory long after they are stilled.

Kirschner threw an armoured leg over the barrel-girth of his towering warhorse and surveyed with satisfaction the pressing throng. Dracula had entrusted to him the charge of foot down the slippery slope to separate the Ottoman infantry from the Kapikulu horsemen. It was absolutely essential that the line advance unbroken. Repeatedly he had plunged into the seething mass, leading reinforcements to buttress a weakening link in the formation.

There, in the insanity of the melee, with mace in one hand and sword in the other, he parried and hacked and stabbed until blood splattered the grey steel of his harness up to the palderons. So numbed were his arms by the relentless deadening impacts, so unconscious his responses, that through the narrow eye-slit of his visor he fancied he watched another man do battle. The constant violent jostle and tumultuous clamor made Hans feel as though he were being flogged on all sides by wet sandbags. Eventually, the sensory overload became so overwhelming that all Kirschner could feel, or hear, was the surge of his own adrenaline, and the roar of his own pulse in his ears.

The line did more than hold. Slowly at first, then with increasing momentum, it advanced. The Turkish vanguard wavered but a second. It was enough. With bile burning in the back of their throats, the Wallachians surged forward with demonic power. The Ottoman fell before the savage onslaught, like trees caught in an avalanche.

Kirschner stood in the stirrups astride the mountain of sable muscle that was his destrier. The advance, he assured himself, was strong and uniform. Only then did his grim smile fade, as the forward progress of the fray revealed the ground over which the battle had joined and was contested for a brutal, bitter hour.

Bodies . . . many twisted into obscene contortions by the trample of a thousand boots. Mutilated and dismembered, they lay in jumbled heaps or strewn asunder, as though sullenly flung by a Titan's tantrum. Nearby a severed limb still clutched a sword in futile, eternal defiance.

But if one could stand to look past the steaming carnage, there remained one horrible discrepancy. One blatant overwhelming wrongness, so palpably conspicuous that it required conscious effort to force the brain to acknowledge it.

It was winter. . . .

The ground was red.

Scattered like pearls in a sea of scarlet, patches of unsullied white brazenly proclaimed their purity. As the prince's men advanced they left in their wake a reeking crimson swath of trodden, sodden snow.

Kirschner wheeled his mount away from the grotesque spectacle, and spurred it to a gallop towards a clutch of Moldavian guardsmen above whom snapped the red and gold dragon standard of the prince. Dracula himself had led the cavalry assault, smashing the Turkish host apart like a splitting wedge through a log. But now, as Kirschner drew up near the guard phalanx, the prince, in his distinctive armour, was nowhere to be seen. This was passing strange; were the prince dead, the guard would scarce be standing about in such a manner. Yet if he were leading men his banner would ride beside him. Kirschner knew the prince's capriciousness, and comprehended a third explanation that he liked not a whit.

"Where is my lord, the Prince?" demanded Hans of the nearest Moldav.

"He has ridden to observe our enemy's defeat," beamed the young guard officer.

Alone, of course, the damn fool, thought Kirschner, although he understood full well the reasoning. Dracula's standard had to remain near the battle as reassurance, and a rallying point. But although Dracula was often rash and impetuous, yet he was not a fool; he would hardly strike out without a guard if he could be recognized. Therefore, he would . . .

Kirschner shouldered his horse between the guardsmen, searching the ground for something he dreaded to find.

There! Near the standard-bearer lay the body of a Turkish sipahi— by the look of his armour, an officer of some consequence, probably an alay bey. But the picture he presented was incomplete in a way his death in battle could not explain. His çiçak helmet, normally secured by a chin-strap, was missing, as was the rich silk brocade surcoat that would normally be worn, cape-like, over his harness.

"Which way?" roared Kirschner, spinning his horse about. Startled by his outburst, the guardsman pointed to the hillside down which Kirschner had led his troops; the only high ground for miles.

Hans thundered off, the drumming of his steed's hooves impelling from him a stream of guttural, imaginative invective.

It was not uncommon for Dracula to make a personal reconnaissance while in disguise, but never in broad daylight under such foolhardy circumstances. Although the prince would naturally seek the high ground, the lower portion of the hill still contained hundreds of Wallachian archers and a small contingent of infantry, stationed to prevent the Turk from using the hill to circumvent the bottle-neck of the engagement and flank their rear. But it was not just the danger presented by his own troops that Kirschner feared. The Sultan's forces included native Wallachian Voyniks. These men, many of whose families had suffered the excesses of Dracula's previous reigns, would not be disposed to merely capture him should he be recognized. His enormous black charger plowed its way labouriously up the hill, snow often reaching near its belly. Kirschner leaned forward onto its thick neck and strained his eyes up the slope, through the bare trees searching for unnatural colour against a background of yet-unsullied white.

Kirschner reigned in his mount and stood high in the stirrups, his eyes narrowing as he tried to feel the ghostly stirring of the proximity of the Gift. Suddenly, through a haze of frosty breath, a flurry of movement danced in his peripheral vision. There, to his right, a small group of soldiers fought through knee-deep drifts to disappear over a shallow rise. Hans snapped the reins and urged his horse forward. Sounds began to reach him as he plunged upwards towards the knoll's crest; vicious oaths and the sharp ring of steel rent the frigid air. He burst through a drift in an explosion of white to see . . .

Dracula. Clad in peacock-blue Turkish silk, his sword flashed in blurred arcs as he kept at bay his two remaining adversaries. Two other figures lay contorted, staining the snow.

The Prince bellowed with rage as he whirled his blade, vociferously proclaiming his title, and threatening the men with the direst of punishments.

Futilely, it occurred to Kirschner. His clothing notwithstanding, Dracula's borrowed helmet had a chainmail aventail that extended around its front, and hooked to the descending nasal bar. Only the Prince's eyes were visible behind its mask. Besides—these soldiers, even though part of Vlad's army, were probably not Wallachian. Almost three-quarters of the royal host were Moldavs and Transylvanians who had probably never seen the Prince up close. And, knowing the presence of Voyniks and Vlaches in the enemy's rank, the fact that this man was raging in Romani would not have lent the content of his invective the slightest credibility.

Kirschner jerked his head to the right. The four soldiers he had circled past were now gaining the pinnacle. Dracula was a fearsomely accomplished warrior, but even Hans could not stand long against six while knee-deep in snow.

Kirschner hesitated; perhaps this was as it was meant to be. After all, he had been attending on this man's death for two years now. What would it serve to his purpose to save him now?

Ruefully, he answered his own question. It was not if, but how he might die that Kirschner could not risk. Were the Prince to be inadvertently beheaded with him this close by, he could not escape being trapped in the fury of the Quickening. After being lashed by such forces, he would be seriously compromised in his ability to defend himself. And if the soldiers merely fled, the tale they would relate could prove inconvenient to him, at the least.

The four reinforcements were closing on Dracula. Thinking sour thoughts Kirschner silently withdrew a yard of well-honed steel from its scabbard. With his left hand he closed his visor with a muffled click, then unhooked the mace from its saddle-ring. He took a deep breath and released it with an even, menacing hiss.

"You damn well better prove worth it," he muttered darkly, a goad of his heels, the giant shire-horse surged forward towards the startled men.

VI

The charger burst through a sparkling constellation of kicked-up snow like a cannon-shot through smoke. Kirschner drove for the two rearmost men, and cut the horse left at the last possible second. Three-quarters of a ton of armoured war-horse slammed sideways into one hundred and sixty pounds of soldier with predictable results. Taking advantage of the momentary distraction, Dracula closed with his two antagonists and, in seconds, a third man lay, a leaking corpse.

Four to two now—the odds were manageable. But one man had a pole-axe, a dangerous prospect for a man in the saddle, and his mount encumbered with the snow. Keeping the horse between himself and the other two men, Hans dismounted and slapped his destrier to one side. The soldiers gave it a wide berth as it thundered past. A riderless warhorse was the proverbial loose cannon on the deck. Lashing out with iron-shod hooves the size of dinner plates, it would stomp anyone but its knight to a paste.

Kirschner took a calculated risk. Hoping the men might recognize him, or at least realize his armour could not possibly be Turkish, he pushed up his visor and yelled.

"Give way, you fools! This *is* the Prince! My Liege—remove your helmet. Let them see!"

The four soldiers hesitated for a moment, but their expressions didn't alter. These were the faces of men assessing a new tactical situation, not considering the plausibility of mistaken identity. Kirschner snarled a guttural obscenity to himself. In his haste, there was one possibility he had not considered. This could well be a deliberate assassination attempt.

Taking advantage of the temporary lull of hostilities, Dracula moved swiftly. With both hands he reached up to wrench the helmet from off his head. In doing so the shoulder-length chainmail aventail dragged over his face, briefly blinding him.

Sensing a singular opportunity, the soldiers fell upon him like famished wolves. Dracula ripped the helmet free and hurled it forcefully at his closest assailant, even as the other two split away to encircle him.

Kirschner managed two labourious strides before the fourth man came upon him from the rear, cleaving a blow to the back of Hans' neck. Kirschner pivoted around, bringing his sword up in a sloping ward that sent the man's blade grazing off to the right. Then, sinking into the blow, he swung down in an anti-clockwise arc, slashing the man under his kneecap. Instantly, flowing with the torque of his cut, he rose forward, twisting to the right. The mace swept up in a blur, and connected with a sickening viscous crunch against the soldier's temple. The man pitched sideways to bury himself in a drift.

Hans wheeled about just in time to witness the conclusion of Dracula's mortal existence. One of his three attackers knelt in the snow, doubled over a fearful abdominal wound, but the two remaining had flanked Dracula on two sides. The swordsman struck first, compelling the Prince to defend. An instant later the pole-axeman lunged forward, driving the weapon's spike through the lower region of Dracula's backplate.

The shock trauma of such a terrible wound would have felled a raging bear. A pity for the assassin that his erstwhile prey was not so predictable a creature.

The thrust snapped Dracula's body to rigid attention. Then, with a demonic roar, he spun towards his stunned killer. The strength of the turn tore the shaft of the weapon from the man's hands, bending the point in the wound agonizingly. The Prince swung his sword straight-armed, describing a curve with almost five and a half feet of reach. The soldier, caught off balance by the unimagined fury of the attack, desperately tried to jerk back out of its range.

Nothing human could have moved that fast. Dracula's sword-tip sheared through the wretched man's trachea with a horrible liquid snick.

The momentum of his superhuman effort brought him to his knees. His sword hung loosely at his side, his head lowered until his chin touched his chest. Then, with a slow, stately grace, the Prince of Wallachia toppled sideways into a downy pillow of snow.

The last remaining attacker had stood almost mesmerized by the sight of his companion's death. Suddenly a thought occurred to him—

there was another. He began to turn; perhaps he saw the sun flare brightly on the moving blade. And then he saw no more.

Kirschner stood in silence and assessed the situation. To his right his mount pawed the ground to uncover grass, munching in a bored, desultory manner. Beyond the crest of the hill, Dracula's horse regarded the scene indifferently. Then, from behind him, came the dull crunch of compressing snow. Hans spun about in a low crouch. It was the eighth soldier, the one he had broadsided with his horse. Stunned and temporarily hors de combat, he had recovered his senses, taken one look at the gruesome tableau, and had decided to do any further thinking with his legs. Kirschner fumed with disgust as he watched the man half run, half roll down the hill, irrevocably beyond his reach.

There lived a witness. He had killed this last man for nothing. Kirschner put away his weapons and began to go from corpse to corpse, turning over bodies, removing helmets and arming caps. Finally, after about ten minutes of quantitative assessment, he chose the first soldier he had slain. So as not to leave drag marks in the snow, he slung him onto his shoulders with a tired grunt and staggered towards the body of the Prince, muttering all the while.

"Couldn't wait, could you? Had to see for yourself. Couldn't stay under your banner with the troops where you belonged . . ."

He dropped the body with a muffled thud beside Dracula. Checking the two men side by side, he assured himself that they were close to the same height. He knelt and began to strip the armour from the dead soldier. That done, he removed the armour first from Dracula's limbs, and belted them onto the nameless corpse that lay alongside. First the legs—cuisse, poleyn, and greave; then the arms—vambrace, couter, and rerebrace. Finally Kirschner required the cloak, breast, and back-plate. He unceremoniously placed a steel-clad foot in the centre of the late Prince's back, took the shaft of the pole-axe in both hands, and wrenched it out to the accompanying squeak of metal. He unhooked the stained brocade, then clamshelled off the back and front of the cuirass. He then unlaced the arming cap and pulled it free, to a cascade of sable curls.

The Prince's eyes snapped open and blazed like green gems held
before a fire. His mouth gaped, and the sharp intake of air drove his
shoulders into the snow and caused his back to arch.

Kirschner sighed resignedly. "Your penchant for bad timing has all
but ruined what was shaping up to be a not unfulfilling day."

Dracula rolled his head wildly first right, then left. "Kirschner!
What . . . ah, of course. So you got the churl that laid me low. Excellent. I'd . . ." His hands went to his chest, he looked down at his arms.
"My harness! What has hap . . ." He stared with alarm at the dead man
beside him. "Kirschner! What in the name of God do you think you
are doing?"

Hans held up Dracula's back-plate. "Calm yourself and listen carefully. Do you see this hole? Do you remember the pain? Now feel your
gambeson over your right kidney. This bastard here put four inches of
a rondel spike into you. Think you a normal man could have survived
such a wound?"

Dracula fumbled a gloveless hand to the area. He inserted a finger
into the hole then held his hand before him, staring hypnotically at the
bloody digit.

"This cannot . . . well, obviously it did but break the skin. A superficial wound that . . ."

Kirschner seized up the pole-axe that lay nearby and held the head
in front of Dracula's face. There was blood staining more than half the
length of the cruel eight-inch spike. "Look you! Does this appear to
have come out of a superficial wound?" Kirschner knelt beside the
Prince and threw the axe to one side.

"My Liege," he implored in a low, even voice, "a miraculous thing
has happened to you as it happened to me many years ago. I shall
explain all when time serves us better, but at this moment it is essential for our safety that we leave here in haste and undetected. Your
army shall soon be informed of your death. Leaderless, they will
retreat to the Citadel, and the Turk will return. And when they do,
they must have a body to find. This man, with his moustache and long
black hair, will serve their purpose as well as ours."

"What?" exclaimed the Prince indignantly as he struggled to stand.

"You would try to pass this base-born whore-hound off as me?" Dracula fairly bristled with pique. "This is insufferable! I shall return to the head of my army—with you!—and we shall grind the Turk under our heel!"

Kirschner placed a restraining hand on the Prince's chest. "You cannot. You were seen to be killed. Damnation, *I* saw you killed! When have I ever given you cause to doubt me? We are not as other men! A whole new realm of existence has opened up to you. All this I shall make known unto you, but not here, not now!"

Dracula almost visibly trembled to contain his mounting rage. He struck Kirschner's hand aside and spoke with rising volume, in a voice that grated like steel on a rock. "Friend or no, you shall not speak to me in such a preemptory manner—*or* touch my person thus! I am the Prince, damn you, and I . . ."

". . . have not the time for this," concluded Kirschner. Then, obtaining the final word in a crude but effective manner, he hauled off with a fortuitously ungauntleted fist, and delivered a mighty lick square to the centre of Vlad's forehead. Three and a half centuries of wielding weapons with this arm made a convincing impression on Dracula. His head snapped back, his eyes rolled up into their sockets, and the ex-Prince of Wallachia instantly lost all interest in the proceedings that followed.

VII

It is said that history is written by the winners. This homily tends to ignore the times, unpropitiously frequent, that it is written by losers scrabbling to salvage the slightest shred of credibility from an otherwise humiliating debacle. When it becomes impossible to pretend that you won, solace can be had in the overly-enthusiastic proclamation that you didn't lose completely.

In the realm of empire-building it is largely unacceptable, strategic disadvantages notwithstanding, for an experienced army of over 20,000 to get their brains slapped out by a motley force of barely 4,500. Therefore, when the body of the Warlord was discovered after the Wallachians inexplicably quit the field, there was much rejoicing among the Turkish host. Or at least as much as the less than 10,000 survivors who had just been flogged within an inch of their lives, and now faced the prospect of freezing to death, could muster under the circumstances.

And so the head of the unfortunate corpse was taken and, along with its insignia of the Order of the Dragon, returned in triumph to the Sultan in Constantinople.

The Sultan received the gift with a combination of stately enthusiasm and guarded skepticism. After all, what had he? A head with the appropriate type and colour of hair, whose finer features had been somewhat inconvenienced by Kirschner's mace and more than six weeks' travel. Added to which, the Sultan had never actually seen Dracula in person, although he had observed several portraits that drew the eye to a distinctive feature. When the court had cleared, his majesty donned a glove and gingerly raised an eyelid on the withered trophy.

Oh dear . . . they were brown.

Now, this was inconvenient. To date, the Sultan had lost well over a quarter of a million men against the Impaler; a long hunt and no coon-skins on the wall, so to speak. Conversely, although this was plainly no princely pate, he had received no word that Dracula had reappeared to claim the Wallachian throne. Afloat in a sea of contradictions, the Sultan did what most statesmen throughout history do when faced with the prospect of continuing to fight without winning. He declared victory, and sat back to see if anyone were imprudent enough to contradict him.

The alleged prize was placed on a stake high over the gates of the city. Quite high, in point of fact. A casual observer might look up to behold an object that looked like nothing so much as a cannon-ball in a wig. However, since the official proclamation held this to be the dreaded Vlad Tepes, well . . . One of the distinct advantages of being an absolute ruler, however benevolent, is the preponderance of people who are tactfully content to give you the benefit of a doubt.

Kirschner bestowed the body upon the monks of the monastery of Snagov, which occupied an island by the same name in the middle of a large lake in the heart of the Vlasie forest. Dracula and his forebears had all made generous grants and endowments to the monastery, to the eternal gratitude of its order. At Kirschner's suggestion, the brothers interred the body in an unmarked grave to thwart desecration by Vlad's myriad enemies.

Meantime, Hans slowly but surely achieved a meeting of minds with his irate and uncooperative captive. However, although Dracula's ego was substantial and accustomed to obeisance, yet he possessed a keen and logical mind. After a few graphic and often painful demonstrations, it became obvious that he and Kirschner were, if not immortal, certainly different from normal men. As far as eternal life were concerned, Vlad finally acceded to remain open to the possibility.

"Ask me again in fifty years," replied Dracula in his usual ironic fashion.

"We'll see," rejoined Kirschner, proferring his hand.

Dracula regarded it for a moment, and then, for perhaps the first time in his life, clasped another's hand as equals.

VIII

The man astride the roan palfrey was barely recognizable as the Dracula of old. His shoulder-length jet locks had been cut back several inches and cosmetically streaked with grey. The broad, droopy moustache that dominated his lower countenance was now gone, changing considerably the overall shape of his face. His skin, which previously possessed a startlingly blanched appearance, was now brown and weathered, the result of an application of stain made from the crushed shells and leaves of walnuts. His armour was subdued and nondescript. Culled from a quantity of corpses to achieve an acceptable overall fit, its mismatched parts bespoke a class of person who had to scavenge his finery. The only visible remnant of his former self, annoyingly undisguisable, were his eyes, green as Venetian glass.

With their war and sumpter-horses trailing on long leads, Hans and Vlad paused in their journey atop a wind-swept promontory and looked back at the receding lights and chimney smoke of Bucharest.

"So—no more to be Prince Vlad," said Dracula, meditatively. "Or Vlad at all, for that matter." His voice, surprisingly, contained no note of bitterness or remorse.

Hans regarded him carefully but without suspicion. "Have you decided on a new name?"

Dracula thought a moment. "Ladislaus, I think." He smiled at Kirschner. "Yes, I know it is both Germanic and Hungarian for Vlad. Is it necessary to give up an entire life in but a fortnight?"

"Wiser, perhaps," said Kirschner, with a raise of his brows. "But what is a name that a man does not make of it? To begin again, tabula rasa—that is one of the greatest parts of the Gift. Through it we learn to write our lives in sand, not carve them in stone. Anonymity is our ally; notoriety, our foe." He turned to Dracula. "To give up a kingdom . . ." He shook his head. "That is beyond my experience. But to my eyes, you sit taller in your saddle now than you did before."

"Indeed," chuckled Dracula, "to wear a crown is to bear a kingdom about your brows. It is surprising to me to admit how little of it I shall miss. Hollow pomp and empty ceremony, obsequious, fawning sycophants, and lickspittle liars. Do you have any idea what it's like to live your life wondering which of your own guards will be the one to drive the knife into your back, or which of your relatives will poison your evening's posset-cup? To suspect virtually everyone of ulterior motives, simply to survive another sunset? No, friend Hans. I have gone disguised among the common man too often to pretend to myself that the simpler life has no virtues." His smile turned briefly wicked. "No, it is over for me. Let my wife's bastard take up the sceptre. If there's any justice in this world, he'll smack her with it."

"Well," said Kirschner, ruffling the fur of his riding cloak up about his neck against a sudden gust of wind, "one of the few genuine consolations of princeliness was wealth. We may travel and live simply but comfortably on my hoard for a time, but come spring I'm afraid we must find employment."

"Which I suppose means selling the use of our swords," mused Dracula. "I killed sufficient to keep one despot in power. I am disinclined to extend the favour to anyone else. No, I was just thinking—

seeing as we are traveling in the right direction anyway—that we should make a short pilgrimage to Snagov Lake."

"You must know that you cannot possibly visit the monastery."

"Oh, not the monastery," grinned Vlad. "I was thinking more of a particular spot near the shore. Fourteen years ago, while fleeing deposition by my disgusting brother Radu, I had the monks, whose loyalty I'd scrupulously cultivated, deposit in the shallows a couple of sealed chests for future contingencies."

Kirschner stared silently with reverential expectations.

"I'm afraid it's not a king's ransom, but"—he paused to savour the moment—"it'll do for an ex-prince and a knight. Several years, I should suspect."

If Kirschner had worn a hat he would have removed it. As it was, he stood mutely, worshipping in silence. Dracula's laughter pealed forth for them both.

Hans gathered in the reins of his mount. "Well then, my student, companion and coin-purse; to Snagov."

"And then . . . ?" queried Dracula as he brought his horse aside Kirschner's.

"You Wallachians have a marvelously vague expression—perhaps you've heard it? 'Mai la munte.' "

"A little further up the mountain . . ." nodded Dracula with an amused smirk. "Of course, as we all know, once you reach the top of one mountain you are most likely to simply see the next, then the next, and so on."

"Exactly," replied Kirschner, smirking back. "Had you made prior arrangements for the next century or so?"

Laughing, the two men rode together into the snowy night.

IX

Dawson left off worrying the keyboard of his computer and stared expectantly at his companion.

"And . . . ?" He drew the word out like a fishing line, making impatient little circles with his hand.

Methos pulled a shirt sleeve over his palm and mopped absent-mindedly at the wet ring his beer bottle had made on the uppermost of one of the many stacks of documents that festooned the coffee table like crennelations on a castle wall. "I don't know, Joe. I wasn't a Watcher back then. Hell, I'd never even been to Romania until the communist government collapsed."

"No, but you were in research for years. You must have run across *something* in the archives—I mean, we're talking about *Dracula*, fer God's sake!"

"Yes and no," said Methos, holding the empty bottle up to the light. "Dead soldier . . ." He rose and ambled into the kitchen.

"What do you mean yes and no?" retorted Dawson, swiveling his chair.

"Well . . . you're talking about the Dracula who's famous for being someone he never was, and doing things he never did. I'm talking about a real man who was a Slavic prince who died, at least for the first time, in 1476." Methos reappeared in the doorway with a fresh bottle applied to his lips.

"And he never had a Watcher?"

"Again, yes and no. It was Kirschner's Watcher that discovered Dracula's immortality, but he apparently lost them both that winter while trying to follow them through the Carpathian Alps. His successor finally picked up on Kirschner over thirty years later, but by that time he and Vlad had separated. There was a Watcher assigned to Dracula, but it was mainly contingent on finding him. According to the records, they never did." He flopped back onto the leather sofa, which gave vent to a long, insolent hiss.

"So," said Dawson, drumming on his knees, "one of the most infamous warlords in history just up and vanishes off the face of the earth?"

"Mmmm . . . well . . ."

"If you say 'yes and no' one more time, you're gonna wear this cane home."

Methos held up his hands in mock consternation. "What I mean is, there are several strange and peculiar reports in the archives attributed to Dracula resurfacing from time to time, although none of them could be officially authenticated." He scanned the table-top briefly for a safe place to deposit his bottle, shrugged, then clenched it in his teeth as he shuffled through several foothills of paper.

"Ergh," he grunted, removing the bottle from his mouth. "Here . . . ah . . . 1535. Vlad's alleged great grand-son, Ladislaus Dracula de Sintesti, receives a patent of nobility from King Ferdinand of Hungary for his distinguished service at the siege of Vienna. A couple of years later in 1537, our lad Lad . . ." He grinned up at Dawson, who deadpanned him with an expression of thinly-worn stoicism. "Ah . . . sorry. Anyway, Baron Ladislaus meets with the famous Doctor Paracelsus who had claimed to have discovered the Philosopher's Stone, the fabled key to eternal life."

"That's pretty sharp," mused Dawson. "Here it is 61 years after he loses a crown. Finally, he gets a title back again. Maybe he'd want to stick around for a while to enjoy it. What better way to explain why you don't seem to be aging than to claim some miraculous potion from a famous alchemist?"

"Perhaps," replied Methos, "but Paracelsus was ostracized from court for his claim and Dracula disappears a few years later. However"—he rooted into another nest of paper, emerging triumphantly with a green-bound manuscript—"about forty years later, a person referred to as the 'dark stranger' shows up at Castle Csejthe in Hungary. I don't know if you recognize the name . . ."

"Sure—play gigs there on weekends."

"Cute," grimaced Methos. "Actually, it was the home of Countess Elizabeth Bathory. Now, the Bathorys were always archrivals of the Dracula clan. In 1537, Ladislaus was suing Count Stephan Bathory, Liz's uncle, for ownership of Castle Fagaras, which had been the hereditary seat of the Dracula family. Stephan claimed it because his grandfather was appointed successor to Dracula—Vlad Dracula—after he was 'killed' in 1476. Dracula, on the other hand, held that the title and estates were successive, not appointive. He was right, but Bathory bribed the royal tribunal, and Drac got screwed out of his homestead. Stephan's last son dies as King of Poland in 1586. Now, out of the blue, a 'dark stranger' turns up at the house of the only living blood relative."

"So the 'dark stranger' is . . ."

". . . wearing a signet ring containing a very distinctive crest. A red shield bearing a sword laid overtop of three wolf's teeth. It's the Bathory device. It's also the personal device of the Draculas."

"So she thinks this guy's a relative? That's convenient."

"Yeah; especially since Elizabeth's husband is a famous soldier, and always off somewhere beating on someone. So, rumour has it, she and the stranger had a lengthy affair right up until her husband is killed in battle. Now, the stranger disappears, and it starts to get a little weird."

"Oh, right!" snorted Dawson, "Like it wasn't already."

Methos ignored him. "Elizabeth is obsessed with losing her beauty, and somehow got the idea that bathing in the blood of virgins was a full-body Oil of Olay. She was finally caught and tried for murder and witchcraft, and walled up in her own bedroom, but only after she'd killed over 650 girls. There was talk that the 'dark stranger' had instructed her in the black arts and he's described in considerable detail in the trial manuscripts by both Elizabeth and others. He *is* Ladislaus Dracula right down to the eyes."

Dawson whistled. "Whoo . . . get your final revenge on your enemies without having to kill anyone yourself. Slick . . . very slick."

Methos stirred some papers about. "There's precious little else after that. In the 1600's, a Count . . . uh . . . Magnus de la Gardie," he muttered, thumbing through another file, "bears a close resemblance to Dracula, supposedly an alchemist and student of Paracelsus. Lived for over seventy years but never appears to be much over forty. Killed at the Battle of Poltova after taking a cannonball through the chest."

"Yeah, that'd do it," winced Dawson.

"That's that," concluded Methos, tossing the folder aside. "From there on everything's apocryphal. Elvis has more reliable sightings." He took a pull on his beer.

"So when did all this 'vampire' nonsense start getting associated with Dracula?" puzzled Dawson. "I don't seem to have heard or read a single thing indicating he actually drank blood."

Methos smiled toothily. "Obviously because he never did. Vampire legends have inculcated almost every major culture for over 2,000 years, although the actual word 'vampire' wasn't coined until 1734. Dracula was described in Romanian and German accounts as 'wampyr' and 'würtrich' but that simply means 'bloodthirsty,' as in 'right nasty bastard.' Bram Stoker did a lot of research before writing his novel, but nobody really thought he mistook the word 'wampyr' to mean vampire."

"Why not?" reasoned Dawson. "Sounds like an honest mistake."

"Because," answered Methos pedantically, "the Romanian words for vampire creatures are Moroi, Strigoi and Vulkodlak, and he would have known that. No, he just liked the ready-made story; and the exotic location—Transylvania—chock full of gypsies and howling wolves, appealed to the Victorian sensibility, and their penchant for gothic horror. Actually, Stoker cribbed a lot of *Dracula* from a novel by John Sheridan le Fanu called *Camilla.*" He crossed his legs methodically. "Did you know I wrote a vampire story myself?"

"Sure—and I used to publish under the pen-name E. Hemingway."

"No, really. It was called 'The Vampyre' . . ."

"That's imaginative. . . ."

". . . and it ran in the April edition of the *London New Monthly Magazine*, in 1819. Of course, I was known as Doctor Polidori back then. But, owing to some lamebrained balls-up by the editor, it got printed under the name of Lord Byron. He almost went off his nut when he saw it." He smiled smugly. "Especially when it was reviewed as the best thing Byron had ever written."

"No kidding? Ain't fame a bitch!" Joe leaned back in his chair and thought for a moment.

"I wonder what the real Dracula thought of Stoker's novel. And then all those movies. I'll bet that's a type of immortality old Vlad never counted on."

"Oh, I don't know," said Methos, sitting up. "In a way it'd actually help obfuscate your past. You know the old saying about the best way of hiding something is to stick it right out in the open."

"Like you becoming the Watcher in charge of finding yourself," suggested Dawson.

"Something like that," replied Methos, thoughtfully. "I kind of wonder if Dracula didn't think about it himself; he is said to have had a rather twisted sense of humour."

"Whaddya mean?" queried Dawson with a narrow look.

"Oh . . . probably nothing," rejoined Methos, pushing back into the cushions with a sigh. "But . . . have you ever seen the portrait of Bram Stoker? It's in the London Stock Exchange, of all places. Anyway, it's a very Victorian piece, highly romanticized. Stoker's depicted as a medieval warrior, wearing a helmet and chainmail. But the really remarkable thing about the work is the depiction of his face." He paused and looked at Dawson. "He has the most amazingly brilliant green eyes. . . ."

A Time of Innocents

by Peter Wingfield

"METHOS": Peter Wingfield

When the role of Methos, the world's oldest Immortal, was created in the season 3 episode of the same name, the possibility of a continuing role for the character was immediately apparent. But we'd tried before to create wise, advisor-type characters to fill the void in MacLeod's life left by the death of Darius (and tragic death of the actor who portrayed him, Werner Stocker), without much luck. Methos would survive his first appearance, but whether he would return—or just return in order to die—depended on the on-screen spark of the actor portraying him.

I think by now everyone's heard the rest of the story. How Welsh-born actor Peter Wingfield's performance as Methos made us cancel development on a story that would have ended his life, replacing it with the storyline that would become the two-part episode "Finale." Peter was back on the set in Paris filming his second and third appearances before "Methos" had even aired in the United States. Suddenly the Highlander *family had a new member, both on- and off-screen.*

In his story "Time of Innocents," set thousands of years ago when Methos rode with The Horsemen, Peter takes a look at an unexamined aspect of Immortality, from his own unique perspective.

⚡

The shock of the air surging back into lungs that should have permanently suspended their rhythmic ebb and flow caused him to cry out involuntarily. And an unformed howl of frightened incomprehension it was, one that echoed his first sound in this world.

The air that newly filled him disturbed more than it refreshed. It was rank. It hung thick and foul with the putrid stench of decay and death.

He blinked his eyes, trying to shake off that undiscovered country from whence no traveller *should* return, and his gaze alighted upon . . .

What?

For try as he might, he could make no sense of the sights that he beheld. The white and the pink; the red and the scarlet; flesh and bone and bruise and gore. Torn cloth, broken steel; wood and stone and dust.

Nothing human stirred.

The only sounds were the patter and plop of claw on carcass and the gentle swooshing of the air under the wings of the vultures, methodically going about their macabre business.

High above in a dispassionate sky, the sun blazed down, mocking and scorching all below.

He lay spluttering for a few moments, trying to reorientate. He wanted to sob, to wail his pain and loneliness to the heavens, but he was too shocked to utter a sound to disturb the eerie peace. His gaze absently took in the bodies around him. They seemed so much a mirror of himself: small, pale, broken children, wrapped in shredded cloths, scarlet stained and torn. Why were they so still and silent when his heart thumped so loud within his chest?

But with a sickening chill he realized the thunder was not inside him. It was in the earth. The whole world was beginning to shake and tremble beneath him. And in a dizzying whirl, they were upon him.

Wild, dark figures, racing across the earth, seemingly stretched from earth to sky, all limb and cloak and double head. Long, spindle legs, stampeding the ground, kicking up a suffocating black fog of dust. And the cries! Blood curdling shrieks that filled the air with hatred and anger and lust.

The Creatures spattered and pounded the ground with their many legs as they eased to a halt before him. Then they split majestically into halves, one wild, masked head separating from another, the fearsome, painted Devil-Heads still screeching and cackling as they tugged at the mouth straps of their anxious, four-legged charges.

And the Devil-Heads began to approach the mass of former humanity from where he viewed their progress. They kicked and prodded the heap, body by body, closer and closer to the spot where he lay, still dazed and disjointed, paralysed with fear, barely able to release the breath from his newly animate chest. Until finally they were rifling the corpses a mere embrace away and he could hold his tongue no longer. His tiny lungs let forth the only noise they knew. He howled!

A howl that screamed for succor to all the powers of eternity!

A howl of fear and frustration; of utter incomprehension.

A howl that vented the pitted anger of his betrayal, and loss, and undefended, impotent vulnerability.

The Creatures stopped in their tracks, momentarily stunned into inaction. Then he heard their calls once more. Low and short and hesitant at first, but quickly gathering confidence. Building in pace and pitch and volume until they were shrieks once more, the shrieks and cackles which had accompanied their arrival.

And suddenly he was in the air. Wailing and flailing. Helpless. Exposed.

One of the Creatures was holding him high above the ground and all he knew now was terror. He screamed and screamed to make it stop. And for a second he was flying, parodying the black birds that patiently waited their turn on the barren branches a dozen yards away. Now he was caught in another calloused hand, shaken and bent like a rag doll and tossed carelessly once more into the fetid air. And again he was in the clutch of a Demon Creature. It poked a strong, angular finger into his defenseless belly and he could smell the rancid breath from its savage mouth. And as he cried and pleaded anew to feel the half-remembered warmth of his mother's breast, he saw the glint of sunlight on steel. And all he felt was the coldness pass through his soul. And the pain was gone.

All was silence.

In a second his lungs were as full as if he were a child's balloon at Christmas. The sunlight stung his eyeballs and the surprised cries of his tormentors brought consciousness flooding back, coalescing into realization. He had wakened from the nightmare, but the nightmare still lived on.

Here again the rotting pile of baby flesh; here again the stench. And as he cried out to the gods once more, an inarticulate plea that begged, nay demanded "Why?," he could hear the cackling Harpies' approach from nearby where they had been engaged in who knew what abhorrent act.

A moment and one of them was at his side. (That same sickly breath!) He cried again and again in righteous indignation, but who would hear and save him? Now he was in its grasp, plucked untimely from his broken brothers' sides, a plaything for a twisted child. He could sense the euphoric joy of his tormentor; deranged, disturbed delight. He could see its teeth, exposed in a mocking grin, salivating at the prospect of the unspeakable games now crowding its degenerate mind, fighting for which would be first. The Creature threw back its head and let out a chilling, jagged laugh and as everything went dark he thought for a second he was tumbling through blackness down its gullet, into its stomach.

But this darkness was warm and soft. Did he imagine, or was it, even, comforting? A second Creature had plucked him from the first and now held him close, shrouded in its furry coat. He was buried in a dark, rumbling cavern, noises issuing from deep, deep inside, indistinct and unidentifiable. He dreamed, or half remembered, a time of peace and safety, another body's warmth surrounding him, nourishing him, its heartbeat lulling his every thought and fancy.

But his hope of Paradise Found lasted but a flicker before a violent hand ripped him from his pouch and held him squealing and squinting in the sunlight once more.

And this hand was cold.

A cold he had never known before.

A cold that had never felt warmth; that could never *be* warmed.

A heartless, bloodless cold that chilled as it stilled the air.

The hand raised him to its master's face and the eye that met him there was icy and still as a glacial fjord. It stared, deep, deep inside him and pondered.

Once more there was silence, and out of the silence came the laughter of the Cold One.

A chill laugh. Misleadingly soft. Full of guile and calculation. Its fearsome hand tightened its grip and held him aloft and the cry he heard was of ironic enchantment; amusement at the fickleness of Fortune, the appreciation of discovered chance.

He was overcome with foreboding, sickened by a premonition of slow, painful dissection and decrease.

When a fourth hand plucked him from out of his frigid prison.

The last of the Creatures had him in its clutch.

And the Creature felt like . . . nothing. He had no sense of it. No anger. No hatred. No fear. No peace.

The hand was soft but firm, unyielding yet not harsh. And the eyes were calm and understanding. They seemed to say, "Don't worry. All will now be well. Leave everything to me."

And as he saw, as if in slow motion, the great steel blade rise high above him, blocking out the sun, the one sole thing he sensed, beyond all else, was the overwhelming feeling that this one, he could trust.

The Other Side
of the Mirror

by Dennis Berry
with Darla Kershner

DIRECTOR: Dennis Berry

Dennis Berry has directed more than thirty episodes of Highlander, *spanning all six seasons. Our most frequent director, he had a hand in many of the most significant developments in the series, including being responsible for much of* Highlander's *signature foggy gloom. The child of expatriate Americans living in France, Dennis's unique personality is a blend of Paris and Brooklyn; his inimitable style was copied by Duncan MacLeod for the "French Director" sequence in the episode "Money No Object."*

A light fog surrounds two figures lying still in a dark alley. The fog continues to roll in as one of the figures, a man, rises to his knees. Duncan MacLeod, the Highlander, staggers to his feet, leaning heavily on his katana that sparkles in the gray haze. As the battle weary warrior regains his balance he is suddenly hit by an invisible force. His back arches and his limbs become rigid. His mouth opens in a silent scream of intense pain as his body begins to tremble. Barrages of small explosions are barely seen as the fog thickens. Duncan MacLeod is completely consumed by the dense dark mist.

"CUT!"

"Get the overhead lights."

"Open the doors, get some fresh air in here."

"Somebody turn off that damn fog machine."

Bright lights suddenly illuminate a small sound stage exposing the chaos that surrounds the filming of a television series.

"Perfect," announces Dennis, the director of the episode, and as he opens his mouth to finish the sentence, he finds a chorus of voices saying it with him, "Let's do it once more."

Adrian, dropping his grave "Duncan MacLeod" demeanor, laughs at the director's predictability. Dennis has directed more episodes of *Highlander* than any other man alive; by now, the crew know his little quirks by heart.

"Dennis," Adrian teases, "I swear you'll be on your death bed getting the last rites, and you'll tell the priest, 'Perfect, let's do it again.'"

Adrian heads off towards his trailer as Dennis and Rick, the Director of Photography, quickly review the footage to see if they can salvage anything from the last take, leaving the 1st AD, Kevin, to deal with the overworked, overtired crew.

"Okay, listen up. We've got to get this shot tonight, guys. You have a half hour break while we reset the blasts," Kevin tries to convey more positively than he feels. The crew is starting their 14th hour and their exhaustion is apparent. It's going to take more than a half-hour break to bring this crew back to life.

Groans and mumbles echo throughout the sound stage. Don, the prop master, removes the "body" of the beheaded "Erik Kling," Evil-Immortal-of-the-Week, from the pseudo alley. Terri and Lisa in craft-services try their best to make the now stale bagels look appetizing.

The PA's with no place better to go find comfortable spots on the set to crash. It's going to be a long night.

A flicker of light and movement of shadows let Adrian know that someone's in his trailer. Taking a deep breath, he begins to open the door, but a high pitched giggle that doesn't sound human makes him pause. He slowly and carefully opens the door just a crack and peers inside. Then he slams the door wide and stalks inside to angrily confront the intruder: Stan is lounged out on his couch, drinking his beer, eating his popcorn and watching his TV.

"What are you doing here?" Adrian asks, in a not-so-friendly tone.

"Watching *The Wizard of Oz;* Dorothy just landed in Munchkinland," Stan answers innocently, his attention focused on the TV.

Adrian growls, plops down in a chair, grabs the remote and turns the channel, ignoring Stan's groans. "No, what are you doing *here?*" He motions his hands in a big circle to indicate a bigger picture. "You're not in tonight's scene."

"I've been practicing with F." Rubbing his sore arms for emphasis, "And the man's a slave driver; the only thing he's missing is a whip. Did you know they have me doing three sword fights in the next episode?"

"You asked for it." Adrian clicks the TV, flipping the channels. "At the beginning of the season, what did you do?" He doesn't wait for an answer. "You called the writing office in LA and complained that Richie wasn't seeing enough action." Stopping the remote on *Twelve Angry Men,* he glances over at Stan, who's still not getting it. "Never complain to the writers."

"Oh boy." Stan groans. He falls back on the couch, going noticeably pale.

"What did you do?" Adrian asks, eyebrows raised.

"I called and complained that they were making Richie too macho."

Adrian doesn't even try to control his laughter. "I hope you like wearing a dress, next thing you'll be . . ."

Adrian's torture of Stan is interrupted by a knock at the door and the AD's voice from outside. "They're ready for you on the set."

• • •

A light fog surrounds two figures lying still in a dark alley. The fog continues to roll in as one of the figures, a man, rises to his knees. Duncan MacLeod, the Highlander, staggers to his feet, leaning heavily on his katana that sparkles in the gray haze. As the battle weary warrior regains his balance he is suddenly hit by an . . .

BONG! BONG!

"Cut!"

BONG! BONG!

"What the hell!"

BONG! BONG!

"What is that?"

BONG! BONG!

"Where is it coming from?"

BONG! BONG! BONG!

"Somebody make it stop!"

BONG!

The studio is plunged into darkness as the unseen clock chimes for the twelfth and last time.

Adrian is first to break the silence of the shocked crew. "That's it, I am out of here." He makes his way through the dark to the outside door.

"Wait!" yells Dennis. The director catches up with the actor and walks with him through the studio door, into the parking lot outside.

"What the . . . ?" Adrian's words fade, his voice can no longer convey his total disbelief.

"What's wrong?" Dennis asks, running into Adrian's back. The actor has come to a sudden and complete stop. Looking over Adrian's shoulder, Dennis sees what's paralyzed him. It takes a moment for the director to realize just what it is he's seeing. Where there should be a studio parking lot filled with cars, trucks, vans and teamsters, is now a dark alley engulfed in fog.

"How—?" Adrian takes a step into the alley, heading for the spot where his car should be. He only gets a few feet when he trips and falls on something he can't see in the fog. Adrian gets to his knees as Dennis comes to his side. Both men see at the same time what Adrian tripped over. Lying in the middle of the alley, mostly hidden in the fog, is the body of Erik Kling. The man "Duncan MacLeod" had slain on film only minutes, hours, or an eternity before.

But this is no prop. This body is horribly, sickeningly real.

Adrian whirls around and heads back to the set, hoping there's some logical explanation, that this is some elaborate practical joke. It has to be. Stan getting even for that stunt with the bananas and the video camera last month . . .

Adrian and Dennis reach the set to find it completely deserted. They couldn't have been gone for more than a few minutes. There's no way everyone could have cleared out this fast. Adrian checks his watch to make sure, but the hands have stopped at midnight. In fact all the clocks have stopped; it is as if all time has stopped.

Then, out of the thick fog that blankets the set, they hear approaching footsteps. A small red light is now visible and coming toward them.

"Gotta get the shot, gotta get the shot, gotta get the shot." The mantra starts as nothing more than a whisper, growing louder and more frantic as it grows nearer.

When the light is almost on them, they can make out the figure of Harvey, the camera operator, carrying a Steadicam. He circles them, zooming in tight. "Gotta get the shot, gotta get the shot, can't go home until we get the shot."

"Harvey! Snap out of it. What the hell is going on?" Adrian grabs Harvey by both shoulders and shakes him until he stops the chanting. "Where is everyone? Did they all go home?"

"Home? Home?" Harvey begins to laugh hysterically until his laughter turns into sobs. "There is no home, this is our home, this is our hell, we're trapped here forever." Harvey's voice turns from pathetic torment to venomous anger. He grabs Adrian's shirt with both fists. "This is because of you, Duncan MacLeod. You mocked the gods." He lets go of Adrian and starts to back away into the fog. "Now, the gods, they mock us."

"Wait!" Adrian calls after the camera operator. "What can we do? How do we fix this? How do we get home?"

"Can't go home, until we get the shot," Harvey's voice answers through the fog. "Gotta get the shot, gotta get the shot . . ."

To Adrian's surprise, Dennis is nodding, as though the strange encounter made sense to him. "Okay, Adrian. Now I see what happened. It's as if we played so much with the game of travelling through time, and we played so much with the rules of natural law by doing fiction about Immortals that suddenly, as a revenge, nature is punishing us." He looks Adrian in the eye. "We are in purgatory, we are stuck with being forever alive"—with a heavy sigh—"on a film set." Dennis then disappears into the fog.

"Dennis . . . wait. . . . Come back," Adrian shouts. Any attempt to pursue his friend is lost as an explosion brings him to his knees. The actor barely has time to cover his face, protecting it from the heat, as a second explosion then a third engulf the soundstage in flames.

What threatened to be a sob comes out as laughter. "Fire! Of course there's fire. After all I'm in hell. You gotta have fire in hell. . . ." Adrian pushes through the exit door and is surprised to find himself in the studio backlot, not the alley as he has expected. He takes off running for the relative safety of his trailer, across the backlot, through the studio door and right into someone, knocking them both down.

"Sorry, ma'am," Adrian hastily apologizes, noting that the person lying under him is wearing a dress.

"Yeah, well, watch it next time and I would appreciate if you didn't call me ma'am." The voice definitely does not belong to a lady of any type.

"Stan! Thank God!" Adrian gets up off the ground and pulls Stan with him. "What the hell are you doing in that dress?"

"Hell is the key word here, man," Stan says, dusting the dirt from his dress. "Richie is getting in touch with his feminine side," Stan's voice turns into a whine. "They're making me a transvestite, an Immortal transvestite. Can you believe this crap?"

"I don't know what to believe anymore," Adrian answers solemnly.

"Sorry man, but you get no pity from me. This whole purgatory thing is all in your hands. But hey, it could be worse, you could be spending eternity in a dress . . ." Stan gives him a wry smile. ". . . and panty hose. Now that is truly hell, they're so"—wiggling for emphasis—"binding."

Adrian puts a comforting hand on Stan's shoulder. "We'll find a way out of this mess; we have to."

CRACK!

"Oh no!" Stan's face pales and he starts to back away.

CRACK!

"Stan? What's wrong?" Adrian asks.

"It's time," Stan says in a small voice.

CRACK!

From out of the shadows of the sound stage emerges F. Braun, the swordmaster. "Time to train," F. says in a low, dangerous voice. The Swordmaster advances toward Stan with a sword in one hand and whip in the other. "Come on, soldier, time to train, now parry!" F. cuts at Stan with his sword. Stan blocks the cut, but his form is very sloppy.

CRACK!

Stan lets out a startled yelp as the whip hits its mark.

"That's no way to fight," F. proclaims angrily, raising the whip again.

Suddenly Adrian is there, pulling the whip from F.'s hand. "What are you doing? We're not at war here!"

F. stares at him for a moment, then: "It's worse, it's worse than war. It's purgatory."

The whip cracks again and Adrian is driven back through the door of the studio. Inside, the fire has died down, leaving an unharmed soundstage. As his eyes adjust to the dimly lit room Adrian can't help but notice the set is now a courtroom. A courtroom with no ceiling and no fourth wall, the "mahogany" walls merely dark stain on cheap plywood. Good enough for camera.

A door by the jury box opens and men start filing in. Cautiously, Adrian takes a few steps towards the jury box, which by now is almost filled. He feels a sense of dread at the recognition of who they are. The twelve men sitting in the box before him are all actors who have guest starred on *Highlander*. Over the years of filming all of these men have played Watchers. Including—

"Jim," Adrian whispers softly, "what is going on?"

Eyes full of compassion, the Watcher responds, shaking his head sorrowfully, "Sorry, friend, this is out of my hands. Nothing I can do."

"What?" Adrian questions emphatically. "What's out of your hands? What's going on?" The Watcher responds only by taking his place in the jury box. "What the hell is going on here," Adrian queries in disbelief. "Am I on trial?"

"That is precisely what is going on here."

Adrian whirls around to see who spoke, to see his Judge. Standing at the judge's podium is Kalas. One of the Highlander's greatest adversaries.

"David?" Adrian asks hopefully. The question lingers between them for a moment. But the laugh that bellows from the judge is all Kalas; no trace of the actor that Adrian had worked with is present in that laugh.

"We are here to find out of you're condemned forever to live on this set or if you can go free, back into the real world."

A speechless Adrian can only mutter a strangled, "Why?"

"You made a deal, a Faustian deal. You dared to pretend to be immortal when you are merely an actor." Kalas's laugh echoes through the courtroom. "I find you guilty," he proclaims, ignoring the indignant gasp from the Watchers in the jury box. "For your crimes I sentence you to live forever in darkness, confined to this horrible little TV set. Because you are always over time, time has stopped for you. Because you are always over budget, you are permanently indebted to this organization, you belong to us forever, you will never escape." Kalas's inhuman laugh gets louder and louder as the room seems to get smaller with every laugh.

The accused turns to flee—out of the soundstage, back out into the fog-covered alley.

His attention focuses on the constant repetitive sound of dripping water. A dripping drainage pipe farther down the alley. The face that returns his gaze from the glassy surface of the puddle is one he cannot recognize. His mind begins to race from doubt. He silently questions his reflection, *Am I Adrian? Am I MacLeod? Who am I? Which life is the real one?* Without receiving an answer, he dips his finger into the small pool of water, causing ripples which distort his reflected features. Adrian closes his eyes, unable to look at the reflection he no longer recognizes. He silently begs for release from this nightmare.

After a moment he opens his eyes; the water is still but another reflection has joined his own.

"Dennis!" Adrian jumps up and embraces his friend. "You're alive! Where have you been? What's going on? Are we totally nuts or is this the Twilight Zone?" As he's firing off questions he begins to take note of Dennis' appearance. The director looks like he's gone through a hell of his own. He's disheveled and his eyes look haunted. "Are you okay?"

"No, my friend." Dennis slowly shakes his head. "I am not okay. We are not okay." The director takes a deep steadying breath before continuing. "I fear we have been taken on a sudden journey, a walk on the other side of the hill, a walk on the other side of the coin, a walk on the other side of the mirror."

"The other side of the mirror," Adrian repeats, his mind flashing to his distorted reflection in the puddle.

Dennis pats the actor on the back and says with a wry smile, "It's not that bad; after all, it's not really worse than certain other horrible productions we've worked on."

Adrian shoots a shocked looked at Dennis, then smiles himself. Whatever is to come next in this nightmare, they'll face it together.

They don't have to wait long. They both turn to see a fog rolling in, filling the alley. Through the fog they see a dark figure standing in the mist. As the fog dissipates, there stands Bill. He is larger than life, with the backlighting and fog giving the Executive Producer an unearthly glow.

Adrian takes a step forward, but stops as Dennis grabs his arm.

"Where do you think you're going?" asks the director.

"To make a deal with the devil," Adrian replies, nodding toward Bill. "I'm going to get us out of this," he finishes with determination.

"Bill, we need to talk," Adrian begins, with all the confidence he can muster.

There's no place like home.

Adrian opens his eyes with a groan. Sitting up he realizes he is back on the couch in his trailer. He stares blankly at Judy Garland on the TV for a moment before turning it off.

"A dream . . ." Adrian says in disbelief, ". . . a damn bizarre dream, but just a dream." He sighs with relief.

He steps out of his trailer into the blinding sun. Adrian is overwhelmed with a sense of calm. He pulls his sunglasses out of the pocket of his leather jacket. Putting the sunglasses on he realizes that he is alone on the studio back lot, but he is at peace. He tries to open the gate to the parking lot but finds it locked. Acting on instinct, Adrian reaches for his sword, which, as always, magically appears. He begins to spin the sword in fast, fluid motions. The blade seems to take on a life of its own, becoming thicker and spinning faster. The blade stretches out over his head and begins to surreally multiply.

Suddenly, the katana is no longer a sword but has morphed into a vehicle. The mini-helicopter lifts Adrian up into the sky, past the studio, past the city, perhaps over the rainbow, perhaps to paradise or someplace else unknown. As he flies away he sings to himself and to anyone who might hear.

"Here we are, born to be kings . . ."